A Seaside Mourning

GW00390858

By the same author

A Christmas Malice
The Seafront Corpse
The Holly House Mystery

A SEASIDE MOURNING

A Victorian Murder Mystery

Anne Bainbridge

GASLIGHT CRIME

One

Sergeant Reeve had seen enough of life to gaze relatively unmoved at knife-wounds, flesh mashed by fists, maggots pulsing in the soft pulp of an old corpse, like the brown patch you'd toss away in an apple. He'd seen the ravages of a vitriol throwing and stomached it like a man. Seeing was one thing, it was the smells that got to him every time.

This one stank of river water. Not so bad in itself but made a filthy brew by the gases rising from the poor wretch's stomach. Reeve did his best to breathe shallowly through his nose, while fixing his mind on the tankard of ale he'd have afterwards. He took a sideways glance at the inspector, who had requested the body be turned over and was studying the back.

'And these marks are?' He indicated the long scratches below the shoulders.

'Boat-hooks,' said the mortuary-attendant. He paused to wipe the dew-drop on his drooping grey moustache and continued in a bored tone. 'Post-mortem, no bleeding, see? From when they fished 'er out.'

Inspector Abbs grimaced. 'It all seems plain enough. She went in over the weir. No marks of violence other than what's to be expected from the body bumping about.' He swallowed quietly. 'And the belly tells the tale.' They looked at the unmistakable thickening around the middle. 'All right. You can cover her, I think we've seen enough. What are your thoughts, Sergeant?'

'Well sir, provided the doc doesn't come up with something unusual, I'd say there's nothing for us here. I don't reckon we'll ever find out who she was, even.'

'Probably not, if no one comes forward to enquire about her missing.'

They watched as the attendant flicked the rough sheet back over the corpse. The water had soaked away all trace of the young woman's visage, leaving a bloated mass.

'Most likely a dollymop thrown out by her employer,' said Reeve. 'Wonder if he knocked her up?'

'Who knows?' said Abbs. 'Nobody cared.' He looked away at the drain in the floor, a hard set to his features. 'I agree she was most likely a servant. A common prostitute would have known where to go to deal with it.'

Belatedly, Reeve remembered hearing some whisper about Abbs having lost a new-born child. It was when he'd joined the detective-branch and Abbs had been pointed out to him as a stickler for paperwork. The inspector wasn't one to talk about himself and though he'd been put to work under him a few times lately, he knew nothing more than that.

'Thank you.' Abbs nodded at the attendant. 'Please tell Dr. Chisholm we're satisfied, pending his report. Sorry we had to miss him.' He turned to Reeve. 'We're done here. Let's get some air.'

Silently, they climbed the basement steps, where the walls were hung with shiny, white tiles like a urinal. As they emerged into the autumn sunshine, Reeve racked his thoughts for something to say. 'A bad business, sir. It isn't the first time we've seen it.'

'Nor the last, Reeve, nor the last.'

~

Adelaide Shaw swung her empty basket as she walked back along the promenade. Her spirits rose in the sunshine, the first half of September having brought constant wind and rain. She picked her way between the puddles to save her hem and avoided the shingle thrown across the road. Pausing, she watched the cart drawn up on the beach and the small boys stooping as they gathered seaweed. Inhaling deeply, she enjoyed the pungent reek of the glossy vegetation strewn in bottle-green heaps.

The majority of Seaborough residents did not share her view. The local businessmen, and town council in particular, feared the noxious smell would disbar their growing town from becoming a stylish resort. Somewhere the fashionable would convalesce and send their children. Fortunately, the seaweed was at its most powerful during spring and autumn tides. And after all, thought Adelaide, the farmers valued its goodness to improve their potato fields.

Turning away from the sea, she walked past the row of beeches on one side of Clarence Square, some leaves turning orange among the green.

'Mornin' Miss.'

She nodded in acknowledgement, as a workman, with a length of wood under his arm, touched his cap and disappeared down the alley beside the town-hall. The sound of hammering came from a door propped open. Few other people were about, though a dray was standing outside the Crown and Cushion, a pile of dung steaming. Across the street, a maid could be seen, busily polishing an upstairs window.

Passing the municipal building reminded her that her father had to go out that evening. His standing in the town required him to take a seat on several of the committees that seemed to increase each year, Mr. Halesworth generally taking the chair, with his cronies at either side, no doubt. She knew her father was considered a well-meaning eccentric in some circles, his concern for the poor indiscriminate, his kindness not confined to the sufficiently deserving.

Memory of a tiny incident, from last spring, still brought a livid flush to her sallow cheeks. She had been attending a musical evening, held, as was customary, at the town-hall. Its purpose had been to raise funds for the Hospital and she had been seeking the supper-room during the interval. Weaving a path between wide skirts and cigar-smoke, clinking glasses and conversation, she'd heard her own name spoken.

'Oh, you know Shaw, he's bound to speak up for those wretches. He thinks his profession obliges him to.'

A burst of hearty laughter greeted the remark. The broad back of the speaker was turned towards her and she could make out the bony profile of Mr. Cox, the druggist, at his side. A group of businessmen were stationed by the supper table and she abandoned her thought of refreshment, returning instead to her seat.

No, she did not care for Mr. Alfred Halesworth, even though he had given her father a cheque for the orphans.

Further down the street, she could see Mr. Cox standing outside his shop and talking to Dr. Avery. The doctor stood by his gig and was stowing a box on the seat, very likely collecting medicines for the Hospital. He had been among the group listening to Mr. Halesworth that evening but he had not been one of those who laughed.

He'd been most conscientious when her father had been laid low with bronchitis, the previous winter. People sometimes thought his manner aloof but everyone agreed, he was a clever doctor.

Reaching the vicarage, she unpinned her hat and picked up the second post lying on the hall table, before following the spirited rendition of *Rock of Ages* coming from the back corridor. The kitchen smelt comfortingly of yeast and onion. A plump woman, enveloped in a holland apron, stood working at the deal table.

'There you are, Miss. Your father's been out in the garden this half-hour nor more, standing on that soaking grass. You know what his chest's like. I told him, summer's long gone and there'll be colds to be had.' This was accompanied by an eloquent slam of the dough being kneaded.

'I'll fetch him in directly. Your preserves were received gladly.'

'You told them we've some clothes put aside for the little 'uns?'

'I did, Mrs Taylor will be up to collect them and now her husband's leg's better, the boat can go out.' Adelaide reached forward and plunged her hand in the enamel bin, scooping out some currants.

'Be off with you, Miss. How's a body to get on, I'd like to know?'

'Sorry, Hannah. I can't resist them.'

'You never could,' the older woman's voice softened. 'Not since you had to climb on that stool to roll your little bit o' pastry.' Her capable, flour-speckled arms gave the dough a final fold and tucked it in a basin. Pulling down a cloth from the airer, she draped it over the top and set it to rise near the range.

~

'Ah, Adelaide, my dear.' Reverend Shaw straightened up from the rose-bed when he saw his daughter appear in the arch of the straggly, yew hedge. 'I fear William Lobb has fared badly with mildew these past months.'

'I'm sorry, Papa. I know it's one of your favourites.' Adelaide peered at the mossy bush her father was inspecting.

'We must hope the frosts are not severe this year. In the meantime, I shall ask Isaac to dig in some manure. You have a letter, I see.'

'I haven't opened it yet.' She did so and quickly scanned the short note, written in neat copperplate. 'It's from Miss Chorley, inviting us to tea next week. Her nephew is paying her a visit at last and I suppose she wants to show him some company.'

'Is that so? I understood Miss Chorley to say she expected him shortly before Christmas, not in September. He will like to tour our Hospital, no doubt. He'll find it very different from his posting. From what I read in the newspapers, the Military Hospital at Netley is like a small town in itself. I shall enjoy conversing with him and meeting someone new will make a pleasant change for you.'

'It will be interesting to see him, after all we've heard, but I should think he'll find us dull fare after Hampshire.'

~

In the upper council-chamber, three men were hunched over a map, its top edges weighted by an ink-well and a decanter. The gaslight popped, its familiar smell mingling unpleasantly with the faint tang of turpentine seeping up the stairs. On this floor, no refurbishments had been deemed necessary, though the ceiling recorded two decades' meetings in an oily sheen of soot and tobacco. A meagre fire smouldered in the grate and the sudden shift of a coal made the bearded man start.

'What's the matter, Hicks? Nervous about your investment?'

'Not in the least, Halesworth. All I say is, there'll be none of your fat profit materialising unless we can get the doings. If Miss Chorley won't sell, we're finished before we've begun.'

'D... it, Hicks. You always look on the black side. Still, it's to be expected in your trade, I suppose.' Mr. Halesworth strode over to the fireplace and added some more coal.

Mr. Hicks laughed and turned to their colleague. 'What say you, Avery?'

The doctor rubbed his hand thoughtfully over his chin. 'Could go either way. She has no real use for the land that I can see but neither does she need the money. I've found she can be stubborn when her mind's set on something.'

'She'll sell,' said Mr. Halesworth, vigorously applying the poker. 'Poor bit of grazing like that, she can't make more than a pittance from it. It isn't as if it's anywhere near her house.' Tossing the tongs back in the scuttle, he returned to the long table.

'Perhaps we've overlooked some suitable plot for our next venture.' Mr. Hicks studied the map.

'We've been over all this,' said Mr. Halesworth, standing between them. 'The cliffs are unstable here, as any fool knows,' he tapped his finger to indicate where he meant. 'The strand's out, though it would make a prime site if that flea-pit were swept away.' He waved airily at the cots and passages of the original fishing village. 'And the land rising on both sides makes it uneconomic to build.'

He traced an area beyond the streets. 'No, it has to be here. Flat and forms a natural extension to the town. A terrace of villas, quickly thrown up.' He rubbed his hands together, good humour restored. 'A steady income for all of us.'

'They won't stand empty?' said Dr. Avery.

'Certainly not. All those clerks and shop-assistants looking to settle down. They'll be queuing up.'

'I think Halesworth's right,' said Mr. Hicks. 'We saw a good return last time. It makes sense to think bigger.'

The doctor gazed at the wall as he considered. 'Salisbury-terrace was a shrewd investment, granted but we sold and collected our profit. These properties would remain on our hands. I'm not a rich man and cannot afford capital tied up without interest.'

'We're none of us rich,' said Mr. Halesworth. 'But I, for one, mean to be.' He slapped Dr. Avery on the back. 'You've no cause to regret using your legacy. Well then, come in again and double your money in rents.'

A slow smile spread over the doctor's face. 'Very well, you've convinced me. I rather like a gamble if the odds are in my favour. Count me in.'

'That's the spirit, good man. Hicks, are you with us?'

Mr. Hicks glanced up at the window as a spatter of rain hit the glass. 'It would be ideal. I pass there when I'm at the new cemetery. I'm in if we can get it.'

'You'll approach her on our behalf, then, Halesworth?' said Dr. Avery.

'As soon as she'll see me. Never fear, I'll get the papers drawn up and we'll have the footings in well before winter.' Mr. Halesworth reached for a stack of papers at the far end of the table. 'Best look lively, the others will be here.' He threw himself on the chair and began to skim through the agenda, as the others replaced the map.

Shortly after, a door banged, followed by a murmur of conversation and footfalls were heard on the stairs.

'Good evening, gentlemen, though it's inclement weather again, I fear.' Reverend Shaw entered the room, shaking out his umbrella, followed immediately by the other committee members.

~

'Thank you, Mr. Hicks. And you, Mrs Lavis, you've both been very kind to me. And Mr. Owen, he'll do a lovely service. I'm sure I never thought such a day would come, even though I took out the burial club.'

The speaker broke off to dab her black-edged handkerchief to her eyes. Turning away a little, she stopped to blow her nose. Mr. Hicks and his assistant waited patiently by the door.

'I know it will all be done proper. You did everything very dignified for my sister's boy. You will be walking yourself, Mr. Hicks?'

Mr. Hicks inclined his head. 'Everything will be done exactly as you wish, Mrs Pardoe. The utmost reverence will be shown to your dear departed. I shall be following the hearse, accompanied by two mutes, as we agreed.'

'Oh, I do like to see men in weepers, it shows proper respect. It's what my Albert deserved.' Mrs Pardoe stared short-sightedly at the undertaker, her round, worn face crumpled within her mourning bonnet. 'He were in good health, 'part from indigestion, which he suffered something terrible. He used to double up with it. I never thought he'd be taken from us so soon.'

She looked, thought Mr. Hicks, like a timid mouse peeping out of a nest in a children's picture-book. He showed the new widow off the premises, as Mrs Lavis replaced the drawer of cheap coffin ornaments.

'Bit of a waste on a Chapel service. If it's what Mr. Pardoe wanted.'

'I don't know,' Mrs Lavis shook her head. 'She's always been Chapel but he certainly didn't sign the pledge. Pity he didn't. I've seen Bert Pardoe a dozen times staggering home drunk from the Compass. He used to beat her, Mr. Hicks. She's had a black eye before now, the poor soul.'

'She's surely suffering, even so. Poor woman indeed.'

Mr. Hicks regarded his assistant with something approaching affection. She was a great asset to his business, with a good head for figure-work for a woman. And being a widow herself, she showed a genuine sympathy to the newly-bereaved.

'I shall take a turn outside.'

Mr. Hicks was quietly proud of his business, without doubt, the leading undertakers in the town. And if not quite a mourning-warehouse, his funeral furnishings emporium endeavoured to meet every necessity for those afflicted by grief or required to make an outward show.

Shelves of crape and bombazine, drawers of mourning gloves, handkerchiefs, armbands, stationery and memorial cards, lined the walls. A glass case on the counter displayed best quality, mourning jewellery, made from Whitby jet. Though the yard behind was where he felt most at home.

The smell of wood-shavings from the workshop took him back to his start as apprentice to a cabinet-maker. The mare was out to hire but Samson in his stable snorted as he recognised his footsteps. The lad was whistling *Maid and the soldier* as he cleaned the new hearse. It looked very fitting with its glass sides, the first to be seen in Seaborough.

Mr. Hicks suppressed a smile before he spoke. 'Let gravity be your watchword on the premises, Bram.'

'S...sorry, sir.' Bram clutched his cap, dropping the leather. His whole figure looked tensed to flee, the faintest softening to his features.

Mr. Hicks gentled his tone. 'It's all right, lad. You've done nothing wrong. Best not to whistle while you're here, though.'

Bram nodded vigorously. 'Right, sir. I been polishing the flowers.' He pointed to the etched white pattern.

'So you have.'

'They're lilies, they are. Missus Lavis told me their name.'

'And you're doing a fine job.'

Two

After listening at the door, Miss Ada Geake moved lightly across the turkey carpet and tried the desk drawer. It had been locked which meant it contained something possibly of interest. Fortunately, the key was in its customary hiding place. Reaching behind the glass case, she ignored the shiny stare of the stuffed dog-fox posed among dried grasses, their colour long faded.

Old Richard Chorley had played the country gentleman, though she had heard he was cold-shouldered by the real gentry of the county. For he was trade, having made his money from a silk and crape factory. She pulled a face at his full-length portrait over the fireplace.

The desk was a flimsy piece with curved legs, designed for a lady's correspondence. Mr. Chorley had picked up his furniture job-lot in country house sales and his daughter disliked change. In many ways, the house was a shrine, thought Miss Geake, with the jumble of walking-sticks still in the hall-stand and the rack of pipes in the rarely used study.

Miss Chorley lived according to her long dead father's edicts, which she quoted frequently, as though he had gone away and was expected back at any hour.

The contents of the drawer were soon examined. Miss Geake ignored the handsome, red morocco diary, knowing, from experience, its entries made dull reading. The interesting discovery was, in fact, an absence. The will had been removed which probably meant it had been taken to read at her bedside. That the unseen nephew was expected imminently, could be no coincidence.

The sound of Miss Chorley's querulous tones made her hastily lock the drawer and return the key. The heavy tapping grew steadily nearer. By the time her employer turned the door-knob, she was standing by the window, looking at the dimly outlined trees and rearranging a vase of bulrushes.

'Do stop fiddling with those, Ada.' Miss Chorley sank into the nearest chair, her hand resting on the ornate ivory handle of her stick. 'There is so much to be done. That foolish girl Sarah has made up the bed, in my nephew's room, with the wrong linen.'

'Yes, Miss Chorley. Would you like me to instruct Sarah?'

'No need, she knows what to do now. I want you to write a note for me and get William to take it round.'

'Certainly, ma'am. Will you dictate it now?'

'You may write it. It is to Mr. Halesworth, the councillor. He asks for an interview with me, as soon as may be convenient.' Miss Chorley sighed, making her grey ringlets stir beneath their old-fashioned lace. 'And my nephew expected at any hour.'

'I understood Captain Selden was not expected until the morrow?'

'You may tell Mr. Halesworth I shall receive him briefly in the forenoon. Briefly, mind. I cannot possibly imagine what he wishes to see me about. I hope he is not presuming on my acquaintance with his wife.'

'Perhaps he wishes to ask for a subscription?' said her companion. 'I hear he has been elected governor of the board school.'

Miss Chorley raised her hand wearily. 'You should not listen to gossip, Ada.'

'No, Miss Chorley.'

'I have a headache come on me and no wonder, with so many calls on my time. This damp air oppresses me. You did tell Cook about the mutton? Gentlemen are always sure to be hungry after travelling.'

'I gave her your instructions.' Miss Geake unpinned the vinaigrette at her belt. 'Here you are, ma'am. Would you like one of your powders or should I send for Dr. Avery?'

'This is sufficient, thank you, Ada. You are most kind.' Miss Chorley held the tiny flask beneath her nostrils. 'I shall rest here quietly for a time. Be so good as to pass me my book before you go.'

'I shall send William directly I have written.'

Miss Chorley opened her volume of Mr. Keble's religious verse but shortly after being left alone, she rose and retrieved some items from her sewing-box. Then she settled herself with the Ladies' Own Paper and a box of violet creams.

~

'It's quite a nasty cut but it won't need stitching.' Dr. Avery dabbed gently as he cleaned the wound across his patient's palm.

'I wouldn't have bothered you, except there could be glass in it.' The young man looked somewhat embarrassed.

'Come over to the window and I'll take a look.' Dr. Avery took a magnifying- glass from his desk and held his patient's splayed hand, tilting it to the light.

The young man looked out of the window, where privacy was achieved by a dense shrubbery of evergreens at the side of the house.

'I can reassure you there is no glass present,' said the doctor, as he straightened up.

'I'm much obliged to you, sir.'

'I'll put some iodine on it against infection and bind it up. How did you come to do it?'

'A second's inattention. I was picking up the fragments of a broken phial and the light was dim.'

The doctor turned round from washing his hands and studied him. 'Phial, you say, then you're a druggist? No, wait, would you be the photographer who's set up in Charlotte-street?'

'I'm glad to hear the word is spreading. Business has been decidedly slow,' the young man grinned. 'Winton's the name. Sorry I can't shake hands.'

The doctor nodded and twitched a brief smile. Mr. Philip Winton thought the rather stern countenance looked younger for an instant. Somewhere in his early forties, Dr. Avery had a haggard look to his clean-shaven face, the kind of fellow who would always be lean.

'Take a seat, I'll be with you in a second.'

Winton sat on the worn leather chair and looked about him with interest. The room held the usual paraphernalia to be expected in a doctor's surgery. A large, serviceable desk, a wooden folding couch and a glass-fronted bookcase full of reference volumes. The desk held a scarred blotter, ink-well, pen tray and wipe with a wooden day calendar. Everything was cheap and functional.

In contrast, a handsome, gentleman's stick stood propped in the corner, its wooden handle carved as a horse's head. He hastily averted his gaze as the doctor stepped back in from the adjoining room.

'This is going to sting a little.'

'Your housekeeper said I'm fortunate to have found you at home?'

'I'm usually at the Hospital at this time of day but I called in to collect some papers.' Avery considered Winton's open face as he deftly held the wadding in place, while weaving the bandage. 'It's possible I might be able to put some work your way.'

Pausing, he reached for some scissors. 'We've been raising funds for a new wing. The foundation stone is to be laid before Christmas and naturally, there will be photographs taken to mark the occasion, our benefactors, the trustees and so forth. I see no reason why you shouldn't have the commission.'

'Really?' Winton looked delighted. 'I'd be honoured and most grateful to you, sir. I could submit some samples of my work.'

'Think nothing of it. See that you favour your hand for a while and don't let any of your chemicals near the cut as it heals.'

'Thank you, Doctor. Now, how much do I owe you?'

~

Mist had rolled in from the Channel overnight and crept through every street, hanging a damp shroud over the slate roof-tops. The morning sounds of hooves stamping, barrels rumbling, shop boys sweeping, the cries of street-sellers and the long, piercing train whistle were muffled and hollow. Mr. Halesworth, impatient with the weather and the stink of seaweed, was glad to climb the long hill that shook off Seaborough and wound inland.

As the land rose beyond the town, a thin sunlight was feebly attempting to pierce the clouds. Halesworth held the reins loosely as the gig rattled along at a steady pace, eventually approaching a crossroads where he slowed to turn off. An empty toll-house stood at the corner, door and windows nailed up, its board torn down and the garden behind choked with nettles.

He remembered the last family there, a widow and her seven children. He'd shared a school-room with two of the daughters. They both lay in the churchyard he would shortly pass, along with their father and a brother, dead of consumption, on a sea voyage. The damp saw off the lot of 'em.

The old church tower was coming into view above the trees, its masonry in a poor state. A woman in mourning was entering the lych-gate, carrying a basket of Michaelmas daisies. The click of the latch sent a flurry of rooks cawing and circling. Halesworth eased his pace as he heard the jangle of harness. A cart, heavily laden with bricks, came round the bend towards him. He nodded as the carter touched his hat to him.

Venning church, together with its rectory built in the last century, stood a little way aloof from the village. Then he was upon The Roll Call, with its smoking chimneys. An elderly man was mopping and casting a pail of water through the open door.

The main street consisted of a straggle of cottages, leaning into one another like a row of drunkards, their thatch, for the most part, ragged and streaked with moss. Here and there, they were interspersed with later dwellings. At the end of the street, stood a plain brick house with a spacious yard to one side, in place of a garden. Halesworth turned in and drew to a halt.

Two men were engaged in conversation beside a long workshop. The ground near its entrance was littered with stone chippings. They were gesturing towards a tall object, shrouded in sacking. They looked up, one clapped the other on the shoulder and handed him his mallet, before strolling towards the gig.

'Jem,' he called and a young boy appeared from round the back. 'See to the horse.'

12

'Good day, Caleb.'

'Mornin', Fred, we're honoured. Don't often see you out this way no more.'

'I'm a busy man.' Halesworth eyed the others. 'We need a word. Can we step inside where it's private?'

Caleb drew on his pipe before gesturing with the long stem. 'Best not, I'm waiting on a delivery of marble. Here will do.' They strolled over to the fence which separated the yard from an orchard, its trees bowing with rosy fruit. 'A tidy crop, nothing like Crimson King for cider,' he said, resting his arms on the top.

'Never mind that,' said Halesworth. 'I came by way of Alma Villas. Seems to me you're well behind with the roof.'

'Rain set us back. No need to fret. We'll soon make up.'

'Well, see that you do. That isn't why I came, though. It's Pardoe's accident. Tell me exactly what happened.'

Caleb shrugged and leant one boot on the bottom rung of the fence. 'Don't rightly know.'

As he waited, drumming his fingers, Halesworth compared their appearance, the one in shirt-sleeves and worn moleskins, his own well-cut frock-coat. Caleb's thinning, slightly greasy hair was in sharp contrast to his own thick head, which unlike his brother's, was as brown as ever. No one would think he was the elder.

'He just fell,' said Caleb, frowning. 'No one saw it, see. One minute he were tiling the roof, next thing was, we heard a cry. We come running, we were round the other side but it were too late. There he was, lying on the ground.' He turned aside and spat, causing his brother to wince. 'It was awful, there was nothing we could do. He gave a sort of shudder and died.'

'Dreadful. What did the police have to say?'

'We sent for them, directly, o' course. The sergeant came himself to see. Had a look at the scaffolding, it were fine. Nothing to be said. We were more concerned about someone telling his poor missus.'

'Had Pardoe been drinking?'

'No more than any of 'em. He were sober when he went up the ladder. I'd stake money on it.'

'Then there's no blame to be attached to us. Tancock was satisfied as to that?'

Caleb nodded. 'He must have slipped, poor devil.'

'There's to be no inquest. That fat fool, Tancock doesn't make work for himself. I think we're clear.' Halesworth brushed some specks of dirt from his sleeve. 'I'll be off, then. We can't afford to have talk, especially in my position.'

Caleb gestured for the boy. 'Reckon not.'

'It can be put behind us.' Halesworth drew on his gloves.

'Mrs Pardoe won't be thinking like that.'

'Eh? No, quite right, Caleb. A sum of money, d'you think? As long as it's understood that it doesn't signify culpability. A good-will hand-out for the widow. I shall see to it.'

'How's Rosa, by the way?'

'Spending my money,' said Halesworth, as he mounted the step of his gig. 'I've another plan in mind that'll bring in all the work you can handle. You may need to take on.' He glanced at his old family home as he began to turn. 'I should get the go ahead on the morrow,' he called over his shoulder.

Three

Nathaniel Hicks hung his hat on the stand and went into the room where Biggs was unpacking his case. He was placing his equipment carefully in a certain order on a white cloth, naming each piece under his breath as he always did. Catching his employer's eye, he cleared his throat and gave a small, self-conscious smile.

'I counted them at the house, of course, Mr. Hicks. It wouldn't do to leave anything behind and offend the family.'

'I know I can count on you, Biggs.'

'That is very gratifying.' Jabez Biggs held a long, flexible metal tube up to the light and breathed on it, before wiping a mark with a soft rag.

Various bottles and jars were placed in a row, followed by scissors, darning needle, an enamel dish, several syringes and a large pump.

'More thread needed,' he muttered to himself. Collecting several of his instruments, he set about washing them in the sink, then seeing they were thoroughly dried.

His large teeth and benign expression, the few strands of hair, plastered evenly over his bald pate, gave him the look of a benevolent grandpapa, thought Hicks. Few would guess his clerk was a man of uncommon skill with the tools of his other trade.

Polishing to his satisfaction, Biggs coughed once more. 'I think I may venture, Mr. Hicks, to say that our melancholy business was concluded most satisfactorily.' He began fitting his implements back in their compartments.

'It all went smoothly enough.'

'And due in no small part to young Mr. Winton, if I may say so.'

Hicks nodded. 'He did well, discreet and efficient.' He glanced at the clock on the wall. 'It was his first time, you know.'

Biggs went to the shelf and added a reel of thread to his wooden case. 'I rather had that impression, sir, although he covered it admirably. The family appreciated his manner.'

'Yes, I'm perfectly satisfied. We shall use him again.'

It had been Avery's thought that he might consider giving young Winton a try. A few of them had been playing a hand at The Marine, the doctor was winning. Avery had been more good-humoured than customary, the cares of his medical work tolled hard on him. He'd mentioned that Winton had taken over Draper's studio.

The old fellow had gone to end his days with his daughter in the north of the county. Draper had been getting steadily more deaf and conversation had been awkward for the past year, being as undertaking required low-voiced hints and murmured asides. Relatives in the next room didn't want to hear the nuts and bolts of the matter.

He'd been uncertain about Winton's probable lack of experience but talking it over with Fanny, she agreed the young photographer should have his chance.

'After all, Nat,' she'd said, 'you had no experience when my father gave you your start.'

And so he had paid Winton a visit, finding him a personable young chap, and engaged him, after emphasising the need for tact and professionalism.

'You do see the necessity for getting it right first time? I know that isn't always easy in your line.'

'I understand, sir and am confident I can provide the service you require.' Winton's manner had been suitably dignified and grave.

He'd not cared for probing about the man's private life but the question had to be asked. 'You have seen a dead body before? Forgive my asking but not everyone can remain impassive.'

He'd wanted to kick himself, seeing the pain flare in Winton's eyes for an instant, like a match that went out.

'I have, Mr. Hicks. My mother died a year ago and I was with her until the last. I should show no untoward emotion at the task.'

Winton had kept his word. The family portrait had been taken with the young daughter arranged on a chaise-longue, her parents standing behind. No one would have guessed that leather straps held the pose, beneath the carefully arranged folds of her paisley shawl.

Biggs's artistry had shaded roses in her cheeks, combed her hair and fanned ringlets on her shoulders. The impression was that of a delicate young girl reclining. And so she had been. The photographer had needed little direction, seeming to go about his work instinctively, his demeanour solemn and unobtrusive.

There was only one moment when Winton had faltered. His auburn head, bent over the body, had stilled for too long, his fingers clumsy as he arranged a locket. Fortunately, the three of them were alone. He and Biggs had effected not to notice.

Another dry cough recalled his attention. Biggs had taken down the ledger and was fussily turning the pages. 'It did occur to me to wonder what brought

Mr. Winton to set up in our small town? His accent is not local and he does not appear to have relatives here.'

Hicks reached for an ash-tray. 'I believe his mother died a while ago. He may have no other family and Seaborough is on the up, after all. It's the right sort of place for a young chap to get on, if he works hard.' Producing his case, he proffered it to his clerk. 'Leave that until the morning. Have a smoke, Biggs, it'll lubricate your throat.'

~

The organ swelled to its last notes and was abruptly still. Adelaide Shaw listened attentively as her father gave the final blessing. Though she was aware of an expectant shuffling of boots and stealthy gathering of handkerchiefs and hymnals. She stood waiting, in the second pew, for Miss Chorley to lead the way down the aisle. Miss Geake accompanied her as usual, with downcast eyes. A small, maroon case for prayer book and Bible dangled, on a gold cord handle, from her gloved wrist. Bringing up the rear was Captain Selden.

Adelaide was intrigued to see him at last, his views on the royal family, the management of hospitals and many other matters, being frequently quoted to Seaborough society. She'd noticed his pronouncements always coincided with his aunt's views, which were trenchantly expressed at every occasion.

Her first thought was that he wore his uniform with a diffident stance. His posture tended to the round-shouldered, rather than the erect, confident set associated with army officers. His sandy, somewhat faded hair, and tentative moustache, contributed to her impression.

She had been told, all too often, that the Captain held an administrative post of some importance at the well-known Military Hospital in Hampshire. He had previously served in India. It was, perhaps, a long time since he had bellowed and stood before his men on a parade ground.

He halted and, meeting her eye, smiled shyly, gesturing for her to go before him. She inclined her head, returning his smile and joined the congregation flowing out behind her papa. As she left, Adelaide caught the clove fragrance from the pink carnation pinned on young Mrs Todd's fitted mantle. She leant on her husband's arm, together with her parents, Mr. Jerrold and his wife, as they waited by the porch door to speak to the vicar.

Hovering by a clipped yew, she watched the townsfolk with lively interest. Miss Chorley had taken up position by her papa, as though they were joint hosts on a receiving line. Her nephew, his cap beneath his arm, shook hands with her papa and stood politely aside for the Halesworths.

Adelaide suppressed a wry smile. She could tell that Rosa Halesworth was pricing Mrs Todd's beautifully-cut costume from head to foot. She'll be cutting out a pattern by the end of the week, she thought.

Mr. Halesworth raised his hat, made a brief remark to her father and strode swiftly down the gravelled path, without waiting for his wife. After the least possible acknowledgement, he had turned his shoulder from Miss Chorley. She did not think it could be unconscious. Certainly, Mrs Halesworth looked surprised as she caught up with her husband by the gate. Grasping his stick, he marched off without a backward glance, his wife scurrying to keep pace.

When the parishioners had departed and Reverend Shaw had had a word with his churchwarden, Adelaide and her papa crossed the churchyard path that led to the vicarage garden.

It was Mr. Shaw's habit to spend some time in his study between services, writing a fair copy of his sermon notes, reading and perhaps dozing a little before evensong. Hannah and Betsey had their free afternoon, having already set out a cold collation.

Adelaide sat in the window-seat, reading the previous day's edition of her father's *Times*. Nothing was ever said but she knew he left it deliberately on the dining-table for her use, often folded at a particular page of interest. It was not the sort of improving reading that Miss Chorley would think fitting on a Sunday. She guessed the day would hang heavily at Tower House.

~

'Thank you, Edwin. That will do very well.' Miss Chorley held up her hand and Captain Selden closed the heavy Bible from which he had been reading. 'Tell me, what did you think of our vicar's sermon this morning?'

The captain hesitated, 'he struck me as a good preacher. He looked a mild, old fellow and he certainly didn't thunder from the pulpit, yet his arguments were quietly compelling. He made you think.'

Miss Chorley sighed. 'The purpose of sermonising is not to make one think. But to instruct people how they must behave. The working-classes need clear guidance.' Her heavily-ringed fingers tapped on the knob of her stick. 'What did you think of the text, Ada?'

'It did seem to me that possibly Mr. Shaw's sentiments were a little too sympathetic towards sinners, Miss Chorley. Although, of course, I am not qualified to judge.' Miss Geake turned to the captain. 'Our vicar is known for his charity.' Her hands were folded idly in her lap. Her employer decreed that stitching was not permissible on the Lord's Day.

'Quite so,' said Miss Chorley. 'Pity has its place but wrong-doers need to be shamed on to the path of righteousness. The vicar is a good man but too unworldly. I shall give him a hint.'

'What was the full text?' Miss Geake quoted softly. *'If we confess our sins, he is faithful and just and will forgive us our sins and purify us from all unrighteousness.'* She smiled sweetly at Captain Selden.

'Who was the dark-haired lady who slipped into the pew behind us?'

'Oh, you mean the vicar's daughter,' said Miss Chorley. 'You will meet her when she comes to tea on the morrow. I have invited several people who will be esteemed to make your acquaintance. Miss Shaw is always useful to make up the numbers.'

'Miss Shaw teaches the Sunday school and often gets to the service just in time,' said Miss Geake. 'She is a great help to her father about the parish.'

'Her duties are no excuse for tardiness. Your grandpapa, Edwin, could not abide lax time-keeping. I share his view.'

'I shall be pleased to meet your friends, Aunt Harriet. It's kind of you to arrange it.' Captain Selden shifted the Bible on his knees, looking about for somewhere he might put it down.

Every surface was covered. There were vases, wax flowers under a glass dome, cases displaying a stuffed fox and an otter. His grandfather's collection of snuff-boxes vied with shells, albums of pressed flowers and china.

'It is fortunate, with your visit being brought forward, that I have managed to arrange some entertainment for you. I wish the army could have spared you for longer but I understand the importance of your duties.

You shall tour your grandpapa's Memorial Hospital while you are with us. Though it hardly compares with Netley, we are very proud of its good work. I know you will be eager to see it and have improvements to suggest to Dr. Avery. He is in charge of its management.'

Captain Selden looked somewhat alarmed. 'I shall be pleased to visit, of course, Aunt but I should hardly care to suggest changes. I know little of medical matters.'

'Nonsense, Edwin, you are too modest. You are an able administrator. In the forenoon, I intend that we visit a photographer's studio, for I have no recent likeness of you.'

'Of course, if you wish it, Aunt.'

'We shall visit old friends of mine in Kempston, our nearest market town and take some drives out to view places of interest. On your last evening, I am giving a dinner, when I shall introduce you to Mr. Jerrold, my man of business.' She paused as the long-case clock in the hall began to chime the hour, echoing through the drawing-room. 'That is settled, then. Ada, kindly ring for tea.'

Four

Thunder rolled over the dark, drenched streets of Seaborough. Rain streamed relentlessly, gurgling along gutters, sleeking the sodden fur of scurrying rats. A weak, blurred glow shone from the window of the small police-station, off the Square. A constable's beat was measured in the regular creak of wet boots and the sway of his flickering lantern. The air stank of decaying scraps, seasoned with salt. Lightning sparked for an instant, out at sea.

Pulling her shawl more closely about her, Mrs Fayter looked at the fire-guard and considered stirring up the dying coals. The small, white dog, on the hearth rug, lifted his head and gave his tail a single thump. The doctor had told her not to wait up for him. He was a considerate employer.

She had decided to sit on in her back parlour. When he returned, he'd be soaked and probably exhausted from battling the elements. He would be glad of hot soup. Her one concession, to the lateness of the hour, had been to unpin her hair, ready for bed. It lay now, a loosely woven plait, still with some brown speckling the grey, across one shoulder.

 However, he might not return for hours. 'Infants will come when they've a mind to and not before,' the doctor was wont to say. The farmer up at Burrow had sent word to say his wife had started her confinement, well before time. A year ago, she'd had a breech birth and the poor mite had been delivered dead, despite all the doctor's endeavours. Now, they were afeared it would happen again and Dr. Avery had promised to be with her when her time came.

It was when she had decided to go up, it wanting only twenty minutes to midnight, that the knocking came. At first, she thought the sounds were another clap of thunder. It made her jump but didn't discompose her right out of her senses, like some.

Plenty of her sex would rush around covering all the mirrors, and crouching under the kitchen table, until a storm passed. Gyp wasn't cowed by thunder, either. He'd jumped to his feet and begun barking. When the sounds came again, she recognised the thud of the brass door-knocker, immediately followed by a pounding of fist.

Again, most women would be terrified at this hour but in a doctor's household, it was not unknown. Some poor soul was in great need of medical attention. But she would have to send their messenger away.

'All right there, I'm a coming. I hear you,' she called. 'It's all right, Gyp. Stay there.' Shutting the kitchen door on the excited terrier, she hurried into the hall, undid the bolts and turned the key as swiftly as she could. When she opened the door and looked out, a great stream of rain cascaded down, as though the gutter was blocked with leaves.

A dark, hat-less figure stood in the porch, his hair plastered to his head, one hand clutching the reins of his horse.

'At last. We need the doctor fetching at once. I've come from Tower House, Miss Chorley's taken badly.'

Mrs Fayter inclined her head towards him, struggling to hear over the storm. There was no mistaking the urgency about him. 'The doctor's not here. He's already been called away.'

'But what'll I do? We must have him, there's no time to be lost.' The fellow raised his voice wildly. His mount shook his head, whinnied and shifted his hooves.

'He might not be back for hours. You must try Dr. Miller. Go on.' said Mrs Fayter, as he stood.

As her words sank in, he flung his leg over the saddle, swinging round. The pale horse cantered away down the dark street.

Five

Josiah Abbs was always struck by the contrast between the staid respectability of the cathedral precincts in Exeter and the teeming, foetid West Quarter. The cool, emerald lawns, overlooked by fine, old buildings, the dignified figures in black, clerical garb, were not much more than a hop and a spit from one of the worst rookeries in the west of England.

Within recent memory, cholera had flared through the dog-leg streets and open sewers, killing a hundred or so poor souls, almost breaching the great, barred gates of the Close.

The old thoroughfare of Fore Street bisected the rookery, climbing from the Town Quay with its barques and barges, warehouses and tannery, towards the municipal heart of the modern city. The rise up the hill was a succession of smells. The throat-catching stench from the tannery, gave way to the brewery, its overpowering reek reminding him of meadowsweet along the lanes of boyhood.

There was the sourness of unwashed clothes and flesh, the fug emanating from the many flash-houses and slops emptied from front room beer-shops. Fried fish, the occasional carcass of dog or cat, in winter the smoke from fires, all stewed together.

All of a sudden, you moved into the order of watered streets, crossing-sweepers, hansoms, men of business, precentors and bells. It was his private opinion that the Bishop and clergy turned their back on the desperate wretches beyond their wall. Many were Irish, a generation after those who'd fled to England, escaping famine.

Though better men than he couldn't make a start on clearing it. A cess-pit, his superintendent called it. The rookery was a dangerous place when night fell. Even in mid-afternoon, a fellow had recently been assaulted while foolishly attempting to hand out temperance bills. Abbs was glad he had not been a constable there.

His had been a village beat in Norfolk, where he'd known every poacher and moucher. Reaching the corner of Queen Street, he glanced back at the cathedral towers, dominating the sky from both worlds. Dismissing them from his mind, he pushed open one of the police-station doors.

'Superintendent Nicholls wants to see you, sir. The minute you come in, he said.'

'Understood, Sergeant. Any other messages for me?' Abbs paused by the desk-sergeant's counter.

'Only that one, sir.'

The sergeant busied himself with sharpening a nib and studying the register before him. 'Whenever he deigns to return' was what the old man had actually said but no need to pass that on.

Had Inspector Abbs generally been a bit more friendly like, he might have given him the nod. But Abbs, though pleasant enough, almost gentlemanly in his manner, wasn't one to josh and pass the time of day with you. Stiff as my pa's gammy leg, that one.

'Now then, missus, what ails you?' He beckoned to a red-faced, elderly woman who sat clutching a bundle.

Ignoring, for the moment, the corridor to Nicholls's office, Abbs entered his own small room. Several reports had appeared in the basket in his absence. The crumbs he'd scattered on the window-sill for sparrows had gone. As he began to untie the top folder, someone tapped on the door and entered.

'Saw you come in, sir,' said Sergeant Reeve. 'There's nothing new there, just the night-watchman's statement on the cracksman and the rest mostly need initialling. And the Superintendent wants you, sir. Word is, he's in a foul mood.'

'I daresay our superior has a good deal on his mind,' murmured Abbs drily. 'I'd best find out what.'

It was more than any officer dared to breeze into Nicholls's office after a perfunctory knock. Abbs waited patiently until the testy voice commanded him to enter. Long enough for Inspector Martin to pull a commiserating face as he stepped smartly into the next room.

'At last. Where the devil have you been hiding yourself? No, don't bother,' said the Superintendent, as Abbs opened his mouth to reply.

'Sit down, man. I haven't all day to waste.' Nicholls fiddled with his pen as Abbs complied, before tossing it on his blotter. 'Ever been to Seaborough, have you?'

'Seaborough?' Abbs had to think where it was for a second. A small seaside town, closer to the neighbouring county than Exeter. 'No, Sir. I've never had cause to.'

Nicholls fingered his pen again, his small eyes fixed on Abbs. 'It's a shithole,' he said with relish. He knew perfectly well that Abbs found his turn of phrase distasteful. 'And that's where you're off to.'

Fixing his gaze on the painting of the Queen behind Nicholls's head, Abbs breathed evenly. 'And the nature of the case, sir?'

'Possible murder.' Nicholls consulted a sheet of paper.

'Someone of quality then, to send for us,' said Abbs, thinking aloud. 'Possible, you say?'

'Local gentry, a female. Taken ill suddenly in the night, dead shortly after. Might be nothing in it but the doctor refused to sign the death certificate.'

Abbs leant forward. 'On what grounds, sir?'

The sheet wavered as Nicholls narrowed his eyes to read. 'Not her usual doctor so he hadn't been attending her. The death was unexpected. She hadn't been sickly until then, no more than any old woman with the vapours.'

'Do we take it the victim was well off?'

'I should say. Enough money to endow the local hospital and other good works. She was a spinster, only living relative a nephew, who just happened to be staying with her. He's some sort of army officer. It sounds a thankless mess.' Nicholls appeared satisfied.

'I take it there was a post-mortem?'

'Naturally. Findings inconclusive. The deceased was a patient of the police-surgeon, name of Avery. The organs have been sent to the capital for detailed analysis. In other words, looking for poison. We should hear in a day or two. Some left-overs are being tested, according to this.'

'The inquest was adjourned, presumably?'

'You presume correctly, Inspector.'

'What about the local station, sir?'

Nicholls shrugged. 'The sergeant will brief you. He won't want to tread on any toes, he's got to live there. He won't have a constable to spare, I daresay, so take Reeve with you.'

'Very well, sir. Shall I clear my desk first?'

'You're not indispensable, Abbs. Hand anything over and be on your way before nightfall.' He grinned without warmth. 'It's probably a mare's nest. Some puffed-up doctor wasting police time. But in case there's something in it, talk to the police-surgeon, interview the servants. Do some digging.'

Abbs glanced at the clock on the mantelpiece. It was already five and twenty past three.

'It shouldn't take the pair of you more than a day or two, so don't go thinking you're on holiday. You can return to present the medical evidence when the inquest reopens. If it does turn out to be foul play, I'll be expecting you to get a quick result. That's all.'

'Sir.' Abbs rose to his feet and was almost at the door when the Superintendent spoke again.

'Oh and Abbs, the victim had some folk to afternoon tea on the day she died. No need to bother the guests at this stage. I wouldn't go offending anyone who matters.' He paused, reaching for his snuff-box, before looking up at him, a flicker of malice in his eyes. 'An official complaint could sink you.'

~

The back room at The Marine Hotel felt decidedly stuffy for September. Dr. Avery would have liked to raise the sash and take in some sea air, but the window overlooked the rear yard and stables. He leant against the bar, sipping his whisky and watching the others.

Halesworth gave a triumphant cry as he clicked the red object ball straight into the furthest pocket. 'My game. Come on, Hicks, pay up.'

Hicks added a coin to the two stacked on the rim of the billiard table. 'My mind's not on it tonight.'

'Nor mine, though I still beat you hands down. Not playing tonight, Avery? Not like you.'

Halesworth returned the three balls to their box and pocketed the coins. 'Go on then, put us out of our misery.'

'Not again, Halesworth. You know, full well, I cannot comment on the inquest. It would be grossly unprofessional.'

'But you examined the body. Surely you could tell what killed her?'

Dr. Avery rubbed his forehead. 'It isn't always straightforward.'

'But you could hazard a guess?'

'Look, it's been a long day. I've been up since I don't know when. I simply called in for one quiet drink. You must wait until the town hears.'

'That won't take long, knowing Seaborough,' said Hicks, reaching between them for his glass.

'No, indeed,' said Avery.

'No one's talking of anything else,' said Halesworth. 'But we need to know how this affects us. When the old woman sent me away with a flea in my ear, that was that. Now we're in with a chance again. Didn't I say something'll turn up?'

'Presumably you didn't finish off the old lady yourself?' said Hicks.

'Didn't occur to me, old man. Maybe it was you drumming up custom?' They both laughed heartily.

'Should we be speaking like this?' said Dr. Avery. 'Miss Chorley is dead, after all.'

'Exactly,' said Halesworth, 'and that changes everything. The nephew must get the lot. We need to get in quick and see if he'll sell the land to us. But if there was any funny business, the estate will be tied up for months. Jerrold will see to that.' Reaching in the pocket of his embroidered waistcoat, he pulled out a cigar which he set about lighting. 'What's more, if it turns out she was murdered,' he said, between puffs, 'this Selden's bound to have done it. Who gets the estate then, eh?'

There was a short silence. Avery stared into his glass before draining it.

Hicks pushed the bell on the counter. 'I think we could all do with another. You can't go around saying things like that, Halesworth. Miller's trying to make a name for himself. He's no friend of yours, is he, Avery?'

Dr. Avery smiled faintly. 'I rather think he would like my position.'

'Exactly so. He wouldn't sign the certificate for your patient out of perverseness.'

Avery shook his head. 'I doubt Miller would go that far. He hadn't been attending Miss Chorley. He behaved correctly in the circumstances.'

Halesworth gave an exasperated sigh. 'Where's Emily got to? I've a thirst.'

'I should be on my way,' said Avery.

The door opened and a man poked his head round, his eyes avid behind his wire spectacles.

'I say, have you heard? Oh, Avery, you're here. Then you have heard.' His voice trailed off, crest-fallen.

'Heard what, Cox?' said Halesworth. 'Don't just stand there, come in and spit it out, man.'

'Well, if you insist. I had it direct from your clerk, Hicks, who's been talking to Sergeant Tancock. Two detectives from Exeter are booked in at the Anchor and expected tonight.' He perched on the nearest stool and paused for effect. 'That proves it beyond a doubt. Miss Chorley was murdered, all right.'

~

By the time Abbs had spoken to Reeve, consulted *Bradshaw* and returned to his house to pack a bag, the cathedral clock had struck five. They had arranged to meet by the book-stall and managed to obtain a second-class compartment to themselves.

'The evenings are beginning to draw in,' said Abbs, as they sat down. 'You know, I can never take a train journey without thinking of the Briggs railway murder.'

27

'That was a rum do, sir. Just after I joined the Constabulary, that was. You'd think he would have been safe in first-class.'

'I followed the case with interest. Talking of which, I see you've brought some reading matter, Sergeant. I shall follow your lead.'

'You didn't bring any sandwiches, did you sir? Only my land-lady was out and I'm fair famished.'

'No, I'm afraid not. They'll give us something at the inn, I'm sure.'

'Unless we're too late.' Reeve jumped up again and leant out of the window. 'Wish I'd bought something on the platform.' The great purple brown engine gave a sudden lurch and whoosh of steam as the brakes creaked off.

'Too late now. Pull up the window, would you?'

Reaching up to get the *Flying Post* from his travelling-bag, Reeve settled behind its pages. Abbs smiled to himself as he opened his copy of the *Fortnightly Review,* turning straight to the next chapter of Mr. Trollope's serial. The train gathered speed above the ever-growing streets.

~

Several country stations later, Abbs placed his periodical on the seat beside his tall hat.

Reeve was wiping the grimy glass and peering at the passing farmland. 'It's a long way between villages, sir.'

'A lonely corner of the county.'

'Seaborough's a sleepy sort of place for murder, isn't it? I mean this isn't like a shiv in the guts down some alley.'

'Murders come in all kinds, not only confined to the lower-classes.'

'Do you know the place, sir?'

'Not yet, Sergeant. I understand it's a growing town, looking to promote itself for the holiday trade.' He had made a brief enquiry of Inspector Martin when he passed on his files.

'The Bank holidays will make a difference to seaside towns, they say. D'you like the sea, sir?'

'I prefer not to be on it. I was taken on a boat trip once as a child and was sick over the side.'

He hadn't thought of it in decades, a hot summer's day in Hunstanton. The family were abroad and the staff had been on their yearly outing. Squashed in a wagonette and confined in his too-tight collar, then stuffed full of oysters. He'd already been close to heaving before the sail on the Wash. The ignominy of being held over the rail by his mother, and soundly scolded, came back to him.

'I'll never forget the first time I saw the sea. My pa took us to Brighton. That's the place, better than anywhere in Devonshire. There's nowhere like it for pleasure. Streets of old houses like bride cakes, grand squares and fountains, even an Eastern palace, old King George's place.' Reeve grinned, as if the scenes passed before his mind like a magic lantern. 'The sea was full of little yachts bobbing. There was the chain pier to walk on and along the front, every kind of food-stall you could imagine.'

Watching his enthusiastic face, Abbs wondered what took his sergeant to Devonshire. His accent, indeed his whole demeanour, spoke of a boyhood spent in London. A certain sharpness of intellect, coupled with an easy, assured manner, stood out among the placid, soft-voiced Devon men.

They were both outsiders. It was no coincidence that Nicholls had started assigning Reeve to him, though he feared the association did his sergeant no good.

The sky was beginning to streak with rose pink weepers when they emerged from a tunnel and began to slow at last. Great coal-heaps, and the looming shadow of a gas-works, presented an ugly first impression of the seaside town. The landscape was seeping into dusk, soon darkness would fall as abruptly as a go-to-bed snuffed out.

The jostle of Exeter felt a long way distant, as they stepped down on to the empty platform. They had reached the end of the line. The locomotive stood hissing and belching, subsiding as the fireman jumped down from the footplate.

'We're to be met,' said Abbs, as they looked about them. Only three other people left the train, vanishing through the door, where the shadowy form of a ticket-collector could be glimpsed.

A stout figure, his stomach straining the buttons of a swallow-tail coat, appeared in the doorway, hesitated and walked self-consciously towards them. He wiped the back of his hand across his moustache, dislodging a few pastry flakes, before greeting them.

'Reckon you'll be Inspector Abbs, sir?'

~

The room was small, as the landlord's wife had apologetically mentioned, but it would do very well. The casement window, set in the roof, overlooked the bay and the furnishings were spotless. There was a good, firm mattress and the paper had a cheerful, sprigged flower pattern. A china plaque, bearing the text *Thou God, seest all,* hung over the bed. Abbs looked in the swivel-glass, noting the shadows beneath his eyes and the strained look they held.

Alone at last, he needed to make sense of all the jumbled information he'd accumulated. It was a relief to be away from Nicholls and the feeling he was walking a tightrope, like an act on the halls. One mistake and his superior would delight in his fall. A man must work and he had no other skill, save a certain facility for ferreting out the truth. Removing his shirt and collar, he filled the ewer on the wash-stand and splashed his face with water.

Sergeant Tancock had obtained a growler and their ride to the police-station had only taken a few minutes. He'd thought the town was only built thirty or forty years ago but he was wrong, for The Anchor Inn dated back to the last century. It had probably been a village inn and Seaborough developed from a settlement of fishing folk.

The police-station was modest, adjoining the sergeant's house, and having only two cells. A constable had made them a pot of tea while they talked. Reeve's guts had grumbled but he was provided for at last. Mrs Gaunt, the landlady, had kindly offered them a cold supper and a private parlour to eat it in.

Tancock had hovered between anxious deference and unease. He'd wrongly assumed they would want to see their accommodation and make a start in the morning.

'Too much time has been lost already, Sergeant. That's unavoidable but we need to get started at once. It's vital to talk to people while their memories are still fresh. Preferably before they compare notes but they will have done that.'

Tancock didn't make eye contact as he listened, though he gave Reeve the once over. 'What do 'ee want to do first, sir?'

'Tonight, I need to get a general picture of Miss Chorley's life. I'd like you to tell me all you can now and make two lists for me. First, the members of her household, including every servant. Secondly, anyone she might have come in contact with on the day she died. I need those first thing, if you will.' Tancock had looked somewhat bemused.

'I'll do my best, sir but I don't rightly know who she saw. She had some acquaintance to tea that day.'

'Give me a starting point and we can build on it later. Straight after breakfast, I'd like you to conduct us to the house. I need to see where the death took place. Reeve and I will interview everyone between us.' He'd sounded authoritative, he knew, but he felt taut with the need to overlook nothing.

'Then I shall need a word with the police-surgeon. Where do you suggest I see him?'

The sergeant leant his bulk against the counter, as he thought. 'He could come here, sir, or you could go to the Hospital. I'll send word round to him.'

'We'll meet him there, if you'll direct us on the morrow. I'm sure he's a busy man. And make me an appointment with Miss Chorley's solicitor, if you please. For late afternoon, if possible.' The sergeant looked increasingly unhappy as he scribbled the instructions.

'Now, Sergeant, tell us about Miss Chorley. As much detail as you can. Did you know her to speak to?'

Abbs lay on the bed, his elbow leaning on the bolster. Feeling tired, and distracted by the rhythmic swell of the sea, he opened the post-mortem report and determined to concentrate.

Six

'I can't wait to be out of there, Hannah and that's the truth for you. Being there now makes my flesh crawl. I stick to the kitchen and scullery, at least there's bars on the windows. But going up to bed, well I don't mind telling you, I took the poker up last night.' The speaker swung her head emphatically and clattered her cup in the saucer. 'Is there a drop more in the pot? It settles my nerves.'

'I'll make some fresh, Bessie. You stay there.' Hannah set aside the spent leaves, for Betsey to do the carpets, and measured out some fresh tea. 'Kettle won't be long. Now m'dear, you can't go on like this. There's no need to be feared in the house. You're not alone at night.'

Her companion sniffed and rammed a loose pin more firmly in her mousy hair. 'Sarah's neither use nor ornament, Jane's a silly goose. William's over the stables so he couldn't save us. I don't know if the murderer's lurking in the grounds, waiting for dark or...' she paused dramatically. 'If the danger's locked in with us. I hear her walking about at night, opening doors where she's no place to be. I say my prayers, then I'm too frightened to sleep.'

'It sounds as though Miss Geake can't sleep either. The poor woman's entitled to open a door, without you thinking you'll be murdered in your bed.' Hannah stirred the brown teapot and picked up the strainer. 'Why should you suspect her? She's to be pitied. She's lost her home and no reference, though I daresay Mr. Jerrold will write a line for her. But some will think she's under a cloud, when she goes for another position. It won't be easy. I should say she's frightened herself.'

'Not that one. You think too well of folk, bound to, being in a vicarage family. Oh, she was always butter wouldn't melt in front of Miss Chorley. Spoke very proper to us below stairs, on the surface, but a tongue dipped in lemon juice, all the same. A regular cat, she is. I can't abide the things. I wouldn't hurt one but they're sly creatures, slinking about and Ada Geake's the same. I'm certain sure she had Mary dismissed.'

'It may be so. You'd know her better than most but I can't believe she'd hurt her mistress. Dr. Miller must have got it wrong.'

Bessie shook her head. 'The police believe him. They've searched all the bedrooms, you know. Even been through the linen cupboard, rumpling the lot. I've had bobbies all over my kitchen this morning, their great boots traipsing in my larder. That inspector wanted to know everything about the mistress's meals, on the day she was gathered, God rest her soul. They asked about the scraps an' had anyone else been ill? He seemed interested in the mushrooms I gave them for breakfast, along with best devilled kidneys. I told them and I'll say to anyone, if the mistress was poisoned, it wasn't from my cooking. Ten years I've been at Tower House and always given satisfaction.'

'Don't take on so, you'll give yourself a seizure,' Hannah patted her arm. 'What were the detectives like?'

'Not from these parts, both London men, I'd say. The one in charge was quite genteel for a policeman. They came to the front door, bold as you like. Miss Chorley would have had something to say about that.' Sighing, she helped herself to more sugar. 'He looked ordinary enough, not very dark nor fair. Quiet, but he had a way of looking right through you. Put me in mind of a school-master. The sergeant was a young fellow, well set up, despite his affliction. A port-wine stain on his forehead. Sarah was making eyes at him. *She* was all sweetness and light, offering them tea.'

Bessie gathered her shawl about her shoulders. 'No, my mind's made up. I've a bit put by. I shall ask Mr. Jerrold to let me have my wages and I'm off to my sister's. You must write to me, Hannah. I'm sorry, I'm sure if it's letting Captain Selden down but I don't want to spend another night in that house.' She leant closer. 'If Miss Geake didn't finish off the mistress, then who did? Answer me that.'

'Good day, Mrs Watkins. May I know the question?'

Bessie started guiltily as she looked up to find Reverend Shaw standing in the doorway, a concerned look on his face and a tea cup in his hand.

~

A large cart, with *Halesworth General Builders* on the side, was standing near the entrance of the Hospital. A man on the rear was handing down a sack to his mate. They looked up as the two detectives passed.

Inside, they followed the corridor, as directed by the porter, until they reached a small, open ward. A tall man in a frock-coat, his back to them, was standing by the bed of an elderly woman, while a nurse held back the bedclothes. As they approached, he looked round, murmured a word to his patient, and came towards them.

'Inspector Abbs?' He looked keenly at them both. 'Avery. How d'you do.' He held out his hand and shook briefly with a firm grip, before turning to Reeve.

'Doctor, this is Sergeant Reeve.' Abbs felt that this man could tell a malingerer at a glance.

Dr. Avery nodded pleasantly at Reeve and shook his hand. 'Shall we go to my office?' Without waiting for a reply, he set off further along the corridor.

'It's quieter here than I expected,' said Abbs, as he caught up with Avery.

'It varies, the commotion's first thing in the morning when the sick turn up at the reception room. Not all need to be admitted, of course. Most receive advice and something from the dispensary. The woman I was with has come in today.' Avery winced. 'An ulcerated leg that won't heal, very painful.'

He drew up at a door, which he unlocked, and ushered them in. 'It's poverty at the root of it. Plentiful good food and coal would help. We do what we can. At least, thanks to Miss Chorley, they no longer have to find their way half across the county for help.'

As he spoke, he swept some newspapers off a chair, mostly the pink sheets of *Bell's Sporting Life*. The doctor carried the chair over to the desk, before taking up a stance by the window. 'Do take a seat, both of you.'

Unusual, thought Abbs, not to take his chair behind the desk and dominate the proceedings. But doctors had a natural authority and Avery, in treating Reeve as an equal, seemed to have a refreshing lack of pomposity.

'We noticed the Hospital name.' The lettering carved into the stone lintel, above the red brick, proclaimed The Chorley Memorial Hospital. 'If Miss Chorley had a lot to do with the Hospital, and you were her doctor, you would have met frequently and known her well?'

Dr. Avery frowned in thought. 'Certainly, I knew her fairly well as her medical practitioner and she did send for me quite often. She took a great interest in the Hospital, naturally. But, as you'd expect, she had nothing to do with its daily management.'

Reeve licked his pencil and wrote a brief note. As the sergeant sat with bent head, Abbs saw Avery give an appraising glance at the disfigured skin on the edge of his brow. The port-wine stain flowed like bleeding into his hair.

The doctor leant against the wall between the window and a door to the grounds, its upper portion glazed. 'Miss Chorley gave this land for a Hospital six years ago, in memory of her father. The building was funded by public subscription. We have twenty beds at present. The town, in fact, has recently completed raising the money to extend the hospital with a new wing. A pity she didn't live to see it built.'

'I've read the post-mortem report and know there was no obvious cause to suggest unnatural death. Could you talk us through the symptoms, as you've been told them? I realise you weren't present at the death-bed.'

'No, it's all hearsay. Before I go on, can I offer you gentlemen any refreshment? It's been remiss of me. I can ring for a nurse if you'd care for some tea?'

'No thank you, sir,' said Reeve gloomily.

Abbs smiled inwardly. He was learning. 'That's very civil of you, Doctor, but we had some at Tower House.'

'In that case, I'll continue. You'll have heard from Sergeant Tancock that Miss Chorley's manservant called at my home, at about twenty minutes before midnight. Unfortunately, I was absent, attending a birth at a farm-house, some miles distant, so my housekeeper advised him to seek out Dr. Miller.'

'He reached Tower House shortly after midnight. Sergeant Tancock interviewed Miss Chorley's household, in your presence, the following day?'

'That's correct. Miss Geake, Miss Chorley's companion, stated that her mistress first complained of feeling unwell sometime after eight o'clock. She mentioned a severe headache and retired to her room, afterwards sending for a glass of brandy.

About an hour later, she rang for Miss Geake, complaining of nausea, feeling hot and stomach pains. She vomited copiously and had recurrent diarrhoea. Initially, as I understand it, she refused suggestions to send for me, as she felt increasingly drowsy. She thought the worst was over, after she'd vomited, and simply wanted to sleep.

Miss Geake sat with her. Miss Chorley seemed to doze but later, became in such distress, with further vomiting and diarrhoea, that her nephew was told. He took the decision to send for medical aid.'

Dr. Avery paused to allow Reeve time to write, then went on. 'Apparently, by the time Miller arrived, she was semi-conscious with laboured breathing and there was nothing he could do. He pronounced life extinct shortly after.'

'Thank you, that's very clear.' Abbs looked steadily at him. 'Tell me, Doctor, would you have signed the death certificate?'

Avery sighed. 'In all honesty, Inspector, having attended Miss Chorley regularly, I would have had no reason not to do so. The symptoms, as described to me, are consistent with a sudden gastric fever or food poisoning. I would have questioned those present about what they'd had to eat that day and I believe, would have been perfectly satisfied.'

Reeve looked up, as though keen to ask something.

'Go on, Sergeant.'

'What about the fact that no one else in the house was taken ill, sir?'

'That wouldn't be unusual. I learned, subsequently, that they had mushrooms at breakfast. Also, potted shrimps were served at afternoon tea. It would only need one shrimp to be contaminated or one poisonous mushroom to be picked by mistake. Such things are far from unknown.'

'Thank you, sir.'

'The post-mortem showed nothing untoward, I perceive.'

'No, indeed, Inspector. There were faint traces of vomit in the mouth and throat. A slight swelling to the female organs, which would be consistent with diarrhoea. I had no reason to doubt the truth of the symptoms described.'

Clearing his throat, Abbs worded his next question with care. 'Sergeant Tancock suggested Dr. Miller might have been over-cautious, due to some element of professional rivalry?'

Avery gave a grim smile. 'All professions include an element of professional rivalry, do they not? You must ask Dr. Miller about that. There was some slight ill-feeling, soon after I came to Seaborough. It must be eight years ago. A young boy was failing to improve under Dr. Miller's care. The family consulted me and our opinions differed over treatment. Medical men do disagree, detectives too, on occasion, perhaps?'

'It isn't unknown.' Abbs glanced at the clock on the wall, hanging above a safe. 'We won't keep you much longer, Doctor. Can you tell us why Miss Chorley was in the habit of consulting you and what, if anything, you prescribed?'

'Certainly. In layman's terms, she was something of a hypochondriac. She was, in fact, in reasonable health for someone of her age, which I would estimate in the mid-sixties. However, she had too much time on her hands and she enjoyed being the centre of attention.'

He shifted his position slightly as he thought. 'That may sound harsh but it's all too common among elderly ladies with money. A working-class woman has no time to spare in dwelling on imagined ailments. Miss Chorley suffered from periodic indigestion, due to over-indulgence in rich food, and headaches, which were probably due to boredom or constipation.'

Abbs felt, rather than saw, Reeve suppress a grin. 'She sounds like a lady who would have expected some medicine to take?'

'She did, of course. I made up some headache powders, distilled from willow and also something to ease her digestion. They were little more than flour, sugar and peppermint. A charcoal biscuit would have sufficed. No powder could help her as well as a little more abstinence at the dinner-table.'

'I think that covers everything. Thank you for your time, Doctor, you've been most helpful.'

'I'll ring for a nurse and have you shown out.'

'No need, we can find our way.' At the door, Abbs paused, his hand on the jamb. 'One last thing, Dr. Avery. Do you think it likely that Miss Chorley could have been murdered?'

'The whole town's talking of nothing else but the idea seems preposterous. Who would do such a terrible thing and why?'

'Why indeed? When I was a green young constable, my sergeant used to say that murder's often done to keep things staying the same. I didn't understand then but he was right.'

'If it was murder,' said Avery slowly, 'then someone's been exceedingly clever.'

'By the way, did you meet Captain Selden when he was here?'

'Only briefly. Miss Chorley introduced us after church on the Sunday. You surely don't think...?'

'I'm just gathering information for the Coroner. Until we get those analysis results, it's too soon to think anything yet,' said Abbs.

~

The afternoon silence in the room was broken only by the lessening cries of a pie-seller in the street outside. Reeve knew better than to interrupt the old man when he was reading. He waited as Abbs turned through his notebook, idly looking round the sergeant's office.

Tancock had made himself comfortable. The horsehair chair, in which he was sitting, occupied the chimney corner. A small table, alongside, held a brass ash-tray and a pipe-rack. On the mantelpiece, incongruous in such a place, stood a shiny pink jug emblazoned with the motto, A Present from Margate.

Behind the inspector was the customary row of ledgers, Snowden's *Police Officers and Constables Guide* and bound *Police Gazettes.* It was a curious blend of officialdom and parlour.

'Two ps in opportunity,' murmured Abbs.

'Righto, Sir.'

Abbs closed the notebook, placing it on the desk, next to his own. The remnants of a late lunch, a plate of cold lamb sandwiches, provided by Mrs Tancock, lay beside them. 'Clear and methodical, Reeve.'

He grinned, taking this as high praise. 'Nothing seemed irregular to me. I can't see any of the servants polishing off the old lady, can you, sir?'

'Not on the face of it, no. What did you make of the lady's companion?'

'She was rattled but most people are when we come calling. She didn't strike me as stupid enough to commit murder, when she'd be a likely suspect. Besides, what would she get out of it? She'd lose her home.'

'People kill for all sorts of reasons. They may seem trivial to anyone else but it matters to them, d'you see? It's finding what matters to them, Reeve.'

'Yes, sir.'

'Though I agree, no one at Tower House seems an obvious prospect. We shall see if Miss Geake gets a mention in the will. I doubt there'd be a legacy worth risking a secure position for, let alone the rope. But she could have hated her employer and snapped. That's what I mean. Murder's been done before now because a party continually cracked their knuckles or picked their teeth.'

Lowering his hand, Reeve thought better of scratching his ear again. 'I thought this Captain Selden would have remained at the house. Surely he knew we'd want to see him?'

'I'm not best pleased. He's the most important witness but, until we hear it's foul play, our authority is limited. He spoke to the Coroner and he was due back from his leave. Perhaps he couldn't bear to stay on at Tower House. We don't know how fond he was of his aunt. At any rate, he'll have to return, army or no, when the inquest reopens.'

'When do you think we'll hear from London, sir?'

'Shortly, I hope. Toxicology tests take time but they'll have priority. We can expect the telegraph at any hour. It's still perfectly possible that Miss Chorley died of natural causes. But Superintendent Nicholls directed us here and you and I, Reeve, must do the job before us.' Getting to his feet, the inspector opened his watch. 'Nearly time we were on our way. If you wouldn't mind taking the tray back to Mrs Tancock, I'll wait outside.'

The police-station was in a short street, lying just off a square, the bottom of which was open to the sea. It was a sprightly sort of day, with the tide coming in and sunlight glinting on the water. A few people were strolling along the seafront. Two women were pushing perambulators, with a small child running ahead. An elderly gent carried a newspaper, someone was pushing a well-wrapped figure in a bath-chair.

Reeve caught up with him on the corner, plunging his bowler on his springy hair and wrinkling his nose. 'Phew, what's that? It was hanging around last night.'

'Decaying seaweed.' Abbs pointed his stick towards the beach. 'It's going over, much worse a month ago apparently. Mrs Gaunt told me, she was quite apologetic about it.'

'I'm not surprised. Enough to put anyone off staying here.' Reeve looked at the sea. 'No pier, I suppose?'

'They don't go in for them much in Devonshire. This way, I believe.'

They made their way across the square. Two sides were edged by a row of beeches, their leaves turning. Several gardeners were at work in the flower-borders, digging up the dying carpet-bedding. In the middle, stood a rather ugly drinking fountain. Abbs halted to read the plaque, stating that it was installed, by public subscription, to commemorate Her Majesty's silver jubilee.

The buildings, edging the modest square, were the usual sort found in any town in England. A town-hall dominated the north side, though a miniature of its city counterparts. It had fresh paintwork of Brunswick green and a squat tower, not unlike the one at Miss Chorley's house, though this was faced with a clock.

There were two solidly imposing banks and on the corner, nearest the sea, stood The Marine Hotel.

'Where the swells stay,' said Reeve.

A scruffy fellow was playing a tin whistle beside the town-hall, rather well in Abbs's opinion. He didn't recognise the air, which perhaps had an Irish lilt to it. Its jaunty melody was at odds with the man's unhappy appearance. His beard was as ragged as his trousers and one leg was thrust stiffly forward, from his stool, at an awkward angle.

As they waited to cross the street, a well-dressed man, finishing a cigar, came out of the town-hall and swept swiftly down the steps. He touched his hat to two ladies, then went up to the whistle player. He was obviously sending the other on his way, for the fellow picked up his stool and cap and set off along the pavement.

A discharged soldier, thought Abbs, watching the man's erect back and pronounced limp. 'According to Sergeant Tancock, Mr. Jerrold's office is along here.'

They crossed the junction behind a grocer's van. A row of limes bordered both sides of the street of distinguished bay-fronted terraces.

'Lawyers always do themselves well,' said Reeve.

Seven

The best chair was, by unspoken agreement, left empty. From time to time, one of the ladies glanced up at it, as though seeing a living occupant. Their voices were unusually subdued as they bent over their work and yet, thought Adelaide Shaw, there was an air of suppressed excitement in Mrs Jerrold's drawing-room.

'I don't know how we will ever grow accustomed to these meetings without Miss Chorley's presence. It is very strange without her,' said their hostess.

'It is remarkable how suddenly things can change,' said Adelaide. 'Life goes on in the same way year after year, a little dull perhaps but familiar and comforting. Then in an instant, everything habitual is gone. Hannah calls it the devil giving the pot a stir.' When no one spoke, she coloured and examined the runner she was embroidering.

'We shall have to decide who will now head our society,' said Mrs Fanny Hicks, having fetched some scissors from the ladies at the far end of the room. 'None of us can keep our minds on our work this afternoon. The rumours circulating are too horrible to contemplate.' Sitting down again, she turned to her neighbour, Mrs Todd. 'Let us think of happier matters, my dear. How is your little one?'

'She is teething at present, ma'am and disturbing the household with her cries.'

'It must be a trying time, hearing the poor lamb suffer. I remember it well with my own. If a ring won't soothe her, you must try a spoonful of Godfrey's cordial. There is nothing like it for making an infant sleep.'

'Thank you, I shall mention it to my nursery-maid.'

'If that doesn't work, you must take your Edie to be looked over by Dr. Avery.' Mrs Hicks lowered her voice confidentially. 'If only he had seen Miss Chorley, she may be with us still. Mr. Hicks and I will never cease to bless him for pulling our Thomas through the diphtheria. We had all but resigned ourselves to losing him but the doctor never gave up. All night long, he sat with Tom until the fever broke. I lost two of mine, you know.'

Her hand strayed to a large mourning broach, pinned on her bodice. The customary good humour in Mrs Hicks's placid face faltered momentarily. 'James was gathered with the measles when he was seven and my Blanche, she is with the angels now. Taken from us at ten months by a chill.' She sighed softly. 'We laid her in her christening gown and placed a posy of snowdrops in her tiny hand. We lost her early in the year and that's all the flowers there were.' Mrs Hicks picked up her thread-work, her fingers puckering the cloth.

'I am very sorry to hear of your troubles, Mrs Hicks.'

'Bless you, dear, my tongue has run away with me, as usual.'

Mrs Halesworth leant forward from her corner of the sofa. 'Has Mr. Jerrold met the policemen yet?'

'We really should not be discussing this,' said their hostess. 'Our purpose here is not for idle gossip.'

'But we all want to know what's going on,' said Mrs Halesworth. 'There's little use in denying it.'

'Did not you say Papa was seeing them today, Mama?' said Mrs Todd.

'Hush, Beatrice. You should not mention matters of business.'

'My husband never discusses his business affairs with me,' said Mrs Halesworth.

'As is proper,' said Mrs Jerrold approvingly.

'So I make it my business to find out.'

'You may as well tell us anything you know, Mama.'

Mrs Jerrold bowed to pressure. 'Well,' she looked around the circle of ladies, confident she had their attention. 'Mr. Jerrold did happen to say he is seeing the detectives from Exeter, this very afternoon.' Glances were exchanged in a satisfying response.

'Finding out what's in the will,' said Mrs Halesworth, rummaging in her work-basket.

'I don't think Mr. Jerrold will tell them the terms before it's read,' said his wife. 'His duty is to Captain Seldon now. He wasn't pleased that the police want to see him, not at all,' she muttered with feeling. 'He was quite short with Ann when she brought in his eggs and bacon.'

'What will happen to poor Miss Geake, I wonder?' said Adelaide.

'She'll have to enquire at a domestic employment agency, I suppose,' Mrs Halesworth shrugged. 'Assuming that is, she's...'

'Ladies, please,' said Mrs Jerrold. 'We should speculate no more. And we ought to discuss the arrangements for our sale of work. I shall ring for Ann. I'm sure we're all ready for some tea.'

'I can't help recalling the last time we had tea together, Adelaide,' said Mrs Hicks as they settled themselves again. 'Thank you, Ann, is that seedy cake, I see?' She paused as the parlour-maid helped her from a cake-stand.

'I've been thinking a lot about that day.' Adelaide accepted a sponge finger and began to break off pieces absently. She gazed at the Jerrolds' piano, draped in buff velvet and covered in silver frames. 'No one else was unwell, that I've heard.'

'Miss Chorley wasn't taken ill for some hours afterwards. I know because Mr. Hicks was there after us. This really is delicious. I must get Cook to enquire for the receipt.'

Adelaide glanced at her companion in surprise. The older matron's soft, features still retained sufficient trace of the pretty, young girl she had once been.

Mrs Hicks swallowed her mouthful and continued. 'He wanted some exercise and walked up the hill to escort me home but we had already left. Captain Selden invited him in for a drink. I expect he was glad of some masculine company.' Adelaide nodded thoughtfully as she picked up her tea cup.

'According to Nathaniel, Miss Chorley had retired to her room but not a word was said about ill health. Surely, he wouldn't have been invited in, if she was taken poorly?'

'It does seem to have happened suddenly,' said Adelaide. 'I know Papa is worried about all the rumour-mongering in the town. I have a feeling he believes Miss Chorley was murdered.'

~

Abbs opened his watch, wondering if Mr. Jerrold was engaged or if keeping them waiting was a deliberate ploy, aimed at reminding them of their place. An elderly clerk had shown them into a waiting-room, his manner stiff with disapproval. That was a quarter-hour ago.

Reeve slumped on a wooden chair opposite. From time to time, filling his cheeks with air and blowing, a regrettable habit of his when forcibly inactive. Abbs knew his sergeant preferred to be up and doing. For his part, he'd flicked through the *Transactions of the Devonshire Association,* on the table between them, and examined the watercolour of Dartmoor over the fireplace, thus exhausting the room's entertainment.

He wondered if the very act of requesting an interview had offended the lawyer and would lead to a complaint landing on the desk of Superintendent Nicholls. An investigation like this could feel like tip-toeing through a covert without setting off spring-guns. The door-knob turned silently and the clerk entered.

'Mr. Jerrold, senior will see you now, if you'll come this way.'

They followed him to a panelled door at the rear of the inner hallway. He tapped softly and a voice bade them come in. The man, behind the handsome walnut partners desk, half-rose as they entered and lowered himself again. He was not about to shake hands.

'Good day to you, Inspector,' Mr. Jerrold regarded them over the spectacles on the end of his nose. 'Abbs. An unusual name, not from these parts, I should say? Sit down.'

Abbs took the other chair. 'Thank you, sir. My name is not uncommon in Norfolk, the county of my birth.' He was aware of Reeve looking around for somewhere to sit. 'I wonder if my sergeant might bring a chair closer. I should like him to take notes.'

'If you deem it necessary, though there is little I am in a position to tell you.' The solicitor waited while Reeve carried an upright chair from a bureau. 'I can give you a few minutes.'

He looked self-important and inclined to be irritable, thought Abbs. He didn't care for the way Mr. Jerrold ignored his sergeant but they were inured to it. Reeve certainly did not regard himself as an invisible servant. Evidenced by the way he opened his notebook with a flourish, pencil at the ready and looked around with unashamed interest.

An old-fashioned, marble fireplace dominated the expensively-furnished room. A side-table held a tantalus and a satinwood humidor. A pair of elaborate silver ink-wells stood on the desk.. The window behind Mr. Jerrold looked on to a neat garden of trim hollies and gravel.

Abbs frowned as he debated how to begin. 'I'm sure you appreciate that ours is a difficult position, sir. We are required by the Coroner to investigate the circumstances of Miss Chorley's demise, while awaiting further medical evidence. We must not delay, in the event foul play has been committed. Yet, we have no wish to give offence to her friends and neighbours, who, no doubt, are grieving.'

Mr. Jerrold settled back in his chair. 'I do see your present difficulty, Inspector. Your sentiments do you credit. Naturally, I'm prepared to aid you with any information within my power to disclose.' He steepled his fingertips together, displaying his manicured nails.

'Perhaps you would begin by giving me your impressions of Miss Chorley. I need to get an idea of her life, the position she held in the community. As her legal advisor, you are in an ideal position to give an unbiased account.'

'Quite. You have come to the right person, Inspector. I was Miss Chorley's solicitor for many years. Indeed, my father acted for her father, Mr. Richard

Chorley. Our firm handled all the family's legal affairs, land transactions, wills and so forth.'

'Miss Chorley was unmarried, I know. Did she have much family living?'

'None at all, apart from her nephew Captain Edwin Selden. Her parents died back in my father's time. She was the eldest of three surviving children. Her only brother pre-deceased her, leaving her to inherit the family home, that is Tower House, and her father's entire estate. Without going into detail, I may say that this was considerable in terms of assets and capital. Old Richard Chorley made his money in commerce, a silk and crape factory to be precise. He was a shrewd investor. A warm man, as they say.'

'Where exactly does Captain Selden fit in?'

'He's the son of Miss Chorley's sister, Caroline, who married a Mr. Selden. Neither of them are living. Captain Selden's mother died of small-pox, I believe. Miss Chorley was anxious her nephew should go into the army, following the footsteps of his uncle. Her brother James Chorley died at Inkerman. He was also unmarried.'

'Am I right in assuming that Captain Selden is Miss Chorley's heir?'

Mr. Jerrold took a visible moment to consider. 'Strictly speaking, Inspector, I am not at liberty to disclose the contents of my late client's will, before it is read. Indeed, I, too, find myself in an awkward position while there is this, what can I say... uncertainty regarding the manner of Miss Chorley's death.'

Abbs made no comment. One of his maxims was that if you let a silence alone, the other person will fill it.'

Mr. Jerrold did so. 'I believe I may say that you would be correct in your assumption.'

'Thank you, sir.' Behind him, Reeve scribbled something. 'And Miss Geake, the companion. Can you tell me if she is mentioned in the will?'

'I should neither confirm nor deny, Inspector. Shall we say that Miss Chorley behaved very properly as an employer?'

'I see. Would that be an unusually large sum, sir?'

Mr. Jerrold pursed his lips. 'Miss Chorley was a prudent lady. I would not say that she was unusually generous, no. She left various charitable bequests and the customary legacies to those in her employ at the time of her death.'

'So you wouldn't say the will contained any surprises, sir?'

'I would not.' Hesitating, Mr Jerrold continued. 'My client was in the habit of sending for me, from time to time, to draw up a new will. This is by no means unusual with old ladies, you understand. However, it was mostly the sums that varied. On occasion, one person or another was omitted but this never applied to Captain Selden. Miss Chorley had a great sense of what was due to family. I have now said all I may on the subject.'

'Thank you, sir. Could you tell us more about Miss Chorley's life in Seaborough?'

'I am a very busy man, Inspector. You must not expect me to do all your work for you.' Mr. Jerrold sighed heavily. 'Miss Chorley was one of the town's most prominent personages, sitting on various committees and known for her charitable works. In fact, there wasn't much she didn't take an interest in.'

'Would you care to be more specific?'

'Miss Chorley was a pious lady, thus involved with the parish church. The vicar, Mr. Shaw, can tell you more about that. I know she gave quite a lot of money for various gifts, she provided an organ, for instance. She took a particular interest in the Hospital, as she had it built as a memorial to her father. She led the subscriptions to raise money for a new wing. Dr. Avery is the one to talk to there. He's the visiting doctor and has a practice in the town.'

'We've spoken to Dr. Avery, as he's also the police-surgeon.'

'Ah, yes. I don't know what more I can tell you. Miss Chorley was in charge of the Ladies Society, as we call it, The Ladies' Society for the Relief of Indigent Widows and Orphans, to give it its full title. My wife is a committee member. I believe they are meeting in my own home at this very hour. They are one of the leading charities in Seaborough.' Mr. Jerrold smiled thinly. 'Doing good works provides an interest for the ladies.'

Eight

'They've b......d off back to Exeter and good riddance to 'em, say I.' Sergeant Tancock raised his tankard in a mock salute before taking a great swallow. 'Said something about they'd done all they could here and the inspector had to report back to his superior. Furriners, what do they know?'

His companion rightly interpreted this as meaning not Devonshire men, or possibly, being from the north of the county. 'Where were they from, in your opinion?'

Tancock wiped his mouth, and abundant whiskers, with a clean handkerchief before answering. 'London,' he pronounced. 'Leastways the sergeant, chirpy as a Cockney sparrow. Must've been made up to sergeant young,' he added reflectively. 'There's more opportunity to show your worth in a big place. Not so easy here.'

'You could always bring the murderer to justice,' suggested his companion.

Tancock preened himself momentarily, then his face fell. 'Not likely is it, they wouldn't let me do any interviews. You wouldn't be making fun with me, I hope, Mr. Biggs?'

'Certainly not, Sergeant.'

Jabez Biggs took a tiny sip of his own ale, pulling a face as he did. 'It seems to me that local knowledge will be what's needed to solve this terrible crime.'

'You may be right there. Now, the inspector, he may've been from London or somewhere else. He weren't from these parts, that I do know. There was a something in his voice.'

'Welsh, perhaps or Scotch?' said Biggs, with interest.

'No, I know those. Northerner, maybe.' Tancock downed some more of his drink. 'Who cares? Not I, he's a starchy so-and-so. Talks to you all polite but eyes everywhere. I saw him through the window, blowing dust off my files, looking like he had a week-old dead cat under his nose. Told me to do up my buttons, b---- cheek!'

'It would pay then, if I might suggest, Sergeant Tancock, to ensure everything is in immaculate order before the detectives return for the inquest.'

'I know that,' said the sergeant. 'Your round.' He set down his tankard with a thump.

'Same again for the sergeant, if you please, miss.' Biggs produced a shilling and slid it across the bar.

'Will you be giving evidence yourself, Mr. Tancock?' he asked, when he'd seated himself again.

'That I will. I was the one Dr. Miller sent for, weren't I?'

'I should like to see that. I shall endeavour to attend, work permitting, of course.'

'Well, your customers will wait, won't they?'

Tancock looked round the crowded room as he spoke, from the old men playing dominoes in the corner, to the young clerks and shop-assistants quaffing at the bar. The landlord of the Dewdrop Inn was no fool. They were clustered round the buxom barmaid, like horseflies on fresh dung.

'Anyroad,' he said absently, 'you won't have long to wait. No sooner got rid of them and they'll be back. Resumed inquest date's been set.'

A sharp intake of breath as Mr. Biggs leant forward. 'You did say it was murder, Mr. Tancock?' he said quietly.

'I never said nothing. More than my job's worth. I suppose Hicks will be hoping to bury Miss Chorley?'

Mr. Biggs flushed and gave his single, dry cough. 'I scarcely think the heir would want less than the foremost undertakers in Seaborough. Economy would hardly be fitting.'

'You'll have your work cut out, I know that much. If you take my meaning.' Tancock grinned and took another swig of his ale. 'She weren't pretty when she were alive and the doctor's taken a knife and fork to her. What with her insides being in a jar, I doubt there'll be much left.'

'We should not speak disrespectfully of the departed, Mr. Tancock. For such is the fate as will befall us all.' Mr. Biggs flexed his fingers as he spoke. 'Oh, I do like a challenge.' Getting to his feet, he pulled on his gloves. 'I shall bid you goodnight, sergeant.'

As he eased past the table, he noticed a young man, with his back to them, slide out from the next settle and make his way to the door. 'That's surely young Mr. Winton,' he said to himself.

A burst of piano music came from the tap-room, as the fellow pushed through the crowded public bar and reached the porch.

'I say, Mr. Winton,' called Biggs, as he stepped into the street. The other man turned reluctantly, he thought, and raised his hat.

'Good evening, Mr. Biggs. I beg your pardon, I didn't see you in there.'

'How are you settling in with us? I trust our small town is to your liking?'

'Oh, quite well, thank you. Yes, I'm finding it very pleasant here.' The young man's face was pale in the dusk.

'Business good, I trust?'

'Slow but steady.'

Mr. Biggs coughed discreetly. 'Perhaps we'll have the pleasure of working together again soon. I enjoyed our last association, melancholy though it was.'

'Er yes, indeed. Perhaps we shall. Good night to you.' Winton bowed and set off rapidly towards the square.

Mr. Biggs stood looking after him a while. As the lamp-lighter appeared on the corner, he watched him reach up to the lever with his long pole. In no hurry to return to his modest home and solitary chop, he waited while first one, then a string of tiny flares and pools of soft light spun along the street.

As the man's footsteps drew near, he turned away. 'Yes, I do like a challenge,' he murmured softly, as he thought over what he had learned.

Nine

The makeshift public gallery was as densely packed as a match-safe. Seaborough being too small a town for its own assizes, the Coroner's court was taking place in the ballroom of The Marine Hotel. One by one, the witnesses had taken the stand, Captain Selden, sombre-faced with a mild manner, Miss Geake, demure beneath a black veil.

The two doctors were as contrasting as Jack Sprat and his wife. Miller was short in stature and portly, swaying on his heels with self-importance, Avery, tall, lean and composed. Then came the servants, over-awed and nervy but they struck Abbs as truthful. He had been aware of the craning of necks as he gave his evidence, could almost sense the furrowed brows take in the medical terms as he read them out.

Casually easing forward a little, he let his gaze drift along the row, where the witnesses resumed their seats. Selden was sitting with an elderly man in clerical dress. Unremarkable in appearance, Abbs had nonetheless noticed him following each statement with close attention. Behind him, Mr. Jerrold leant over to say a word to them both.

Whispering and rustlings suddenly ceased, as the door opened at the end of the long room and the twelve jurors filed back in. Abbs watched their self-conscious faces, trying to guess their occupations, shopkeepers, saddlers, carpenters and clerks. The Coroner requested the foreman to give their verdict.

The fellow stood stiffly, in his best suit, swallowing. His voice, when it came, was as cracked as his well-polished boot leather. 'Wilful murder by person or persons unknown.'

The resultant gasps and blatant asides caused the Coroner to rap his gavel on the table before him. Captain Selden sank forward, nibbling one of his nails. Though Miss Geake's expression was impossible to see, Abbs did not miss her gloved fingers clenched on the black-edged handkerchief she held, the sole outward expression of grief to be seen.

Avery was shaking his head in disbelief. Dr. Miller seemed almost elated, turning instantly to his neighbour. A man, in the front row of the public seats, whispered urgently to his dark-bearded companion. The quick movement of his head, with its thick brown waves, set Abbs wondering where he'd seen him before. Then he had it, outside the town-hall, the man admonishing the whistle-player. Beside him, Sergeant Tancock shifted his fat thighs on the hard bench, his tall hat held on his knees.

When the room was silent again, the Coroner spoke for the last time. Florid-faced, with the look of a gentleman who'd rather be exercising his hunter, he discharged the jury and formally released custody of the deceased's body back to the care of the sole relative.

The hotel lobby was thronged with people in no hurry to leave. Abbs pushed past their backs in Tancock's wake. The strain of giving succinct evidence and the press of voices were bringing on one of his headaches. A dull beat was beginning on one side of his forehead, like a lightly tapped hammer, regular as a blacksmith.

The intensity of the blow would gradually strengthen until the only recourse was to lie down in dim light and above all, quiet. Such an antidote was rarely possible for a working man. Fresh air and solitude could suffice, if taken early.

'Let's get out of here, Sergeant.'

'I reckon the doctor wants a word, sir.' Tancock indicated Dr. Avery making his way towards them.

The police-surgeon paused briefly as a benevolent-looking, older man halted his progress. Stepping in his way with a husky cough and consoling expression. At the foot of the stairs, the other doctor, Miller was at the centre of a small group, two of whom turned to stare at Avery as he passed. He caught up with them as they waited by the front entrance.

'Do you mind if we talk outside, Doctor?'

'I'd prefer it, Inspector. I suppose I must get used to being taken for a fool.' Avery halted on the pavement, shaking his head. 'I can't understand it,' he said slowly, half to himself. 'I've been going over the post-mortem in my mind, retracing the steps I took. I don't know what I could have done differently. It's a methodical process.'

'It weren't your fault, Doctor,' said Tancock awkwardly. 'You didn't miss nothing. The Coroner said so. Dr. Miller would've done the same.'

The three men stepped against the wall to allow a lady to pass. She ushered a small boy in front of her, a red balloon bobbing on a string from his hand.

'The Coroner underlined the fact that your findings were perfectly proper, Doctor. The cause of death was inconclusive. Further tests on organs were no reflection on you.'

Avery looked thoughtful. 'Thank you, both. I know, medically, you're correct. I examined the stomach contents carefully. There was no sign of anything unusual.' He rubbed his chin as he considered. 'Forgive me, it makes unpleasant listening for laymen. I had no reason to conduct the Marsh test, which is the only reliable indicator of arsenic in a recent cadaver. But that won't stop people thinking me a poor doctor,' he added, his voice hardening.

'S'cuse me, sir,' broke in Tancock. 'He's a reporter,' jerking a thumb at a man hurrying towards them. 'Shall I see to him?'

'Please do,' murmured Abbs. 'I'll see you back at the station.'

They saw Tancock bar the pavement, placing a beefy hand on the fellow's shoulder, as they turned away.

'It's irrational but I can't rid myself of the feeling I've let Miss Chorley down. She was, in many ways, my benefactress,' said Dr. Avery. 'Without her, I should not have my position at the Hospital.'

'Your feelings do you credit but there's only one person to blame. God willing, they'll answer for this at the end of a rope.'

'The results of the left-over food analysed were clear, you said?'

'That's right. No arsenic was found but of course, most of the tea had been consumed.'

Avery glanced curiously at Abbs, as they strolled. 'Are you unwell, Inspector? You grow pale.'

'A slight headache, nothing more. It was airless in the hotel.'

'In that case, the sea breeze should help. Is your own sergeant not back with you?'

'He was needed elsewhere but he's on his way.'

'You'll have much to do. And I have patients to attend, if they still trust me, so I'll bid you good day.' Raising his hat, Avery tucked his stick under his arm and strode purposefully in front of a waiting brougham.

Crossing the street, Abbs wandered along the promenade and leant against the sea wall, separating it from the beach. It was all shingle, apart from a narrow strip of sand along the seaweed-heaped frill, left by the tide. The sand was a curious reddish brown hue, looking grubby and unappealing.

Inspector Martin was right. Although a pleasant enough town, Seaborough did not look to have the attributes desirable in a resort. No pier, pierrot or Punch and Judy to be seen.

A small tan and white dog came racing along the beach, his owner pottering behind, poking among the pebbles with his stick. Taking in some deep breaths of the pungent air, Abbs watched the contented dog and master, feeling his tension gradually begin to uncoil. He was surprised to find himself aware of Reeve's absence. They were short-handed, back in Exeter. Superintendent Nichols had grudgingly said Reeve could follow on, since it was now officially a murder inquiry.

A sudden burst of raucous, plaintive cries erupted as a few seagulls soared across the sky. As he idly watched, two men reached the bathing-machines and began to push and wheel the first one, bumping it up the beach.

~

Supper had been a sorry affair, from the moment Papa had finished saying grace, thought Adelaide. He'd toyed with his beef, his thoughts clearly elsewhere and even Hannah's stewed blackberries, with a thick crust of cream, had failed to revive his absent spirits. Rising from the table, she went to the sideboard.

'May I fetch you some cheese, Papa?' She waited patiently for him to look up.

'What is it you say, my dear? Ah, some Stilton. No, I think not, tonight. I fear I have little appetite.'

'You usually love blackberries and this was the last of them, it's almost Michaelmas.'

Her father looked down at his bowl, as if wondering how it came there. 'I'm sorry to waste Hannah's labours.'

'Never mind, Papa, shall we sit and be cosy by the fire?'

The vicar smiled gratefully at his daughter. 'I should like that, Adelaide.'

When they were settled on either side of the fireplace, Adelaide took up her embroidery, appearing intent on choosing which colour thread to use next. Her father took his tobacco jar from the mantelpiece, setting it on the small table by his chair. His pipe lay in his hand, as though there were comfort in holding its shape. He made no attempt to fill it.

The coal blazed steadily, its flames reflecting in the fire-dogs. The bottle green, velvet curtains were left open to catch the last vestige of light. To an onlooker, the vicarage drawing-room presented an inviting scene.

After some time, the vicar began to speak. 'The inquest was a great ordeal for Captain Selden.'

Adelaide looked up instantly. 'I suppose none of us can imagine his feelings, the horror of having a relative murdered.'

'Quite so. It has come as a terrible shock to the poor fellow. He had seen very little of his aunt for some years but one always thinks there is time.' Her father was gazing into the fire, then his eyes met hers. 'This cannot be said to be God's will, Adelaide. I wish I could believe it the work of a stranger but I cannot.' He grasped the stem of his pipe. 'Someone among us has done this appalling deed.'

Setting aside all pretence of industry, Adelaide considered her father's words. 'You don't think Captain Selden then...?' She felt unable to be any more direct.

Removing the lid of the tobacco jar, Samuel Shaw began trailing the mixture through his fingers, before packing a little into the bowl of his pipe.

'He seems a perfectly agreeable man but people are saying... well, we don't really know him.'

'I know what people are saying,' said Mr. Shaw. 'No, I don't believe Captain Selden came visiting his aunt, supplied with arsenic. Quite apart from his good character, no one in their senses would do something so likely to throw themselves under suspicion.'

'But Papa, surely whoever did this has lost their senses. Won't they be insane?' Someone has quietly lost their mind, without anyone noticing.'

'In the meaning that they've lost all sense of right and wrong, I agree, my dear.' said Mr. Shaw, between puffs. 'But as a man of God, I must make a distinction between insanity and evil. It seems to me that Miss Chorley's murder has been carefully planned. Quite possibly, in such a way as to lay suspicion on the Captain.'

There was silence while Adelaide considered this. 'I can't believe it to be one of the servants, we know them all. Nor Miss Geake, she's been with Miss Chorley for years. Companions don't kill their mistress because they're bored or been a little condescended to.'

'The police will surely focus their attention on her and that will be a most unpleasant experience. I shall offer her my support on the morrow. Together with any constructive help I can give, such as writing a character reference.'

'You are going to Tower House, Papa?'

'Captain Selden wishes to discuss the funeral service. Because of the circumstances, he thinks it proper that it be less elaborate than one would usually expect.' The vicar shook his head sadly. 'He went to make the arrangements with Mr. Hicks, after the inquest. Because there's already been a great delay, it must take place with all urgency. It is to be in three days' time. Miss Chorley will be interred with her father, of course.'

Adelaide nodded. Richard Chorley was laid to rest in a large, square plot ,surmounted by a tall, marble cross. 'Your diary is free, fortunately, Papa.'

Her father looked warmly at her. 'I do not know what I should do without you, Adelaide. The Captain has been given leave of absence until after the funeral, then he talks of having the house shut up. I don't know his plans thereafter but it doesn't sound as though he intends to make his future home in Seaborough.'

'I suppose the policemen from Exeter will question him first?'

'The detective-inspector spoke to him before the inquest. He wishes to call on the Captain and Miss Geake in the forenoon.' Mr. Shaw knocked out his pipe on the grate. 'Even tobacco will not comfort me this evening. I must give a great deal of thought to my sermon this week.' He glanced up at the window. 'Darkness has fallen. Will you shut out the night, my dear?'

'Of course, Papa.' As she did every evening, Adelaide looked across at the low spire, rising like a finger pointing heavenwards, between the line of holm oaks separating the garden from the churchyard.

The moon was a thin sliver. The garden looked faintly sinister, with shapes of ink-black darkness and chess-piece shadows. She told herself not to be so foolish, knowing full well that morning would return them to sundial, yew hedge, monkey puzzle and fir.

'Have you spoken to the detectives, Papa?' she asked as she drew the curtains.

'Not yet. I saw the inspector give his evidence. He struck me as an intelligent man. You will have to prepare to meet them yourself, Adelaide. No doubt, the police will wish to question us both, in due course.'

She spun round in surprise. 'But we cannot help them, we know nothing.'

'We knew Miss Chorley and we were present at Tower House on that last day. Don't look so alarmed, my dear. The police can only work by speaking to everyone and piecing information together. We will, all of us, have a little to tell.'

Ten

One of the traits, Abbs was beginning to like in Reeve, was his enthusiasm for his work. Most subordinates waited passively for orders. Reeve was full of questions and keen to play his part in solving their inquiry. He was minded to allow him to speak to the servants again, by himself.

Abbs looked up at the house, with its sash windows and drawn curtains. It had stood, if he was any judge, before the town was built and been remodelled in the present century. The eponymous, square tower stood at one end and a large, tiled porch was an after-thought. An ugly pile, its additions sprouting like warts on an old face.

'Which door this time, sir?'

'The front.'

As was customary, the knocker was bound with crape. Its muffled thuds brought the young parlour-maid, wearing black ribbon on her cap, to admit them.

'Captain Selden said to show you into the library. Shall I take your things?' She tapped on a door further along the hall and entered.

'If you please, sir, it's the detectives.' Eyeing them with open curiosity, she bobbed a curtsey and withdrew.

The room was dominated by a large, oil painting, hanging above the fireplace. Its hazy gun-carriages, smoke and patchy, red figures caught the eye, before the man who moved forward to greet them.

'Good day, Inspector.'

Abbs introduced Reeve and the three of them sat on a pair of sofas, arranged near the window. 'We're sorry to disturb you at such a distressing time, Captain, but you'll understand the urgency. A good deal of time has been lost.'

Captain Selden inclined his head. 'Of course. I'll answer your questions as well as I can. Naturally, I want my aunt's murderer caught.' He swept his hand before him. 'Though frankly, I don't see what use I can be.'

In Abbs's opinion, witnesses who prefaced their statement with frankly, rarely were so. However, innocent people were often nervous when interviewed by the police. He decided to keep an open mind for the moment.

'It's a question, sir, of taking statements from everyone in Miss Chorley's circle. Each person adds information to build an overall picture. We look for someone with motive, means and opportunity.'

The Captain was examining his nails, which were badly bitten. His hands were on the small side for a man and lightly freckled. He looked up as Abbs finished speaking. 'Where do you wish me to start?'

'I have to ask you, sir, if you have any knowledge of a motive for this crime. Did your aunt speak of anyone with a grudge against her, or a quarrel in her private life or business affairs?'

Hesitating slightly, Selden shook his head. 'I can think of nothing, Inspector and I've thought of little else. I still believe my aunt's death might have been an accident. Nothing else makes sense.'

'You heard the medical evidence at the inquest, sir. I'm afraid that's been ruled out. While ladies do use arsenic for cosmetic reasons, it's extremely unlikely that anyone would take such a hefty dose.'

Selden picked at the side of his thumbnail as he listened. 'Very well, I accept what you say.'

'The truth may lie somewhere in Miss Chorley's character. Forgive me, but would you say she was a lady who made enemies?'

'You must understand, I have not seen my aunt for several years. Until a little under a year ago, my regiment was in India. Since my return to this country, I've been settling into an administrative post. My aunt invited me to visit her and this was the first chance to do so.'

'Nothing comes to mind that Miss Chorley mentioned in a letter? An incident that sounded trivial at the time, perhaps?'

'Not that I recall.' Selden watched Reeve make a note. 'I have almost no knowledge of my aunt's circle. She wrote at regular intervals and mentioned her charity work, the local Hospital, orphans and so on. I know she took a great interest in the church but I didn't pay a great deal of attention. It all seemed a very long way off.' His gaze fell on the brown-shaded globe, standing in an alcove.

'To be honest, Inspector, my aunt was of a somewhat forceful disposition. She meant well, had people's best interests at heart and all that. But she always thought she knew better than they did. She pushed me into the army at a young age, solely because her brother had served in the North Gloucesters. My father gave way to her and I had no say in the matter.'

Couldn't stand up to her, thought Abbs.

Selden was settling into his stride, nerves forgotten, his soft voice taking on a hard-done-by tone. 'I certainly don't mean to speak ill of the dead, Inspector.'

'That's understood, sir.'

'Thinking about it, I suppose it's possible my aunt unwittingly got someone's back up.' He shrugged, falling silent.

'Your candour is appreciated, Captain. We have a list of everyone invited to tea here on the day Miss Chorley died. D'you have it, sergeant?' Reeve handed him the paper.

'My aunt wanted me to meet some of her acquaintance. There were three ladies, all involved with her charity work, I believe. Her neighbour, an elderly gentleman, on the Hospital board, and the vicar.'

'Did you see or hear anything unusual, throughout the afternoon?'

'Not at all.'

'What about anyone near Miss Chorley's food or drink?'

'No, but one doesn't pay attention to such things. The maid passed her plates and the cake-stand. Miss Geake poured tea for her several times, I think.'

Abbs nodded. 'You didn't see a guest anywhere in the house that they shouldn't be?'

Captain Selden touched his neat moustache with the back of a knuckle. 'I saw nothing out of the ordinary. People did move about. The ladies went off to the conservatory to look at plants. And I suppose to wash their hands and so forth.'

Reeve cleared his throat, hunching further over his notebook. Abbs gave him a look. 'Did Miss Chorley see anyone else that day?'

'As a matter of fact, yes. I escorted her to a photographer's studio in the forenoon. She wanted a recent likeness of me in uniform.'

Abbs and Reeve exchanged glances. 'Miss Geake didn't mention this.'

'I daresay it slipped her mind. She didn't accompany us.'

'Where was this, Captain Selden?'

'Just off the high street, I don't recall the name. The photographer was a young chap. New to the town, I believe my aunt said.'

'We'll find him. Were you offered any refreshment?'

'By Jove, yes. Now you mention it, my aunt accepted a cup of tea, while she watched. I'm almost sure it was accompanied by some small tarts. But the photographer was a stranger to her.'

'Just routine. We'd be failing in our duty if we didn't account for all the food and drink Miss Chorley had that day.'

'Yes, of course. There's one thing, I had a drink, early that evening, with a gentleman named Hicks. His wife was one of the guests that afternoon. He called to collect her but she'd already gone. I invited him in but he didn't even see my aunt.'

'What time was this?'

'About six, I should say. My aunt was upstairs and unaware that Mr. Hicks was in the house. We had a whisky and soda in here. Fact is, I was glad of some masculine company.'

'Had you met Mr. Hicks previously?'

'We were introduced briefly after church. He expressed an interest in India. I've seen him since. Turns out he's the undertaker.'

'Did Mr. Hicks leave your presence, while he was here?'

'He didn't leave this room but I did, for a short time. I went to my bedroom to fetch a map to show him. He stayed around a half-hour. But my aunt wasn't taken ill until eight or thereabouts.'

'The maid said Miss Chorley rang for a glass of brandy, after she went upstairs. Would that have been obtained from the tantalus in here, sir?'

'It's the only one I've seen. Yes, I suppose it would.'

'And this was after Mr. Hicks left?'

'Yes, though I don't see where this is leading.'

Abbs rose to his feet, Reeve at once following his lead. 'You've been very patient, Captain, thank you.'

'I hope I've been of some use.' Selden paused by the fireplace, where Reeve was gazing at the painting. 'Inkerman, Sergeant. My uncle lost his life there in the fog. That's his regiment, the 28th Foot. My grandfather had it done.'

'Mr. Jerrold mentioned you'd be having the house closed up after the funeral, sir? 'said Abbs.

'I've changed my mind,' replied Selden, as he rang the bell. 'I've asked Miss Geake if she'd be willing to stay on for a while, until everything is resolved. It makes sense as she'll need time to inquire after a new position. I shall return to Hampshire straight after the funeral. When this nightmare's finally over, I shall sell.'

'Perhaps Sergeant Reeve could have another word with the servants, while I see Miss Geake?'

~

'She was in here,' said the parlour-maid uncertainly. Her face cleared as she saw the door ajar. 'She must have stepped outside.'

'Don't worry, I'll find her,' said Abbs. 'It's Sarah, isn't it?'

'Yes, sir.' The young woman looked gratified that he remembered.

'Would you take the sergeant to see Mrs Watkins, please. He'd like to ask you all a few more questions. Nothing to worry about,' he added.

Sarah nodded and turned on her heel, the sway of her skirt indicated she was aware of Reeve following her.

Left alone, Abbs looked around the conservatory. Sunlight through the upper glass was reflecting red, yellow and blue lights across the tiles. They seemed to quiver fractionally and move as he did. Maidenhair fern, mother-in-law's tongue and ivies spilled from clay pots along the wide window-sill.

He halted before a Wardian case, thinking there was something unpleasant about the way the plants were trapped. The smell of watered compost took him momentarily back to boyhood, to the orangery at the Hall, with his father. Pushing away the past, he circumvented the iron seat and table, leaving by the garden-door.

Miss Geake was standing before a flower-border. A thin, black figure in a paramatta dress, scissors in her hand and a flat basket at her feet. She watched him walk towards her along the brick path, a spray of bronze flowers raised to her face.

'Do you care for chrysanthemums, Inspector? What could be more appropriate for a house of mourning? I always think they smell of death.'

Country folk likened them to cats' piss. He knew what she meant. They were the scent of decay, a cemetery flower. In autumn, he always purchased a bunch from the old woman outside the gates, perhaps it was because they lasted well.

'Good day, Miss Geake. I can't say I've given it any thought.'

'Ah, a ladies' companion has plenty of time to think, you see.' She turned away from him, as she laid the stems in her basket.

'I don't doubt you've been thinking about Miss Chorley's death.'

'Of course.' She selected a stem and cut it, discarding a spent bloom. 'Really, the gardeners have become lax but then, they are no longer admonished.' She smiled archly at him, as though she were pouring tea.

'They don't live on the premises and they weren't here the day Miss Chorley died.' Abbs recalled his earlier visit. Sergeant Tancock's men had spoken to them.

'We wouldn't want them looking in the window, at their betters.' Miss Geake gave a vicious snip to another stem.

Abbs sighed inwardly. 'Miss Geake, your employer was murdered. I need to know if you can think of any reason for her death, or any unusual event in the last weeks? No matter how trivial.'

'I believe I can, Inspector.'

'Perhaps you'd care to sit?' He gestured to a nearby, wooden bench and picked up her basket. 'This is a pleasant, sheltered corner.' He waited until she had arranged her skirt and began to speak again.

'Have you encountered Mr. Alfred Halesworth?'

He shook his head. 'I have not, though the name is familiar. I know a Mrs Rosa Halesworth was a guest here, on the day Miss Chorley died.'

'His wife.' Snip, went the scissors as she began to trim the ends of the stalks. 'He's a councillor and regards himself as one of the leading men in Seaborough.'

'Was he a friend of Miss Chorley?' asked Abbs, noting her choice of phrase.

Miss Geake sniffed. 'He would like to have been. No, she thought him a parvenu. And she would know,' she remarked, in an aside. 'She saw Mrs Halesworth often, through the Ladies' Society, hence the invitation. That's where the comfortably-off ladies of Seaborough meet to gossip and interfere in the lives of their inferiors. I was required to attend to thread Miss Chorley's needle and carry her work-box.'

Abbs wondered about the change in Miss Geake's demeanour since their first meeting. He glanced discreetly at her face. Handsome, though with too strong a nose to be considered a desirable specimen of womanhood. They were much of an age.

Her eyes sparkled with malice and a fierce intelligence. Was it the knowledge that a legacy was coming, together with a few weeks' respite from seeking a new position? She seemed to have the measure of her former employer. Surely, she did not anticipate enough money to set her free?

'A few days before Miss Chorley died, she asked me to write a note to Mr. Halesworth, agreeing to his request for an interview.'

'Do you know what this interview was about?'

'I do not. At first, I thought he was after a subscription.'

'What changed your mind?'

'He came the following day, on the morning before Captain Selden's arrival. I was not asked to be present and overheard nothing. But I happened to be entering the hall when Mr. Halesworth left.' She paused before continuing. 'He pushed by me, ignoring my greeting. He grabbed his stick so hurriedly, he almost upended the stand. Then he wrenched the door open, without waiting to be shown out. I think he would have slammed it, had he dared. He was furious.' She sat back, in unmistakable satisfaction.

'Thank you for telling me,' said Abbs. He took out his notebook.

'There is something else you should know, Inspector.'

'Indeed, Miss Geake?'

She was clearly enjoying herself. He could understand, it was a relief to say what she thought, without picking her words. Though, he did not care for her relish.

'A few weeks ago, a parlour-maid was dismissed for stealing. No doubt, she bore a grudge against Miss Chorley.'

'What were the circumstances?'

'The girl stole a garnet ring from her mistress, probably thinking it a valuable ruby. It was missed and a general search made. It was found hidden among her possessions. She was dismissed at once.'

'Were the police called?'

'No,' Miss Geake looked sideways at Abbs and smiled. 'Miss Chorley did not care to have the Constabulary in the house. Mary was sent back to her family, without a character.'

'Surely she could have had no access to this house afterwards?'

'You might think that but I happened to see her in the lane, the day before Miss Chorley died. If she had nerve enough to steal, she could have been visiting one of the servants. She was friendly with them, I daresay.'

'Where might I find this Mary?'

'Her father keeps a small farm beyond Venning. That's the nearest village if you continue past the house.' Abbs made a note, as she gave him the name and further directions.

'Did you also happen to see Mr. Nathaniel Hicks call on the day of the tea party?'

'No, I did not.' Miss Geake sounded surprised. 'Are you sure about that, Inspector? He was not invited, unlike his wife. She's a good-natured, vapid creature who never stops talking.'

'I'm quite sure, Miss Geake.'

'Nathaniel Hicks, you'll find, is a close friend of Mr. Halesworth.'

'One thing more,' said Abbs 'and I won't take up your time any longer. To your knowledge, has arsenic ever been purchased for this household? For the gardener or groom for instance, or for Miss Chorley herself?'

'For her complexion, you mean? Not for the stables, as far as I know. I've never heard tell of rats there but you'd best ask William. As for Miss Chorley, it's not something she ever confided in me but she was vain enough.' Miss Geake picked up her basket, setting it on her lap, preparatory to moving. 'Her hair was thinning and she wore a false piece, though she'd never admit it. She preened herself when Mr. Emerson sat by her at the tea-table, though he's past seventy. He had ample opportunity to poison her.'

Abbs recalled Miss Chorley's dressing-table, with its ivory-inlaid brushes and hand-glass. Among the trinket trays and scent bottles, there'd been a china hair-holder, with some long, grey hairs saved.

He found such intimate sights distasteful and sad. Murder had many consequences, loss of dignity for the victim was one of them. Many a small secret would be laid bare, before he and Reeve were done.

'You'll find many things about Miss Chorley were false. You saw the library, shelf upon shelf of books in their fine bindings. All for show. Her father bought them, to impress callers with his learning. They've never been read and I daresay never will be. I was not permitted to borrow any.' Her voice shook with suppressed ire.

Standing abruptly, Miss Geake faced him as he rose. She snipped each word, in the same way she'd wielded the scissors. 'And the brother, the distinguished hero of Inkerman. She was always vague about exactly how he died. No medals for valour ever mentioned and believe me, they would have been. I should enquire of Captain Selden. It's my belief his uncle died of the flux.'

'I'm grateful for your candour, Miss Geake.' Abbs followed her inside, her flare of temper seemingly snuffed out.

She sounded subdued, as she turned to him in the conservatory. 'I must get these in water. I'll bid you good day, Inspector. The maid will show you out.'

Reeve, waiting in the hall was eyeing a stag's head mounted over a door. Abbs, minded of Miss Geake's scornful outburst, doubted it had been shot by a Chorley.

He elected to walk back, knowing Nicholls would not countenance any cab fares on expenses. It would give them a chance to get the measure of the town. When they were a few yards from the gates, a brougham slowed past them and turned in, affording a glimpse of the clerical gentleman, who'd been at the inquest.

'Shame you weren't in the kitchen, sir,' said Reeve. 'Mrs Watkins insisted I try her lardy cake.'

'You're confident that nothing new emerged, since we were here previously?'

'Yes, sir. The cook's still livid that someone put poison in her food. The scullery-maid's terrified we think it was her, that's the gist of it.'

Abbs nodded, deep in thought. 'Miss Geake, on the other hand, was fulsome in her fresh information.'

He related all he'd been told, as they walked along the hedgerows, clusters of ripe elderberries bending over their heads. A woman in a donkey-cart passed them. They reached a wagon, so laden with hay, it was having difficulty turning from a by-way. A fellow had jumped down and was gesturing encouragement at the horse and driver.

As they turned into a bend, Seaborough lay spread out below them. Grey, slate roof-tops with drifting smoke, a cemetery with a chapel, its headstones bunched in a corner. They saw the drum of a small gas-works, with its heaps of coal, a church spire, the town-hall square and the dirty-looking beach, nibbled by the sea. They began the long descent into the residential streets. The hollow, damp hoot of a train sounding, as it chugged on its way.

'We'll have to talk to Mr. Halesworth. The question is how best to approach him. We can't very well, ask him bluntly, why he quarrelled with Miss Chorley. He'll only deny it. There's the photographer to be seen, the undertaker and the guests at the afternoon tea. Plenty to keep us busy.'

'What about the maid who was dismissed, sir?'

'I shall send you to talk to her, Sergeant. She might be more forthcoming with someone nearer her own age.'

'Righto, sir,' said Reeve, grinning with pleasure. 'You reckon I'll know if she's lying?'

'Trust your instincts, Reeve.' They reached a hump-backed bridge and both paused to look over the parapet at the railway-line beneath. 'We'll head back to the police-station now and find out where this photographer has his place of business. His name's Winton. Sergeant Tancock is sure to know. We shall call on him this afternoon, but first, I could do with a cup of tea. You were obviously well looked after in the servants' hall.'

'I wouldn't say no to stopping off for a pie along the way, sir. This sea air's giving me an appetite.'

Eleven

It was a most ordinary street, in a fair-sized market town, and that was the beauty of it. Small enough to be a pleasant place for a young widow to settle, yet large enough for her to make a modest living and above all, to be anonymous. One of the more useful amenities of this ancient settlement, with its coaching inns and crumbling butter-cross, was a station. In a westerly direction, the line eventually ran to Exeter but long before that, a line branched off to the small, seaside town of Seaborough.

Mr. Alfred Halesworth had quite forgotten it was market day in Kempston and found that when he alighted on the platform, a good many people followed suit from the inferior carriages. He had elected to wear sober attire and carried a stick with a derby handle of plain cow horn, as befits a shop manager or clerk, rather than the fine silver pommel he usually favoured. Though his appearance was unremarkable, his spirits were good. His confident stride, and jaunty air, still caught the eye of more than one young woman.

Perceval-street was situated conveniently near the station. Its houses were small and respectable, spotless cream or écru lace hung from every bay, despite the proximity of soot. The entrance to an alley lay between each short terrace, the earthen paths free from weeds and rubbish.

The thoroughfare was empty, yet Mr. Halesworth glanced back before extracting a house key from his coat pocket. A few paces on the tiled path took him to the front door of one particular house. Cheerful, scarlet geraniums still bloomed in the diamond-shaped border of its diminutive front garden.

In the scullery, a woman, at the sink, caught the sound of a key scratching in the lock. Hastily drying her hands on a cloth, she unfolded her cuffs and smoothed the wisps of her fair hair as she hurried to the front door.

'Oh Fred, it's you,' she exclaimed, her complexion warm with pleasure. 'It isn't your day. There's nothing's wrong, is there?'

'Nothing at all. Some council business was postponed and I fancied getting away. Aren't you pleased to see me?' His voice was teasing as he hung his hat and coat on a peg.

The hall was so narrow that a person could touch both walls, leaving no space for a stand. An oak barometer hung to one side, its round edge decorated with carved leaves and acorns. Opposite, hung a small looking-glass. Below, a slender shelf, hardly more than a ledge, served for letters.

'Oh, Fred, you must know how pleased I am. It's only, imagine what would I do if I had a pupil?'

Halesworth chuckled and caught at the strings of her apron. 'Luckily you're alone and can devote your time to me, Nelly.'

'The fire's lit, go through and I'll bring us some tea.' Nelly folded her apron as she spoke and ushered him through the half-open door.

In the front parlour, everything was trim and welcoming. The piano took pride of place, with its twin stools and tidy pile of sheet music on top. Some sort of fern stood, in a brown glazed bowl, on the table in the window. Tobacco-coloured button-back chairs were arranged invitingly by the hearth.

Looking about, Halesworth idly wondered why he always felt so at home in the unassuming room. He sat back, closing his eyes for a moment, soothed by the sounds of a kettle on the range and the rattle of china.

'How are Miss Lavinia and little Myrtle?' said Nelly, when they were sipping their tea.

Halesworth grunted. 'They're off having their photograph taken to mark Vinnie's birthday on Sunday.'

'How lovely for them. And does she still practise?'

'Their mother sees to that sort of thing. I don't see much of them. Let's not talk of Seaborough. How's the boy doing?'

'Very well. He's in good health and working hard at school. Can you stay to see him? He would love to see his uncle.'

'I don't see why not. I'm glad to hear he's getting on. He's a bright boy, a credit to you. Does he need anything?'

'No, thank you. You're ever so kind but I'm managing. Alfred wants for nothing.'

'Come now, no false pride. You would say, Nelly? I don't want the lad going to school in tight boots.'

'Truly, we're doing all right. You're already so good to us and I don't want to take advantage.' She smiled fondly at him. 'You look tired, Fred. You work so hard for all of us.'

He felt touched by the concern on her pretty face. What a contrast to Rosa and her never-ending list of things needed for herself, the house and their daughters. Only that morning, she'd ruined his breakfast by prattling on about the wretched photographer. Never mind that Cook had overdone his chop and a chap liked to read *The Times* in peace.

'I do have a lot of concerns at present,' he said, setting his saucer on the hearth and stretching. How pleasant it was to put his cup where he liked, without his missus objecting. 'Mind, one obstacle has been removed. I always get what I want, one way or another.' He patted his lap invitingly. 'Come sit by me, Nelly. We'll go upstairs presently.'

~

P. Winton. Portrait and Landscape Photographic Artist was inscribed in freshly painted lettering. The window held three large photographs displayed on stands, against a maroon curtain. Two of them were conventional portraits, a single gentleman standing and a family group seated.

The other was more interesting in Abbs's eyes. It depicted a stream tumbling down a rocky chasm in woodland, with a pattern of dappled sunlight on the leaves. A selection of *cartes de visite* were laid out in a fan shape and a framed notice of black-inked terms completed the display.

'Negatives carefully kept. Copies may be had at any time. Charges extra for children,' said Reeve. 'Because of keeping them still, I suppose.'

'I imagine so,' said Abbs. 'I daresay spoiling the plates comes expensive.'

A bell jangled as he pushed open the door. They entered a cramped room which seemed full of people. A smartly dressed matron was seated by a desk, where a young man, in a frock-coat, was scribbling something. He looked up, with a harassed expression.

A young girl was sitting against the wall, together with a nurse-maid, who was attending to a much younger child. The girl threw them an indifferent glance and looked away.

'Good afternoon, gentlemen. Please take a seat and I'll be with you in one moment,' said the young man.

'Put your arms through, Miss Myrtle, that's right,' murmured the maid. She stooped over the wriggling child and attempted to button her into a jacket. Although there were two empty chairs, Abbs and Reeve elected to remain apart from the family group.

'You'll send them round before Sunday, Mr. Winton.' The customer had her erect back to them. Her firm tone was an underlining, rather than an enquiry.

'Certainly, Mrs Halesworth.' Abbs raised his eyebrows at Reeve, who grinned back. 'You'll have the cabinet prints in good time for your daughter's birthday. And these are the measurements you require for the frames.' He handed her a folded slip of paper. 'Thank you again for your custom. It has been a pleasure to work with such charming sitters.'

'I trust you don't charge extra for flannel, young man.' Mrs Halesworth rose, tucking the paper into her reticule. 'Come along, Lavinia.' The older girl stood, wearing a bored expression.

Removing his hat, Abbs stepped forward. 'Excuse me, ma'am, Detective-Inspector Abbs of the Exeter City Police.' Mr. Winton looked up abruptly as he bowed. 'This is a fortuitous meeting. I wonder if I might speak to you, concerning the tragic event at Tower House?'

Mrs Halesworth looked him up and down, ignoring Reeve. 'I presume you're speaking to everyone, Inspector? You've no particular grounds for seeking me out, I trust?'

'That is so, ma'am, it's a matter of routine. We're seeing everyone who was with Miss Chorley, on the day of her demise.'

'Well, I can be of no help to you. No one buttered the sandwiches in my presence. It was a perfectly normal social occasion. Rather dull, if you want the truth.'

Abbs summoned his considerable reserves of patience. 'I'd like to hear your impressions in more detail, ma'am. Perhaps, when you've had more time to recall them?'

She gave an abrupt nod, setting her pendant earrings moving. 'Very well. You may call on us in the forenoon. I believe my husband will wish to be present.'

'I'm much obliged, Mrs Halesworth.'

'Ten o'clock will suit. Come along, Jessie. Mr. Winton will let you have our address.'

Reeve sprang to hold the door, as Mrs Halesworth swept out with her elder daughter. The nurse-maid followed more slowly, encouraging the child.

Reeve darted over to the chairs and retrieved something, calling after the young woman. 'Excuse me, miss, the little girl left this.' He held out a piece of fawn, woollen cloth.

'It's her scrap of shawl, she will take it everywhere.'

Crouching, he held it out to the child. She stared at him, suddenly chuckling with glee, as she took the cloth and held it to her cheek. Reeve composed his features and the nurse-maid smiled her thanks, before hurrying out to the waiting carriage.

'Now, sir, perhaps we can have a word with you?' said Abbs.

'Certainly. Inspector, you said? I'll just put the catch over the door,' said Mr. Winton, turning his sign to *Closed*. 'Now, how may I be of assistance to you, gentlemen?'

'You'll have heard what I said to Mrs Halesworth. I take it, you're aware of the death of Miss Harriet Chorley and the circumstances.'

Mr. Winton nodded soberly. 'It was reported at length in the local newspaper. You'll want to ask me about her visit here? I recall it well.'

'Good. What can you tell us about it?'

The photographer moved behind his desk and produced a ledger from a drawer. 'She came in late morning, accompanied by a gentleman in army uniform. He was to sit for the photograph. I believe he addressed her as Aunt.' Turning back a page, he found an entry. 'Yes, here's the order.' He rotated the book and indicated the line.

'Two copies. Is that customary?'

'Not always, but I recall Miss Chorley saying the gentleman should have another for himself. I understood that the photograph was for her to keep.' He looked from one to the other. 'Is there anything else you'd like to know?'

'Did Miss Chorley take anything to eat or drink, while she was here?'

'Yes, she drank a cup of tea and I think she may have had a small pastry with it.' His voice trailed away and he waited for Abbs to speak again.

'Is that customary, to offer refreshments?'

He shook his head. 'Not to everyone but better-off customers rather expect the attention. Mrs Halesworth had a cup of tea while she watched her daughters. I had the idea from the studio where I was apprenticed. Sitters often bring someone with them, especially ladies and it's quite a long wait. First, there's a discussion about the requirements, then the sitter's posed and the process takes time. Would you like to see?'

'If you please, we'd be interested to see where you work.'

'Through here.'

They followed Mr. Winton into a large studio, which held a haphazard assortment of furnishings and articles. The space might resemble the back-stage of a theatre, thought Abbs.

Skirting his tripod and camera apparatus in the middle of the room, Winton showed them a corner, where a sofa and armchairs were grouped by a side-table. It held a tea tray with a single cup and a plate of arrowroot biscuits. The nurse-maid, presumably, had not been thirsty.

'There's a small kitchen at the back and I've converted the scullery to my dark-room. Would you like to see?'

'No need, thank you. I take it the chemicals are safely stored?'

'Oh, certainly.' Winton looked alarmed. 'There's no possibility of a mishap.'

Reeve wondered over to inspect the varied props. A velvet-upholstered chair had been positioned in line with the camera. A rocking-horse stood at a little distance.

A large screen, painted to suggest a garden, stood against the wall, together with a wooden pillar and a section of balustrade, made to resemble stone. An ornate, wooden chair was placed by a rattan plant-stand displaying potted ferns. A chaise-longue stood next to a tall, reading-desk.

'That looks like a device of medieval torture,' he remarked, eyeing a wooden neck-clamp with a heavy base.

Winton laughed nervously. 'They can be uncomfortable, I'm told but they're often necessary. The ladies can find it difficult to hold a pose for long.'

'Can you recall what Miss Chorley and her nephew talked about, Mr. Winton?'

'I don't consciously listen to the conversation of clients, Inspector. Actually, the person sitting cannot speak. I'm sorry, I can't recall anything significant.

Miss Chorley was deciding on the pose her nephew should take. She wanted a three-quarter stance.' Winton rested an index finger on his moustache, as he thought. 'I had the idea that Captain Selden wasn't keen to be here. He had no real enthusiasm for having his likeness taken, it was to oblige Miss Chorley.'

'How did you get the little girl to keep still?' said Reeve, with genuine interest.

Winton turned to him, his features relaxing. 'Oh, that's easy. Her sister stood right by the chair. The child stood on the fur and her sister had an arm around her waist. Sometimes, I pose them with a hand on a pile of books. It all depends on what the mother wants. I have albums to show them and they pick out the setting they like.'

'Sounds as though you could do with an assistant,' continued Reeve. 'You've a lot to do, with fetching tea and arranging all this stuff.'

Winton picked up a child's riding crop from the floor, tucking it into a box. 'It is a great deal to organise. There's my dark-room, of course and accounts to be done. I hope to be able to employ an assistant in the future. I should like to advertise more, although word of mouth is the best recommendation.'

'I like the landscape you have displayed in the window,' said Abbs.

The young man's face lit up. 'Do you, really? You're the first person to mention it.'

'Where was it taken?'

'In Derbyshire. I was experimenting with light effects.'

'You're a long way from home, then,' said Reeve.

'Oh, I was on a walking tour.'

'I didn't think you had a north country accent,' said Abbs pleasantly. 'Though I believe someone mentioned you haven't been long in Seaborough?'

'No, I moved here from the next county.'

'What made you come here?'

The photographer bent over his camera, his face hidden. 'Seaborough is a growing town and I read that a studio was closing. I'd been looking to set up on my own for a while.'

'Do you live on the premises?'

'Yes, I have two rooms upstairs. If that's all, I'll write down the Halesworths' address for you.'

Handing Abbs the direction, Winton hesitated. 'Mr. Halesworth is a prominent person in the town. He's my landlord. Affable enough, but best to keep on the right side of him, so they say.'

~

The evening train was already in, when Mr. Halesworth hastened through the ticket-office and across the platform. The smell of cinders was in the air and the engine steamed like an impatient cart-horse. The guard blew his whistle, as he flung open a door in a first-class carriage and clambered swiftly aboard. The compartment he lurched into was empty, save for a fellow buried behind the open pages of the *Flying Post.*

Catching his breath, he lowered himself on the opposite corner seat and shook open his own copy, purchased on the way to the station. It was fortunate he had not missed the train and had a long wait, but events did tend to arrange themselves as he wished. The day had been a rewarding one and he had the enjoyable feeling of having played truant.

The lad and his mother had been gratifyingly pleased to see him. Far more so than his elder daughter and her mama. However, life couldn't be all play. With these considerations, Halesworth dismissed the day from his mind and gave his attention to the stock prices.

It was only when they'd passed the Venning tunnel and the train began to slow for the terminus, that Halesworth put aside his paper and took the slightest notice of his fellow passenger. He had been vaguely aware that the figure had slumped lower in his seat, no doubt, snoozing beneath his broadsheet.

Getting to his feet, he felt the other man seemed little inclined to leave the compartment. Glancing at him, Halesworth suddenly saw the other's face reflected in the glass, lit by the last rays of the evening sun.

'Good grief, Avery. What the devil are you doing, hiding yourself away there?'

Lowering his newspaper, the doctor met his gaze. Outside, the lamps were being lit on the platform. Above the sound of doors being heaved open, the voice of a porter could be heard. '... at Seaborough. This train terminates here.'

'Halesworth,' said Dr. Avery in a tone of resignation. 'You must excuse me, I was dozing and didn't realise it was you. I little thought to see you here.'

'Nor I, you. What's the matter with your face?' Halesworth stared curiously at Avery and the livid, dark bruise across the side of his jaw.

The doctor brushed it with his fingertips, as if surprised to feel it there.

'It's nothing, I was asked to attend someone, who turned out to be a drunk. In his stupor, he lashed out and accidentally caught me. We had better get out.' He indicated the porter, who opened their door, touching his cap to Halesworth.

'Where's your bag of tricks?'

'What?' Avery got stiffly to his feet as Halesworth stepped down.

'Your medical doings.' Halesworth waited on the platform as the doctor climbed down, wincing and holding a hand to his side.

'I don't take my bag everywhere. I wasn't expecting to see a patient. I'm extremely tired and not in the mood for an inquisition, Halesworth.'

'Steady on, old man. You look as though you fell down a flight of stairs as well. That's what comes of trying to do someone a good turn, eh?' They walked towards the way out, Halesworth slowing his pace. 'You didn't bring your stick either, I see.' Dr. Avery ignored him. 'Well, I can see you've had a rough day of it. I won't enquire what you've been up to.'

'Decent of you but I've nothing to hide. Nor have you, I'm sure.'

'No need for the sarcasm, Avery. I've been to see someone on a bit of business, that's all. I'd as soon it wasn't bandied about.'

'No one will hear anything from me,' said Avery coldly.

'Obliged to you.' They reached the station forecourt and halted on the corner by *The Railway Tavern*. 'Care to share a cab?'

'Thank you, no. We go in opposite directions.'

'Then I'll bid you good night. I'm for my supper.'

Avery looked on while Halesworth climbed into the waiting cab. As the sound of hooves receded, he leant against the wall. Halesworth was as great a gossip as the washer-women at the hospital. Their meeting would be regaled and embellished to Hicks, and anyone calling in at the billiard-room of the Marine, were it not that Halesworth had obviously been on some dubious enterprise.

There was no other cab. Avery set about the slow, painful walk to his house, where he would bind up his ribs and attempt to disguise his condition from the concern of his kindly housekeeper.

Twelve

'Now you've slept on it, Sergeant, does anything strike you about the witnesses we interviewed yesterday?'

Scratching his ear, Reeve felt his way cautiously. In his experience, it wasn't common for an inspector to ask his subordinate's opinion. Generally, they stuck to giving orders without explaining their thinking. Abbs was an exception. You felt he was training you up. He was prepared to listen to what you said, was interested even. Reeve found he didn't want to say anything foolish.

'Well, sir, about Mr. Winton. I might be wrong...'

'Go on.'

Abbs waited, without showing impatience, which was one of the things that made him good at questioning people. Reeve had noticed that people responded well to that quiet, gentleman-like way of his. He let them talk and tell him things, like the solicitor. He'd reeled off the important points in the will, while saying he couldn't comment. Abbs didn't bluster like Superintendent Nicholls, nor crawl to his betters, though he'd seen him flatter witnesses to disarm them.

'I thought he seemed uneasy the whole time, sir. That's common enough when talking to us. But it worsened when you asked him where he came from and why he moved here.'

Having stuck his neck out, Reeve waited for the response. There was little space in the small room Sergeant Tancock had given them. The air smelt musty. It was used as a repository for the dormant files, lost property and equipment found in every police-station. They still had a few of the old-style, larger rattles on a shelf, even truncheons painted with the initial of the old king.

'I thought so too. Our Mr. Winton struck me as evasive about his background and his reason for setting up shop in Seaborough.' Abbs frowned, then seemed to come to a decision. 'We'll leave it there for the moment. We've plenty of people still to see. There may be nothing in it. People have all sorts of secrets which are nothing to do with murder. We'll bear it in mind.'

'Will do, sir.' Glancing up at the small casement, Reeve noticed the rain showed no sign of lessening.

'I was curious as to why Captain Selden has changed his mind about shutting up the house. You recall, he said he intends leaving Miss Geake in charge.'

'Could it be simple kindness, sir? So she has a roof over her head while she obtains her next employment.'

Abbs shook his head slowly. 'It's a thought but I don't believe so. No employer shows that kind of consideration for their staff, inherited staff too. He's had no long contact with them, they're strangers. We know now that Tower House isn't his childhood home, so he can have no sentiment about it. He told us he does intend to sell.' Pausing, Abbs drained the cooling dregs of his tea. 'Why incur unnecessary wages? It would be more usual to pay off the servants and shut up the house, until it can be sold.'

'Whatever his reason, it's a help to Miss Geake.'

'Indeed. I've a notion that lady is quick to turn events to her advantage. I'm afraid we shall both get wet, Reeve. You know your way?'

'Sergeant Tancock gave me directions, sir.'

'Then I shall see you back here.'

~

Mr. Hicks was privately of the opinion that every funeral he had orchestrated had been a dress-rehearsal for this one. Miss Chorley's cortège would be the most prestigious he had presided over. He regretted that the dreadful circumstances dictated a smaller scale than would have been expected. Nevertheless, there was an air of expectancy about his premises and the lists, on his desk, put him in mind of a general conducting a campaign.

The outlay was considerable, from the hire of extra horses to the provision of four mutes to lead the procession. Then there was the necessary call at the hospital mortuary. The long delay since death rendered the customary lying of an open coffin at the deceased's home, quite impossible. Finally, everything was ready and at short notice too.

'But how magnificent it will be, sir. I should say, the finest cortège ever seen in Seaborough. What a feather in our cap.' Mr. Biggs clapped his hands together, his eyes twinkling.

'I'd like the weather to look up,' said Hicks. 'It'll be a shame if the mourners get soaked at the graveside and the plumes bedraggled.'

Biggs nodded, his expression solemn in an instant. 'Alas, that is beyond our control. Sunshine would seem equally inappropriate. A grey day would be best, sombre, yet dry.' He indulged in his dry cough once more as Mrs Lavis manoeuvred through the door with a laden tray. 'Ah, a veritable angel.' He cleared a space on the desk, moving a box of black sealing-wax and a torn open package from the stationers.

'Thank you, Mrs Lavis, that's very welcome,' said Hicks. 'What do you think of this?' He handed her a stiff, black-edged card.

'Shall I be mother?' Biggs proceeded to pour.

'That does look fine quality,' said Mrs Lavis, as she examined the wording.

'Very dignified,' added Biggs, over her shoulder. 'A fitting sentiment. She'll be sadly missed, I don't doubt.' Mrs Lavis and Hicks exchanged glances. 'Though only one family carriage needed and a single, family mourner. One could wish for more. May I?' Taking the card, he studied it, running a long fingernail over the raised flower engraved to one edge. 'And the border, which flower did you decide on, Mr. Hicks?'

'It's coltsfoot. Seemed the most appropriate for murder.'

'Ah yes. *Justice shall be done.*'

A small silence fell. Mrs Lavis looked through the smeared office window at the yellowed leaves of the plane tree, hanging like limp handkerchiefs in the rain. Hicks helped himself to a piece of shortbread.

A discreet cough broke the lull. 'Changing the subject, Mrs Lavis, have you seen Mrs Pardoe lately?'

'It's funny you should ask that. I did see her in the street this week. She seemed quite light-hearted. She was telling me, she's ordered her winter coal, I don't know how. She's been the length of the alley asking to borrow a shovelful before now. And I happened to see both her lads were wearing new boots. I'll be glad if the poor body has had some good fortune come to her at last.'

Biggs licked his lips. 'An inheritance, do you think?'

'I wouldn't have thought so. Bert Pardoe spent most of his wages in the Compass. She often had to fetch his suit out of hock. I can't think he had anything to leave her and I don't believe she has any family of her own.'

Biggs slurped his tea noisily and set down his cup. 'Now that I come to think of it, Mrs Pardoe was wearing a new bonnet, trimmed with jet, at Chapel last Sunday. Not one of ours, from a milliner's. Could she have earned something extra, I wonder?'

'Not by washing sheets at the Hospital.'

'I daresay Caleb Halesworth has given her something.'

Biggs spun round to his employer. 'I believe you've hit on it, Mr. Hicks. That's one small puzzle solved. I do like to get to the bottom of things.'

~

75

As he waited, rain trickling down the back of his collar, Inspector Abbs reflected on how much time he spent on doorsteps. That, and the writing up of notes and reports, was the mainstay of his work.

He had woken from a disturbed sleep, filled with repetitive dreams, as though he were awake and working. All the strangers he had recently met blurred together, becoming a treadmill of questions, sifting words and watching faces. Desperately trying to find a discrepancy or a lie. The loose end of a thread, that followed, would lead to the truth about Miss Chorley's murder.

He awoke with a fading thought that there was something he should have registered. A look on a face, a gesture? He could not grasp at the lost impression, nor could he afford to fail.

Abbs forced himself to concentrate by studying the Halesworths' home. It was a prosperous house, built within the last few years. The spacious, front garden still had a raw look to it. The row of holm oaks, behind the boundary wall, were young and spindly. It would be a long time before they did justice to the name Oakhurst, inscribed on one of the brick pillars at the gate.

The roof was many-gabled, edged with heavily-ornamented, barge-boards. The red brickwork was decorated with diamond patterns of contrasting grey bricks. This was a house intended to impress.

The middle-aged parlour-maid looked pointedly at his damp boots, as he entered and followed her down the hallway. Through an open door, he glimpsed a highly-polished dining table, a ruby glass lustre at its centre.

'The policeman, sir.'

She stood back for him to enter what was probably a morning-room, situated as it was, on the east side of the house.

The man standing by the fireplace, ostentatiously consulting a gold watch, was the one he had noticed at the inquest, in the front row of the public benches. He was alone.

'You're on time, at least. I can only spare a few minutes. I'm Councillor Halesworth, my wife'll be along presently.'

'Detective-Inspector Abbs, sir, of the Exeter City police.'

'I know who you are. Saw you in the witness-box. Sit if you like.' Mr. Halesworth waved at a chair.

'Thank you, sir. You know why I'm here?'

'To hear what my wife has to say, about who might have murdered Miss Chorley.' Abbs smiled faintly at the other's directness. 'I doubt you'll get anything useful out of her. Women aren't observant, to my mind, not unless it's another woman's hat and so forth.' Halesworth grinned.

Suddenly, Abbs could see how people might find the councillor charming, when he cared to take the trouble.

'I daresay you're right, sir. I do see that it's distasteful for the ladies to be questioned. But in your position, you'll understand I have to see everybody who visited the house on that last day.'

Visibly relaxing, Halesworth straddled the hearth-rug, one thumb planted on his fob chain, from which a small seal dangled.

Looking, thought Abbs, as though he were posing for his official portrait.

'Quite so. You have your duty, Inspector.'

'Perhaps you can tell me more about Miss Chorley, Councillor Halesworth. Did you know the lady well?'

'You'd better understand, Inspector, that this is a small town. Everyone, in the same position in society, knows one another. I wasn't a close friend of Miss Chorley but we encountered one another often enough. We may be small, but we pride ourselves on our activities here in Seaborough. Charitable works, concerts, and so on. I'm called to serve on so many committees, I need never spend an evening at home.'

Abbs nodded, deeming it best to keep his notebook in his pocket. 'I assume you can shed no light on Miss Chorley's death, at all?'

Halesworth spread his hands before him. 'It's baffling. She was an innocuous, old lady. In such cases, I imagine you always look to see who benefits? Cui bono, Inspector. That's my advice.'

'Thank you, sir. One of the servants, at Tower House, mentioned you called, a few days before Miss Chorley died.'

Discreetly studying Halesworth's reaction, Abbs decided that most women would find him very nearly handsome, with his thick, brown hair and soft moustache. His countenance was unbalanced by a thin mouth, which hardened, for an instant, into a straight gash.

'Now I come to think of it, I believe I did.' There came a slight pause, which Abbs did not intend to fill. 'It was of no account. I merely called in connection with the orphans, a request for a subscription.' The door opened and Mrs Halesworth came in. 'There you are, Rosa. Inspector, you've already met my wife.'

Ignoring the sofa, Mrs Halesworth perched on a chair by a davenport, in the corner. When Abbs resumed his seat, she looked at him, her hands folded in her lap.

'What is it you wish to ask me, sir?' She glanced down at the watch pinned to her bodice. Checking the time seemed to be a family trait.

Abbs had the distinct feeling he didn't have long. 'On the day Miss Chorley died, at what time did you arrive and depart from Tower House, Mrs Halesworth?'

'I was there shortly after three, that was the time specified. It would have been acceptable to call later but these occasions are best at the beginning, if you ask me. When people are fresh.'

'Otherwise the tea and the gossip are stewed, eh?' said Halesworth, by the window. His wife threw him an irritated glance.

'I was the first lady there. Apart from Miss Geake, of course, who doesn't count. Old Mr. Emerson was already installed at the tea-table and Mrs Hicks arrived shortly after me.'

'That's very helpful. So, you were in a position to observe the other guests as they arrived?'

'You could say so, though I don't make it my business to watch other people.'

'I think the inspector means to imply that not much gets past you, my dear,' said Halesworth.

Mrs Halesworth looked at her husband. 'I know what you're going to ask me next, Inspector. I shall save you the time. You want to know if I saw anyone behaving out of the ordinary. Being somewhere they shouldn't be?'

'Quite so, ma'am.'

'Well, you're in luck. Thinking it over, after we met yesterday, I did remember something of use to you. I saw Miss Shaw, the vicar's daughter, slip through the door that leads to the servants' quarters. She took care that Miss Chorley didn't see her.'

~

The stink of the seaweed had not been left behind in the town. It seemed to linger in the fields thereabouts. The journey had been a single stop on the railway but a long, wet trudge from the station. The place was smaller than he expected, more of a small-holding than a farm. It seemed to consist of a few scruffy fields, carved out from wild heath of furze and a scattering of low scrub.

He didn't hate the countryside, or even dislike it, decided Ned Reeve. It was more that it wasn't his world. His first ten years had been spent in the jostling streets of London, in the part of St Pancras, where his father had been a cabby. Helping with the horses, and peering through the railings of the Regent's Park, had been the nearest to the countryside he'd ever known.

Even when his Pa died and his Ma followed within months, after he'd been fetched by his uncle to Exeter, he'd seldom ventured far from the cathedral city, except in the course of policework. There were vast areas of Devonshire he'd never seen. Including, until now, this lonely corner, which had little to commend it.

There was an emptiness to the country that made him feel uneasy and vaguely discontented, unlike himself. Though he'd been in many a tight spot, alleys and wharves where you didn't venture after nightfall and didn't linger by day. He understood their lurking menace and knew how to defend himself. Wide, open spaces made him feel he was the mark of invisible watchers.

Burrow Farm appeared to be mostly laid to vegetables. Rows of thick, yellowing stalks were growing on long ridges of the claggy, red earth. He didn't know what they were. The fields nearest the track had been recently harvested, the soil churned up and littered with old leaves and stems.

Near the buildings, he could see signs of life, a single cow of the same red as the land and bedraggled, brown hens pecking. The place had a dismal aspect in the rain. The wet had lessened to what he had learned to call mizzle. The soft, damp, west country mist you scarcely noticed, until it soaked you through.

No dog barked on his approach. There were nettles growing in the corners of the yard and a few tiles slipping on the mossy roof, gave the place a run-down look.

As he neared the out-buildings, the farmhouse door opened. A woman, of indeterminate age, stood waiting. Her scraped-back hair, and sun-browned complexion, gave her a harsh appearance. When he reached her, Reeve could see it was made up of fortitude and tiredness.

'Would you be the policeman?'

'That's me, Sergeant Reeve. You'll be Mrs Tucker?' He smiled in a way he hoped would disarm her. For at close-quarters, he could see the anxious expression on her face.

'The constable told us to wait on your coming, only I thought you'd be in uniform.'

'I'm with the detective-branch, ma'am. There aren't that many of us in the county, as yet.' After nigh on nine years, he still enjoyed saying that. He did not say, as he might have done, that he was the youngest sergeant in the

County Police. Made up before his ten year service, on account of a particular incident.

'You'd best come in, only...' Instead of standing aside, Mrs Tucker took a step into the yard, drawing the door half-to behind her and lowering her voice. 'Only I'd take it kindly if you'd keep your voice down. My man's upstairs, he's laid up with his chest.'

'By all means.'

'Our Mary's a good girl. Not the sort to bring the police to our door. Her father's not best pleased about you coming and he's in no fit state to come downstairs. Everything's been said and he don't want it gone over again.' Her fingers kneaded a fistful of her apron as she spoke.

He hastened to set her fears at rest, speaking quietly. 'Miss Tucker isn't in any trouble, I assure you. Because of Miss Chorley's murder, Inspector Abbs, my superior, needs to know everything that happened at Tower House in recent weeks. Especially any event out of the ordinary. Let her tell me all about her dismissal and that will be an end to it.' Unless, of course, she killed her mistress, he added silently.

Mrs Tucker looked earnestly at him and held back the door, waiting while he used the boot-scraper. He followed her into a dark passage with an uneven, flagged floor. A steep, boxed staircase rose from one side. Motioning him through a door on the right, Mrs Tucker shut it quietly behind them.

A young woman got to her feet, scarcely more than a girl, and smoothed down her skirt. He explained again, moderating his voice. Mary Tucker gave him a pleasant smile and invited him to sit.

'Let me take your wet jacket, Sergeant and my mother will make you some hot tea.'

'That's very good of you both. I don't want to give any trouble.'

'It's no trouble, we have it ready. It only wants the water.'

She busied herself arranging his things over a chair before the hearth, while Mrs Tucker left them. There was an awkward silence, which he spent looking round the room.

They had shown him into the parlour, which smelt of polish and had a chilly, unused feeling, with the fire recently lit. On the mantelpiece, with its draped scarf, two silvery-grey shells caught his eye. They were like the two halves of a giant oyster, standing at either end, behind a candlestick.

Mrs Tucker returned directly with a teapot. He guessed it was their best china, taken from the corner cabinet. Gladly accepting a cup, he swallowed a scalding mouthful, produced his notebook and looked at their apprehensive faces.

'Miss Tucker, can you tell me how it came about that you lost your position with Miss Chorley?' The young woman didn't answer immediately, so he tried again. 'No need to be embarrassed, miss. You wouldn't believe the things I've heard. Tell me how it was in your own words.' His words sounded foolish to himself, as he imagined the inspector listening.

A hint of anger flashed in her eyes, though she began to speak in a self-possessed manner. 'Beg pardon, sir, I'm not embarrassed. It makes me furious to think of it and I was just wondering how to begin.'

'Mary... best not make trouble,' said her mother, placing a hand on her arm.

'No, ma, I shall tell the truth.' Mary turned back to Reeve, looking at him directly. 'I was dismissed for stealing a valuable ring, sir, only I never did such a wicked thing. I was happy at Miss Chorley's house and my parents raised me to be honest. It's true, when a search was made of the servants' quarters, the ring was found in my drawer...' She drew herself up straighter and continued in a firm voice. 'But I never put it there. I've sworn on our Bible there and I'll do it again for you.'

'You're not in court, miss. I shall write down your words and show them to my inspector.' Reeve took several hearty gulps of tea while he worked out what Abbs would likely ask next. 'Do you have any ideas on who did put it in your room?'

'I do, sir.' She shushed her mother with a gesture. 'I'm not feared to say it under this roof. I believe Miss Ada Geake, Miss Chorley's companion, did it to get me disgraced.'

'Why do you think that, miss?'

'Because I knew she'd been looking in the mistress's desk. The ring was missed later that very day and I was packed off by nightfall.'

'I see,' said Reeve, busily scribbling. The old man was going to find this very interesting. He was glad to have something of significance to report back. 'Let me get this right, you happened upon Miss Geake opening the desk, did you?'

'Not exactly. I went to the drawing-room to dust and I was deliberately moving quietly because Miss Chorley had gone to lie down with a bad head. She'd already reprimanded Sarah, that's the other maid, for making too much noise when she was brushing the stairs. The mistress was very sensitive to the slightest sound. Am I going too fast for you?'

'No, go on,' Reeve smiled at her.

Sitting side by side, he could see Mary resembled her mother, only young and pretty at present. It was sad that women came to look careworn and pinched. Looking at Mrs Tucker's calloused hands, he could understand why a position as parlour-maid, in a fine house, would seem an easier situation.

'When I entered the room, Miss Geake was reaching up behind the case with a stuffed fox in. I saw her, not directly, but in the looking-glass. Well, I wondered what she was about. At first, I thought she was wiping her finger to check for dust, that's what the mistress would do. But it was a strange action, so when Miss Geake had left, I felt there myself...'

A burst of hoarse coughing erupted suddenly, from somewhere on the upper floor. The two women exchanged anxious looks.

'Father's awake. Shall I go to him?' They listened but the sounds subsided.

'I'll see to him presently. Finish your tale.'

'I pulled out a small key and knew it to be for Miss Chorley's desk drawer. I'd seen her fit it in the lock often enough, but not where she kept it, so I knew what Miss Geake had been doing.'

'How did she know she'd been rumbled?'

'I don't know. I couldn't prove she planted the garnet ring from Miss Chorley's porcupine box but I know she did.'

'Did you tell Miss Chorley any of this?' Reeve found himself believing the girl.

'What would have been the point? There was the ring tucked among my night-gowns.' Blushing, she went on. 'Miss Chorley saw it found, herself. She was disgusted with me, after she'd given me my chance. She was always talking about honesty and moral rectitude.' Mary looked down at her lap, her voice fading away.

'Hush now,' murmured Mrs Tucker, patting her arm once more. 'You know your father and I believe you,'

'Miss Geake was too clever to be there when the search was made. Mrs Watkins, who's cook-housekeeper, had to do it. She begged Miss Chorley to send me home, without calling the police. Otherwise, I'd be in Exeter gaol. But I am innocent of all wrong-doing.'

'You won't take my daughter away, now she's told you this?'

'Don't worry, ma'am,' he said cheerfully. 'It's over and done with. Even if Miss Chorley were alive to lodge the complaint, there's no evidence now. Try to put it behind you, I'd say.'

Privately, he thought she'd been lucky. There'd been evidence aplenty, coming from a wealthy employer.

Mrs Tucker nodded. 'That's for the best. I'll tell her father what you said.'

'But what about justice?' Mary's voice rose in a burst.

'Hush, girl, remember what I told you.' Her mother gestured towards the ceiling. 'Justice don't put food on the table.'

He got to his feet and gathered up his things. 'Thanks for being so frank, miss.'

'We won't have to have anyone else here, will we?' asked Mrs Tucker.

He dared not speak for Abbs, in case he wished to see Mary himself. 'I can't give you an assurance, it isn't within my power. Anyways, the inspector's a decent sort. If he does want to see you, there's nothing to worry over. I don't reckon he'll need to.' A sudden thought struck him, just in time. 'By the way, miss, have you been near Tower House at any time, since you were sent away?'

Mary looked evenly at him. 'I have to pass there. It's the only lane down to Seaborough. Once, I waited for Sarah on her afternoon off. But I've never set foot in the grounds of the house since, nor wanted to. No matter what anyone's said.'

The coughing started again, as though someone were bent double, trying to rid their guts of a blockage. It was painful to hear each effort more feeble.

'I'll have to go up. Mary will show you out.' Mrs Tucker hurried to the door.

'Thanks for the tea.' They followed more slowly. His bowler was still damp.

Mary took a step in the yard with the door half-pulled, as her mother had done. 'The rain's stopped at last.'

'I'm glad of it. Is it just you and your parents here?'

She shook her head. 'I've a brother and sister at the school in the village. My elder brother's at sea.'

'What will you do now?'

'My father won't get better. I'm needed here now.' Her arms folded against the chill, Mary Tucker gazed at the long years across the empty fields.

Nodding clumsily, Reeve turned away. There was no more to be said.

Thirteen

'Reeve's not back yet, I presume?'

Sergeant Tancock cursed under his breath, as his nib spattered ink on the ledger. 'No, sir, it's a good walk from the station the other end.' Dabbing with blotting paper, he looked up at the inspector, who'd put his head round the door. 'Can I be of assistance, sir?'

As Abbs came into the room and pulled out the other chair, he caught the sour tang of pickles on the sergeant's breath. A greasy screw of waxed paper lay in the basket under the desk. He'd called back at the Anchor for a quick repast of bread and cheese, while he mulled over his meeting with the Halesworths.

'I'd like you to send one of your constables round all the druggists, to check their poison-registers. Have them copy out the names for the last three months, if you please. We'll see if anyone familiar turns up.'

'I'll get someone on to it straight away, sir.' Tancock made to get up but Abbs motioned him to stay.

'In a moment will do, Sergeant. Tell me, what do you know of Councillor Alfred Halesworth?'

The sergeant lowered his ample buttocks and pursed his lips thoughtfully. 'Bit of a mixture really, sir. He's a big man in these parts, fingers in lots of pies. Likes to think he practically runs the town. You'll find a lot of folk'll speak well of him. He's generous with money for the needy and quite a favourite with the ladies, so I've heard. He's full of energy, a great one for getting things done.'

Abbs waited but Tancock seemed to be finished. 'And the others? Those that don't speak well,' he prompted.

The sergeant grimaced. 'It's like this, sir, Mr. Halesworth is all for change. He talks of building up Seaborough to be a smart resort. Why not, says he? Now we've the railway to bring more people in. We've only had the line two year, you see. Afore that, you had to go by road from Kempston Junction.' He broke off to belch discreetly. 'Anyway, says he, We've the sea like Weymouth and Brighton and any fine place. He talks of building better-class hotels. We've only a few, and the Marine's the only one you could call select. Then he thinks of pulling down the old town, that's beyond where you're staying, and even building a pier.'

Abbs thought of Reeve's fondness for lively seaside entertainment. 'And this is upsetting some residents?' Especially those poor devils whose abode is the old town.

Tancock leant back in his chair, more relaxed than he'd been since their return. 'People don't like change, do they sir? The thing is, it's all very well to talk of investment and how it will help shop-keepers, hotel-owners and the like. Fact is, it will help those already rich. Don't everything?'

'I agree with you about people disliking change. I daresay many residents like Seaborough the way it is.'

The sergeant nodded emphatically. 'That's it. There's a lot to be said for a quiet life. Why, imagine the crime it'd bring.'

'Tell me about Mr. Halesworth's background, if you know?'

'Oh, I know all right. He were a local boy. Come from Venning, the nearest village north-west of the town. That's where Sergeant Reeve took the railway to, this morning. His father were a small-time builder. That's where the money comes from. Alfred Halesworth and his brother built it up and up. Now, his brother, Caleb that is, runs the business and Councillor Halesworth keeps his distance. He'll never climb a ladder again, not in his fancy weskets.'

Abbs was beginning to be amused by Sergeant Tancock's pictorial way of description. He'd noticed Mr. Halesworth was sporting a rather loud waistcoat for the morning. 'If he's part-owner of a building business, that does explain why he's so keen to expand Seaborough.'

'He's quite the landlord too. Buys up empty shops and they built a row of small villas near the church. I did hear they were snapped up. Some by a titled gentleman, to lease out.'

'I interviewed one of Mr. Halesworth's tenants, Mr. Winton, a photographer.'

'Don't know him. I'd heard someone had taken over the premises in Charlotte-street. Mr. Halesworth is known as a hard man in business. A bit quick to evict, you might say.'

'A man of contradictions,' said Abbs. 'Though, I suppose that can be said of most of us.'

'Dr. Avery might be able to tell you more, sir. He's well acquainted with Mr. Halesworth, I believe.'

'That's useful to know.'

'He's joined some council committee or other, on account of public health. I've heard him mention it. Mr. Halesworth's closest crony is Nathaniel Hicks, the principal undertaker in the town. Him that's burying Miss Chorley on the morrow.'

Abbs cast his mind back to the inquest. 'Is he, by any chance, a broad-shouldered man with a dark beard?'

'That's him. He's well-liked, of a cheery disposition, for all his calling. There's none looks more solemn when he's leading a procession. His wife's a pleasant lady. My brother's girl does the rough work in their house and she speaks well of the household. Mrs Hicks engaged her and spoke kindly to her.'

'Does everyone in Seaborough know one another?'

'It sometimes do seem like it. The worthies of the town all congregate in the back room at the Marine. They say there's more committee-work decided there than at the town-hall.' Sergeant Tancock unbent so far as to scratch his belly while he reflected.

A thought struck Abbs. 'Do you happen to know if Miss Chorley owned any land in the town, an empty parcel or a dilapidated building, perhaps?'

Tancock shook his head. 'She owned the land the Hospital stands on. No more that I know of, sir, but you don't always know who owns what.'

'No matter, I'll look into it.' He stood up, yawning, 'I must get back. My thanks, Sergeant, you've been most helpful. Is the vicarage by the parish church?'

'That's right, sir.' Tancock showed him on the street map pinned to the wall. 'Now, Mr. Shaw's a different kettle of fish. You won't find any to say a bad word about him, particularly not among the poor.'

'I think it's time I consulted the wisdom of the church.'

~

As Abbs walked briskly across the square, he decided his opinion of Sergeant Tancock's perspicacity was somewhat improved. He and Reeve would be required back in Exeter soon enough and Superintendent Nicholls would expect the murderer found. The answer might lie in sifting some fact of background knowledge. Tancock's understanding of the suspects could be invaluable.

He couldn't resist taking a look at the church before calling at the vicarage. They would be there on the morrow, to watch the interment from a distance, but it would be impossible to view the interior at leisure.

He had a liking for old churchyards with their sloping headstones and ancient yews. They were peaceful places. Cemeteries were very different.

They were desolate towns of the dead, with their neatly laid-out avenues, the chapel, their park-like railings, benches and lodge. Even their visitors, dutifully attending the departed populace.

The parish church of Seaborough was a disappointment. Its counterpart was to be found in the majority of English towns. Built in recent years, in blocks of grey stone, with the addition of a short spire. Pausing, he read the board, St Edward the Confessor, before passing through the iron gates.

The churchyard was not very large and crammed with plots. He recalled seeing a new cemetery, as he and Reeve walked down the hill into the town. A path, to one side, led off to a gate in the hedge. He could see the eaves of the vicarage through the trees.

Rising from the midst of a row of headstones, was a prominent white marble cross. The shingle in the large plot had been heaped on the turf. Sacking, weighted with bricks, stretched over an open grave.

The rain had stopped, while he was writing up his notes, but the darkening clouds threatened another downpour. Jackdaws were strutting about the tombs, making their curious, harsh croak. Their grey heads always put him in mind of judges' wigs.

A woman emerged from the church porch, carrying an armful of golden-rod. She waited for him, smiling shyly as he drew near. 'Good afternoon, do you wish to look over the church?'

Abbs touched his hat. 'Good afternoon, ma'am. I should like to do so, if it's convenient, but I'm looking for Reverend Shaw.'

She had an expressive face, one which would make it difficult to conceal her thoughts. 'He is presently at home, sir. I'm his daughter. May I be of any help to you?'

'My name is Abbs, I'm an inspector with Exeter City Police. Here to investigate the demise of Miss Harriet Chorley.'

'I see.' Her face became pensive. 'Of course, my father said you would wish to speak to us both.'

He nodded pleasantly. 'Perhaps I might speak with you now, Miss Shaw? It shouldn't take long.'

'Excuse me, if I just throw these away, then I'll take you to the vicarage.' He followed her a few yards, where she tossed the stems on a heap by the wall. 'They would have lasted a little longer but they aren't suitable for a funeral service. Too cheerful,' she added, half to herself. 'We had the harvest thanks-giving on Sunday. This is a sad contrast. I came to make sure nothing has been overlooked.'

He glanced up as fat drops of rain began to patter down. They took cover in the porch.

'Are you in a great hurry, Inspector, or shall we talk here? You said you would like to look over the church.'

'I should think this shower will pass over soon enough. It seems more like April than late September. Perhaps we could wait inside, while you finish what you were doing, Miss Shaw.' He stood aside, carrying his hat, as she led the way. 'I know you and your father were among the guests at Tower House, on the day Miss Chorley died. I take it, you knew her well?'

She stopped by the table bearing hymn-books. 'I'd known her since childhood and I met her often socially but I don't really believe I ever knew her well.' She obviously thought more explanation was required. 'I was so much younger than Miss Chorley. She talked a great deal when we met but we were never intimate. She said what was expected of a lady of her age and class.' Miss Shaw coloured. 'Excuse me, Inspector, I've said too much and find myself rambling, without answering your question.'

'No, no,' Abbs motioned with his hand. 'I know exactly what you mean, Miss Shaw. What sort of things did Miss Chorley talk about?'

'The royal family, Mr. Gladstone, the responsibility of the poor for their own plight. If there was any gossip at the meetings of our charitable ladies' society, she would have decided views on that. She spoke often of her nephew, when he was in India. She was very proud of his achievements in the army.'

'I've been told Miss Chorley took a keen interest in the church?'

'She did. Sometimes, my father would have preferred it to be a little less, I think. And there's our town Hospital. Miss Chorley gave the land and led the subscriptions.'

Miss Shaw wandered a few paces towards the aisle. 'What I was trying to say, was I don't know what she truly felt. I sometimes think we women meet over the tea cups and say the same things all the year. We comment on the weather, who was at a social occasion, good works. There is rarely anything fresh and none of us are saying what we really think. It would not be proper.'

'I believe it to be much the same with gentlemen,' said Abbs. 'Perhaps only the working-classes have the luxury of saying what they mean.'

'If that's so, it's the only one they have,' said Miss Shaw soberly. 'Would you like a moment to look round by yourself, Inspector? I said I'd check all is ready in the vestry, for my father.'

'Please take all the time you require, Miss Shaw.'

'I shall only need a moment.'

Abbs paced slowly about the nave, his footfalls echoing on tiles patterned with fleur de lys. An ornate crucifix stood on the altar, above which, St Edward was depicted in richly patterned glass. An enormous organ dominated the wall nearby and the air held a lingering whiff of brass polish. That composite odour he rather liked in old churches, made up of damp hymnals, mice and the mustiness of centuries, was absent.

'I'm afraid we have no treasures to show you.' Miss Shaw echoed his thoughts as she returned. 'What you see here is largely Miss Chorley's doing. She gave the organ and the crucifix and altar-cloth. My father would have preferred a plain cross and a simpler cloth.'

Abbs recalled the books by the bedside. 'Miss Chorley was a devotee of Pusey and the high church movement?'

'She was. I think my father secretly wishes he had an ancient church with medieval brasses and a Crusader's tomb. He has an interest in antiquities.'

'I can understand that.'

'Then he will enjoy speaking with you. He rarely meets anyone new who shares his interests.' Miss Shaw's enthusiasm faltered. 'I was forgetting, Inspector, you are here on quite different business. What would you like to ask me?' She sank into the nearest pew. He joined her, leaving space between them.

'Perhaps you would cast your mind back to the afternoon tea on the day Miss Chorley died. Did anything unusual strike you about the occasion?'

'Only that it was unusual for us to meet Captain Selden. We ladies had never seen him before and we were curious, I confess.'

'Did you like him?' Miss Shaw seemed to have a lively insight, looking beyond social pleasantries.

'Yes, I did, he seemed a kind man, most attentive to his aunt. But he did not say a great deal. Miss Chorley was very... forceful in her ways. She often answered remarks intended for another. Captain Selden was quieter than I'd imagined an army officer. I felt he was more at ease conversing with Mr. Emerson and my father.'

Miss Shaw looked up at a memorial between the nearest windows. Following her gaze, Abbs saw it was dedicated to the memory of Miss Chorley's brother, James. *Fought bravely at the Battle of Inkerman, died of his wounds 6th November 1854, aged 32 years.* The day after the battle, if he remembered rightly.

'He was quite a lot younger than his sister. I believe Captain Selden's mother was a year or so younger than Miss Chorley. The Seldens come from somewhere in the north.'

'I'm aware Captain Seldon served in India. But I have the impression he's never before visited his aunt here. Would you know, Miss Shaw?'

'I suppose he was away at school, then the army. I have heard his mama died when he was quite young, so perhaps the connection was not closely kept up. I've lived in Seaborough since I can remember and do not believe he's been here. Miss Chorley would stay in London every year, so they may have met there.'

Abbs found himself studying her. Miss Shaw was past her youth, turned thirty. A little older than Reeve, he thought. While she would not be considered handsome by many, he found her countenance agreeable. He wondered irrelevantly if she was contented in her lot.

'Did any of the guests leave the drawing-room at any time?'

'All we ladies did at one time or another. After we'd eaten, Mrs Halesworth expressed a wish to see Miss Chorley's fern collection, so she escorted us to the conservatory. The gentlemen stayed behind and yes, Miss Geake returned before the rest of us. She was at the rear of the party and I recall seeing her slip out. There's nothing to be read into that,' said Miss Shaw hastily. 'She probably had a headache. I think her life was not always easy with Miss Chorley. I mean, she was treated kindly but it must be exhausting to be always at another's beck and call.'

'Please go on.'

'Is this really of use, Inspector?'

'I know it must feel distasteful to be questioned about your friends and neighbours but an old lady has been murdered. I'm afraid it is necessary.'

'It's so hard to believe that someone among us could be a murderer. Someone we see every week, who smiles and speaks of the weather.' She was silent for a moment, then fixed her serious gaze on him. 'May I ask you a question?'

'By all means, though it may not be possible to answer.'

'Do you think one of us poisoned Miss Chorley?'

A sudden sound reverberated in the church like gunshot. Abbs spun round as Miss Shaw flinched and looked over her shoulder.

The door-latch had been lifted and a woman stood, shaking an umbrella, silhouetted against the porch.

'Adelaide, my dear, your papa sent me to fetch you. It's stopped raining.' She called out in a Devonshire accent, rich as cream, as she negotiated the single step, holding her wide skirt. 'Beg pardon, I thought you were alone.'

Miss Shaw slipped out of the other end of the pew. 'Inspector Abbs, may I present Mrs Hicks.'

'I'm glad to make your acquaintance, ma'am.'

Mrs Hicks returned his gaze with warm interest, as though she had happened upon an unexpected treat. 'And I you, sir. Though the good Lord knows, it's a terrible thing that's brought you to us.' Mrs Hicks looked meaningfully at the altar, as though the Almighty should have known better. 'One occasionally hears of these dreadful things of course, but not in Seaborough.'

'I'd intended to call on you, Mrs Hicks. Miss Shaw has been describing to me the tea you attended at Miss Chorley's house on the ....'

'Day she died. Don't let me interrupt you, sir. I shall sit here and wait, if I may.'

'I think Inspector Abbs needs to question us all.' Miss Shaw smiled at her friend.

'Yes, to be sure he will. It is like one of Mrs Braddon's novels.' The cherries on Mrs Hick's bonnet bobbed in agreement, as she sat, spreading her skirt.

'I was relating how we went to see the conservatory,' said Miss Shaw.

'You want to know who had the means to poison the food and drink, Inspector? Of course we are all suspects,' said Mrs Hicks, with relish. 'There was ample opportunity for someone to have poisoned Miss Chorley. When we returned from the conservatory, the drawing-room was quite unattended and plenty of food was still laid out. Do not you recall, Adelaide?'

'Yes,' said Miss Shaw, a shade reluctantly. 'The gentlemen had gone to look over something in the library.'

'An atlas. Captain Selden had been telling them about his time in India. Of course, poor Mr. Emerson finds it tiring to walk far. Is this the sort of thing you want to know, Inspector?'

'Thank you, Mrs Hicks. Where was Miss Geake at this time?'

'She came in from the terrace, saying something about feeling stifled and needing a breath of fresh air. Miss Chorley always had early fires in autumn. She liked her comforts. Mind you, Miss Geake could have put something in the food before any of us returned.' Miss Shaw looked horrified and was about to protest. 'I know what you are going to say, my dear but there it is.'

'I went to the kitchen myself,' said Miss Shaw. 'Our cook, Hannah, wanted me to ask Mrs Watkins whether she'd like any plums for Miss Chorley. We've had a great many and they don't last.'

'It's the wasps,' said Mrs Hicks. 'They're still around and they do love plums.'

Abbs smiled politely, mentally dismissing one query.

'Is there anything else you can add, Mrs Hicks? Have you any suspicions regarding Miss Chorley's death?'

Shaking her head, Mrs Hicks looked regretful. 'I wish I could help you, Inspector, but it is a great mystery, to be sure. Somebody must have hated poor Miss Chorley but no one can work out who, or why. We have all thought of nothing else.'

Not quite true, thought Abbs as he thanked them. One person among you knows. Though they were not necessarily among the guests on that day.

'Shall you come and meet my father now?' asked Miss Shaw, as they made their way to the door.

'I should like to, if he can see me. I daresay he will not be free at all on the morrow.'

'After the service, he is going to Tower House. Mr. Jerrold has asked my father to attend the reading of the will, which means Miss Chorley has left a bequest to the church. Come with us now and he will help you in any way he can.'

Both the vicarage and its incumbent were welcoming. The outer door stood open to all callers. In its way, the exterior of the house was as ecclesiastical as the church, with leaded glass and lancet windows.

Inside, were all the appurtenances of a much-loved home. Following the two women, Abbs had an impression of crimson turkey carpet, walls hung with water-colours and a rich, inviting aroma of something like mutton stew. Mrs Hicks placed her umbrella in the hall-stand, as though she were an accustomed visitor.

The vicar was in the drawing-room. Miss Shaw introduced him to her father.

'You are most welcome, sir. Abbs... correct me if I'm wrong, but does not that name hail from eastern England?'

'You're quite right, sir. My family came from Norfolk.'

Samuel Shaw's face lit up. 'The locality of some of the finest churches in England. As a young man, I once had the privilege of a few days walking-tour there. I have never forgotten those enormous skies and the unusual, round bell-towers.'

'Would you care for some tea, Inspector?' Miss Shaw rang the bell and cleared some space on a low table, her arms full of books.

'Thank you, Miss Shaw, I'd be most grateful.' Abbs took an ineffectual step forward to help but they were deposited on the window-seat, before they toppled.

He found the room unexpectedly disarming. How pleasant it would be to sink into one of the armchairs, with a cushion behind his head, and eat hot buttered muffins by the fire. To sit in good company and talk of books, or nothing at all. To be still and watch the burbling fire.

Mentally shaking himself, he found the vicar watching him. His eyes, behind his wire spectacles, held a solicitous expression.

'We'll have tea now, if you please, Betsey,' said Miss Shaw, as the maid appeared. The girl stared, wide-eyed, at him as she left. He was beginning to feel an object of curiosity to everyone in Seaborough.

'I suggest we retreat to my study and leave the ladies to their conversation,' said Mr. Shaw. 'Through here, Inspector.'

The study window overlooked a rose garden to the side of the house, sheltered by a yew hedge. While the vicar busied himself removing the fireguard and rattling the coals into a good blaze, Abbs looked unobtrusively around. It had become instinctive, over the years, to make a swift survey of rooms to get the measure of their owner. An unpleasant habit, he thought.

Shelves held Bibles, collected sermons and other devotional works, along with histories of Devonshire, its antiquities, geology and flora. There was also an extensive selection of poetry. A pipe-rack stood on the desk, beside a volume of Mr. Tennyson's verse. Some inked papers were held down by a chunk of flint.

'Ah, I see my axe-head has taken your eye. It is remarkably fine, don't you think?' Mr. Shaw handed it to him. 'See how skilfully it was worked. It displays craftsmanship the equal of any in our industrial age.'

'I agree, sir.' He examined the flint with interest, tracing an edge with his forefinger. 'Where did you find it?'

'A mile back from the cliff, there is a hill-fort. From which, Seaborough derives its name. It's a favourite tramp of mine, when trying to tease out a sermon. You must view my small collection of arrow-heads and other knapped flints, for I can see your enthusiasm is genuine, rather than simply courteous.'

Indicating a cabinet, Mr. Shaw pulled out a shallow drawer. They bent over the exhibits together. 'This one is particularly good. I am indebted to the rabbits who excavate the earth around their burrows. Though I fear that does not stop me enjoying their meat. However I digress, I hear the sound of our tea coming, then you must ask me your questions.'

A cursory tap on the door was followed instantly by a plump, grey-haired servant, bearing a tray.

'Thank you, Hannah.'

'Thank' ee, sir, I can manage. You sit yourself over there in the warm.' Abbs sat meekly in the armchair, while a cup of steaming tea was placed at his elbow, together with a plate of fruit cake.

'You're most kind, that looks delicious.'

'You're very welcome, sir. Now Reverend, you won't forget to eat some? You'll see that he does, sir?' Fixing them both with a stern look, she nodded and left them.

'Hannah has been with us for many years. We are very fortunate to have her devoted service. She is much more to us than Cook.'

'I appreciate your hospitality, sir.'

'It's the least we can do, Inspector. You come to restore order to our shattered community. What is it you wish to ask me?'

Gone was the absent-minded air of a kindly, country cleric. Mr. Shaw looked intently at him, a steely resolve in his quiet voice. Abbs felt he was catching a glimpse of how he held his congregation from the pulpit.

'You've known your parishioners here for many years?'

He nodded. 'That is correct. At least, insofar as they allow me to know them.'

'Miss Shaw said something similar, when I asked if she knew Miss Chorley well.'

'My daughter has a shrewd mind for a young woman. Still waters run deep, as the saying has it.'

'There is no obvious motive for Miss Chorley's murder. I want to ask if you have any theory, sir? From your long observation of the people concerned.'

There was a moment's silence before the vicar spoke. 'On rare occasions, someone in my position may gradually become aware of a troubled soul among our midst. There are small acts of malice perhaps, a word dropped into the wrong ear, in seeming innocence. Someone who seems perfectly ordinary but in truth stands apart, manipulating for their own ends.'

'You are saying that you know such a person? Someone in Miss Chorley's circle?'

'Ours is not a confessional church, of course,' replied the vicar in a gentle tone. 'Even so, if an individual had confided in me, something which could be construed as a motive, I could not repeat it to you, Inspector. That would be a breach of trust. By the same token, I cannot give you the name of a parishioner whom I fear, may have a warped character. I could be quite mistaken. Judgement is the prerogative of the Almighty, you see.'

'I understand your position, sir. And that this town is your home. My sergeant and I will be long gone, when the repercussions of Miss Chorley's murder still linger.'

'Sadly, that is so.' Mr. Shaw looked away at last, his bald head pink in the firelight. 'I see you understand human nature very well, sir.'

'No death brings more loss than murder. There is not even a... a clean sort of grief for the mourners. One of the losses is privacy. I must come in and sort through people's lives. Turning over their secrets, and all the small matters they prefer to keep hidden, like a scavenger sifting through a dust-heap.' Abbs took a mouthful of tea, as though to swill the distaste he heard in his voice.

'Your work must be extremely difficult, Inspector, and receive little gratitude. But you are the instrument of justice. No man should feel apologetic about his honest work.'

'I don't know about justice, sir. I leave that to the courts. I'm here to catch a murderer.'

'Indeed.' The vicar added some sugar to his cup, stirring his tea slowly as he thought. 'You mentioned grief. One of the saddest things that occurs to me is the lack of mourners for Miss Chorley's death. She never married and had no family left, apart from Captain Selden.'

'And he had seen little of his aunt over the years. I do get the impression that Miss Chorley had long acquaintance, rather than close friends.'

The vicar bowed his head in agreement. 'You have not spoken to Mr. Emerson yet, I think? He was her nearest neighbour and knew the family well for many years.'

'I intend visiting him after the funeral.'

'To answer your question, Inspector, I have no one in mind who could have perpetrated this terrible act. To take another's life – except it be judicial – is to risk salvation for one's soul. There may be some redemption for a desperate wretch who kills on the spur of the moment, if they truly repent. But surely, this poisoning was a premeditated act?'

'It had to be. The poison may have been carried around, awaiting an opportunity, but the cold decision to kill had been made.'

'Be assured, Inspector, if I knew of someone I thought capable of such an act, I would tell you. I saw nothing untoward at Tower House that afternoon. '

'Thank you, sir. It is useful to be able to speak frankly with you.'

'Is it possible this was an act of revenge, think you?'

'There's nothing to suggest that.'

'Then if the motive was not pecuniary, I wonder if the murderer was not in some kind of danger from Miss Chorley?'

'Danger?' Abbs was taken aback for a moment. 'You mean because of something she knew? It's an interesting thought, sir.'

'We are accustomed not to speak ill of the dead, Inspector. The people of Seaborough owe much to her charity. However, Miss Chorley made a difference between the deserving and the undeserving poor, if you follow me?'

'A common feeling, surely.'

'One you share?'

'No, sir. I've seen enough misery and despair, in the backstreets of Exeter, to know the poor need decent food and lodging. How they came to that state matters little.'

Mr. Shaw smiled warmly at him. 'I hope you'll come and see us again, Mr. Abbs. The vicarage door is always open. Now, please sample Hannah's fruit cake or she will never forgive me.'

'You're most kind.'

After a little, the vicar grew serious once more. 'Miss Chorley prided herself on being righteous. If she discovered some damaging secret about another... I fear she would not be merciful.'

Fourteen

A weak sunlight was seeping through the branches of the sycamores above the stable wall. There was a chance now that the rain had done, thought Bessie Watkins, that they'd have a fine day for the funeral. But if she knew Seaborough and she did, the damp with a mild air would bring fog. The old stick barometer in the hall said *Change,* when she'd rapped it earlier. It had been too much to resist, Miss Chorley had allowed no one else to touch it.

She stood looking out of the window, for this was the quiet hour of late afternoon. When Jane had prepared the vegetables and it was not yet time to set the dinner on.

The Master and Miss Geake had both ordered a tray again, seeming to avoid one another's company. He spent every evening shut away in the library, the tantalus always within reach, smoking and going through old papers. Sarah had reported the state of the ashes with burnt fragments fallen in the hearth.

Miss Geake had taken to having her dinner in her room and she spent the evenings in the drawing-room, in her dead mistress's old place on the sofa. She'd even had the sauce to sit openly at Miss Chorley's desk, rummaging through her stationery.

Bessie looked around her domain, thinking that she would never cook dinner for the mistress again. Ten years had woven grey threads among her hair, and thickened her waist, but there was vigour in her yet. She was luckier than most, for never again, would she have to take herself to an agency and plead to strangers that she was a good, plain cook, careful with her accounts.

Lilian had assured her, she only took a very genteel sort of boarder in Tunbridge. There were streets of fine shops to see, theatricals and entertainments of every kind. She'd see a bit of life and be more or less her own mistress at last. There was even the prospect held out of seeing London. Tunbridge had three stations and a trip to the capital could easily be had in a day.

Well, she supposed she didn't regret Mr. Jerrold persuading her to stay on another month. The extra wages were welcome but she would be glad to go to her sister, all the same. Good riddance to Seaborough. She wouldn't miss the sea at all.

Through the open, scullery door, Jane could be seen scouring one of the copper pans, the sink reeking of vinegar. Funny to think, she'd normally be putting up jellies and preserves at this time of year. What would happen to all the utensils she'd used, year in year out, which felt very like her own possessions? The china on the dresser made her think of the big tureens in the cupboard beneath.

She'd always loved that naval-blue pattern and wouldn't they be going begging? Miss Geake hardly came into the kitchen, no further than hovering in the doorway when she passed on her orders. Even she would have more to think about than china. The best service was kept in the sideboard, in the dining-room, and that would be accounted for.

Deciding regretfully, she could hardly have them packed up with her boxes, she dismissed the idea. She'd always coveted the lovely set of silver fish-knives and they'd been forgotten in one of the sideboard drawers, for a year at least. Miss Chorley had given up fish, after that time she'd choked on a bone. Ada Geake would never think of those and surely, she was entitled to a little present to send her on her way.

That happy thought led to a ripple of excited anticipation turning in her belly. She was to attend the reading of the will. Captain Selden had come into the kitchen, looking embarrassed, and told her himself. That meant Miss Chorley had remembered her or her name wasn't Bessie Watkins.

There was little to be done for the morning. In the circumstances, Captain Selden was not receiving the mourners at the house, after the funeral. Only those summoned to the reading of the will would be offered refreshment. And little enough, at that.

Miss Chorley, who had prided herself on keeping a good table, would be turning in her grave. Her poor spirit would have no rest until the murderer were found. Captain Selden had been to the cellar, himself, to bring up the port and sherry. The funeral biscuits lay covered in the larder.

Entering the kitchen, with a rustle of her black, bombazine skirt, Sarah came to an indignant halt by the table, putting an end to her wool-gathering. 'Imagine what Miss Geake's doing now, Cook.'

'I don't begin to guess, Sarah. It could be anything with that one. Tell us, then.' Jane had come to the scullery door to listen, red-faced, with a strand of damp hair stuck unbecomingly across her brow.

'The master rang from the Tower Room. It fair gave me a fright to see that bell jangle. When I got up there, he's just inside the door and Miss Geake's standing in the middle of the carpet, looking pleased with herself. You know that tiny smile she does?'

'I've seen it often enough, behind the mistress's back.'

'You wouldn't credit it. The master told her to go through Miss Chorley's things and box them. Take any garments you wish, Miss Geake, he said. I have no use for them.' Sarah looked from her to Jane, to savour the full effect of her news.

Bessie folded her arms to her bosom. 'It isn't even as though she were a ladies' maid. Mind, I doubt Captain Selden would know how things should be done. She's a bit taller, but she can sell the dresses for a goodly sum and there's plenty she can wear. Did he include gloves and bonnets and such like?'

'I don't know, I'm sure.' Sarah pulled out a chair. 'Everything, I shouldn't wonder. He'll want it all gone.'

'Fill the kettle, Jane.' She took her place at the head of the table. No, she wouldn't miss the seaside at all. And if there were pickings going, she didn't see why she should miss out. Some real, silver flatware would look a treat on Lilian's walnut sideboard. They wouldn't give them to the boarders, mind.

~

'Commercial travellers,' murmured the landlord's wife, as she removed their supper plates. 'They're in good voice tonight. I hope they aren't bothering you, sir. I can ask them to keep the noise down.'

'Let them be, Mrs Gaunt. They aren't disturbing us.' Abbs smiled at her, seeming in unusually good spirits, thought Reeve.

'There's baked apple to follow, or cheese if you prefer.'

'I've had sufficient, thank you. What about you, Reeve?'

Brightening a little, he asked for pudding. The inspector didn't often appreciate the importance of sustenance, having a poor appetite himself. He'd been on tenterhooks, lest Abbs had suggested they leave the table and talk in his room. Though he wasn't one to invite you into his private quarters.

Mrs Gaunt had explained apologetically, that there was no spare parlour for them, this time. He'd eaten his beef-steak like a starving man and mopped up the gravy, until the plate was polished, with the remainder of Abbs's bread.

He was feeling thoroughly disgruntled with Seaborough, Inspector Abbs and their fellow diners. Their work was done for the day. They'd nothing better to do than get steadily corned and exchange convivial stories. The travellers had pushed two tables together, in the middle of the room, and were calling to the waiter for more port. A few of them had nudged one another, turning quite openly, as he and Abbs had taken their seats.

It had been a long trudge, in still-damp apparel, to catch the train back after interviewing Mary Tucker. Then a bone-rattling, on the hard benches in third-class, and a further walk back from the station. He'd missed his grub and Abbs was off interviewing the vicar without him.

He'd felt obliged to fall in with Sergeant Tancock's suggestion, that he accompany a constable round the druggists, which meant more tramping in wet boots. His feet were smarting and the old man didn't seem as interested in his report, as he'd expected. Abbs hadn't even inquired about the poison-register, yet.

The jug of hot custard, that accompanied his bowl, brought a small comfort, were he allowed to eat in peace. Pouring it liberally over his apple, Reeve listened gloomily as the inspector, after glancing at their companions, spoke again in a low voice.

'I was saying, it occurred to me that Mr. Halesworth may have been proposing some kind of business deal with Miss Chorley. He may have an eye on some old property she owned in the town. According to Sergeant Tancock, he has grand plans for more hotels. That would keep his labourers in work for a good while.'

'We know she sent him away with a flea in his ear, at any rate,' said Reeve indistinctly. 'It doesn't sound like a motive for...' Watching the worsted, check backs at the other table, he tailed off. 'You know, sir.'

'I agree but we need to clear away anything unexplained. I intend a further word with the solicitor. He'll be able to tell us if there's anything in my theory.'

'Won't he be busy all day, with the funeral and the reading of the will?'

'Undoubtedly, but I'll catch him before he leaves for the church. It won't take long. As her man of business, he must know all she owned.'

'Do you reckon the servant girl's cleared away then, sir?'

'Oh, I should think so. Unless we have fresh reason to look at her anew. Most of what we find will be irrelevant but it will take us nearer the solution. We mustn't be downhearted, Reeve. Think of it as holding a thread in a labyrinth. We follow it to daylight.'

'Right, sir.' There were times when Abbs had a curious way of talking. Most like, on account of the books he read. His head down, he concentrated on scraping the remains of his custard.

'We've achieved a good deal in a short space,' continued Abbs, folding his napkin. 'Only two more people to interview. But first, we'll have to get the funeral out of the way.'

'That reminds me, sir.' Pushing aside his bowl, Reeve felt in his jacket pocket. He passed Abbs a paper. 'You haven't seen the list compiled from the druggists,' yet.'

'Ah, yes. Were there many premises to visit?'

'Only three. One in Fore Street, another, just off it. The third was a poky place in a back street. That's where I spotted a name we recognise.'

'So we do.'

'He'll have an explanation, sir, like the vicar's daughter. They're all respectable as can be.' He sighed heavily.

'One of them is not. We shall ask him, soon enough. He has a pressing engagement on the morrow.'

~

The gas flickered and dipped behind the glass shade, casting a fan-shaped luminescence on the patch of ceiling above where Miss Geake sat. She was not given to superstitious fancies, but this was no ordinary evening. When a door shut overhead, she found her ears straining in expectation of the familiar footfall and tap of a stick. The glass, on the wall, behind her, was covered with black crape. In the hall, the long-case clock was stopped. It felt as though the house was waiting.

She had taken to usurping her erstwhile employer's corner of the sofa, the best-lit place in the room for reading. At first, she'd felt that the upholstery still bore the imprint of Miss Chorley's form. Like the mustard-brown velvet, worn shiny along the arm, where her thin sleeve had rested and the bent old fingers fidgeted.

When the door opened slowly, she did not admit to relief, to see Captain Selden step just inside the drawing-room. Brushing a finger across his moustache, he spoke distantly, looking somewhere to her left.

'I have your reference, Miss Geake.' He held out an envelope with its flap unsealed. 'I've written what you wanted.'

'Thank you. You may leave it on the desk.' She enjoyed speaking coolly and watching him do as she wished. He returned to the door, before hesitating.

'Was there something else, Captain?'

'Do you have any idea when it will suit you to leave here? I shall return to my post on the day after the funeral. Mr. Jerrold tells me the cook is anxious to be gone.'

'I do not think I shall need accommodating for much longer. I have made all the enquiries I can about a new post and am waiting to hear any day.'

Looking relieved, Captain Selden stiffly bade her good night.

Miss Geake sat on, deep in thought. An owl hooted several times, each sound more distant, a ghostly echo of itself. The coals sizzled and burnt low. Eventually, she rose and began to pace the length of the room. Holding aside a curtain, she stared out. The night sky was clouded.

Finally, she sat at the desk, pushing away the envelope on the blotter, without reading it. Taking a sheet of black-bordered paper, she dipped her pen in the ink and began to write.

Fifteen

When Abbs emerged from the front door of The Anchor, he found the sea opposite was gone, shrouded in fog. Somewhere nearby, a muffin-seller was ringing his hand-bell. His cry, vanishing down a side-street, sounded oddly discordant, as though the fog were swallowing his voice. The herring-gulls, usually raucous at breakfast time, were silent.

It was the day of Miss Chorley's funeral. At various places in and around the town, the mourners would be preparing to attend. As would he and Reeve, though in their case, from a distance. Before then, there was Mr. Jerrold to be consulted. As he stood, he could hear the water washing on to the shore. A curious sensation, when nothing could be seen.

A seaside mourning. Abbs recalled his conversation with Mr. Shaw. A sad business, with the majority of mourners present only to show respect and no one truly grieving. Perhaps, that was as well. Grief was not to be wished on anyone.

He turned his back on the coast, able to see a few yards ahead, with the end of the street lost in mist. As he walked cautiously, he wondered how the murderer was faring. Whether they felt safe, or did they fear him and his powers of deduction? He could not afford to fail. And if he should, Reeve would be tainted by association with him.

Reasoning that Mr. Daniel Jerrold was unlikely to call at his place of business before the funeral, Abbs followed Tancock's directions to his home. At the junction with a busier street, he saw that a carriage and pair, emerging through the fog, had almost collided with a grocer's van. Both drivers were exchanging insults as they steadied the horses.

He took a wrong turning, finding himself in a quiet road of large, detached villas. The pavements were empty, saving the footsteps of an elderly person somewhere behind him. They were guiding themselves with a stick, tap-tapping on every railing with the regularity of a blind man.

When he found Navarino-road, his pace was slowed further as he kept stopping to make out the name on a pillar. Ivydene had the solidly prosperous appearance, he expected. An enormous monkey-puzzle dominated the front garden, its stiff branches reaching through the fog, towards the upper sash windows.

The door was opened by a fetching parlour-maid. On explaining his business, she shook her head doubtfully.

'I'll inquire, sir, but I doubt the master's receiving visitors.' She left the front door ajar.

Waiting in the porch, Abbs, who possessed excellent hearing, caught the dismissive tone of the solicitor's response.

'I'm sorry, sir, it's as I thought. Mr. Jerrold cannot see anyone today. He says you're to make an appointment to see him at his place of business.'

'Please tell him, I regret disturbing him at this hour but need to speak with him on police business. It will take only a moment of his time.' As the parlour-maid withdrew again, Abbs wondered if he'd been unwise to press the matter.

He had no more time for reflection. The door opened wide enough to admit him and he was shown into the hall.

'Who was that, Ann?' called a voice on the stairs. Looking up, Abbs saw a grey-haired matron, dressed in a dark plaid, poised with one hand on the bannister. 'Do try to keep the damp air out.'

Before the girl could answer, a door to the right opened and Mr. Jerrold came out.

'It's nothing for you to concern yourself about, Alice,' he said testily and turned his back on the lady. Her eyes met Abbs's for an instant, with a hint of sympathy. She retraced her footsteps and disappeared along the landing. Mr. Jerrold frowned dismissively at the parlour-maid, who bobbed and left.

'What is the meaning of this intrusion, Inspector? Anything further you wish to ask of me can wait until this day is over. Have you no respect, sir?'

Knowing he trod on suddenly shifting ground, Abbs hesitated a second too long in selecting his reply.

'Well? Have you nothing to say for yourself, now you've thrust your way in at the *front door* of my private dwelling?'

'I apologised for presenting myself here. But you know the business that brings me, Mr. Jerrold. I'm trying to catch a murderer. Time is crucial. I cannot question anyone today and must do what I can to further my enquiries.'

His reasoned tone failed to pacify the solicitor. Jerrold was already wearing a black cravat. His silk mourning scarf hung from the hall-stand, together with his black top-coat and tall hat.

Deliberately consulting the clock, Jerrold eyed him, as though a street-urchin were oozing mud on his carpet. 'Five minutes, Inspector. I may say, I strongly object to your manner. I hardly need reminding that my late client has departed this life at the hands of a ...' He glanced at the galleried landing, 'of another.'

'I won't waste any more of your time, sir. What I need to know is this, did Miss Chorley own any other property in Seaborough?'

Jerrold stared at him. 'Property, is that all?' As Abbs waited in silence, he continued in a chilly tone. 'Miss Chorley owned some cottages in the old town, which were inherited from her father. When the railway came, and adjacent streets were laid out, I purchased several terraced houses on her behalf. This was in my capacity of managing my client's investments. In addition, Miss Chorley owned various, small properties in Exeter. Does that answer your vital question?'

'Partly, thank you. Did Miss Chorley own any parcels of vacant land in the town?'

'There is one field on the edge of the town. It is presently let to a farmer for rough grazing.'

'Would this be on a long lease?'

Jerrold gave an exasperated sigh. 'My son dealt with it. Without consulting our records... I believe it is let by the half-year.'

'I've only one further question for you, sir. Would Miss Chorley, in your opinion, have been likely to sell any of her holdings?'

'On no account. She lived on her rents and never touched capital. She believed there was no greater security than property.'

'My thanks for your time, Mr. Jerrold. The information is most helpful. I'd be obliged if you would have a copy of the will left at the police-station, after the reading.'

'Your officer may collect it from my clerk, late this afternoon.'

'As you wish, sir. I'll bid you good morning.' Bowing, he turned to leave.

'One moment, I am dissatisfied with the manner in which you are conducting your investigation. Instead of enquiring after strangers, you appear to spend your time questioning Miss Chorley's own acquaintance. Furthermore, you are troubling highly respectable gentlemen such as Councillor Halesworth. I think you forget your place, Abbs, and take too much on yourself. You are a public servant, man. I wish to take the name of your superior officer.'

~

The cortège had made its stately way along Fore Street, moving at slow walking pace and passing the lowered shop blinds beneath their awnings. People stopped to watch the procession, falling silent, the men pulling off their hats and bowing their heads as it drew near.

The featherman, carrying his staff of swaying black-dyed, ostrich plumes, led the way. Followed by the town's principal undertaker, carrying his black wand. Four solemn mutes walked behind Mr. Hicks, two by two, their weepers streaming down from the back of their tall hats.

The hearse was a sombre spectacle, pulled by two pair of glossy, black horses. Their feathers dipped and nodded as they moved under the direction of the coachman, his whip decorated with black ribbon bows. The hearse was an unusual model with etched glass sides. Through which, the oak coffin could be seen, its lid heaped with silk flowers.

As the cortège, looming out of the fog, reached the church gates, a single bell began to toll. The clear, hollow ring sounded insistently over the mourning-carriage wheels, following the hearse. The chief mourner descended first and was led into the church by Reverend Shaw.

The others followed, Mr. Jerrold close to Captain Selden, the Coroner, Dr. Avery, among many others they could not know. Sergeant Tancock, in his best uniform, represented the Constabulary. Their dark garb put Abbs in mind of a straggling line of rooks.

'You probably reckon this as really bad, sir. But it's not, you know, nothing like.'

'What?' said Abbs belatedly, as the words sank in. He turned to look at his companion, who was leaning against a tomb. He frowned at Reeve's stuffing his hands in his pockets.

'The fog. This is absolutely nothing compared to a real London particular. For a start, it's mostly from the sea, isn't it?'

With an effort, Abbs dragged his thoughts back to where he was. 'Yes, mostly a natural phenomenon here, though the fires don't help.'

'Nor the gas-works. If you ask me sir, Seaborough stinks something rotten. That seaweed could be rotting corpses.'

'Best not to repeat that at the station, Reeve,' said Abbs drily. 'I've some sympathy with your view, mind.'

'Oh no, course not, sir. I wouldn't go carping at a man's home and they're all very decent coves. I'm only saying this doesn't compare with the fogs I mind from boyhood. You could pass within a yard of your own ma and never know. Folk stumbled along clutching at walls, else you'd find yourself run down. This is bad for Devonshire, mind,' conceded Reeve generously. He paused to scrape some mud off his boot, along the kerbstone of the grave beside him.

He was right at that. The sickly stench, emanating from the Seaborough Gaslight and Coke Company, permeated the fog and crept into Abbs's throat, making him choke. A weak, yellowy light was attempting to penetrate the fog behind the cross on the church spire.

'Feeling better?' he asked. The discourse on the weather had been delivered in his sergeant's customary cheerful tone.

Reeve grinned sheepishly. 'The landlady kindly dried my boots.'

Throughout the distant strains of organ music, Abbs returned to thinking about Mr. Jerrold. Trying to work out whether the man's dignity would be assuaged by his parting remarks, or if he would complain to Superintendent Nicholls. Even if Jerrold did not act on his veiled threat, he did not expect them to be allowed much more time in Seaborough.

On one matter he was determined. If he had to defend his conduct of the case to Nicholls, he wanted to keep Reeve out of it. Mind, Nicholls would have to think hard before dismissing an officer with a commendation for bravery. There was a chance, however, the sergeant could find himself out of the detective-branch.

'Here they come, sir.'

Mr. Shaw, wearing his funeral surplice, was emerging from the porch. Leading those of the mourners who wished to follow behind the coffin to the grave. The undertaker's men carried the elaborate coffin along the gravel path, turning between the graves to the edge of the waiting hole.

From their position, discreetly hidden by an evergreen oak, the two detectives should have had a good view of most of the churchyard, were the scene not blurred by the shifting fog.

The male mourners stood, with bent heads, as the vicar spoke the final words. One of the undertaker's men stood behind Captain Selden with the customary box of earth to be scattered on the coffin.

Reeve turned to Abbs, whispering rapidly. 'Over there, sir, we've got company. D'you see behind that angel? Someone else is watching.'

Abbs looked to see a muffled shape crouching behind a winged stone figure. A man, certainly, but the mist made it impossible to tell if the watcher was someone they'd met.

'See if you can get round the other side and find out if it's anyone we know,' Abbs instructed quietly. 'But whatever you do, don't let the funeral party see you.'

With a swift nod, Reeve moved off silently, taking a wide circuit. Abbs watched tensely, one eye on the sergeant and the other on the mourners. Thankfully, their attention was on the coffin, now being lowered into the grave.

Reeve had disappeared from sight, making his way behind the church. When Abbs looked again, a second later, the figure had vanished. No purpose in staying where he was any longer, so he made his way to the gates and prepared to lurk unobtrusively behind the last carriage.

Shortly after, the first members of the funeral party began to leave the churchyard. Abbs stepped back, not wanting to run into Mr. Jerrold. He saw no one he recognised, Captain Selden was probably receiving condolences and speaking to Mr. Shaw. Then he did see a face he knew, a gentleman was taking leave of Dr. Avery. The police-surgeon turned to step into a carriage. As he did so, Abbs noticed an ugly bruise spread along his jaw.

He was alone again, the carriages having set off, when Reeve appeared, red-faced and panting with his exertions.

'Sorry, sir, I lost him. He saw me and made himself scarce. Went and bolted through a gate in the hedge and down someone's drive.'

'The vicarage,' said Abbs, while Reeve straightened up.

'I followed him but I went and tripped over. Time I got to the street, he'd disappeared. He didn't come this way?'

Abbs shook his head. 'A pity but not your fault, this wretched weather.'

'It doesn't matter, sir. I know where to find him. I recognised him.' His breathing returning to normal, Reeve looked pleased with himself. 'It was the photographer chap, Mr. Winton.'

~

When she finally heard the brougham, Adelaide put down her sewing and hurried to the window. The fog had cleared and the night sky was scattered with stars as she watched her father set down, in the light spilled from the open door. By the time she reached the hall, Isaac was already turning on his way to the stable and Betsey had taken the rug from Papa.

Adelaide watched approvingly as she helped him off with his travelling-coat and collected hat and gloves. A good, willing girl, she was coming along nicely. She enjoyed helping Betsey with her lettering and fine stitching. The girl was filling out with plentiful good food, her face losing the pinched look she had when she came to them.

'That will be all for tonight, thank you, Betsey. I'll see to it, if we need anything else.' Adelaide dismissed the girl, knowing she had little enough time to herself. Although she hoped theirs was not an arduous household, Betsey would still be up at six to see to the fires. At least, she would have an easier time with them, than straining her eyesight in some Exeter manufactory.

She watched her father fondly as he replaced his town stick in the hall-stand. He was very attached to his handsome, partridge wood stick with its silver collar. Inscribed and presented from the congregation of his first parish, on the occasion of his leaving. It lived beside the sturdier blackthorn he used on his country walks.

'Would you care for some refreshment, Papa?'

'Nothing, thank you, my dear. Captain Selden and I dined very well. I am glad to be at home though, the nights are turning chilly.' Mr. Shaw held out his hands to the drawing-room fire. 'That feels better. The rooms at Tower House are of such proportions as to be draughty, away from the hearth. Despite its grand furnishings, it is not a comfortable house.'

'Nor can the occasion have been, I should think? It was kind of you to keep the Captain company.'

Mr. Shaw took his tobacco jar from the mantelpiece and began to fill his pipe. 'It was the least I could do. He's most anxious to return to his home in Hampshire, for the time being, at least. Whether he intends to leave the army, I know not. He is now very comfortably off but he is adamant that he will sell the house. It is good of him to keep it open until Miss Geake can leave.'

'It is, indeed. I'm sure she is grateful.'

Pausing while he opened the match-safe, Mr. Shaw continued. 'He is away in the morning. It is probable we shall not meet him again. What a tragic end to his long-promised visit.'

'At least he saw his aunt once more. Had he not brought forward his visit, he would not even have had that. He knows that seeing him made her last days happy.' Adelaide looked at her father, when he did not answer. 'Papa? Are you very tired?'

Mr. Shaw smiled gently at her. 'It has been a long day. I hope you are right, my dear. It occurs to me that Miss Chorley may have been murdered because of the Captain's visit.' He fingered the bowl of his pipe, 'though it makes no sense at all.'

'Unless he was intended to be blamed,' said Adelaide slowly. 'A kind of scapegoat.' She shivered and drew nearer the fire. 'Do you think Inspector Abbs will find out the truth?'

'He struck me as a most intelligent man. A sensitive mind, which must make his work more difficult, I should think.'

'He had rather a sad face in repose. But then, I suppose a detective would be, with all the awful things they see.' Picking up her thread-work, Adelaide resumed briskly. 'How was Miss Geake this evening?'

'She did not join us at dinner, pleading a headache. I believe she was being tactful. She told me, beforehand, that she has heard from a prospective employer only this morning. A widowed lady residing in Guildford.'

'I hope she obtains the position and the lady is amiable. This must be an anxious time for her.'

'Quite so. Were Inspector Abbs less shrewd, she might even have been arrested.'

'Do you really think so?' said Adelaide. 'I only meant it must be alarming to lose her home and have to suit a new employer.'

'The poor lady has had a most unhappy time.' The vicar drew on his pipe, hesitated and went on. 'I know I can trust your discretion, Adelaide. Miss Geake has received a legacy but it is not large. It may, I felt, have been smaller than she was expecting.'

Adelaide nodded but did not comment. Privately, she was not surprised. Miss Chorley had been generous with her funds for charitable endeavours. But she had noticed, long ago, that petty economies were practised on her household. She'd seen Miss Geake dispatched on a trivial errand, on foot in the wettest weather, and heard Miss Chorley remark that the exercise would do Ada good.

Miss Chorley had a habit of speaking about her paid companion, as though she were not present. Hannah too, had often reported that Mrs Watkins was instructed to be less extravagant with the servants' food.

'However,' said Mr. Shaw, his expression brightening, 'Miss Chorley has left an extremely generous sum for the Church, one hundred pounds.'

'Oh Papa, that is a huge amount. You must be so pleased.'

'It is a chance to do some real good. Miss Chorley has left a similar sum for provision for the Hospital. Some of the legacy is to be used on charitable works, as I see fit. A portion has been set aside for the erection of a lych-gate. in her memory. It will be a handsome addition to the churchyard and of practical benefit in poor weather. We shall make sure it has benches. It cannot be constructed yet, of course.' He looked gravely at his daughter. 'It would not be fitting until justice has been done.'

~

It had been a long, tedious day. The work of a detective necessitated hanging around for lengthy spells of time. But at least, as a uniformed constable, he had been moving at his own pace. A change to the detective-branch had involved learning how to follow criminals surreptitiously. The skills of loitering, seemingly aimlessly, observing the suspect through shop-windows, dodging into alleys to avoid being seen.

He'd learnt to trail someone through a crowd without losing them, watching all the while for flimps and fine-wirers. To wait outside shady lurks, all without being spotted, and with an eye to your back.

With promotion, came longer hours at a desk and finding ways to question the quality without giving offence. It seemed he had failed dismally at the latter.

Thumping his pillow again, Abbs flung himself on his back and stared into the darkness, gradually making out the shapes of curtain, chest of drawers and wash-stand. His head was too peopled for sleep to come. Jerrold was a pompous fool and probably would enjoy writing a letter of complaint to Superintendent Nicholls.

He had a couple of days' grace before any summons back to Exeter, to explain himself. Even then, there was a fair chance he'd be allowed to continue, there being only four detectives of his rank in the county. It depended on what criminal activity was taking place elsewhere. He would resent being taken away from this case. It presented a great puzzle. But there was a solution and he meant to find it.

Which led back to Philip Winton. He had spent part of the afternoon reading through his notes. What was it the photographer had said? I grew up in the next county. He had been careful not to name it. Would not it have been more natural to say Cornwall, Somerset or Dorset?

There was little point in speaking to him again at present, he still felt. Reeve, like an eager terrier with his tail a-quiver, had been all for going straight to the photographer's studio. He'd pointed out that curiosity was no crime. If Winton had some stronger reason for watching the burial, he was unlikely to tell them. Best, for the moment, to leave him unsure whether Reeve had recognised him.

Frustrated, Abbs wished he could recall whatever was knocking at the edge of his memory. He felt there was something he'd missed, when they visited the photographer's studio. Try as he might, he could not retrieve it. Nor was it to be found in the careful memoranda he'd made after their meeting.

Life had seemed much simpler in his early days. First, working his beat in a small, market-town, then being appointed constable in a village, much like the one where he'd been raised. He could name every poacher and the gypsies who visited the district each year. A useful life but he had been keen to get on.

Promotion and transfer to Norfolk's fledgling detective-branch came in time, encouraged by his own inspector, who brought him forward. Later, came meeting Ellen and her not wanting to give up her Devonshire home for him.

Abbs slammed shut the door on his past and determined to compose himself for sleep, shrugging the eiderdown about his shoulders. It was a long while before his breathing slowed, in rhythm with the susurration of the waves.

Sixteen

No one was on the desk and the empty room resounded with yells and cursing, coming from the short corridor that led to the pair of cells. Beneath it all, came a repeated groaning.

'What the devil's going on?' muttered Abbs. He'd slept badly and sent Reeve on ahead, saying he wanted a word with the landlord.

'S'cuse me, sir,' said a young constable, emerging from the other door. He passed Abbs with a tray bearing several tin mugs of tea. 'Got the cells full to bursting. There was an affray outside the Compass last night. We had to arrest five of them. It's been like Bedlam here since dawn, this might quieten them down. You'd think they'd have slept it off by now. Two of them's Irish.' Pulling a face, he made for the passage, slopping the hot liquid as he went.

'Is Sergeant Reeve about?'

'He's gone for the doctor, sir,' called the constable. 'Seems now one of them reckons he's broken his arm. Sergeant Tancock's in there with him.'

Abbs followed to see for himself. The floor of the corridor had a large, recently cleaned patch, a mop and bucket stood against the wall. A pungent reek of tar soap overlaid, but did not conceal, the sour taint of vomit.

'Give it to me.' He took the tray while the constable reached for the key hanging beside the door and unlocked it.

'Thank 'ee, sir. Now then, Paddy, pipe down. The Inspector's here and he doesn't want to hear your foul language. Drink this and shut up, begging your pardon, sir.'

Abbs looked in at a sorry sight. The dishevelled fellow, who'd been making all the racket, was already grasping the mug and gulping down his tea. One of his eyes was blacked and half-closed. His knuckles were scraped raw and there were blood-stains on his ripped sleeve. He seemed none the worse for it, grinning at him, revealing several brown, crooked teeth, as he wiped his hand across his mouth and belched.

His mate lay across the narrow cot, his arms behind his head. After an indifferent glance, he ignored them and the tea set down beside him. Dried blood was caked about his nose and had dripped down his waistcoat. Abbs guessed his assailant had come off worse.

'It's Constable Dean, isn't it?' he asked when they were back in the cramped passage. 'You took Sergeant Reeve around the druggists'.'

'That's right, sir.'

The other cell door was ajar. Sergeant Tancock eased himself through as they spoke.

'Mornin,' sir. If you're wanting your sergeant, he offered to fetch Dr. Avery. The doctor shouldn't have left for the Hospital yet, so they'll be back soon. Sorry about all the row,' he finished awkwardly.

'Not your fault, sergeant. How's the injured prisoner?' Abbs looked into the crowded cell. One man crouched by another, sitting on the cot and nursing his arm, white-faced. A third was slumped against the wall behind the door.

'He'll be all right. He were fairly quiet for most of the night but now he's been complaining fit to wake the dead. Best to let the doctor see him, I thought. I'm a man down after arresting them. He's gone off duty with sore ribs and the others are out on the beat.'

'D'you often get this kind of trouble?'

Sergeant Tancock yawned copiously as they moved back to the entrance.

'Every now and then. It'll be quiet for months, then there'll be a rumpus in one of the lowest pubs. Often, it's between the fishermen like, but this lot are labourers. Three are working on the town-hall, the others work for Halesworth's. They'll have had their pay. Tempers flare when there's strong drink taken, as you know, sir.'

'Not long since, Halesworth's had a death on their building-site,' said Constable Dean. 'One of them fell from scaffolding. He was a regular customer of ours for being disorderly.'

'Was his death an accident?'

'Oh yes, sir,' replied Tancock. 'I looked in to it, myself. He wasn't drunk and no one was near him when he fell. E'd been feeling ill, according to several accounts, his widow and others, complaining of his guts, like. Probably shouldn't have been up there but no one could say it was Caleb Halesworth's fault. Bert Pardoe wouldn't have said anything. They can't afford to be sent home or laid off.'

Abbs nodded. Losing your work was the path to ruin.

'Get you a cup of tea, sir?' asked Dean.

'Not now, thank you. I'll step out for a bit.'

Fresh air would do more to clear his head. No sign of the others as he looked along the street. A quiet, grey morning, the day seemed as little awake as he felt himself. At least, it was dry and clear.

He'd reached the bottom of the square and was strolling past one of the imposing bank premises when he heard his name hailed. A brougham was pulling in to the kerb. Captain Selden had his head out of the window.

'Inspector Abbs, I was on my way to see you.' He stepped down, glancing up at the coachman. 'I won't be a moment, William.'

'I'm glad you saw me, Captain. What may I do for you?'

'It's nothing like that, I thought I should inform you that I'm returning to Hampshire. I'm on my way to the station now.'

'I see. My thanks for letting me know, sir.'

'The staff are on notice, but the house won't be closed up until Miss Geake leaves for her next post. Call, by all means, if you need to question the servants again. Mr. Jerrold will see to paying them off and having the place sold.'

Abbs noted the stony face of Miss Chorley's man, William, sitting on the box, the reins held loosely in his lap. 'That's good of you, sir. On behalf of the Constabulary, I should like to offer our condolences once more. I assure you, we are doing our utmost to solve the crime. You will be kept informed, Captain.'

Flushing slightly, Selden looked at his boots, rubbing his moustache before meeting his gaze. 'Thank you, Inspector, your sentiments are appreciated.' He looked round at the promenade and the line of beeches behind him. 'It's all been well... terrible. Frankly, I shall be glad to get out of Seaborough and never see nor hear of this benighted place again.'

'That's understandable, sir. I wish you a good journey.'

Selden got back in, rapping on the roof with his stick, when he was seated. Abbs stood watching as William set off along the foot of the square and across the far side. A few russet leaves drifted down in their wake.

~

'What's been going on here? I thought the outside was all finished?'

The workman, who'd been tunelessly humming through closed teeth, jumped at the sound of a voice at his shoulder. Carefully setting down the pane of glass he'd been holding up, he turned to answer. The sarcastic reply died unspoken as he saw Councillor Halesworth.

'A pane got cracked last night. Won't take a minute to whip out.'

Mr. Halesworth looked the fellow up and down, from the stub of pencil behind one ear to the scuffs on his boots. 'Mind you do a neat job, then. I shall inspect it when I leave. I'll be having words with Sergeant Tancock about this.'

With a self-satisfied nod, he dismissed the fellow from his mind and entered the town-hall. Even so, his good mood was not sullied. While an assault on what he almost considered his private fiefdom was an outrage, he would rather relish giving Tancock a verbal leathering. Public order was a serious matter.

He grinned to think how expertly he could have handled the putty and replaced the glass himself. How astonished the fellow would be. He was not one of brother Caleb's labourers. He could not be seen to hand a contract for refurbishing the town-hall to a business he part-owned, more's the pity.

A small pile of letters had been placed on his desk, together with the minutes of the recent meeting of the sanitation committee. Halesworth grimaced as he poked a cursory finger through the opened letters. Nothing of interest there and an evening's talk of drainage to look forward to. Avery, who'd only been appointed for his medical knowledge, would side with the vicar. They'd all be forced to listen to a boring discourse on how the poor needed an adequate water supply.

Let the poor get off their arses and work harder, if they wanted homes like their betters. He'd had to. The truth, and this the vicar would not see, was that the poor were perfectly happy as they were. He was all for town improvements, no man more, but you couldn't try to raise a man's station in life for him.

Why, it went against the natural order of things. Fact is, there were two kinds of men in the world. Those who had ambition and those who had none, take brother Caleb, for instance.

Halesworth looked out at a view that never failed to give him satisfaction. Clarence Square was the heart of Seaborough. Home of its municipal buildings, banks, post-office and superior hotel, all dominated by the town-hall. The streets were filling up with conveyances. Townsfolk were constantly crossing the public garden and greeting each other on the pavements.

As he gazed beyond them at the grey edge of sea, his mind's eye saw fine pier buildings on girders straddling the waves. Eager holiday-makers queuing for a pleasure-steamer. He had added a comfortable, gentlemen's club, rooms for billiards, smoking and coffee-drinking, when the clock, striking the half-hour, recalled him to the present.

Taking up his official correspondence, he revealed an envelope unopened by his clerk. Addressed to him in a neat hand, it was marked *Strictly Private*. Slitting it with his letter-opener, Halesworth dropped into his chair and extracted a single sheet. As he read the contents, he felt his guts turn to ice.

Crumpling the paper in a ball, he hurled it ineffectually at the empty grate. Fumbling for his box of matches, he intended to destroy the letter, only to retrieve it seconds later. Smoothing out the sheet, he folded it and placed it in his pocket-book. While his lower regions still felt icy, a vein throbbed in his forehead, as though at risk of apoplexy. A knock at the door made him jolt.

'Come in.'

'Good morning, sir. Some letters for you to sign, if you please.' The clerk bent deferentially over him, as he laid the papers on the blotter.

'Leave them, I'll do them later.'

'As you wish, Councillor Halesworth. But if you could see your way to signing them now, they would catch the post.'

'Oh, have it your own way. Give 'em here.'

'Not so bad out today, sir. The fog seems to have left us.'

Halesworth glared up at him, oily fool. 'Get out of my light, will you?' He strived for his usual voice. But as he reached for his pen, the pier, and its projected theatre, seemed to collapse in to the sea.

~

Handing a coin to a news-seller, Abbs took a 'paper and returned to the police-station. A gig now stood outside, with a lad holding a brown horse. Behind the front desk, Constable Dean was in patient conversation with two women, one young, the other of middle years, both looking anxious.

Escaping in search of Reeve, he found him in the end cell with the police-surgeon. The other two men had been removed, the remaining space filled by Sergeant Tancock.

'Be steady, man, how can I aid you if you won't let me examine your arm? Help me remove his jacket, will you?' asked Avery.

Reeve pulled the garment off the labourer's good arm and they gently eased the fustian off his other shoulder. The fellow groaned heavily, cradling his right arm again. Sitting on the cot, Avery gently straightened the injured limb, flexing it cautiously.

'It isn't broken,' he said at once. Catching Abbs's eye, he nodded at him. 'Good day, Inspector.' Abbs returned his greeting, watching him at work, with interest.

'If it ain't broke, it's a fracture, Doc. I'm in agony, I ain't puttin' it on.' The workman screwed up his face as Avery felt his wrist.

'No one said you were,' he remarked mildly.

''E did,' said his patient, shooting a vicious look at Sergeant Tancock.

The sergeant sniffed and shifted himself. 'I'll see you outside when you've finished, Doctor.'

'Does the pain run the length of your arm to your fingers?'

'Too right it does, like red-hot pokers.'

Avery nodded and began probing his shoulder, while manipulating his upper arm to see the movement.

'Ow, watch what yer doing, will yer.'

'I thought as much,' said Avery straightening up. 'It isn't your arm at all, it's your shoulder. Fall on it, did you?'

'Landed on it like a sack of taters with me mate on top of me. But 'ow can it be me shoulder? It does 'urt but not as bad as me arm. I told yer, I'm in agony. Call yourself a doctor?'

'You have a sprained shoulder,' said Avery. 'In the course of fighting, you tore the muscles around the joint, probably when you fell. No doubt, they are severely inflamed. You're experiencing pain running from the injured muscles along your arm. Such displaced pain is frequently worse than at the source.' The fellow greeted this information in sullen silence.

'A sling will help, and I'll give you something for the pain, but there's nothing else I can do. Time will heal it and rest will help.' Avery stood up, moving stiffly himself. His mouth tightened, as though in discomfort.

At close quarters, the bruise along his jaw was turning from indigo to yellow. He rummaged in his medical bag. With a jerk of his head, Abbs indicated to Reeve, they should leave the doctor to his patient.

Back in the reception area, Sergeant Tancock was leaning on the counter, talking to the constable.

'Inspector Abbs,' said Dean, 'message just come for you, sir.'

Abbs tensed, expecting to see a telegram from Nicholls, until he was handed a folded sheet of paper.

'Thank you, Constable.' Rapidly reading the few sentences, he turned to Reeve. 'This is from Mr. Emerson. He assumes we'll need to speak to him and he invites us to call this afternoon, if convenient. He's offered to send us back in his carriage. Decent of him.'

'Do we see Mr. Hicks first, sir?' asked Reeve.

'Yes, we'll be off there now.'

'Did I hear you propose calling on Hicks?' said Avery, as he joined them. 'Only I happen to know he's away today.'

'Is that so, Doctor? I'm obliged to you.'

'He mentioned he's travelling to Exeter to see a supplier. Mrs Hicks is accompanying him, they won't be back before nightfall.'

'Very well, he'll keep till the morrow.'

'Mr. Emerson isn't actually a suspect, I take it, sir?' said Sergeant Tancock. 'Not with him being a retired magistrate?'

'No, we need to see him as he was present at Miss Chorley's tea-party. I understand he knew the family for many years.'

'I've patched up your man, as best I can,' said Dr. Avery to the sergeant. 'At least his arm isn't broken. The injury lies in his shoulder. It will heal in a few weeks but I hope he has some savings. He cannot manage physical work until it does. Are you going to charge him?' he asked abruptly.

Tancock scratched his belly. 'Ought to by rights, he were part of an affray.'

'Surely he's suffered enough? He clearly came off worst. I doubt he can afford a fine.'

'What do you think, sir?'

Abbs shook his head. 'Not my jurisdiction, Sergeant. I should take the advice of your police-surgeon.'

'I suppose it'd cut down on paperwork. I'm charging the Irish, specially the one who did for my constable.' Tancock turned to Dr. Avery. 'You look like you've been in the wars yourself, sir.'

'So everyone keeps saying. If you must know, I fell down a flight of stairs, thanks to a loose rod.' Avery snapped shut his bag. 'I must be at the Hospital. If that's all, I'll bid you good day, gentlemen.'

'Funny, that,' said Tancock, when the door had swung to behind him. 'I overheard him telling someone at the funeral that he'd attended a drunk, collapsed in the street, and caught a flailing fist from him.'

'That bruise looks like it came from a fist,' said Reeve.

Looking over the frosted lower window, Abbs watched the doctor climb gingerly into his gig. The lad started down the street, whistling, and Avery moved off with a flick of his reins. Abbs gazed thoughtfully after them.

Seventeen

'Laetus House, wonder what it means?' said Reeve, as they approached the gate-post.

'Happy,' replied Abbs, 'or glad, if I remember rightly.' He stopped to catch his breath, looking round at the deepening autumnal colours of the lane they had climbed. The home of Mr. Emerson was further on than Miss Chorley's house and its only near neighbour.

From where they were standing, a wide sweep of the bay could be seen. A small cargo vessel was making its way down the Channel, perhaps heading for the ship canal at Exeter, though trade there was declining.

Reeve glanced at Abbs in surprise. 'Did you study Latin then, sir?'

'For a while,' said Abbs as they began walking along the drive. He felt some explanation was necessary. 'I grew up in a servant's cottage on an estate. For a time, I studied with the local rector's pupils.'

Laetus House had been built, he thought, at the end of the previous century. Unlike its neighbour, it had not been ruined. Its rows of sash windows were three storeys high. The fawn-coloured stucco was mostly hidden by the fiery red leaves of a Virginia creeper.

'You'd need plenty of bunce to keep this up,' muttered Reeve, just before the door was opened.

Abbs agreed silently, wondering if the house lived up to its name. The person who greeted them was not the usual servant. A stocky man, in shirt-sleeves, took their things. A battered face, he looked about fifty.

His features did not quite seem to agree somehow, as though his bulbous nose wanted to look in a different direction from his chin. His sharp eyes darted everywhere. They agreed, on comparing notes later, that he could have plied any dubious trade in his youth, from a prize-fighter to a peter-man.

'Mr. Emerson's seeing you in the smoking-room. This way,' he said, in a gravelly Scotch accent. He led them to the rear of the house, gave a cursory knock and put his head round a door. 'The police for you,' he announced, pronouncing it *pollis*. 'Two o' them.'

'Bring them in,' said a husky, refined voice.

Its owner was sitting in a high-backed armchair by the fire, a rug over his knees. Mr. Emerson was probably in his seventies, elegant in appearance, with neatly-brushed, thin, grey hair. He wore an old-fashioned wing-collar, above a maroon smoking-jacket.

His breathing was noticeably laboured, his head back on a cushion. Despite his unhealthy pallor, his eyes were bright and his smile warm.

'Excuse my not rising, gentlemen,' he said, when Abbs had made their names known. 'Do make yourselves comfortable.'

Thanking him, they took their places on the sofa. Reeve took out his notebook.

'May I offer you both some madeira and a biscuit?'

'Not on duty, sir, thank you.' Abbs flicked a severe glance at Reeve, who looked disappointed.

'It's good of you to visit me here, Inspector. I'm afraid I can get out little these days, Miss Chorley's invitation to tea being a rare exception. I'm that tiresome article, an invalid, most frustrating.' As if in illustration, Mr. Emerson broke off in a fit of coughing. The manservant, who'd been hovering in the doorway, moved quickly to his master's side.

Abbs looked discreetly at their surroundings, which revealed so much about a person. Reeve, a picture of healthy youth, studied his empty page.

They were in a wholly, masculine room, dark-panelled walls hung with political caricatures. A table held a revolving book-stand and bound copies of periodicals. Another, against the opposite wall, was laid out with humidor, pipe-rack, tobacco jars, vesta cases and silver cigarette boxes. An open lid showed the contents divided into compartments.

Abbs recognised the slim, dark smokes which came from Russia and the fat, creamy-papered, Turkish variety. The display was a regular tobacconist's emporium. A pair of tall windows overlooked the garden. Beneath one of them, the window-seat was replaced by a modern wash-basin.

Though the brass ash-tray by Mr. Emerson was clean, the air was heavy with the trapped odour of stale tobacco. There could be no doubt, even to a blind man, of the room's purpose, designed for the convenience of male guests.

As his coughing died away, his man held a glass of water to Mr. Emerson's lips. He then helped him sit upright again, his muscular arms raising his master effortlessly.

'Forgive me for that unedifying exhibition. Thank you, Logan, I'll be all right now.'

'Don't be letting them tire you out, sir,' said the manservant. He gave them a stern glare as he left.

Mr. Emerson regarded them both, with some amusement. 'You are wondering how Logan came to be here? The Scots always seem to wander far from home. We encountered each other long ago, in the course of my tenure as a magistrate. I have taken an interest in recidivism and prison reform. I trust that does not put us at odds, Inspector?'

'It does not, sir,' said Abbs. 'I'm for any means that bring us fewer customers.'

'How about you, Sergeant? Do you believe that regular employment can reform a rogue?'

'I don't see why not, sir,' said Reeve. 'Depends on the man. There's some wicked just for the pleasure of it, 'cause they're made that way. But most criminals want to keep body and soul together, to give their families decent things... same as the rich.'

'Well said,' Mr. Emerson nodded. Reeve contrived to look both surprised and pleased. 'Logan decided on a change of direction, I'm pleased to say. He's proved loyal and a great help to me. But he's a little uncomfortable around officers of the law.'

'Thank you for your message, Mr. Emerson,' said Abbs. 'I was about to get in touch with you.'

'I knew you'd want to question me at some point. My old friend, Sam Shaw suggested I invite you here. He seemed to think you might find it useful to hear more about Miss Chorley's background.'

Abbs raised his eyebrows. 'That was very kind of Mr. Shaw. I'd be glad of anything you can tell us, sir. To begin with, did anything seem odd or out of place to you during the tea-party?'

'I've gone over the events of that afternoon many times. I can think of nothing, no possible indication of what was to come. Harriet, Miss Chorley, was unusually animated. Delighted, of course, to have her nephew with her.' Pausing, he sipped some water. 'She was in her element, parading him before friends and neighbours. Captain Selden was somewhat diffident. An uncomfortable trait for an army officer but he was a shy little fellow, as a boy.'

'Did you know Captain Selden well, Mr. Emerson?' asked Abbs.

'Not at all, I saw him two or three times when his mother brought him to stay. Caroline, Mrs Selden, was Miss Harriet Chorley's younger sister, though they were close in age.' He smiled reminiscently. 'She was a pretty, lively girl, quite unlike Harriet. Our families knew one another well, as the only near neighbours. Their parents weren't accepted fully by the best families hereabouts. New money, you see, from trade.'

'Indeed, sir?'

'Ridiculous snobbery. My own parents were fairly new to the area themselves. The families struck up an acquaintance. When Caroline Chorley married a chap from the north, her father wasn't best pleased, so she visited without her husband. Selden was in business and old Richard, her father, wanted her to marry gentry and improve the family. Poor Caroline, she was dead from the small-pox by her early thirties. Now, you mustn't let me bore you, Inspector. I spend too much of my time in the past. It seems closer than the days before me.'

'Do please continue, if you will, sir. It's most interesting. If I can understand Miss Chorley, I believe it will help to solve her murder.'

Mr. Emerson looked keenly at him. 'You theorise that the victim's character will explain the motive?'

Abbs thought for a moment. 'I believe so, in part. Certainly in a domestic case like this.'

'You may well be right.' After some ragged breaths, Mr. Emerson turned over his memories. 'Harriet worshipped her father but sadly, her affection wasn't reciprocated. She was quite passed over in favour of Caroline and James. Harriet was plain, not to put too fine a point on it, and she lacked social graces. Richard Chorley would have liked a son first, of course. After Caroline's birth, they had probably resigned themselves to no more, until along came James, ten years after.'

Open-mouthed, Mr. Emerson breathed evenly for a spell, his chest wheezing softly.

'Can I get you anything, sir?' said Reeve.

Mr. Emerson held up a hand until he felt able to speak again. 'I lack nothing, thank you, Sergeant.' He gestured at his table. 'I can ring if need be. There is nothing Dr. Miller can offer me, apart from pills and an insistence on rest. I would consult Dr. Avery, if I believed he could make any difference. I know Miss Chorley thought highly of him.'

Abbs looked at the paraphernalia of an invalid, the water glass and jug, folded handkerchief, inlaid pill box and hand-bell. A pocket volume of Mr. Borrow's *Wild Wales* lay close at hand, together with a cigarette case and matches. Mr. Emerson reached for them as he watched.

'This will help me more than any physic.' They both declined as he proffered the case. 'No?' Waving the spent match, he placed it in the ash-tray. 'Ah, that's better. Where was I?'

'You were about to tell us of Captain Selden's uncle, sir.'

'Ah, yes, thank you, Inspector. I can't claim to have known James intimately, you understand. I was so much older, several years senior to the girls. But I remember he was, not unnaturally, his father's pride and joy. Old Richard had his male heir, long after giving up hope. Every good thing was lavished on him. Fortunately, Harriet adored her little brother. It could so easily have gone a different way.'

Abbs was as interested as in a novel. He had seen their portraits, could imagine the Chorleys, and Tower House as a busy family home. It must, he thought, have been a sad husk of former life, when Miss Chorley lived there alone with Miss Geake. 'What happened to Mrs Chorley, sir?'

'She died a year or so after James's birth. Never recovered properly from her confinement. Harriet soon became a little woman and gradually took on the duties of running the household. Caroline eventually married Mr. Selden and left. Harriet was passed over.' Mr. Emerson shook his head sadly. 'It's unfortunate when a woman does not have marriage and children to fill her time. Harriet was of an energetic disposition, though wearied in recent years. She threw herself into charitable works, particularly the Hospital. You know she established that in her father's memory?'

'We met Dr. Avery there.'

'Of course, he's police-surgeon also. What else can I tell you? James went in for the army and lost his life at Inkerman. He was a young blade, sowed plenty of wild oats in his youth. Miss Chorley encouraged Mr. Selden to buy her nephew a commission. But I don't believe Captain Selden had the same taste for military life as his uncle. I had the impression that the Paymaster's office suits him better than campaigning.'

'Service in India wouldn't suit everyone,' remarked Abbs. 'I don't believe I could stand the heat.'

'I'm with you,' said Mr. Emerson, 'Captain Selden was describing summers at the hill stations, which did sound somewhat more congenial. I understand the social life was very good. Miss Chorley was most interested, wanting to know every detail. It's a blessing that Selden was able to bring forward his visit. At least, she saw her only family again, after so long.'

'So Captain Selden was expected later in the year?' said Abbs. 'I didn't realise that.'

'I don't suppose it occurred to him to mention it. Originally, he was due in the weeks preceding Christmas. Miss Chorley had hopes of his spending the festive season here. Apparently, the army wanted him to take his leave this month.'

It was painful to watch the poor gentleman, thought Abbs, as he extinguished the fag end of his cigarette and sank back. His breathing became more laboured, like machinery in want of grease.

'You've been extremely helpful, sir. Thank you for inviting us to your home. We mustn't take up any more of your time.'

'On the contrary, Inspector, it's you and your sergeant who have been indulgent to an old man. It's pleasant to relive times long gone. Logan will have the carriage ready for you. I should not, I daresay, enquire how your investigation fares?'

'I believe,' said Abbs, as he rose, 'we may finally be getting somewhere. We have one or two leads to pursue.' Reeve glanced sideways at him.

Mr. Emerson reached up to clasp his hand. 'Poor Harriet didn't deserve to be poisoned in her bed.' His hoarse voice was little stronger than a whisper. 'Find whoever did this, Abbs.'

'We shall, Mr. Emerson,' he promised.

~

Some of the seaweed on the beach had been cleared, in consequence, the stench was fading. Abbs leant on the railings as he considered his next course. Reeve had been invited to take a drink with one of the constables, when he came off duty, while he sought the open air again.

If Jerrold had acted on his implied threat to contact Superintendent Nicholls, he was likely to hear on the morrow. He felt as though a storm were about to break over him.

While they were walking to Laetus House, he'd remembered what he'd seen in Philip Winton's studio. Mr. Emerson had indirectly made his suspicion seem more likely. The question was how best to find confirmation? Better to find proof before confronting Winton, lest he give them a flat denial. When he returned to the police-station, he would compose a telegram requesting the services of Scotland Yard.

Even so, he was not wholly convinced that Philip Winton was their murderer. Mr. Emerson had set him thinking on a quite different line, though he did not know what it meant.

Idly watching a line of sea-gulls, as they flew beyond the oldest quarter of Seaborough, Abbs recognised the slight figure of Miss Shaw walking towards him. Raising his hat, she smiled in recognition as he greeted her.

'I didn't expect to see you here, Inspector. Are you exploring?'

He looked down at her, some wisps of dark hair escaping from her bonnet and lifting in the breeze. 'I'm escaping my temporary quarters. I find I think better outside.'

'My father says the same. But in that case, I mustn't disturb you.'

'Not at all, I'm glad to see you, Miss Shaw. I've been visiting Mr. Emerson and find his invitation was arranged by your father's forethought.'

'They're old friends. My father visits him every week for a game of chess.'

'Will you please convey my thanks to him? I appreciate his help.'

'Of course, but you can thank him when next you meet. He would like to see you again, I know.'

'You're most kind, I enjoyed talking to Mr. Shaw very much.'

She smiled at him, clearly pleased by a compliment to her parent. 'It must be tedious to leave your home and stay in a strange town. Unless you are accustomed to doing so, in your work?'

Abbs thought of the small, dreary house he rented. 'Not often but it saves time travelling back and forth from Exeter, in this case. I don't mind too much where I am, as long as I've a book with me.'

'Books are the best of companions. I've just been visiting a family and trying to persuade them to send their children to the new board-school. It's hard for people with no money to spare.' She looked back at the tiny cottages, beyond the end of the promenade.

'They say basic schooling will be made compulsory in a few years,' remarked Abbs.

Miss Shaw nodded. 'A good thing.'

'Is it mostly fishermen who live down there?' He gestured towards the huddled buildings. In front of them, women were sitting on the pebbles mending nets.

'Yes, though some of the families have little work. As you see, the men can only launch small boats from here.'

'The town could do with a harbour.'

'You sound like Mr. Halesworth,' said Miss Shaw. 'There was one here in the last century, when Seaborough was a village. The harbour wall was swept away one night in a great storm and it's been silted up ever since.'

'And now the town seems to be developing in another way.'

'I suppose it was inevitable, once we had the railway.'

Turning their back on Seaborough's past, they began strolling towards the heart of the town.

Abbs found Miss Shaw's company unexpectedly restful. Unlike most women, she seemed content to remain silent. Perversely, he found himself wanting to converse further.

'Do you enjoy living in Seaborough, Miss Shaw?'

'It's a pleasant town. Our friends are here, my father is contented and I have never known anywhere else.' She glanced at him, her face serious. 'Even so, part of me would like to feel that freshness of beginning anew. Instead of life being dull and always knowing what's ahead.' A wistfulness faded in her voice. 'How remiss of me, I forgot about Miss Chorley for a moment. Life here will never feel predictable again.'

He was at a loss what to say to her. Any words of reassurance would sound trite. From what he knew of human nature, most people were not sensitive. They would carry on, much as before. Harriet Chorley would become a worn name on a memorial, unread and forgotten.

'How about you, Inspector? Do you enjoy living in Devonshire?'

He searched for the right words. To his dismay, he did not hear himself uttering the polite, meaningless remarks, he would have made to anyone else.

'It wasn't my choice. I've never really become accustomed to living here. The topography is very different from where I grew up.' A pull of longing, for his Norfolk home, tugged almost physically in his chest.

Miss Shaw looked quietly sympathetic as they walked on. He was grateful that she said no more.

Eighteen

'Mr. Hicks, I think you'd better come. It's Bram, he's worked himself up like a top and I... Beg pardon, I didn't know anyone was with you.' The woman hurrying in from the rear of the shop, her words tumbling before her, stopped abruptly as she saw the men standing with her employer and Mr. Biggs. Her hair a tweedy grey and brown, she had a kind face, which told of a placid disposition.

'This is Mrs Lavis, my assistant.' Mr. Hicks turned back to her. 'These gentlemen are detectives.'

'Good day to you, ma'am,' Abbs touched his hat.

Returning their greeting, she stood deferentially, her hands folded against her dark blue merino.

'What's the matter with Bram? He's the lad who helps with the horses and suchlike,' said Mr. Hicks to Abbs.

'He's in with Samson now and won't come out. He's got it in his head that he saw a ghost in the churchyard last evening and Joe's been teasing him. Mr. Biggs and I can see to him. I wouldn't have called you if I'd known you had visitors.'

Pulling out his watch, Mr. Hicks compared the time with the clock on the wall. 'Joe should have taken Delilah down to Towser's by now. Sorry about this, Inspector. We hire out the horses when they're not needed. Towser's are a removal firm.'

'He's just left, sir,' said Mrs Lavis.

'Good, then shall we go to my room?'

'Actually, sir,' said Abbs, 'I should like to hear the lad's tale.'

'In that case, I'll show you the stables. Though I must warn you, Bram's perhaps not the most reliable witness.'

Mr. Hicks's clerk had been silently studying them, his head tilted to one side. Like a thrush watching a juicy worm, thought Abbs. He recognised him as the feather-man who'd led the funeral procession and he'd approached Dr. Avery, immediately they left the inquest.

Mr. Biggs gave a slight, hollow cough, preparatory to speaking, and tapped the edge of his forehead with a forefinger. 'The boy's touched.' He held out an arm, ushering them after his employer. 'This way, if you please.'

Abbs and Reeve followed them behind the counter and through a short passage, leaving Mrs Lavis in the shop.

Emerging in a good-sized yard, they saw stables, a coach-house and a workshop built across the end wall. High wooden gates gave on to the street. Through the open door of the workshop could be seen a coffin on trestles, a plane resting on the lid.

Reeve wandered over to the occupied loose-box and spoke softly to the horse looking out at them, Mr. Hicks joined him. 'He's a fine beast, sir.'

The undertaker smiled appreciatively, through his thick beard. 'Isn't he, just? This is Samson, he knows I've usually a sugar lump about me.' He felt in his waistcoat pocket. 'Here we are, care to give it to him?'

Reeve held out his palm for the stallion, patting his head while the offering vanished. 'He's in peak condition, isn't he? Glossy coat, black as night.'

'Yes, they have to be, of course and have a good, steady temperament. I wish you could see the mare, they're perfectly matched. Quite hard to come by. So many have a white blaze.'

Samson nuzzled Reeve's head, showing a large set of teeth. Not unlike Mr. Biggs, thought Abbs.

'You obviously like horses, Sergeant.'

'I grew up around them, sir. My pa was a cabman.'

'He knows you like him. I'd better see if I can winkle Bram out.' Mr. Hicks leant over the door of the other stall, peering in the shadows. 'Bram, come on out, will you? Joe didn't mean any harm.' There was a few seconds' silence. 'Come on, lad.'

A rustling of straw and a figure shuffled out of the end door, his arms hanging limply. He was a tow-haired, gangly youth, with a slight, but unmistakeable looseness to his features. Abbs felt a sad pity as he caught sight of Bram's face. Life was hard enough without being marked out.

'So what's all this about, Bram? Tell us what you told Joe.' Mr. Hicks leant against the stable wall. He spoke kindly, absent-mindedly rubbing Samson's head, as he looked at the youth. Bram gave a quick, nervous glance at the two strangers before staring at his boots.

'Now then, cat got your tongue?' said Mr. Biggs, stepping forward. 'This gentleman's an important policeman. He'll lock you up if you keep him waiting.' His jocular tone, likely intended to be kind, would have terrified a child.

Abbs threw him a sour glance. Bram twitched, his fingers picking at his hands. Abbs saw they had reddened patches with sore, flaking skin.

'No one is going to lock anyone up,' he said quietly. 'We've come for a talk with Mr. Hicks, Bram. We're interested to hear what you saw. There's nothing to worry about. Will you tell us?'

Bram jerked his head and edged closer, stopping near Reeve. 'I see to Samson,' he announced.

'He's a credit to you.' Abbs smiled at him.

Appearing mollified, the youth began again. 'I was goin' by the churchyard last night and I saw her.'

'Who did you see?' asked Reeve, in a friendly manner.

'The old lady, the one we buried. It were her ghost. All in grey, she were. I was walkin' past the wall and I saw her. Joe wouldn't believe me but I did.' His voice wavering, Bram examined each face in turn.

'What was the lady doing?' said Abbs lightly.

'Flittin' between the graves. She'd risen and she was going to the church. I ran afore she saw me and tried to take me with her.'

'Do you have a pocket-watch, Bram?'

The youth shook his head.

'Was it dark when you saw her?'

'Dusky. I bin to Liddlow's for some scrag end for my ma. He lets you have it cheap when he's closing. Liddlow's fat boy was sweeping out the sawdust. I don't like him.'

'Ahem, surely it was someone cutting through the churchyard?' said Mr. Biggs. 'Miss Shaw, perhaps, she's the vicar's daughter.'

Bram shook his head vehemently. 'T'wasn't Miss Adelaide, I knows her. She wouldn't frighten me.'

'Bram attends Miss Shaw's Sunday school,' murmured Hicks. 'He would recognise her, I think.'

'Have you any particular reason to be interested, Inspector?' Mr. Biggs looked avidly at him.

Abbs shook his head, 'Idle curiosity.' Dismissing the matter, he turned to the undertaker. 'Perhaps we might have that word now, sir?'

'Of course. Off you go and see Mrs Lavis, Bram.' Hicks led them back inside to his office, his clerk bringing up the rear. Abbs was determined that Biggs be firmly shut out. He wouldn't be surprised to find him listening at the door.

'Would you care for some tea?' asked Hicks, over his shoulder.

'Thank you, no. Too soon after breakfast for us, isn't it, Sergeant?'

'Yes sir,' said Reeve, his voice lacking conviction.

The undertaker's room was subdued. Arranged in muted, good taste with grey-green paper and furnishings. There were already two comfortable chairs drawn up to the desk. Abbs spared a passing thought for all the unhappy individuals who had taken them. No miasma of grief hung in the air, though.

Indeed, there was a pleasing scent of cherry pie from the small jug of heliotrope on the desk. Their mauve shade was appropriate for mourning. He wondered if that was intentional. Remembered Miss Shaw thinking her bright yellow flowers unsuitable for a funeral service

Hicks leant back in his chair. 'How may I assist you?'

'I understand you purchased some arsenic several weeks ago,' began Abbs. 'Will you begin by telling us why you needed it?'

Hicks laughed. 'By Jove, I hope you don't have me in mind as the Seaborough poisoner. It was for the rats. Every now and then, you'll always get a problem with stables. You'll know this, Sergeant.' Reeve nodded. 'We could do with a cat but people will drown kittens as soon as they're born. My wife has asked around if someone will keep one back for us. I know you met my wife with the Shaws.'

Abbs studied the undertaker, intent on weighing up his character. 'I see, sir. Will you tell us about your calling at Tower House, on the evening Miss Chorley died?'

'There's little to say. It was looking like rain, there was a tremendous storm later that evening, I recall. My wife had been invited to afternoon tea, as you know. I decided to call and escort her home.'

'But she'd already left?'

'That's right. I was shown in to Captain Selden and he invited me to stay for a peg or two. I didn't see Miss Chorley. But it must have been before she was taken ill, or surely I would not have been asked in?'

'Quite so. Did you have any ulterior motive for trying to see Captain Selden?'

The undertaker looked puzzled. 'I don't follow you, Inspector.'

'Perhaps you should know that I've spoken to Mr. Halesworth, sir. I should like you to confirm matters.'

Hicks grinned again. He toyed with the glass paperweight on his blotter, his hands perfectly relaxed. 'Very well, Inspector, you're quite right. I did have an ulterior motive.'

Reeve made a brief note and looked up, his expression keen.

'I don't know how much Halesworth told you but he, Avery and I are hoping to invest in a building venture. Halesworth approached Miss Chorley, as she had a parcel of land that was ideal and little used. Seaborough needs to expand but there's limited building land with the topography. The old lady declined to sell, her prerogative, of course. I thought there was no harm in sounding out Selden, in case, he was amenable to using his influence. It seemed to me that Halesworth might have rubbed her up the wrong way.'

'And did you ask him, Mr. Hicks?'

'The right opening didn't arise. Selden wanted a drink and some undemanding company. I suppose I thought I'd established cordial terms and there'd be another time.'

'And now there's every likelihood that Captain Selden will sell the land to you,' said Abbs pleasantly. 'Will this building deal make you a wealthy man?'

'Steady on, Inspector, we're simply three professional men clubbing together to make a modest investment. We didn't murder an elderly lady to further our ends. The idea's outrageous.'

'No, sir, I don't suppose you did. But we need to sift through everything that concerned Miss Chorley.'

'That's reasonable enough in the circumstances,' said Mr. Hicks. 'I confess I'm surprised Halesworth told you. Or was it Avery? Though he plays his cards close to his chest.'

'We didn't know Dr. Avery had business dealings with you, Mr. Hicks. Councillor Halesworth didn't mention any of this when I met him. His ambitions are widely known in the town. It seemed quite possible that Miss Chorley had a building plot of interest to him.'

Hicks stared at him before breaking into a rueful laugh. 'I see everyone's secrets will be laid bare, Inspector.'

'Do you have any arsenic left, sir?'

'No, it was all laid down. Under strict supervision, what with the horses. We had a pile of dead rats to show for it.'

'I believe you were left alone in the library, at Tower House?'

'Look, am I a suspect, Inspector?'

'Please answer the question, sir, it's simply routine.'

'You already know, by the sound of it. Selden slipped out of the room to fetch a map. I was alone for a few minutes. I looked out of the windows, glanced at a few of the book titles, and examined the contents of a cabinet table.' He grinned. 'It was the first time I'd been inside the house. I was rather curious.'

Abbs glanced at Reeve, indicating they were finished. 'We've all done it, sir.'

'I'd watch it, Sarge,' said Constable Dean. 'Your inspector's had a telegram and he didn't look too happy when I went in.'

'Righto, thanks for the tip-off,' said Reeve.

'What's it like in the detective-branch?' Closing his ledger, Dean leant confidentially over the counter. 'A sight more exciting than dealing with drunks and pick-pockets, I bet.'

Reeve sauntered over, hands in his pockets. 'It's not all murders, you know. Mostly it's thieving, house-breaking and serious assault. Bit of forgery,' he added, 'this sort of case is a rarity.'

'Have you worked on one like this before?' Dean's attention hung on every word.

'Not exactly like this. I've done a few murders among the criminal-class. They're straightforward enough. Most times, you don't have far to look for the culprit. This is really something to get your teeth into.'

'Reckon your inspector will find who done it?'

'Course he will. It's a tricky case but Inspector Abbs is known in Exeter for his perspicacity. He's one of the very best in the force.'

'Is he a hard man to work for?'

Reeve considered. 'He works you hard, expects you to be thinking about the case all the time, and keep your notes tidy. There's no taking it easy but he's straight. He wouldn't do the dirty on you, like take credit for your idea.' He scratched his head as he thought. 'He actually asks what you think and listens when you tell him.'

'Sergeant Tancock 'ud never do that,' said Constable Dean. 'Anyways, Inspector Abbs asked for a *Bradshaw.*'

'I'd best see what's afoot.' Giving a cursory rap on the door, in case the old man was in one of his stickler moods, Reeve found Abbs at his borrowed desk. The inspector looked up, breaking off his scribbling.

'Ah, Sergeant, there you are. Just in time. I've been summoned back to Exeter. Superintendent Nicholls requires a report of our progress, or otherwise.' Getting up, Abbs shut the door fast, hesitated, then made up his mind. 'Actually, that's not all there is to it. The Superintendent does want a report but I've been summoned to account for a complaint made by Mr. Jerrold. I told you what passed between us.'

'Yes, sir.' Reeve frowned, that was a bad turn.

'There you have it. I shall leave at once and return first thing on the morrow, or possibly this evening. Failing that, I won't be required to return to

Seaborough at all. I'll grab a bag now and have a word with the Gaunts about my room.'

'Am I not to accompany you, sir?'

Abbs shook his head. 'Your name hasn't been mentioned. I think it's best you're out of harm's way. It's me Jerrold has found fault with. I was alone when I saw him. I shall tell the Superintendent you aren't involved in any way.'

'It's not that, sir. What if the Superintendent does pull us off the case? I mean... no offence intended, sir.'

Abbs grimaced. 'If another officer returns, it will be up to you to brief him and hand over our findings. I hope it won't come to that, I should like to see this through but we must abide by the Superintendent's decision.'

Reeve opened his mouth to argue, catching his eye, thought better of it. 'Sir. What shall I do while you're away?'

'Expect the telegram from the Yard. I stressed the urgency, so it could come at any time. Read it, of course, but don't act on it. I hope we may see Mr. Winton together. You can go over everything we've written down. See if anything fresh occurs to you. Now, I'll be on my way.' Abbs picked up his hat. 'There's a train at half-past midday I can catch.'

Reeve accompanied him to the entrance, watching as he hurried down the steps and along the street. Giving way to an old lady, who still wore a wide crinoline, swerving round stooping children, playing marbles in the gutter, his long stride scattered blown leaves. His lone figure was swiftly lost to view. Reeve found himself hoping Inspector Abbs would return.

~

Reverend Septimus Owen's knees were remarkably uncomfortable on the hard boards, as he tried unsuccessfully to concentrate. He rested his clasped knuckles against his forehead, his elbows supported on the edge of the front pew, as he began again to intercede with his Maker.

Unfortunately, the next thought that floated across his consciousness was that perhaps, he had been too hasty in rejecting the suggestion of hassocks. At the time, they had seemed too comfortable, effete even. Typical of all that was complacent about the well-to-do Church of England parishioners. No doubt, Samuel Shaw would scorn to kneel on a hard floor.

Mr. Owen sighed and thought again how much he needed a helpmeet. If only the Almighty would see fit to send him one who would support him in his work. She who would gratefully receive his stern, affectionate guidance. Provide the small comforts his home woefully lacked.

His thoughts were straying to precisely what form those comforts might take, when he heard the outer door swing open.

He waited just long enough to hear someone step inside the chapel and see him at prayer. A female footfall, he judged, before rising gracefully, as though unaware he was no longer alone. It was with a slight sense of disappointment that he beheld the dumpy figure of Mrs Pardoe, a familiar member of his congregation.

Surely the Almighty did not mean to send her to his aid? The fact that she was at least ten years his senior would not, in itself, deter him, if a lady were suitable in other respects. A new widow, in her unbecoming bombazine, she was neither prosperous nor pretty. In addition, being burdened with two strapping boys.

A man in his position deserved to meet a lady of quality. Someone sweetly submissive, who was called to serve her Maker, by assisting his humble minister. She would preside equally well over hearth and tea-urn, pantry and pamphlet, untiringly devoted to easing his labours.

'Mrs Pardoe. And what brings you here at this hour? Have I mistook the ladies' cleaning day?' Bestowing a brief, though gracious smile, Mr. Owen strolled over to the black-board. Consulting a jotting in his pocket-book, he proceeded to chalk some hymn numbers.

'Oh no, sir, that's Monday.' The widow Pardoe watched him for a moment, the only sound being the dashing of the chalk. 'Your washing's by the door, Mr. Owen.'

Irritated by her information, reminded anew of his uncomfortable domestic situation, he frowned as he dusted off his hands. Really, had the woman no sense of propriety? Such trivial, earthly matters had no place in His house. Was he so little valued, that he was to be accosted by any washer-woman?

'My thanks to you. Mayhap, in future, you would take it to my door, rather than our place of worship?'

'Yes sir. I was on my way there. Only being as I was passing, thought I'd look in and see.'

'Very well. I trust we shall see you at the temperance meeting next week?'

'I'll be there, sir, along with my boys. I don't want them to go the way of their poor father.'

Mr. Owen turned away hastily, as tears glistened in her eyes. Effecting to check the marker in the Bible on his reading-desk, he hoped she would leave. But it was not to be.

'Was there something else?' he inquired resignedly. The little woman had stopped dabbing her eyes at last, yet still lingered.

'The truth is, I was hoping for a word with you, sir.' At a stand-still again, she peered at him.

He recalled seeing her wear wire spectacles when she sang from her hymn-book. Most unbecoming in a woman. 'What is it you wish to say to me, Mrs Pardoe?'

'I don't rightly know where to start, sir. I'm in that much of a dilemma. It's been hanging over me. At first, I was that pleased... I thought the Good Lord Almighty had answered my prayers. For when my Albert was first took from us, I didn't know how we were going to manage. My wages from the Hospital wouldn't provide for the rent and feed us. Two shillings a day, I get. And with two lads always growing out of their trousers ...'

'Mrs Pardoe, please desist. Do not distress yourself so, good lady. Sit down and tell me clearly, what is your problem. Do I understand that you wish to ask my advice?'

Sinking on to the nearest bench, Mrs Pardoe looked up at him gratefully. 'Yes please, sir. I must have your guidance. Only, I don't want to be a thief. Poor but honest, my family have always been. Well,' she amended, 'not wanting to tell a falsehood in the house of God, my Albert had been light-fingered in his time. But never since we were wed. He promised me and it does say in the Bible, that each of us is tempted. My poor Albert always did say I told a tale backwards.'

'Am I to believe you have acted dishonestly, Mrs Pardoe?' The minister looked sternly down at her. 'Tell me, at once, how you have sinned. No more shilly-shallying and remember this, the Almighty is listening.'

Mrs Pardoe sat up straight. 'It's like this, sir. I always knew my Albert had a hidey-hole, beneath a loose floorboard, in our room. After he died so sudden, it was a while before I thought about it. Mr. Hicks's burial club paid out for his funeral, thank the Good Lord. The tiny bit I had put by, went on rent and mourning clothes. I couldn't afford to get it all from Hicks's.'

'Yes, yes, so you looked in your husband's hiding-place? What did you find?'

'Twelve pound, seven and eight,' said Mrs Pardoe, in a rush. 'I couldn't believe it, Mr. Owen. I came over all weak and had to sit on the rug for a time. It didn't seem real. Then I counted it and hid it in my hat-box, where I keep my mother's topaz brooch, pinned to a piece of flannel. I had to keep it there.

My mother had it from her own mother, on her wedding day. I feared Albert would pawn it, if he could lay hands on it.'

'Never mind the brooch, Mrs Pardoe. Come to the point.'

She looked earnestly up at him. 'He was a good man, sir, for all he'd never come to Chapel, but strong drink was his weakness.

Mr. Owen frowned. 'I really am at a loss to know why you are telling me all this, Mrs Pardoe. You don't know how your late husband came by this money. And you believe he stole it, is that it?'

Flinching as though she'd been struck, Mrs Pardoe nodded. 'It truly did seem like a miracle at first. I paid the grocer and got our coal in, the cellar's full to bursting. I bought new boots for young Bert and John. But, as the days have gone by, it's been on my conscience. Growing and growing like a carbuncle.'

'I see,' said Mr. Owen severely. 'You wish me to tell you what to do.'

'I've thought so hard, sir, till my head nearly bursts. I don't know how my Albert could have come by that money honestly.'

'It is a strange sum. I should think it had started out a round amount and been broken in to.'

'Them's my thoughts, too, sir.' Mrs Pardoe tucked her handkerchief into her glove.

'Had Mr. Pardoe been spending extra money in his last weeks?'

'He'd been spending more time in the Compass and he seemed real pleased with himself. Like he had a secret but he wouldn't say what. He didn't give me any extra, no, sir. What do I do, Mr. Owen? Should I go to the police with what's left?'

'No, Mrs Pardoe, you cannot do so. In truth, you have nothing to tell them. No knowledge of any criminal act. Can you think of no one who might have given your husband a sum of money? Could he have done some work for someone, or applied to a relative for a loan?'

'There's no one, sir, and Albert couldn't have done any extra work without my knowing. There aren't the hours.'

'In that case, I believe you may never know how he came by it.'

A sudden ray of sunlight shone through one of the clear, latticed windows, illuminating them both. It occurred to Mr. Owen, in passing, what a fine painting they would make. The Wesleyan Methodist minister, gravely giving counsel to his sister in Christ, as she gazed beseechingly at him.

Half-turning, he pointed dramatically towards the cross. 'Only the One-who-sees-all knows the truth of it.' Drawing himself up, he looked down at the washer-woman. 'You are innocent of all wrong-doing, dear lady. You have done the right thing in telling me. Let your conscience be eased.'

Mrs Pardoe's face brightened. 'You don't know how thankful I am, Mr. Owen. You've properly set my mind at rest. I feel so much better for coming to you.' Gathering her skirts, she rose to her feet, shuffling awkwardly out of the pew. As she made her way to the door, a thought struck her and she halted. 'In your opinion then, sir, it's quite all right for me to spend what's left?'

Pursing his lips, Mr. Owen struck a further pose, his hand slipped in his frock-coat. 'That I did not say, Mrs Pardoe. While there is doubt in your heart that the money could be ill-gotten gains, it is surely tainted. The only way in which it can be cleansed is to give it to some worthy cause. To those whose need is far greater than your own.' Flinging out his arm, he gestured meaningfully at the poor-box.

Mrs Pardoe faltered, the relief drained from her face, once more. 'Oh... If you think that's right, sir ...'

'I have given you my guidance as your minister.' How pleasingly his ringing tones resounded through the chapel.

There came a small, desperate hesitation. Then submission. 'I shall do as you say.' She sighed and began to undo her worn reticule.

Nineteen

Left alone, Abbs remained seated before Nicholls's desk for a few minutes. Their meeting had scarcely begun before the superintendent had been called away by a grizzled sergeant, a generation older than Reeve. Nicholls had been unusually subdued, he thought, seeming about to get down to business without a sarcastic preface. The reason was plain to see. His gravelly voice had been a dried husk of itself and a tin of menthol and eucalyptus lozenges lay on the desk.

Stretching, he moved to the window. A good hour in the train carriage had made him want to loosen his limbs. He looked out at pigeons shifting on the window-sills and elaborate ledges of the Albert Memorial Institution. The splendid building, which was said to rival the great museums of the capital, dominated the corner of two streets, with its warm sandstone and vast arched windows.

It was intended, according to the press, to be a cathedral of learning. A steady flow of visitors were entering. Those with sketch-books beneath their arms doubtless, bound for the School of Art, others to the School of Science. He'd first been to view the museum when it opened three or four years ago, admiring the collection of antiquities.

Had Mr. Shaw studied them, perhaps corresponding with other learned gentlemen there? The best of the place, he considered, was the free lending-library and reading-room. Not everyone agreed with its charity, the Superintendent among them.

It was another of those grey, nondescript days. Looking down on the crowded roofs of carriages, the loads of open carriers, a shrimp of a crossing-sweeper expertly leaping clear at the last second, Abbs felt strange to be back in Exeter. In the space of a week, the quieter streets of Seaborough, and the changing light on the sea, had become familiar. Hearing a door bang and footsteps along the corridor, he returned to the chair.

When the door opened, a constable came first, bearing two cups of tea. That is, a flowered china cup and saucer set on the superintendent's side of the desk and, Abbs was amused to see, a tin mug for him.

Nicholls seated himself heavily and took up his cup, wincing as he swallowed. 'We're all run off our feet here while you're taking the waters at the seaside.' The cup crashed carelessly back in the saucer.

That was more like the Nicholls they knew, thought Abbs. He really shouldn't rise to it. 'We're hardly there for our health, sir.'

The superintendent grunted. 'Don't talk to me about health. I should be at home in bed but I'll be stuck here. The place won't run itself. This cold's laying men down like nine-pins. Then, to cap it all, Martin's broken his ankle. Though I'm beggared if I know why he isn't back working at his desk with it.'

'I'm sorry to hear that. How did it happen?'

'B..... fool fell through a rotten stair. He was after seeing a suspect in a crib.' Nicholls jerked his thumb at the wall, which Abbs interpreted to mean in the rookery of the West Quarter. 'As well he had two men with him or he'd have been dumped in an alley, minus his clothes and watch.'

He poured a little of his tea in his saucer and blew on it, raising it to his lips. Abbs set down his mug without drinking.

'Now then, you were saying afore we were interrupted, you've interviewed every suspect?'

'That's correct, sir. Everyone Miss Chorley saw on the day she died, Servants, guests and a photographer whom she visited in the forenoon. We've ruled out a visitor who called at the house in early evening and didn't see Miss Chorley.'

'So who's your money on?'

'Difficult to say, sir, it's a baffling case.' Abbs paused, taking up his tea again.

'You're not paid to be baffled, Abbs. This wasn't some old woman in a slum. Her murderer must be brought to justice.' The superintendent sneezed, producing a large, cambric handkerchief.

'Miss Chorley's position is irrelevant, sir. I hope I'd be just as eager if the victim were impoverished. I was about to say that the photographer, Mr. Philip Winton, has drawn our attention. I have an idea about him and await confirmation, before questioning him again. Sergeant Reeve has remained in Seaborough, on my orders, waiting to hear from Scotland Yard.'

Sniffing and loosening his collar, Nicholls's small, dark eyes looked sharply at him. 'If this Winton's your man, that cocky young sod Reeve had better not let him scarper.'

'He won't, sir. Reeve is competent and Mr. Winton has no idea we're looking at him. I don't say he's our man but his actions need explaining.'

'What are these suspicions? And who said you could contact the Yard on your own authority? I don't want them poking their long noses in, thinking we can't cope with a murder.'

'I agree, sir, but they're on the spot to visit Somerset House. I did think of sending Reeve to London, but knew you'd be mindful of the expense,' said Abbs innocently. He proceeded to explain his theory about Winton.

'So what it amounts to, you could be right, or could be talking out of your arse,' croaked the superintendent, when Abbs had finished. 'Lot to pin on what could have been a trick of the light.'

'It was no trick of the light. They had the same gesture,' repeated Abbs. Reserves of patience were needed when negotiating a meeting with Nicholls. Fortunately, he possessed them. 'Something was nagging at me when I met Mr. Winton, some thought I couldn't catch hold of. Meeting Captain Selden again, as he was leaving, must have jolted my memory. Later that day, it came to me.'

'I still say you're clutching at straws.'

'I believe it's worth checking out, sir. Both men have a way of holding a finger to their top lip, when they're thinking. Strange similarities do come down from our forebears. Once that set me wondering, there's a faint likeness, if you know to look for it. It isn't obvious. And they both have reddish hair. You don't notice any similarity because the Captain's was sandy and is now greying. Mr. Winton has a sort of chestnut hue. I'm sure they're somehow related. Add to that, the way Winton was watching the funeral but didn't intend to be seen.'

'You'll look a fine fool if it comes to nothing,' muttered Nicholls. He flicked through the remainder of Abbs's report. 'Mind you keep me informed. Anyone else a possibility?'

Hesitating, Abbs shook his head. 'Not so far, sir. There are one or two anomalies but that's always the way. I'd like to get this matter cleared up first.'

Sneezing a fine spray of droplets over the paper, Nicholls wiped his nose. 'Poison's generally a woman's weapon.' He helped himself to a lozenge. 'Though when you think of the Road murder...'

'Point taken,' agreed Abbs. The savage murder of the infant child, of a prosperous family, had shocked the entire country, over a decade earlier. The gory details were poured over by everyone who could read. The obscure Wiltshire village of Road had become known to all.

The victim's own sister had been suspected from the start, though it had taken five years to bring her to justice, after she had suddenly confessed to the killing. In the summer of 1860, he had been a young constable and had followed the case with interest. The family, he now recalled, had once lived on the Devonshire coast at Sidmouth, some miles west of Seaborough.

'You'd best stop wasting time and get yourself back there,' said Nicholls.

'I'll do that, sir.' Concealing his surprise, Abbs picked up his hat, preparing to rise.

'Not so fast. I've had a letter of complaint about you.' Abbs made no comment. 'Didn't take you long to get someone's back up. I warned you.' Nicholls pulled open a drawer and tossed a long envelope on the blotter. It lay between them, Abbs glanced at it and looked away.

'It never pays to get on the wrong side of an attorney. Can't stand 'em, myself,' said Nicholls. 'Pompous swine, thinks he can tell me how to do my job.' Snatching up the envelope, he threw it back in his drawer. 'I couldn't give a tinker's cuss how much you offend him, if you nail this murderer, Abbs. This b....r wants you replaced but I don't dance to his jig. Anyways, there's no one of rank to spare. He can have you back and lump it.'

His voice cracking, mopping with the white handkerchief like a flag of surrender, Nicholls waved his hand irritably at him to leave.

~

Abbs let himself in through his front door. Everywhere seemed smaller, odd and diminished, as home always does after even a few days' absence. Not that he thought of it as home. Since his wife's death, it was simply a place where he slept and kept his things. A letter was on the mat, recognising his sister's hand, he pocketed it to read on the train.

The terraced house was tiny, a few paces led to the scullery at the rear. He stood at the sink, where the dish-cloth hung curled and stiff from a nail, and a sifting of dust filmed the wooden draining-board. A rusty stain bled towards the plug-hole where the tap had dripped.

He already regretted the eel pie he'd consumed at a coffee-stall, before walking the short distance to Sidwell. For the first time, he wondered in which neighbourhood Reeve lived. He had no knowledge of his life beyond their work.

The window looked out on a back wall, with a bolted gate to a narrow alley, and the roof-tops of the street behind. A hundred chimneys puffed soot across the oyster-shell sky. The small yard was bare.

Nothing survived of Ellen's attempts to make a garden. That had blackened beneath his neglect and the ashes he'd dumped on the single earth bed. The only greenery was a hideous spotted laurel, which had been there when they came. He'd always disliked the blotched leaves which thrived in the darkest corner, beside the coal-shed. Perhaps, when the case was over, he would dig it out.

Taking the stairs with a new determination, he entered the back bedroom, with its single bed, found some clean linen and set about returning to Seaborough with all speed.

Outside the railway-station, a legless news-seller, propped on a miniature cart, was decrying the headlines. There'd been an 'orrible slaying in London and Mr. Gladstone had, after all, managed to form the government.

'Thank 'ee, Mr. Abbs.'

Though run together in one breath, presumably the two events were not linked, he reflected, as he nodded at the speaker, adding a coin to the hat. 'How are you, Micah? No grandson today?'

'Gorn ter school,' the old man replied simply, pride evident in his voice. 'Took yer advice.'

'Glad to hear it.'

~

The streets were wet in Seaborough. Abbs caught a waft of damp earth, in front gardens, as he walked through the town. The sun had come out with the soft light of October, low in the sky. He had often noticed how, at the end of a drab day, there would sometimes be an unexpectedly lovely hour before nightfall. His meeting with Nicholls behind him, he felt as free as a lad let out of the school-room.

He smiled to himself as he passed the board-school, with its entrance at either end, *Boys* and *Girls* carved in the stonework. A newly-built school-house stood across the puddled yard, where a young woman was opening a window. He sometimes wondered about the lives of people he glimpsed for an instant and never saw again. That was, perhaps, in the nature of a detective.

The tap room of the Anchor was half-empty, though Reeve was there, talking to the landlord, his back to the door. Next to him at the bar, Abbs recognised the undertaker's clerk. Quite why he should seem sinister, when his appearance was benign and respectable, Abbs didn't know.

Partly his calling, no doubt, and something more. The way he kept utterly still as he listened, watching with barely-suppressed inquisitiveness. He had his large eyes fixed on Reeve's face as the sergeant picked up his tankard. The landlord caught Abbs's eye, just as Reeve saw him in the etched glass behind the bar.

'Evenin', Mr. Abbs. You've come back to us, then.' Reeve and Mr. Biggs both swung round.

'My business in Exeter was concluded earlier than I expected.' Abbs nodded to Reeve, who was grinning broadly.

'Will you be wantin' a bite of supper? I'll tell the missus. Your room's all ready and waiting for you.'

'Thank you, Mr. Gaunt. I'll dine with the sergeant as usual, if it's no trouble.'

'None at all, sir, I'll give word.' The landlord disappeared in the back.

'It's roast pork and hot mustard,' said Reeve.

Mr. Biggs gave what Reeve described as his graveyard cough, preparatory to speaking.

Abbs raised his eyebrows at Reeve, while trying to evade the clerk's gaze.

'You've been all the way back to Exeter, Inspector?'

'I have, indeed,' said Abbs pleasantly.

'Urgent police business, no doubt?'

'No doubt at all.'

'I don't suppose you can give a hint as to the progress of your investigation?' persisted Mr. Biggs. 'Only people are naturally fearful, with a murderer among us.'

'I'm sure you appreciate, sir, that I cannot comment on our inquiries.'

'You've been to report to your superior. I should like to have been a fly on that wall, Inspector.' Mr. Biggs smiled into his sherry at his small pleasantry.

Nicholls would have soon swatted you, if you were, thought Abbs. He smiled, thin as watered milk. 'How about a turn outside, Sergeant? I could do with some fresh air after being cooped up in the train.'

'Good idea, sir,' said Reeve, promptly sliding off his stool. 'Just the thing before supper.' They escaped before Mr. Biggs could suggest accompanying them.

'I thought I'd never shake him off. Good to see you back, sir.'

Abbs nodded in acknowledgement. 'Let's cross over. I wouldn't put it past our Mr. Biggs to follow.' They halted on the promenade beneath one of the lamps.

'He was telling me he's not just a clerk. He does the laying-out and embalming,' Reeve pulled a face. 'He started going on about how he pumps fluid through the veins and how he removes stuff. Can you imagine the stench? He's a strange cove. You can tell he loves his work, artistry he calls it.' Giving a sepulchral cough, he produced a fair impression of Mr. Biggs's sepulchral tones.

Abbs suppressed a smile. 'I take it the telegram has come?'

'It has, sir, I don't know what you'll make of it.'

'Tell me, if you please.'

'Right.' Reeve leant against the railings. 'It's back at the station, of course, but I copied it in my notebook, in case you returned.' He held the page up. 'Here we are, though I know it off by heart, anyways. Born on 24th March 1847 at an address in Gloucester, county of Gloucestershire. That makes him in his twenty-seventh year. Mother Margaret Winton.'

'Go on,' said Abbs as the sergeant paused. 'The father?'

'Father unknown.'

'Poor woman,' muttered Abbs. He spared a thought for the ignominy she must have felt on registering her son's birth. Though it was hardly uncommon. 'That's it, then? A dead end.' Dismayed for a second, he suddenly stared at Reeve. 'Hang on, you looked pleased with yourself.'

Grinning, Reeve flourished his notebook. 'I saved the best till last. You were dead right, sir. Name... Philip Chorley.'

Abbs gave a low whistle. 'Philip Chorley Winton. So what do we have? The mother didn't dare give the father's name on the certificate. But she did bestow it on his son, as a Christian name. What's more, if my memory serves me correctly, Captain Selden mentioned his uncle served in the North Gloucesters. Our Mr. Winton has to be Selden's cousin.'

'Which gives him quite a motive for Miss Chorley's murder,' said Reeve. 'By all accounts, she wouldn't have been the kind to acknowledge him. But Captain Selden might take a kinder view, if Winton makes the relationship known to him.'

'It's possible.'

'We've got him, sir. Winton can't have much money and the Captain could set him up for life, now he's inherited. He'll be planning to leave a decent interval before he contacts him, I would. I bet he has something up his sleeve, family documents he uncovers, something like that.' Reeve shook his head. 'He seemed a regular sort of cove.'

'Hold your horses,' said Abbs gently. 'We'll see what he has to say for himself on the morrow.'

Puzzled, Reeve looked at him. 'But you were right, sir. Don't you think it's him, now?'

'Let us keep an open mind.'

'Leastways, we're still on the case, are we, sir? Er.. everything's all right?'

'We're still on the case, Sergeant. And it seems we're not the only ones.' Abbs indicated Mr. Biggs, in the doorway of the Anchor. He peered in both directions, shielding his eyes with a hand, before heading purposefully towards them.

Twenty

As it turned out, Reeve had to contain his impatience a while longer. Lying awake before dawn, Abbs surrendered to the familiar headache that brought debilitating pain and nausea in its wake. By day-break, he knew it would be impossible for him to continue work that day.

Dragging himself to his feet and dressing, he knocked at Reeve's door and gave him the day off. Refusing his offer to send for the doctor, Abbs returned to his room, while Reeve elected to journey back to Exeter.

~

The next day saw Abbs still pale but able to appear at breakfast. He'd tried to occupy the hours in reading their notes and thinking over the case. The landlady had been very kind, bringing him soup. He was relieved it was Sunday and visiting Mr. Winton might be postponed.

A walk would set him right, fresh air and solitude would be his remedy. The landlord readily supplied directions to the hill-fort, mentioned by Mr. Shaw, confessing it were many a year since he'd been up that way.

After the recent rain, it was a muddy climb up the great hill. The claggy earth gave off a strong reek, in a way particular to autumn. Abbs knew that the sticky, red clay of east Devonshire would soon make roads treacherous and the old ways, nigh on impassable.

The coming of the branch-line must have been a boon to Seaborough, though perhaps it had given the town, what his mother would have called, ideas above its station in life. He'd not intended the pun. Words were a strange business and the wrong ones could even hang a man.

He did not think Philip Winton was their murderer, but much depended on his answers. Sufficient evidence was piled against the young man. If he were taken off the case, another inspector might seek no further, especially with Superintendent Nicholls at his shoulder.

And if Winton was innocent, where should they look next? Reeve would be asking him on his return and as yet, he had no answer. He could think of nothing he'd neglected to do.

His spirits lifted somewhat as he neared the top of the incline. His headache had quite gone at last. The enclosed land left behind, the narrow path between hedgerows had opened onto rough heath. Countless cobwebs were draped among the browning bracken, made unusually visible by the heavy dew.

He idled away a pleasant half-hour tracing the sloping ramparts of the ancient fortification. The banks were thickly strewn with mouldering leaves, a ditch at their foot. Pines grew around the perimeter, their shapes twisted by the wind. The breeze soughed through their tops and their trunks creaked ominously. The sound of church bells reached him from Seaborough and the villages across the distant vale.

The grassy middle lay bare. To the south, the sea shone like polished pewter. When he reluctantly stepped down the far bank, Abbs decided to find his way back to the town by a circular route. He was tired of being cooped up in other people's rooms. A steady tramp in the open air was conducive to thinking.

After a mile or so, the way descended towards a lane with farmland beyond, autumnal shades making a rag-rug of the landscape. As he reached the road, he became aware of dogs barking. Several traps and gigs were drawn up on the wide verge, their tethered horses grazing, oblivious to the retreating sounds.

A group of men were walking along a track towards a large barn. It had a dilapidated air, with slates slipping and brambles encroaching on the blank rear wall. Some of the men looked like farmers or estate-workers. Others, despite their old clothes, had a prosperous air. Mr. Halesworth, Dr. Avery and Mr. Hicks were among them.

They were just too far off to make out what they were saying, though he could tell the party was in good spirits. The doctor, in the fore-ground, was more animated than he had seen him previously. Laughing heartily at something said by one of his companions and gesturing with a stout, country stick.

Avery, and several others, were accompanied by excited terriers, alert and yapping, straining ahead on tangled leashes. Abbs watched them from the shelter of a great elm. There was no one else he recognised. So, he thought, the three of them were not only speculative builders on the side. They were ratting gents.

He decided to see Mr. Shaw again. Small puzzles bothered him. He wanted to know why Captain Selden had changed his mind about shutting up Tower House immediately.

The vicar had hinted there was someone among his parishioners who made him uneasy. Who could say if that had any connection to the murder? But he wanted to know who it was.

On the edge of the town, the lane led through a ford with a narrow footbridge. Tired, but somewhat restored, Abbs determined to find Reeve. He'd lost them time and somehow, they had a murderer to find.

Twenty-one

Rosa wanted something, no doubt about it. For one thing, she couldn't sit still, hands fidgeting at the cruet. Jumping up to adjust the curtain so the sun didn't fade the furnishings, never mind him trying to read the paper. Then she was watching him surreptitiously, gauging his mood, angling the best line to take. Well she would find he was no pike to be played.

And then, this being the real clincher, there was her meek tone of voice and air of solicitude for his comfort. Before his eggs and ham, Cook had sent in kippers. Rosa usually made a fuss about ordering kippers, his favourite, complaining about the lingering odour. But oh no, nothing was too much trouble for him this morning.

The instant he set down his knife and pushed aside the plate, she jumped up and tugged the bell-pull. Mr. Halesworth watched her in return, his attention seemingly fixed on his folded copy of *The Times*.

'Was the ham to your liking, Fred?'

'So-so,' he murmured, one eye on a report about interest rates. There was talk, in the capital, that a financial crisis was on the way and they wouldn't hold at their present nine per cent.

'I bought the kippers myself, knowing how you like them.'

No answer, as he turned the page. It amused him to see her eyes narrow, as she bit back some tart remark. The dining-room door opened and the girl came in with his toast. Rosa had finished toying with her meagre breakfast and generally left him alone, after running through all the errands she had to do. Another sign that she was after something.

'Thank you, Liddy. Tell Cook that the master enjoyed his kippers.'

'Yes 'm.' The girl dumped the toast rack, slumped her shoulders in what passed for a bob and left.

She was a pinched little thing, all bones and no meat, but that was Rosa's choosing. His missus, despite knowing a handsome parlour-maid reflected the status of the family, took care to employ ones who were past their youth or on the plain side.

'Marmalade, Fred?'

She was at it again. Passing the dish of Dundee, that only he liked, though it was within easy reach. Then she was fiddling with her napkin ring, tapping the ivory lightly on the damask tablecloth. Wait for it, any moment now, he reckoned. as he scraped butter and preserve lavishly, cramming a corner of toast in his mouth.

'Fred.' She made two syllables of his name, drawn out in a wheedling voice. 'I've been thinking...'

'Eh?' he grunted. Setting down his half-eaten toast, he unfolded his paper and shook open the full pages.

'Oh Fred, don't disappear behind that, when I want to speak to you.'

'Can't it wait?'

'You're hardly at home these days. No, it can't wait or we'll lose it.'

Might as well swallow the medicine. See how much it was going to cost him. His mind slid to the great crisis hanging over his head. All women wanted from a fellow was his money, one way or another.

'How much, this time?'

'What's that you say, I don't follow you?' Her brow furrowed unbecomingly.

Spying round the page, he could see her mother on her face. Fortunately, the effect wiped away, as though rubbed from a slate. He scowled to think that one day, the likeness might be permanent.

'New dresses, is it? Something else for the girls?'

'I don't know why you should take such a tone, Fred Halesworth. The girls and I hardly ask for anything new.'

That's more like it, he grinned to himself. She was bridling now in her customary manner. 'Riding habit for Vinnie, not a month since.' He rustled the page to indicate the conversation was at an end.

Rosa sniffed in that way women had. 'Most men would take a pride in their wife and daughters being well turned-out. Perhaps you'd rather your daughters were a laughing stock? Anyway, it's not as if we can't afford it.'

She was right, he thought, that in the general way of things, he was careless of what she ordered from her dress-maker. He liked to be known as a generous fellow and it did look well of him that his females were the best dressed in the town. She was not to know he had the expense of keeping up two establishments.

'Order what you want, within reason.' He turned a page noisily, hoping having gained her victory, she would leave him to finish his breakfast in peace. 'Any more coffee?'

'Let me pour it for you.' She set the cup by his hand. He reached for it by feel. 'That's very cordial of you, Fred, but it isn't garments I want to talk to you about.' Swallowing his coffee as he tried to read, he effected not to hear. 'It's something much more important. Do put that down and listen.'

Reluctantly, Mr. Halesworth lowered his paper. 'Let's have it then. I've to be off, soon.'

His wife took a deep breath. 'I've been thinking for some time now that we're a mite cramped in this house. It isn't anywhere near as convenient as I thought it would be. It seems to me, we'd all be much happier if we packed our boxes and moved.'

'Eh?' said Mr. Halesworth, after a few seconds' silence. 'What the devil's got in to your head now, woman?'

'Getting on, Fred Halesworth. That's what's got in to my head. Something I thought you were all for. And no gentleman would speak to his lawful, wedded wife in such a way.' Rosa jerked her head in emphasis as she finished speaking. Sitting back with her arms folded.

Her husband knew that look of old. The opening round in a skirmish had been fired. 'But we did take a great step up when we moved here,' he said, genuinely baffled. 'We haven't been in this house above two year. Why, you had that put in this autumn.' He glanced up at the elaborate gasolier above their heads. 'Cost me a pretty penny that did. It isn't even tarnished yet.'

'We can have it done again. Tower House will need improvements, I'm sure.'

'Tower House? Have you taken leave of your senses?'

'Don't shout, Fred, the servants will hear. Now just stop and consider.' The wheedling manner was back. 'You're head of the council, one of Seaborough's foremost citizens. You should have the right setting to take you still further. Background matters, you know it does.'

'Don't go getting above yourself, Rosa. You didn't marry a gentleman, but the son of a village builder, if you remember. And your background's a tuppenny ha'penny beer-shop, with a ma who could add up all right but scarcely sign her name.'

His missus slammed down the salt-cellar, fit to crack it. 'My mother ran a small brew-house, as well you know. And she saved enough to give you a good start when you took it. I know that's the only reason you married me.' The words hung in the air but were not taken up and refuted.

The door opened and the girl appeared again, with the post on a tray. 'Your letters, sir, ma'am.'

Glad of the distraction, perhaps he had gone too far, Mr. Halesworth quickly flicked through the four envelopes. A cold relief pooled in his chest. Any day could bring a communication to the house. He couldn't possibly be at home for every post.

'One for you, my dear.' He tossed an envelope, bearing the name of a milliner's, towards his wife. They waited in leaden silence while the maid removed the chafing-dishes from the sideboard and left with her stacked tray.

'What's brought this on?' asked Mr. Halesworth in a more reasoned tone. 'I thought you liked this house?'

'I did, but don't you see it, Fred?' Rosa leaned forward eagerly. 'Tower House is one of the very finest properties in Seaborough. 'What would living there say about you?'

'That I was mortgaged up to the hilt.'

'It has such an air of distinction.'

'True. I'll grant you that, I suppose.' Mr. Halesworth thought back to the day when he and his business proposal been dismissed by Miss Chorley. He'd admired the fine architecture, when he'd been waiting at the front entrance. For an instant, he saw himself drawing up to that portico in a smart, new carriage.

His wife saw the softening of his expression. 'That long drive adds a lot to the property. And you wouldn't say garden, it would be grounds. Good-sized stables, out-buildings. It's almost like an estate in miniature. Think what a good marriage Vinnie could make from a home like that.'

Shaking his head, Mr. Halesworth looked thoughtful. 'I don't say you're wrong in principle, Rosa, but it would stretch us too far. I doubt we could manage it.'

'Mrs Jerrold told me that Captain Selden wants it on the market any day. Miss Geake's leaving and the servants are on notice. Mr. Jerrold thinks he'll take a fair price for a quick sale. You did make yourself known to him at the funeral, did you not?'

'Jerrold introduced us, I made sure of it. Hicks, Avery and I want to buy some land from Selden.'

'It's too good a chance to miss.'. She laid her hand on his sleeve. 'Fred, at least think it over, do.'

'I suppose there's no harm in inquiring what Selden wants for it,' said her devoted husband. 'But that's all, mind.' Giving up on his paper, Mr. Halesworth drained his cup and stood up. 'I'm off to the town-hall.'

'Is there anything particular you fancy for supper?'

'Don't wait for me. I may look in at the Marine this evening and get a bite there.' He waited for a sharp comment but she smiled sweetly. 'Celebrate my winnings,' he added. He held up a hand as she opened her mouth to say something. 'I shall be seeing our Caleb later. No more nagging and I just might find time to go over some figures.'

~

Breakfast had been a hasty affair, both having been too keyed up to speak over-much. Though, as Abbs remarked, Mr. Winton may have a photographic sitting booked first thing and they couldn't interrupt that, in all decency.

'After all, he has to live here. No need to make him the talk of Seaborough, if he's innocent. He has a living to make, as well.'

'You really don't fancy him for it, do you, sir?' said Reeve, when they reached the police-station.

'I think what we've found would be enough to hang him. He had motive and opportunity. Anyone could purchase the means. I know it would please our superiors if this case were wrapped up quickly. But as I'm not in the murdering business myself, I require something more than circumstantial evidence. We'll give him a chance to convince us of his innocence.'

Waving the sergeant ahead of him, he resumed when they were in their room. 'I'll just see the telegram for myself and we'll be off. No, I don't see our Mr. Winton as a cold-blooded poisoner. I must confess I rather liked him.' Taking the slip, he studied it carefully. 'It's a delicate subject. I doubt he will care to discuss his mother with us, but I fear he has no choice.'

~

The photographer's door was locked, the closed sign turned to the street. All that could be seen of the dim interior was a chair, the curtained door to the back, and a hat-stand. Stepping back, Abbs looked up at the two sash windows belonging to the premises. Their faded curtains were drawn back unevenly. In one of them, a fly-paper could be seen hanging. The business next door was a boot & shoe maker's, beyond that a linen-draper.

'There he is,' said Reeve.

Mr. Winton was at the corner,, holding a loaf under one arm and a paper bag besides. On seeing them, he faltered, dismay crossed his face, then he continued slowly towards them.

'You're seeking me, gentlemen?' More a resigned statement than a question.

He stood between them. The paper bag he held was sticking to its contents, a crimson stain already seeping through. Seeing Reeve eye it, Winton held it aloft. 'Oxtail. My supper for the next few nights. What is it you want with me? I've already told you all I can.'

'Not out here, sir,' murmured Abbs. Though the side-street was quiet, they were attracting glances from the few passers-by. The shoe-maker was standing in his doorway.

Winton produced his key and led them inside. 'I'll just get rid of this.'

They followed him through the studio and into a kitchen. Ignoring them, the photographer put down his loaf and took an enamel plate from the rack over the sink. Dumping the butcher's bag on it, he left the plate in his small larder.

Washing his hands, he dried them and turned to face the two detectives. 'I can fetch another chair from the studio,' he said reluctantly.

'We'll manage,' said Abbs. He leant against the table, indicating Reeve to take the chair. 'Perhaps you should sit down.' The photographer sank on to the Windsor chair by the range.

'You look alarmed, Mr. Winton,' began Abbs. 'Are you quite certain you don't wish to tell us something more?'

The young man looked up at him, then at Reeve, busy folding back his notebook. He licked his lips, as though to speak. They waited until he felt obliged to fill the silence.

'I told you, I know nothing about Miss Chorley's death. Why won't you believe me?' His voice wavered like a candle flame in a draught.

'Perhaps if you'd been honest with us from the start?' said Abbs evenly. 'It would have saved us some effort inquiring into your background.'

'You had no right.' Whey-faced, the photographer half-rose.

'We have every right, in the name of the law. Sit down, Mr. Winton,' said Abbs, his voice hardening. 'Why were you hiding in the churchyard, watching Miss Chorley's funeral?'

'I did no such thing. You must be mistaken.'

Abbs glanced at Reeve. 'You were there all right,' he said indignantly. 'You ran for it when you saw me. I gave chase and would have caught you but for the fog. You scarpered down the vicarage drive. No point denying it.'

'What if I was there? I've done some work for Mr. Hicks, the undertaker. He told me himself, the funeral was to be a great spectacle. It's natural I should take an interest.'

'Quite so,' said Abbs. 'Many people watched on the pavements. No one else felt the need to skulk behind a headstone.' He watched the photographer redden. 'Let us stop wasting one another's time. We know what is written on your birth certificate.'

Winton leant forward, his hands over his face. Abbs studied the cramped room, where the window gave on to a brick wall. Another fly-paper hung from a meat hook on a beam overhead.

It occurred to him that a patient person could soak them to extract the arsenic. But he did not believe that had happened in this shabby room, with its painstaking efforts at homeliness. The rag-rug and cushion were some years old, he thought, carefully fashioned by some female. There were times when he disliked what he had to do.

As they waited, somewhere nearby, the chimes of a deep, echoing clock began to sound the hour.

Winton gave a shuddering sigh, smoothed his fingers over his hair and sat up. 'It's the town-hall,' he said. 'It woke me at first but you get used to it. You get used to anything.' He looked straight at Abbs. 'You know then that I'm a Chorley by birth, if not by name. I'll answer your questions and I regret not being frank with you. But I did not murder Miss Chorley, you have to believe me.'

'Tell us if you will, of your connection with the family and why you came to Seaborough.'

He looked away, his hands on his knees. 'My mother had... an affair of the heart with a young army officer. She met him at a regimental dance in her home town. Gloucester. My mother was... a respectable girl, the daughter of a clerk. She was not given to such behaviour, but she was very young and blinded by love. In a just world, no blame should attach to her. The young man was the one at fault. It was the old story.'

The bitterness seeping in his tone reminded Abbs of Miss Geake, as she described the Chorley family.

'Her seducer promised marriage but he was of good family and a coward. When he was told that the inevitable had happened, my mother never saw him again. The regiment left and she was sent away to relatives, to hide her shame.' Gazing unseeingly at the range, Winton went on haltingly. 'My mother spoke well of him all her life. She laid any blame on her not being good enough for his family. She said she understood. She was a gentle creature, the best of women.' At this he looked angrily at them, as if they would refute his claim.

Reeve was, Abbs knew, tense with excitement, as the truth was revealed. Quite without malice, he was young enough to enjoy the chase. Had not been long enough at the game, to know how the necessity of harrying a man left a sour taste in the mouth.

'Would you like a glass of water?'

The photographer swallowed and nodded. 'Please.'

Reeve got up and looked about him. They waited while he ran the tap and handed him the glass.

'Thank you.' Winton gulped several mouthfuls and wiped his mouth. 'Sorry about that. Where was I?'

'You were coming to where Miss Chorley fits in, I think,' said Abbs.

'My father was James Chorley, her younger brother.'

'Forgive me, did you always know his name?'

'Yes. As I said, my mother would speak of him. Not frequently, but often enough over the years. She had obtained from him a lock of his hair and this she kept in a locket, with her own likeness. He died at the Battle of Inkerman, serving under Major-General Bentinck. She was told this by my grandfather, who made it his business to find out. My mother would tell all she knew to me, in order to instil a filial pride.' He grimaced in distaste. 'As a b..... growing up without a name or father, I saw things differently.'

'Did you and your mother return to Gloucester?' asked Abbs.

He shook his head. 'My grandfather didn't want us in the town. I only saw him once. We remained in Bristol. My mother lost her home and her family as well. She made a living with her needle. Her health was never strong and we were always poor.'

'And your decision to move to Seaborough?'

A shadow of sadness passed over Winton's face. 'My mother died about a year ago. She'd developed a weakness of the heart. I'd managed to save a little money from my work as a photographer's assistant. With the sum my mother had put by, there was just sufficient to rent premises and try setting up on my own. I knew my father's family home was at Seaborough. When the opportunity arose, I decided to come here. It was as good a place as any, for a fresh start. There was nothing to keep me in Bristol. I prefer to live somewhere smaller.'

Reeve shifted on his chair. Abbs raised his eyebrows, tacitly inviting him to take over.

'You can't expect us to believe, that's all there was to it. Was it not your intention to approach Miss Chorley for help?'

'No, I .... I don't know what I intended.' Winton's voice rose in agitation. 'Until I came here, I didn't even know if there were any Chorleys still alive. Of course, I was curious about my father's family. But how could I make myself known to them? I can't prove any claim to kinship and I've no legal claim on the estate. To be illegitimate, Sergeant, is to have no name.'

'That wouldn't stop Miss Chorley helping you if she wished,' said Reeve. 'Or paying you off, in order to protect her dead brother's reputation. By all accounts, she thought a lot of him. From what we've discovered of her, she wouldn't want the Chorley name covered in scandal. She wanted her family known for charitable works. And now she is dead, Captain Selden may be easier to tap.'

Winton looked about him, beads of sweat glistening on his forehead. 'I don't deny I have very little money. My business is not yet flourishing as I hoped. But how could I apply to Captain Selden, with his aunt murdered? Would not that, at once, make me the chief suspect?'

'Not if you left it for a year, then concocted a good story,' said Reeve. 'He would, perhaps, settle with you to avoid besmirching the family name. Or he might even give you a lump sum, out of decency.'

'I swear to you, I am innocent. Please. You must believe me.'

Studying him, Abbs decided it was time to intervene again. 'Thank you for telling us this. It cannot have been easy to speak of it.'

Shrugging, Winton looked away again. 'In some ways, it's a relief. There's never been anyone to tell.'

'Do you know anything that would help us discover who murdered Miss Chorley?'

'Nothing. I wish I did.'

'Then we'll leave it there,' said Abbs. Reeve catching his eye, rose to his feet.

'You aren't going to arrest me?' said Winton.

'No, sir. You've answered our questions satisfactorily. If you had told us this from the beginning, we'd have saved time.' At the door, Abbs swung round as he was leaving. 'Take heart, Mr. Winton, I hope your business picks up soon.'

'Sir?' Reeve looked questioningly at him as they walked along the shabby street. 'Do you think I was too hard on him?'

Abbs sighed. 'No, Sergeant, not really. It's the nature of our job.'

'He isn't fit to do more than sit by the fire and sip beef tea. He mustn't even think of going outside today. I made sure I told him so.' Using her arm, Hannah brushed a lank lock of hair off her forehead and glared at Adelaide, who was drying the breakfast dishes. The range was alight and the kitchen warm and damp, smelling of lye on linen brought in from the scullery.

'There's no need to be so fierce, Hannah. I agree with you. Papa would be best off in bed but go, he will not. At least, he's warm and can doze in his chair. He won't hear of sending for the doctor.'

'I reckon he's right there, miss. There's no physician can do more for the Reverend than we can. We know his chest. Goose-grease, rest and good food's the best medicine.'

'His appetite is very poor. I wonder if you should call at the druggist and get something made up to ease his cough?'

'Best thing for that's an onion with a dollop of honey. My beef tea'll soothe his throat and we've some calves-foot jelly left in the larder. That's a blessing, the way you hand it out to all and sundry.' Hannah emptied the greasy water. 'Nothing like it for strengthening an invalid and it's easy to take, when you've no appetite.'

'I must go over and open the church. Papa will fret terribly if that isn't done. Then I shall keep him company, if he wishes.'

'And I must see how far on Betsey is, afore I'm away to the grocer's.' Unpinning her apron and taking her basket, Hannah went in search of the maid, muttering to herself all the while.

~

It had rained again the previous evening and a blowy night had brought down more leaves, making the path to the churchyard slippery. Adelaide paused, as she always did, on reaching the grave of her mama. Green lichen was spotting across the white marble, obscuring the first line of lettering, *Grace, dearly beloved wife.*

The two of them would clean it with a stiff brush again in the spring. It was pointless to try before winter, when the staining would return, spreading like mould through cheese. She wished she could remember her mother. She knew of her only through the portrait in the drawing-room, the unaccustomed softness in Hannah's voice, when she spoke of her, and the precisely lettered inscriptions in books.

Come the new year, the grey-green spears of snowdrops would cover her grassy mound, then celandines, the yellow stars of spring. Adelaide shivered as she thought of her Papa's weak chest. A sudden breeze gusted, lifting the dead leaves.

When she rounded the corner of the church, her first impression was that a bundle of grey clothing lay blocking the entrance to the porch. As she looked, she knew it was a woman's body lying on the ground, half out of the open archway.

She ran the few yards, not waiting to pick up her skirt and treading on the hem. It would be some poor creature weak with hunger. Please God, it was not yet cold enough for someone to die of exposure.

As she went to kneel by the woman, her eyes took in the matted hair. Hidden, as she'd approached, by the bonnet, which was dislodged but still held by its ribbons.

As her mind struggled to make sense of what lay before her, something between a choke and a gasp emerged from her throat. A wave of nausea swayed her, but she stayed on her feet. Much later, she was quietly glad that she had not disgraced herself by screaming.

There was no possible hope that the woman could be roused and taken into the warm. She was long gone from that place. A wound on the side of her head had been shattered, like an egg-shell with a teaspoon. Amid the dark, clotted blood, more black than red, she glimpsed horrifying flecks of white, before tearing her gaze away.

Before she did, Adelaide saw enough to recognise the face.

~

'So what do you think?' finished Abbs. 'Have we missed something? Don't be afraid to say, I welcome your thoughts.' Usually someone who sat still, he fiddled with a pencil as he spoke, a measure of his frustration.

Reeve opened his mouth to answer, as the door was thrown open.

'What is it, Sergeant?'

'You'd best come quick, sir. Both of you. Word's just come from the vicarage. There's been another murder.'

'Who is it? Who's been killed?'

Reeve's chair went over backwards with a crash, as he leapt to his feet. Abbs stood more slowly, his mind racing. He stared at Sergeant Tancock's red-veined face, his throat dry. 'Tell me, man.'

'It's Miss Chorley's companion. They found her at the church.'

'Miss Geake.' Reeve's eyes were lit with excitement. 'How was she killed?'

'Head bashed in.'

'Who's reported this?' said Abbs.

'Isaac May, sir. He's the vicar's groom.'

'Let's get over there,' said Abbs crisply. 'We'll take him back with us. We'll need you as well, Sergeant. Send a constable for Dr. Avery. Ask him to meet us at the church and organise transport to get the body moved to the mortuary. I want to view the corpse, then back here to notify my superintendent and send word to the Coroner. Got all that?'

'Yes Sir.' Sergeant Tancock hurried out.

'Blimey, sir, we didn't see that one coming,' said Reeve, as they strode into the vestibule.

'We should have done,' muttered Abbs grimly.

The groom was being attended to by an older constable, he knew only by sight. Isaac May was in his fifties, a sturdy, balding man of middling height. He stepped forward as the constable gave Abbs's rank.

'I know who you are, sir. Saw you from the garden when you called on Mr. Shaw.'

'Who found the body, Mr. May?'

'Why, it was Miss Adelaide, sir. She came haring up the path and saw me first. She'd been across to unlock the church. White as marble she was.'

'Was she unharmed? Did she see anyone else?'

'She's not hurt, sir, but shocked, I'd say. I don't believe she saw anyone or she'd have said. Miss Adelaide's strong-minded. She's often sat with the dying and helped to lay them out. But not like this.'

'Have you seen the body yourself?'

He shook his head. 'Not I, sir. The mistress said it was important you knew, as soon as could be. It was quicker to go on foot than get the carriage harnessed.'

'She was quite right. We'll accompany you back now. Is anyone waiting with the body, do you know?'

'Miss Adelaide was going straight back. Soon as she ran in to tell Mr. Shaw. He's laid up poorly. Said she had to prevent anyone else seeing the body. Once the vicar knows, he'll be there, sir, sick or not. He'll say it's his duty.'

Sergeant Tancock, puffing, came back through the front entrance. 'Ready when you are, sir. I've flagged down a carter.'

'Good thinking, Sergeant.'

'Thank 'ee, sir. I'm leaving you in charge 'til I get back, Colley, so keep your wits about you. Lord knows when any of us'll get off duty now.'

As they hurried along the main path through the churchyard, Miss Shaw and the vicar stood waiting for them, partially blocking a view of the corpse. When they both moved forward to meet them, Abbs saw the sprawled figure on the gravel. Isaac moved awkwardly to the vicar's side, peering behind him at the body and dragging off his cap.

'Inspector, thank you for coming so swiftly. We have touched nothing and fortunately, no one has approached the churchyard.'

Mr. Shaw did look unwell, thought Abbs. His features were drawn, the clerical cape hung heavily about his shoulders.

'Thank you, sir. We appreciate your remaining here until we arrived. If you'd like to take Miss Shaw back to the vicarage, I'll join you as soon as I can.' He turned to the vicar's daughter. Despite her pallor, she appeared to be composed. 'I'm sorry that I'll have to speak to you presently, Miss Shaw, but you'll understand the urgency.'

'Of course, Inspector,' she murmured and placed her arm through her father's. 'Come, Papa, let us get you out of the chill.'

Moving round the Shaws, Reeve approached the body. Standing well back, his eyes searched the vicinity. Abbs knew he was looking for marks in the gravel, indicating a struggle.

Tancock joined Reeve, with a stifled curse as he saw the smashed skull.

'No, Adelaide.' Patting his daughter's sleeve, Mr. Shaw stepped away from her. 'I shall remain here.'

'Please, Papa, you're not well enough to stay out here,' said Miss Shaw. 'There's nothing you can do.'

'You are mistaken, my dear,' replied Mr. Shaw gently. 'I shall endeavour to keep out of your way, gentlemen, but I must wait with the body. Miss Geake was my parishioner.'

Abbs knew when he was beaten. 'As you wish, sir.' He turned to Isaac. 'Would you take Miss Shaw into the house?'

'Gladly, sir.' The groom looked pleased to have a purpose.

'Adelaide,' called the vicar, when they were a few yards off. 'Keep Hannah away when she returns.'

His daughter nodded in acknowledgement but did not speak. Abbs could see she was apprehensive about her father. Their eyes met, she turned away to follow Isaac, her back rigid.

Joining Reeve, who was now crouching by the corpse, Abbs inspected the wound. Sergeant Tancock hovered by them, with his notebook. 'First thoughts, Reeve?'

He scratched his head, unconsciously touching the same area as that on the broken skull. 'The blow's to one side and nearer the temple. I'd say she was turned away. Someone standing behind and on her right side. Right-handed? That's most of the population, so no help at all.'

'Any facts help us. I agree, so the first question is, did she see her attacker? Was it someone she knew, or an assault by a stranger?'

'Someone she knew,' said Reeve promptly. 'The same person who murdered Miss Chorley. She wouldn't let a stranger get that close. She didn't think she was in any danger, or she wouldn't have turned her back on them.'

'Sound reasoning,' said Abbs. 'Is this path used, other than for visiting the church? A short-cut perhaps?'

Tancock shook his head. 'No, sir, the only other way out's through the vicarage garden.'

'We know Miss Geake had no family buried here. Is it possible she was visiting Miss Chorley's grave, I wonder?'

'Possible, sir, but she didn't seem to like her much,' said Reeve. 'There are no fresh flowers.' They looked over to where the wreaths were placed on the raw earth.

Abbs studied the corpse, carefully lifting the right hand an inch. 'No visible clues then. No unusual button or scrap of paper clutched in the palm to aid us, as there undoubtedly would be in a novel.' He looked meaningfully at Sergeant Tancock, who coloured and looked away. He'd found a well-thumbed volume by Mr. Wilkie Collins in his borrowed desk drawer.

Glancing at Mr. Shaw, Abbs felt ashamed of his levity. He wished he could explain that a gallows humour was the detective's defence in the presence of violent death. The vicar's bent head and folded hands suggested that he was employing his own defences.

'There's no sign of a lady's reticule, sir,' said Reeve suddenly. 'They mostly carry something for money and handkerchief, don't they?'

'Well spotted, Sergeant.' Abbs scanned the grass and nearby graves, without seeing anything. The sound of clattering hooves distracted him.

They watched an ambulance van draw up by the gate. Soon after, the tall figure of Dr. Avery came crunching along the path, Constable Dean at his side. Dean manhandled a stretcher.

'Thank you for coming, Doctor.'

'My job, Inspector.' Dr. Avery stared down at the corpse. 'A bad business.'

'Indeed. I'd be glad of anything you can tell us now.'

'Give me a moment.' The doctor squatted in his turn and examined the wound, his fingers delicately probing round its broken edges. He lifted the outstretched arm, stiff as a branch. The other arm, caught beneath the body, was bent at an unnatural angle.

Finally, he felt one of the legs through the grey wool skirt, gauging its rigidity. Looking up, he caught Dean's face, suffused with embarrassment. 'A necessity, Constable,' he said austerely. 'To determine rigor.' Straightening up, he dusted his handkerchief over his fingertips and directed himself to Abbs. 'There were at least two blows, possibly more. Delivered with some considerable force.'

'Does that rule out a woman?'

Dr. Avery hesitated, while he considered. 'No, a woman could have struck them. But they would have to be as tall as Miss Geake. The angle of the blows is downward. They were carried out with the arm raised.'

Abbs had noticed how the doctor was a man who measured his words. Not perhaps, a physician with an easy manner at the bedside. But one whose opinion, he felt, could be trusted implicitly.

'What about if Miss Geake was bending?' said Reeve. 'Suppose she was stooping to pick something up and the murderer seized their chance?'

'It's possible.'

'Can you make any guess at the weapon, Doctor?' continued Abbs.

His brow corrugated, Avery continued to gaze upon the corpse. 'Something rounded, no sharp edges. There could be a splinter impacted when I examine her on the table.'

Constable Dean pulled a face. Tancock, wandering a little away, spat on the grass and dashed the back of his hand across his mouth.

'Something like the pommel of a walking-stick?' asked Abbs.

'That sort of thing. A life-preserver, perhaps.'

'How about the time of death?'

'Tricky when the body's been outside.' The doctor pushed the toe of his boot in the gravel, tracing lines as he worked it out. 'Rigor mortis is fully established. As I presume you know, that takes half a day. Say twelve, thirteen hours or thereabouts, not less.'

Glancing up at the church clock, Abbs calculated aloud. 'It's almost ten now so that gives us ten o'clock last evening or an hour or two earlier. Would you agree with that, Doctor?'

'Broadly speaking but, as I say, it's impossible to be completely accurate. For one thing, the temperature of an October night would slow the onset of rigor.'

'Long after dark at any rate. She certainly wasn't visiting the church. We might be able to narrow it down, once we know when Miss Geake was last seen alive.'

'She didn't die at once.'.

'Really, even with the skull smashed like that?'

'It is remarkable how the body can survive for a short time after severe trauma. I'm no detective but it appears to me, the poor woman tried to crawl, probably only a foot. You see the bloodstains here? Then she would have lost consciousness and mercifully, known no more.'

'Maybe the murderer was disturbed?' ventured Constable Dean.

'Could have been,' said Abbs. 'No one's come forward to report anything. But someone could have disturbed the attack, without being aware, I suppose. You can enquire at all the houses nearby, Constable, and the public-house on the corner. Someone may have seen something. Miss Geake arriving, or the murderer leaving, if we're fortunate.'

'Sir. Shall I get on to that as soon as we've moved the body?'

'There'll be someone to help at the hospital,' said Avery. 'If you could assist in loading the stretcher, I can manage alone.'

'I think we're almost ready,' said Abbs. 'Yes, Constable. One of the problems with a murder enquiry is that everything needs doing at once. People's memories fade quickly. We need the surrounding area searched, lest the weapon was discarded.' He felt the sleeve of Miss Geake's mantle, as he spoke. 'Damp. The ground beneath the body is dry. Does anyone know what time the rain started last night?' They shook their heads but Mr. Shaw came over to them.

'I looked out of the window at about five and twenty past seven. It wasn't raining then but it started a few minutes later. I can be sure as it was soon after the church clock sounded the half-hour.'

'Thank you, Mr. Shaw. That helps with the timing.'

'You don't look well, sir,' said Dr. Avery. 'I would recommend you go indoors and take a glass of wine.'

'You are very kind, Doctor but I cannot abandon my vigil.' There was a quiet dignity about Mr. Shaw which befitted his calling.

'Miss Geake's body will be taken up now, sir,' said Abbs. 'When will you be able to perform the post-mortem, Doctor?'

'With all urgency I presume? It shall be done this afternoon, if Mr. Biggs is available. Do you wish to be present?'

'Mr. Biggs?' said Abbs frowning.

'He's clerk to Hicks, the undertaker.'

'We've met.' Reeve and Abbs exchanged glances.

'He's acted as my assistant on occasion. We have no need for a full-time mortuary attendant in a place like Seaborough. He's very useful.'

'We don't need to be present, if you'll give us a verbal summary.'

'Then shall we say four? I'll aim to be finishing then. The porter will direct you.'

'Until then, doctor. Would you lend a hand, Sergeant?'

Moving aside, Mr. Shaw made the sign of the cross as Tancock and the constable lifted the corpse on the stretcher. They shuffled down the path with the doctor walking behind. One arm stuck out incongruously, as though in a theatrical gesture. The actress had finally left the stage.

'I shall return to the vicarage,' said Mr. Shaw. 'We are at your disposal, Inspector. The door will be open. Come straight in when you are ready.' He sounded weary and sad.

'Mr. Biggs again,' said Reeve, as they waited for Tancock and Dean to return.

'If he tries to listen in, eject him,' replied Abbs savagely. 'Arrest him, if needs be.'

'What do you want doing now, sir?' Sergeant Tancock was breathing heavily as he came to a standstill before them. Dean looked decidedly more enthusiastic about the tasks that lay ahead.

'Set your men to searching for the weapon and a lady's reticule. Try the vicarage drive. As I recall, it has a dense shrubbery.'

'What exactly do we look for with the weapon, like?'

'You heard the doctor. Something rounded and weighty. Obviously, with a shaft long enough to be wielded. If it were a walking-stick, the murderer will still have it, so look for a life-preserver or a cudgel. Keep an eye out for a likely length of wood, or a branch, even. It could be some distance away or flung in a garden.'

Tancock nodded unhappily. 'Right, sir.'

'Then knock on doors alongside Dean. You are asking if anyone saw Miss Geake or anyone else last evening. Not only entering or leaving the churchyard, or the vicarage drive, but in the street. If they saw anyone, get descriptions and times. Remember, our murderer would have been trying to blend in. Speak to someone at the gas company. Find out which lamp-lighter worked this street and question them. Question the beat constable.'

The sergeant chewed his lip. 'Do I take men off the beat?'

'Certainly, this takes priority, Sergeant. Reeve and I are going to speak to the Shaws, then I must call on the Coroner. You sent someone to inform him, as I asked?'

'I did, sir.'

'Good, he'll expect me to report to him in person. He'll call an inquest and adjourn tomorrow, I should think. I believe he lives some distance away. Can you get hold of a conveyance to take me out there?'

'There's a fellow hires his pony and trap by the railway-station, I'll get him to take you, sir.'

'Thank you. Have him wait at the police-house in about an hour. Dean, you can go to Tower House with Sergeant Reeve, later. He'll meet you back at the station when Sergeant Tancock's finished with you here.'

Dean's spirits rose as visibly as his superior's sank. 'Yes, sir.'

'It will be good experience for you.'

'Excuse me, sir,' said Tancock. 'This is goin' to take hours. People won't be in and we'll have to keep going back.'

'Best get to it then, Sergeant. Shifts will end when the work's done and not before.'

Reeve followed Abbs along the path where he'd chased Mr. Winton. If he felt some sympathy for Sergeant Tancock, who was reeling with instructions, he was wise enough not to show it.

'I doubt there's much the Shaws can tell us,' said Abbs. 'This shouldn't take long. I should like to go with you to Tower House. But we need to get it searched before the servants have a chance to touch Miss Geake's things. The Coroner takes priority. I know you won't miss anything.'

'Do my best not to, sir. Dean looks gratified to be singled out.'

'He seems keen. I shall telegraph to Exeter when we're done here. Superintendent Nicholls must be told there's been another murder.' Abbs's voice was carefully neutral. 'You might see how Sergeant Tancock and his men are faring on your way back. Diplomatically,' he added.

Reeve grinned. 'They have it easy in a country place like this. They wouldn't know what hit 'em in a big town.'

'Ah well, I'm a countryman myself, Sergeant. We wouldn't wish the rookeries on these good people.' He paused as they reached the gate to the vicarage garden. 'I've another job for you when we leave here. Mr. Jerrold must be informed. Call at his place of business, if he's absent, leave an urgent message with his clerk. If you see him, tell him you're on your way to Tower House. Should he object, remind him this is a murder inquiry and refer him to me.'

'I'll do that, sir.'

The outer door of the vicarage was open, as before. A stout figure could be glimpsed waiting for them, as they crossed the wet lawn.

~

'Come away in, sir.' The housekeeper greeted them in a greatly subdued manner, compared to their previous meeting.

'Thank you, it's Hannah, isn't it?'

'That's me, sir. The vicar and Miss Adelaide are waiting for you in the warm.' Looking down at Reeve's boots, she sniffed as she took their hats.'

'Did you know Miss Geake, Hannah?'

'Only by sight. You get to know most people that way in Seaborough, when you've lived here as long as I have. I saw her when she called here, the day afore yesterday. Whoever would have believed the poor body were in mortal peril? I had no foreboding when I rose this morning or ...'

'Thank you, Hannah,' said a quiet, sonorous voice. Miss Shaw held open the door. 'Please come in.'

'Thanks, miss.'

Abbs followed the sergeant into the drawing-room. Miss Shaw's composure appeared to him as thin as ice on a puddle, would bear as little weight. He pushed away his picture of the shattered depression on Miss Geake's head.

'This is Sergeant Reeve, with me from Exeter.'

Rising from his chair, the vicar invited them to take the sofa drawn up near the fire.

'May we offer you any refreshment?'

'Thank you, no. It's very good of you, Mr. Shaw, but we'll take up as little of your time as possible.'

'Of course, Inspector. We must not delay you.'

Abbs turned to Miss Shaw. 'I'm sorry you've been subjected to such an ordeal and for having to ask you about it.'

'It's quite all right, Inspector, really. Nothing matters, except the work you have to do.'

'We have but a couple of questions for you both. At what time did you go to the church, Miss Shaw?'

'About ten minutes after nine. I saw the kitchen clock as I left.'

'And at what time is the church usually locked?'

Miss Shaw turned to her father, who leant forward. 'Soon after four in the afternoon, on a week-day. On Sundays, we have evensong, of course and the bell-ringers practise on a Thursday evening. I believe the house of God should be open for prayer as long as possible but in practice, people would not come to us any later.'

'Did you, by any chance, pick up anything from near the body, ma'am? A purse or reticule, for instance. You might have done it without thinking.'

Miss Shaw shook her head. 'No, I saw nothing. I went to put my hand on her arm, I didn't know she was dead, you see, and then I saw her head...'

He watched the blood drain from her face, her hands tighten. Hands were always revealing when a person was being questioned. It took a skilled dissembler to keep them loose, when they were lying. Someone as genial as Mr. Hicks, he thought. Halesworth would more likely bluster and lose his temper, Winton would look embarrassed. Miss Shaw would lie only to avoid hurting someone. She would make a poor fist of it.

Looking away from him to Reeve, she continued. 'I couldn't take it in at once. When I first saw the body, I thought it was a bundle of old clothes and someone had placed a bonnet on top. I feel dreadful that I could have been so stupid. People do sometimes leave things for the poor, you see. Usually here or at the church-hall.'

'You mustn't be hard on yourself, miss,' said Reeve. 'You've had a bad shock. No lady should ever see what you've had to.' Miss Shaw smiled sadly at him.

'Mr. Shaw, do you think it possible Miss Geake was on her way to visit you?' said Abbs. 'If she was coming from the direction of the square, might she walk through the churchyard and use the gate to the vicarage?'

'I don't believe so, Inspector. No one uses that gate except our household. No, she would carry on past the church and up the drive. If her purse is missing, could she not have been attacked for money?'

'Do you really believe that, Mr. Shaw?'

'You do not, then, sir.' The vicar sank back, diminished, in his winged chair. 'No, you are right, of course. I am an old man who does not want to acknowledge the evil in our midst. To murder someone on consecrated ground...'

'Papa.' Miss Shaw reached out to her father, letting her hand fall away.

Breaking the small silence that followed, some embers collapsed, dislodging a glowing coal, teetering on the edge of the hearth. Reeve grabbed the tongs, lobbing the lump back in the flames before it fell on the rug.

'We are obliged to you, Sergeant Reeve,' said the vicar.

'Your housekeeper said Miss Geake called on you two days since?'

'That is so, Inspector. She came to tell me she'd obtained a new post. She thanked me for her reference. She seemed...' Mr. Shaw thought back. 'Light-hearted. She told me she was off to Surrey in three days. She spoke of being glad to leave Devonshire and Seaborough in particular, I fear. I am sorry she was unhappy among us.'

'Did you see her, Miss Shaw?'

'No, I was out visiting. I hadn't seen Miss Geake since the day Miss Chorley died. She stopped coming to the Ladies' Society. She was in mourning, of course but I don't think she liked coming very much, only Miss Chorley expected it.'

'Did Miss Geake say anything else, sir?'

'I'm afraid not. She stayed only a few minutes. She was saying good-bye.' The vicar cast a wistful glance at the mantelpiece. Abbs guessed he was seeking his pipe. 'Do you recall when we met, Inspector? You asked me if there was anyone who... troubled me, shall we say, among my congregation?'

'I remember, sir.'

'I admitted there was one person who gave me cause for disquiet.' Mr. Shaw looked steadily at him. 'At that time, I felt unable to be more specific.'

'Will you tell us now, sir?'

'I regret to say that the person who worried me, was Miss Geake.'

Reeve carefully avoided looking at Dean, as Mrs Watkins raised her handkerchief to her eyes again. Try as she might, it was still perfectly dry. The two maids were true to their feelings. Sarah, the pretty one, looked quite indifferent as she sipped her tea. Jane, the scullery-maid, stared at them with eyes like chapel hat-pegs.

Attempting a choked sob, Mrs Watkins settled for shaking her head from side to side. 'Who'd of thought it, foul murder going on while decent folk were abed. Thinking she was safe upstairs and all the while, that poor creature was lying in the churchyard. In a pool of her own blood.'

'Have some more tea, Mrs W,' said Sarah, lifting the pot. 'We none of us liked her.'

'Hold your tongue, miss, you're so sharp you'll cut yourself,' said the cook, rounding on her. 'It don't do to speak ill of the dead.'

'You spoke plenty when she was here. No sense in denying it.' Sarah smiled at them, revealing a gap in her lower teeth. 'These two want the truth, not gammon. You do, don't you?'

'Yes, miss, that's what we're here for,' said Reeve. 'So none of you had any idea Miss Geake was missing, until she didn't come down for breakfast?'

'That's right.' Sarah watched him scribble.

'Didn't you take her early morning tea?'

Sarah and the cook exchanged glances. 'Not since the master left.'

'Nothing's been what you might call normal here since Miss Chorley died,' said Mrs Watkins. 'Miss Geake couldn't expect to be waited on, same as when the mistress were alive. She'd nothing to do with herself all day, after all. We've been waiting to shut up the house and go our separate ways. I don't mind telling you, I leave this house tomorrow. There's been two murders at this door and I've no intention of making the third.'

'What'll I do, Mrs Watkins?' said the scullery-maid, speaking for the first time.

'Go back to your family, you silly girl. Your mother'll take you back, won't she?' Jane nodded, her expression uncertain.

'Are you fixed up all right?' Reeve inquired of Sarah.

She tossed her head, making her cap-ribbons swing. 'It's all the same to me. I'm to be married in the spring. I can go home for a while.'

Reeve returned his attention to the matter in hand. 'What did you think when you saw Miss Geake's bed hadn't been slept in?'

'We didn't know what to think,' said Mrs Watkins. 'Since the master left, she'd taken to going out walking. Leastways, she didn't ask William for the carriage, but she'd never gone missing all night afore. I'd 'ave said she'd just upped and gone but her things were still in her room.'

'She always did like to go for a walk,' said Sarah, 'when Miss Chorley was resting. Aren't you going to write what I say?'

'Not everything,' replied Reeve shortly. 'What time did Miss Geake leave the house yesterday?'

Sarah turned to the cook. 'It's no good looking at me,' said Mrs Watkins, 'I was having my lie-down.'

'She rang for tea in the library at four o'clock,' said Sarah. 'I didn't see her go out.'

'Was she there when you went back to clear it away?'

'No, but I saw her on the stairs when I was in the hall.'

'So she could have been on her way out?'

'She might have been doing anything.'

'Didn't she order dinner?'

'No, I forgot. When I brought the tea, she said she wouldn't require a tray. She'd taken to having a tray in her room, instead of sitting at that long table by herself.'

'Didn't you think it odd she didn't want any supper?'

Sarah shrugged. 'Not my place to. Suppose I thought she had a headache. We were glad of less work.'

'What about you, miss?'

Addressed directly, Jane started. 'I wouldn't see anything from in here.'

'We'll see Miss Geake's room now,' said Reeve, standing up.

'You take them up, Sarah,' said Mrs Watkins. 'I'm sure I'm too afflicted by the shock.'

'What she means is,' confided Sarah, when they were on the stairs, 'she'll help herself to some brandy for her nerves.'

'Aren't the spirits locked away?' asked Dean.

Sarah glanced scornfully at him. 'There's brandy and sherry kept in the pantry for cooking. Don't you know anything?'

The constable's ears reddened. Taking pity on him, Reeve broke in. 'It's this end room, isn't it? You can leave us to it.'

'I'll keep you company. After all, you might pinch something.' Following them through the door, Sarah plumped down on the edge of the bed.

Reeve stood in the middle of the bedroom, deciding where to start. He was rather enjoying himself with an audience, and aware of Dean, awaiting his instructions. They were in a good-sized, corner room, with a pair of windows overlooking the front lawn and furnishings in a chilly, peacock blue.

In the middle of the carpet, stood a large trunk with an open lid. Taking a look inside, he saw it was part-filled with layers of neatly folded clothing, interspersed with paper.

'She'd started to pack for leaving,' said Sarah. She got up again and wandered over to stand behind him. 'Didn't get very far.' Moving to the dressing-table, she tilted the looking-glass, admiring her reflection. 'The wardrobe's still full of Miss Chorley's things, that Captain Selden gave her.'

'That was decent of him,' said Dean. 'Worth a good bit if she didn't wear them.'

'Was it, though?' said Sarah carelessly. 'Was he being decent?'

Reeve knew perfectly well she was watching him in the glass. 'What's that supposed to mean? If you have any information, spit it out. We're in a hurry.' Sarah smiled sweetly at him and wetting her finger, wound a curl in her front-knot. 'Or would you rather tell Inspector Abbs? He doesn't like time-wasters.'

'I don't know anything,' she admitted. 'But I wouldn't be surprised if Miss Geake had something on the Captain.'

He decided not to take out his notebook again, nor show how interested he was. 'Go on, let's hear it.'

'Well before the mistress died, it struck me he was funny with Miss Geake. That is, he didn't like to stay alone in a room with her.'

'Sounds like he was keen on her, and on the shy side, to me.'

'You're wrong there. He was a mite shy but that made him speak nicely to everyone. Anxious to please, he was with the mistress. It was more like he was half-scared of Miss Geake.'

Leaning against a tall chest of drawers, Reeve ignored Sarah as she perched on the dressing-table stool. He turned his attention to Dean, standing self-consciously by a window, his hands clasped behind his back. 'Make a start on the wardrobe, Dean. Feel in all the pockets, check for inside ones and don't forget the hat-boxes on top.'

'Right away, sarge.'

'You seemed to have noticed a lot, miss. Surely you didn't see that much of them?'

'When the mistress was alive, I was in and out of the drawing-room, fetching and carrying. As well as serving them at meals.'

'If that's all you can tell us, we'll get on,' he said, in a bored voice.

'I've not finished yet. Why did Captain Selden change his mind about shutting the house up, directly after the funeral?' It was almost, word for word, the question Abbs had asked.

'Well? D'you know why or not?'

'Something Miss Geake said to him. It was the last time they dined together. When I took in the main course, they were making polite remarks to one another. Time I came back, to clear before bringing in pudding, you could cut the air with a knife. She sat there looking pleased with herself. He got up, blurted out something about not being hungry, and left the room. Next day, he sent for Mrs Watkins and said about keeping the house open a while. He asked us to stay on until Miss Geake left.'

Sarah smiled pertly at him, ensuring her profile was displayed to best advantage.

Her neat, high bosom put him in mind of fresh apples. 'Anything else you want to tell us?'

'I heard you interviewed Mary, so you know what Miss Geake done to her.'

'Cut along then, if that's all,' he said, enjoying himself. 'We've work to do, if you haven't.'

Tossing her head, she flounced from the room, banging the door.

'She's a saucy one,' said Dean. 'There's nothing here. Where now?'

'I don't envy her betrothed. Try those drawers. I'll take the dressing-table. Take out any writing. She may have kept a diary, though that might be in there.' He indicated a writing-box and tried the lid. 'Locked. Keep an eye out for a key. Oh and if you come across any books, shake 'em out.'

'Are you walking out with anyone, sarge?' asked Dean, his face hidden as he stooped over a drawer.

'No one in particular. I'm too fly to be caught yet awhile,' said Reeve loftily.

~

Parting the slices of bread, Abbs eyed the lamb, with its white frill of congealed fat and lump of gristle. It was no good, he couldn't face sandwiches before a post-mortem, even though they didn't intend to be present at the carving-up. No doubt, Reeve would oblige by disposing of them, lest they gave offence to Mrs Tancock.

Pulling a sheet of paper towards him, he dipped his pen in the ink and began to make a list. Some twenty minutes later, he heard footsteps. The sergeant's breezy countenance appeared in the doorway, followed by Constable Colley with two cups of tea.

'How did you get on?' he asked, when they were alone again.

Reeve laid two bank-notes on the blotter, with a flourish. 'These were in the deceased's writing-box, sir. It was locked but Dean managed to find the key.'

'Where was it?'

'Shoved in the toe of a boot and wedged with a handkerchief.'

'Good work. I suppose she didn't want to carry it with her. Did you ask about Miss Geake having a latch-key?'

'Yes, sir. In the general run of things, she'd ring to be let in, as you said. They locked up and bolted all the doors before dark. No specific time, all except for a side-door on the terrace. Miss Geake was in the habit of strolling out there, for a breath of air, before going up to bed. The door would be locked but she would bolt it, before she turned in. The keys were kept hanging in the corridor off the kitchen. When I got the cook to check, the one for the side-door was missing.'

'So Miss Geake must have had it with her and probably intended to slip back, without the servants knowing she'd been out? Her mantle didn't have pockets, as far as I could see. She must have carried a reticule. Sergeant Tancock and the others aren't back yet.'

'The cook noticed the side-door wasn't bolted this morning, sir, but thought Miss Geake had forgotten. They're doing as little as possible, I'd say, with no one to stand over them. The cook was adamant she's leaving on the morrow. Mind, she was saying that when we first went up there.'

'They'll all go now. Captain Selden won't want to pay their wages any longer.'

'The parlour-maid, Sarah, had something interesting to say about him.' Taking a seat, Reeve repeated what she'd said.

'Now that is useful,' said Abbs when he'd finished. 'She might not have told me. You've done well, Sergeant. How did you find Constable Dean?'

'Keen to learn, sir. He took his searching diligently.'

'You ensured he missed nothing?'

'Yes, sir. There was nothing else of interest. The only papers were this small notebook, she seemed to use for recording expenses, and a letter stating the terms of her new post.' Reeve placed them next to the money. 'Not much to show for a life.'

'No.' Abbs began to leaf through the notebook. 'I suppose a diary or journal was too much to hope for.'

'It's a fair amount of money. Do you think it came from the legacy Miss Chorley left her, sir?'

'Definitely not,' said Abbs. 'Probate won't be granted for some time yet. It's a tidy sum for a companion to have lying around. We don't know what savings she had and she would have needed cash for her travelling arrangements, but even so. The bank manager will tell us, in the circumstances.' Without pausing, Abbs proffered the plate. Reeve accepted a sandwich gratefully.

'Did you see Mr. Jerrold?'

The answer came indistinctly while Reeve swallowed his chewy mouthful. 'He wasn't there as it turned out, sir. These are good. I saw that same snooty clerk and told him. He didn't turn a hair.'

Abbs nodded, thinking the solicitor would doubtless feel he hadn't been treated with due deference. 'The inquest's being called tomorrow afternoon and will be adjourned as soon as the formalities are done. I've also contacted the Hampshire force. I want someone to discreetly check that Captain Selden is back at work in Netley.'

'D'you reckon he could have sneaked back and killed her, sir? Two counties away, it's a fair way to travel.'

'He's had sufficient time to get back here and do it. It all depends on the motive for Miss Geake's murder. It's a long shot, I agree, but we can't afford to overlook anything. There's been so much to get underway, I've barely had time to formulate any theories yet.' Cradling his cup, Abbs drained the last of his tea. 'I don't know, Reeve. Selden has to be checked. With any luck, we'll hear from Hampshire by nightfall. Eat up and we'll be on our way again.'

~

A large horse-chestnut overhung the street, from the garden of the house next to the Hospital. Spiky, bright green seed cases were scattered on the pavement. Some had burst, revealing glossy conkers, which were being picked over by small boys. A coalman's trolley stood near the entrance, the blinkered horses waiting patiently. A great rumbling, as of coals down a chute, was coming from the side of the building.

A young nurse opened the door, as a thickset fellow in porter's uniform hurried round the corner to catch them. 'Sorry to keep you waiting, gents. Had to see the coal in. The sacks all have to be counted. It's all right, nurse, I'll show them the way. It's easiest if I take you. It's right down the back.'

The porter led them along a corridor, at a swift pace. They passed a small ward on either side. Although similar, this was not the way Dr. Avery had taken them on their previous visit. They glimpsed a dispensary, outsized sinks and a latrine. The tiles, on wall and floor, gleamed with disinfectant. Overlaying that, as they reached the end double doors, was a reek of carbolic and chemicals.

'Straight through there. The doctor's expecting you.' Abbs tried not to inhale the grim odour, familiar from the Exeter mortuary.

'Good day to you both.' Dr. Avery was in his linen, unfolding his sleeves, as he turned to greet them. Mr. Biggs held out his dark frock-coat, for him to put on. 'Well timed. As you see, we're done here.'

The body lay on the table in the middle of the room, beneath a large gas-bracket. Decently covered by a sheet, the bare feet protruded. The breasts were covered, a raw, red line scored between them, reaching almost to the bottom of the neck and held together with fresh stitching.

Mr. Biggs hovered at Dr. Avery's elbow, his eyes downcast and features composed so solemnly that Reeve stifled a laugh. He concentrated instead on a large glass jar, containing something like tripe.

'You're both all right in here, I take it? Not likely to keel over?'

'We've seen our share of post-mortems,' said Abbs evenly.

'I don't mind what I see, Doctor, it's the stench,' said Reeve.

'In that case, I wouldn't venture too close,' said Avery, gesturing at a kidney-shaped, enamel dish, next to the jar. 'Those are the stomach contents.'

'What do you have for us, Doctor?' asked Abbs.

'The stomach matter contained morsels of semi-digested dried fruit. In other words fruit cake. There was no trace of an earlier meal remaining.'

Abbs nodded. 'We now know she was served afternoon tea, before she went out. Can you get the time of death any closer?'

Avery shook his head decisively. 'Not possible, I'm afraid. The state of the stomach indicates the contents were ingested about two to three hours before death. That merely corroborates your earlier theory.'

'It's looking as though the murder took place roughly between six o'clock and about half-past seven,' said Abbs.

Mr. Biggs coughed discreetly, fixing them with his shrewd, bright eyes.

'So the poor lady was meeting someone at dusk?' he said softly. 'A terrible business. We estimated the lady's age at about forty, Inspector.'

'I doubt that will help Inspector Abbs find the perpetrator,' said Avery irritably.

'Could you learn any more from the wound?' Abbs turned his back on the clerk.

'Again, no more than I surmised at the scene.'

Abbs studied the head. The hair had been shaved away from the edges of the wound. At such close quarters, a few greying strands could be seen. There were incipient pouches beneath the eyes, a patch of coarse skin on the cleavage.

He knew he was reputed to be a cold fish. Indeed, he felt despicable for noticing such blemishes, even while his dispassionate mind recorded them.

'No foreign particles embedded, unfortunately. If you examine the extent of the haematoma, which can be seen more clearly now, the bruising pattern indicates considerable force, applied by a smooth-edged weapon.' Avery handed Abbs a magnifying-glass. On either side of the table, Reeve and Biggs moved closer.

'My thanks, Doctor,' said Abbs, as he straightened up. 'A life-preserver still looks likely, then.'

'I should say so. Lead-weighting would fit with the severity and spread of the trauma, while being a smooth-surfaced weapon.'

'It would fit in a coat pocket,' said Reeve.

'If Miss Geake was confronted by a raised weapon,' said Avery, 'she would have put up her arms to protect herself. It's instinctive. A man might try to grab the weapon or hit out. A woman would try to shield herself. The fact that there are no defensive injuries on her hands or arms,, suggests she saw no danger before the impact.'

Nodding thoughtfully, the soft sound of Biggs's tongue, clicking behind his teeth, made Abbs look at him. The clerk looked as though he were about to polish silver in a butler's pantry, were it not for the darker stains on his green apron.

'A terrible business, to be sure, Inspector.'

'It is indeed.' He supposed it churlish to ignore the fellow, who presumably meant well.

He had little patience with obsequiousness, nor those who devoured penny dreadfuls and lurid newsprint accounts of mayhem. The idea that some poor devil's horror was entertainment to the masses, disgusted him. And yet, thought Abbs, as Avery showed Reeve the wound, his working life was spent looking in dark places.

Beyond the circle of light, their shadows were thrown giant-like against the bare wall. As he watched, one detached itself from the rest and loomed over him. The gas flickered and the undertaker's clerk coughed tentatively.

'It would appear, Inspector, that one small mystery has been solved. Young Bram was telling the truth, as he saw it, after all.'

'What's that you say, Biggs?' said Dr. Avery.

The clerk gestured to the pile of grey clothing, folded on the work-bench.

'Bram's ghost,' breathed Mr. Biggs.

~

The tide had retreated a long way out. The beginning of water could be discerned only fitfully, as the wind blew clouds to and fro across the pale sliver of moon. Somewhere far out, a single light burned, marking a vessel. Abbs stood at the promenade railings, relishing the cool night air after the fug in the Anchor.

Reeve had gone up to his room but he needed a few moments alone, to think in the darkness, before retiring to the small chamber under the eaves. A clock sounded across the streets, whether from the town-hall or the church, he knew not. His over-tired mind roamed back over the events of the long day.

At this time on the previous evening, Miss Geake already lay dead. He felt a stab of pity for the needle-tongued, clear-sighted woman he had met. Unhappy and not without goodness. Gone now, gutted like a fish on the mortuary table.

He rubbed a hand over his brow, knowing he should have remembered Bram's tale at once. What he most feared was happening, he was weary and missing things. The telegram from Superintendent Nicholls, at the station on his return from the Hospital, had been circumspect in its wording. Nicholls, for all his coarse bluster, would observe the proprieties.

He was a great one for discipline and would not have lowly, uniformed constables in Seaborough reading a dressing-down for a senior detective. But the order had been uncompromising. A few days more to solve the murders. Or the case would be taken from them.

Jabez Biggs, who could stitch a gaping incision in a corpse, more neatly than some women might hem a sheet. He was right, of course, about Bram's sighting of the ghost in the churchyard. Miss Geake had evidently taken to half-mourning since he'd questioned her.

Could Biggs be more involved than appearing at every opportunity? He could see no motive but that was so for everyone connected with Tower House on the day Miss Chorley died. Biggs had not even been there.

Philip Winton had told them of his fear that the clerk knew something about his background. How, when they'd worked together, Biggs had adroitly questioned him about his past. He was not a blackmailer, decided Abbs, rather, one of those people who avidly collect information, simply for the pleasure of its possession.

Miss Geake though, he believed, had tried her hand at blackmailing and paid with her life. Sergeant Tancock had returned, both disgruntled and triumphant, with two discoveries to present. A lady's reticule had been found in the churchyard. An elderly widow, residing nearly opposite the church, had seen a woman of Miss Geake's description entering the gate at around a quarter before six.

No response yet from the constabulary in Hampshire. Deciding there was no point in trying the station again, at that late hour, Abbs walked back to the inn. His footsteps echoed in the empty street. The sky was as dark and clouded as his thoughts.

Twenty-four

The reticule, dark blue beadwork with a drawstring, tassel and wrist loop, lay on the desk between them. It had been found behind the heap of dead flowers in a corner of the churchyard. The few contents were spread out, a handkerchief with the initial *A* embroidered in one corner, a tiny flask of smelling-salts and a key. There was no money.

'Miss Geake leaves Tower House at some time after half-past four, when Sarah collects the tea things. It takes a half-hour to walk down to the town, maybe forty minutes for a woman. We don't know what time she left. But a female in a grey costume is seen entering the churchyard at a quarter before six o'clock. It all fits.' Abbs sat back in his chair.

'Lucky the old lady was looking from her window,' said Reeve. 'She was expecting her son to call and keeping an eye out.'

'Bram saw his ghost on his way back from the butcher's, as it was near closing. Which according to Sergeant Tancock, would be about six. It looks as though Miss Geake met someone in the churchyard at least twice. Probably at six o'clock and she made sure to be there early.'

'Funny place to meet, though, sir.'

'I was giving it some thought, last night. How many places are there where two people can meet out of the way, somewhere perceived as respectable for a woman, and dry if it rains?'

'They can't go in a public-house and they don't want to use one of their homes. Let's see, they could meet in a tea-room or take a stroll.'

'They don't want to be seen together,' said Abbs promptly. 'They don't want questions asked.'

'A sea-front shelter, then or... the church porch. In the middle of the town, respectable, with the vicarage close by and villas opposite, yet not too overlooked and sheltered from bad weather,' finished Reeve.

'I think so,' said Abbs. 'At dusk, they were unlikely to be disturbed. Too late to visit the church or bring flowers. Most folk don't care to frequent graveyards at that time but Miss Geake was a strong-minded lady.'

'But who was she meeting and why?'

'I don't believe she was having assignations with a lover,' said Abbs. 'I think she was blackmailing the murderer.'

Reeve started to whistle under his breath and catching Abbs's eye, stopped. 'Putting the black on. She was taking a big risk, sir. Didn't expect to be battered over the head, then.'

Abbs winced. 'No, I think we can assume Miss Geake felt safe. She thought she had the upper hand and miscalculated.'

'Then we're looking for a man?'

'Dr. Avery did say a woman could have managed the deed. It isn't easy to imagine one female doing that to another. But blackmailers are killed from desperation, fury or fear. I think it would be a mistake to assume the murderer is male.'

'She would have felt safer with another woman.'

'That's a good point. What do you think she could have known in order to blackmail someone, Sergeant?'

'Information about Miss Chorley's death,' said Reeve, at once. 'She must have seen something. Which means it was at the tea-party, or when Mr. Hicks called later. That puts Mr. Winton in the clear. Miss Geake didn't go to the studio with Miss Chorley and Captain Selden.' He looked pleased with his reasoning.

'What I'd like to know is this,' said Abbs. 'Did Miss Geake know the identity of the murderer from the start, or did she realise something over the days since?'

'But sir, doesn't this make it Captain Selden?' said Reeve, excitement shining on his face. 'We know from Sarah, it looks like Miss Geake was blackmailing him?'

Abbs shook his head. 'Not necessarily. She had some hold over him, certainly, and we need to know what. But I can't see her sharing the house with a cold-blooded poisoner.'

He regarded his sergeant with concealed approval. The morning sun, finding its way through the small window, was in Reeve's face, making his eyes crinkle. At eight-and-twenty, if he recalled correctly from his record, Reeve's enthusiasm was still fresh. Abbs found himself hoping that the nature of their work would not turn Reeve into another Superintendent Nicholls, by his middle years.

It was a long while since he'd thought about his small brothers, dead before grown to be companions.

'Sir?'

Abbs realised Reeve had been speaking. 'What were you saying?'

'I wondered how many times Miss Geake had an assignation with the murderer?'

'I doubt she met him or her more than twice. Think about it, she contacts the poisoner, possibly at a social meeting, but more likely by letter. Miss Shaw said she'd stopped going to the Ladies' Society. Although the servants said she was taking walks. They meet once, the poisoner needs to hear what she has to say and possibly hands over a down-payment. A second meeting is arranged to hand over a larger sum. Miss Geake was leaving Seaborough, remember. This would have been their only chance to kill her.'

'It makes sense. Who could Miss Geake have seen do something, so she realised they were the murderer?'

'Let's look at it logically. We're satisfied it wasn't Mr. Winton and we'll leave Captain Selden to one side. I can't see any motive for the servants, Mrs Watkins, Sarah, William and ...'

'Jane. I can't believe it was Mary. No opportunity.'

Abbs rubbed his eyes. 'Which brings us to the guests on that day and Mr. Hicks. What do you think about the Shaws and Mr. Emerson?'

'Can't see it was Mr. Emerson, myself. He's a retired magistrate, part of the gentry and he was keen to help us.'

'That wouldn't necessarily be a character reference,' said Abbs drily. 'I agree in this case. There could be something in his past that Miss Chorley knew, I suppose but I'm blowed if I can come up with any motive for killing her now.'

'Same goes for the vicar,' said Reeve. 'I'm not sure we should forget Miss Shaw though.'

Abbs looked at him in surprise. 'Go on, Sergeant.'

'Don't get me wrong, sir, I thought she seemed a very nice lady. But we don't know anything about her private life. Suppose Miss Chorley came in possession of some secret about her? Something that would ruin her, if made public. Miss Shaw could have met Miss Geake at the church porch and slipped home in no time.'

'An enterprising theory, Reeve, if you really see Miss Shaw capable of striking another woman over the head. I don't share your view. Besides, from what we've learned of Miss Chorley's character, she would have revealed any misdemeanour as soon as she knew of it. She'd have seen it as her painful duty.'

'S'pose you're right, sir.'

'Which brings us to the others. Mr. and Mrs Hicks and Mrs Halesworth. Let us take the ladies first.'

'I didn't meet Mrs Hicks, if you recall, sir, and I only saw Mrs Halesworth briefly.'

'So you did. Mrs Hicks seemed pleasant and kindly, a talkative lady and a close friend of the Shaws. I'd find it difficult to imagine her a murderess. Now,

Mrs Halesworth, I could see as determined and tough as any man. But she is direct, not devious, I fancy.'

'Might she act on behalf of her husband?'

'Quite possibly, but I can't believe she'd poison someone. I should think Alfred Halesworth is unscrupulous. Dodgy dealings on the council, very like but more than that, who knows?' Abbs shrugged and glanced down at his notes.

'That only leaves Mr. Hicks, sir.'

'As likeable as his wife. I doubt the murderer purchased their arsenic openly in Seaborough. Someone must be wearing a mask, Reeve. I think we need to take a closer look at the business plans of our councillor and undertaker. Perhaps one of them had a pressing need for their building deal to happen and Miss Chorley stood in their way.'

'Money's always the best motive, if you ask me, sir. But if we ask around, they'll get to hear about it.'

'I thought to ask the third partner in their business dealings. As a medical man and police-surgeon, Dr. Avery will understand the need for discretion. He shouldn't object to discussing his friends, in the circumstances. In fact,' said Abbs, glancing at the clock, 'he probably has lunch at home. I think I'll try to catch him.'

'Right, sir.'

Seeing Reeve's expression fall, he added, 'I'll see the doctor alone to make it easier for him, if he feels he's breaking a confidence. Besides, I need you here to await the confirmation from Hampshire.' Taking up his hat, Abbs paused at the door. 'Go through the reports again. If I'm not back, I'll see you outside the hotel at ten to three.'

~

Dr. Avery's house proved to be a medium-sized, detached villa, built in the local brick. It had decorative, terracotta roof-tiles, a sharply-pitched gable with brown-painted barge boards and a large porch, its upper half glazed. A sign indicated *Surgery* to the left, where the path vanished in a gloomy shrubbery.

As Abbs turned into the short drive, the front door opened. A small, white terrier bounded down the steps and raced towards him. In the doorway, were an elderly lady and the doctor.

'Gyp, to heel. Come here now,' called Avery.

The dog paused his careering in circles, glancing back to his master and then at Abbs, his tail wagging in friendly fashion.

'He won't bite you,' said Avery, as Abbs came towards them. 'It's more that he'll cover you in hairs. For a short-haired coat, he sheds them everywhere, don't you, sir?' The little dog, having trotted obediently back to him, he bent and rubbed his head before encouraging him gently back inside with his foot.

'I'm used to dogs,' said Abbs easily. 'He's a fine specimen.'

'I had him from a farm,' replied Avery. 'He was the runt of a litter, so they were only going to drown him. As you say, he filled out well and he's a great ratter. Thank you, Mrs Fayter. I expect to be home this evening.' The grey-haired lady smiled at Abbs, bidding him good day as he raised his hat.

'As you see, you've only just caught me. Is it urgent?'

'I wanted to ask your help, Doctor,' said Abbs. 'It's rather delicate.'

Avery, raised his eyebrows. 'Now you have me curious. Walk with me. I'm on my way to see a patient but it's a duty call, gout. A few minutes won't go amiss. I keep my gig at the livery stables round the corner.'

'Thank you. I've seen your dog before. I happened to see you out ratting on Sunday. I'd been exploring the hill-fort and saw you all making for a barn.'

'You're thinking it a poor occupation for after church?' said the doctor humorously, as they walked. 'I did attend the morning service.'

'That's more than I did,' said Abbs. 'I went up there to get away from Seaborough and think about the case.'

The doctor nodded. 'Life in a small town can be stultifying. I like the country air, myself. A man should have exercise. I find fishing gives me a chance to think. My cares seem easier when I'm sitting on a river-bank.'

'I haven't fished since boyhood,' said Abbs. 'You were accompanying Mr. Halesworth and Mr. Hicks, when I saw you.'

Pausing to raise his hat to two ladies descending from a clarence, Dr. Avery looked sharply at him. 'What is it you wish to know about them, Inspector?'

'There you have me, Doctor, I don't know myself. They are your friends, yet as police-surgeon, you'll see my problem. We haven't found a motive for Miss Chorley's murder. I find myself wondering about the building land she refused to sell.'

Dr. Avery appeared dumbstruck for a second, before breaking into a rueful grin. The relaxing of his stern features shed years from his countenance, so that when he sobered, he looked all the more austere. 'How did you find out about that? Halesworth was anxious for it to be kept quiet.'

'Mr. Hicks told me. He hasn't mentioned it?'

Avery shook his head. 'I've seen little of them lately, apart from our sporting afternoon, and then we were in close company. I doubt Hicks has told

Halesworth you know, for all they're old friends. I regard them more as colleagues and associates. Hicks is a good fellow but Halesworth and I have had our run-ins.'

'Mr. Hicks did say that you'd been part of a previous business deal with them.'

'That's perfectly true. They approached me to put up a third, knowing I'd recently been left a legacy to invest. It was a good deal. I know nothing of building but property will always give a sound return. You can see bricks and mortar.'

'Indeed. What I want to ask is, do you know of any problems either of them might be facing? A pressing need for money that they don't want known? Was this prospective land deal vital to one of them?'

The doctor listened attentively, his eyes on Abbs, his head slightly to one side. The bruise had gone on his face now and he moved with ease.

Abbs suddenly wondered if he'd tumbled in a river and made up a tale, not wanting to look a fool. He could imagine Halesworth guffawing and repeating the story about the town.

'I'm sorry, Inspector. I can think of nothing that would help you.' Avery knitted his brows in thought. 'Hicks is fairly cautious. I don't believe he would over-reach himself. He's built a leading business in the town, by doing it steadily and providing good service. Most people go to him, if they can afford to, which is not to say he overcharges. In fact, he's well-known for a soft heart. I believe him to be happily married. Mrs Hicks is in full possession of his confidence regarding money and business matters.'

'Really?'

'You look surprised. Fanny Hicks has helped her husband build their small empire. She knows the value of a pound.'

'And Mr. Halesworth?'

'Now, he may well over-reach himself, I'm not privy to his financial dealings. He and his wife live extravagantly but his prosperity and influence always seem to be increasing. He has a shrewd eye for business or I wouldn't consider investing with him again. In fact, I haven't committed myself. Miss Chorley's parcel of land was the only one well-placed for Halesworth's scheme. He was extremely keen to get his hands on it, but not desperate. He doesn't care to be thwarted but then, do any of us?'

'Do you happen to know where either of them were, two nights ago?'

The doctor looked at Abbs while he considered. 'Say what you mean, man. In early evening, at the time Miss Geake was killed?'

Abbs nodded. 'I'm sorry to involve you but it's necessary. Time is of the essence.'

'Do you think they'll kill again?'

Abbs gazed down the street. A sweeper was coming gradually towards them, his task rather hopeless as the limes, planted at intervals in the pavement, were half-bare. Their leaves were thick in the gutter, every now and then, another fluttered down. He knew how the man felt.

'That depends on the motive, Doctor. You see why I have to ask.'

'I can't say where either of them were on that evening, as I wasn't with them. More often than not, one or both will stop off at the Marine. The professional men of the town tend to congregate in the bar at the rear, as a sort of informal club. You can make discreet enquiries there. A young woman named Emily usually serves behind the bar. There was no council meeting that night. I can tell you that much.' The doctor pulled out his watch. 'I must be on my way, shortly.'

'I appreciate your help.'

'Not at all. You'll want to know where I was that evening. Sitting by the fire in my study, immersed in a medical journal. My housekeeper cannot vouch for me as I didn't require anything. Only Gyp could tell you.'

'My thanks, Doctor.'

'Don't have a mind to Jerrold,' said Dr. Avery unexpectedly. 'Seaborough is a very small pond with too many big fish.' He bowed. 'Good day, Inspector, I shall see you later at the inquest.'

~

'Take a pew,' said Halesworth, waving him to the chair before the desk.

Mr. Hicks watched his friend curiously as he stood before the window, stretching and gazing down on the Square garden they'd just crossed.

'People still coming out. Half the town's down there.' Halesworth laughed without humour. 'There goes your long-faced clerk, trotting behind Avery. I saw he had a ring-side seat again, practically licking his lips, he was.'

'We attended ourselves, to be fair,' said Hicks, crossing his legs. 'Why have we come up here, did you say? We'd be a lot more comfortable at the Marine.'

Halesworth shot him an irritable glance and returned to philosophising on the scene below. 'The detective's a po-faced one. He'd never make a councillor, his voice is too quiet. There's his cocky sergeant. You know Jerrold complained about the inspector's high-handedness? You weren't there when he was telling us.'

'I did hear something about it, from Fanny. The fellow has his job to do. Abbs was all right to me. Decent to Bram too, not everyone would have been.'

'That half-wit.' Halesworth grunted, as though his mind was elsewhere. 'Don't see why you ever took him on. What good is he?'

'He makes himself useful. I can't afford to keep anyone who doesn't work.'

'You're too soft, Hicks, that's your trouble.'

'If you brought me here to quarrel, I'd rather we do it in the bar,' remarked Hicks lightly.

'Mind, I've been too soft, myself.'

'Eh? Nobody could accuse you of that, surely?'

'The vicar's daughter stepping in her carriage. Everyone wanted to hear the gory details. She stood up well in the box, mind.'

'Yes, she was most composed. Fanny wanted to accompany her but Miss Shaw wouldn't hear of it.'

'No Shaw, though. Word is, he's unwell. Always looks as though a puff of wind would blow him over. He must be over sixty. Could be a fee coming your way.' Hicks made no comment. 'Who the devil is it, now Selden's out of the running?'

'Murdering defenceless women? If I knew, I'd be telling the police.'

'Abbs and his lackey must be running out of time. I thought the Coroner gave him an easy ride, but loss of public confidence and all that. Seems to me, he'll be taken off the investigation.'

'Then we'll have to tell it all again to someone else from Exeter.'.

Halesworth swung round. 'Can't see it, they'll send in Scotland Yard.'

Hicks wondered what was on his friend's mind. As fond as the next man of gossip, Halesworth was not normally one to prevaricate. He was making small-talk to delay his real reason for bringing them somewhere private. The fellow looked decidedly rattled.

'A man could die of thirst around here.'

'Oh, beg pardon, Hicks. What'll it be?' Halesworth moved swiftly to the tantalus. 'I could do with a drink, Lord knows.'

'Whisky, if you please. Better make it a small one, it's early yet.'

'I'll join you, small be beggared.' Pouring two hefty measures, Halesworth passed one across the desk and took his chair, at last. 'You asked why I brought you up here,' he continued, after taking a large swallow. 'No listeners.' Another generous mouthful.

Hicks began to feel somewhat alarmed. He sipped his own drink, then set down the glass.

'Is something up, Halesworth? Has Captain Selden turned down our offer for the land?'

'What? No, I'd have told you. Jerrold hasn't heard back from him, yet. This is nothing to do with business. Do try and concentrate.'

There was nothing for it but to be patient. Hicks looked encouragingly at him and waited.

Halesworth cleared his throat. 'Fact is, I'm finished if this gets out and you know what an old tattler Cox is. I couldn't take the risk of anyone overhearing.' He subsided again. 'The thing is, old man, I could do with your advice. I'm in a spot of bother.'

After the story had been spilt, Hicks considered in silence, for a moment, what he might say. 'It seems to me, you have it all worked out.' He rubbed his beard as he thought. 'I don't know what you could have done differently, in the circumstances.'

Brightening, Halesworth nodded. 'It's a relief to talk to someone sympathetic, nor do I. I've behaved very handsomely. It's not my fault if Nelly's been so careless. I can't be expected to ruin my life, can I?'

'No. There's your wife and girls to consider.'

'Exactly. Have another, old man. I knew you'd see things my way. It'll be all right, won't it? These things blow over.'

'If you can trust the lady not to make trouble.'

'She's never shown the slightest sign that way. She was perfectly amenable the first time, but you can never rely on women. My great fear is that someone's put her up to this. She's mentioned a neighbour, once or twice. Some shop clerk, scraped an acquaintance, invited her to a concert, obviously sniffing about. Naturally, she gave out she's a widow, you see, so she looks available to any sharper. The best thing is if she leaves Devonshire.'

'She can't afford to turn down your offer. You said there's no family to cause trouble or support her?'

'None, which is just as well,' said Halesworth. 'It's a pity about the boy, but it can't be helped. He's a fine lad. Great pity Rosa and I weren't blessed with a son. Proves it's her fault, mind.'

Extracting a key on his chain, he unlocked his desk-drawer and felt for something. A photograph landed between them, face down, the cardboard mount slightly creased from handling.

Hicks picked it up and studied it. 'Very pretty. A fine lad, as you say.'

'I daren't keep it at home. I wouldn't trust Rosa not to rifle my pocket-book or desk, but she never comes here. I've been on pins, lest a letter comes to the house, I can tell you.' Halesworth accompanied this with a grin as he raised his glass, satisfied all his troubles were behind him.

~

As turned into the street, they saw Sergeant Tancock coming out of his house, next door to the police-station. He buttoned his jacket, as he saw them, and brushed some crumbs from his protruding front.

'Afternoon, sir. How did it go, might I ask?'

'Much as expected, Sergeant. The Coroner heard the evidence of finding the body, and the post-mortem, then adjourned.'

'Well, sir, your telegraph from 'ampshire has come.'

'At last.' Abbs hurried up the steps, Reeve at his heels.

They waited impatiently for Tancock to join them and pass through the opening in the unmanned counter. With maddening slowness, he removed the flimsy from a docket spike and presented it to Abbs.

Scanning it swiftly, he handed it to Reeve. 'What do you make of that, Sergeant?'

A grin spread over Reeve's face as he read the few lines. He looked questioning as he handed back the message. He's learning not to jump to conclusions, thought Abbs.

'Captain Selden's unwell and not back at his desk.'

'From a Sergeant Webber,' said Abbs, studying the paper. 'Offers any further assistance, most cordially.'

'No one at the Military Hospital has actually set eyes on him since he came back from Seaborough.'

'So it would seem. Let me have your *Bradshaw* again, would you, Tancock?' Abbs led the way to their room. 'I'm going to have to do some calculating, but I think Captain Selden could have killed Miss Geake and just about returned to Hampshire that night. He might have travelled via London and stayed the night there. It would be imperative to get away from Seaborough, as fast as possible, without being recognised.'

'He wouldn't be known at the railway-station,' said Reeve.

'No. I shall want you to ask if the station staff recall any passengers for the late train on that evening. I shall go to Hampshire tomorrow. I need to speak to the Captain again, in any event.'

'I'm to stay here, sir?'

'You are, Reeve. I need someone I can trust here, meaning no offence to Sergeant Tancock and his men.'

'Understood, sir.'

'Dr. Avery said something that made me think. I made a chance remark about running out of time and he asked if I feared the murderer killing again. It set my thoughts on a different line. Poisoning is a calculated way to remove someone. People do it for two reasons. One, so they don't have to be present at the death. Two, because they hope it will be passed off as natural causes. With me, so far?'

'Yes, sir. Dr. Avery admitted he'd likely have thought Miss Chorley died of gastric trouble. It was only Dr. Miller's being awkward, brought us in.'

'Suppose we're looking at this the wrong way round? We see Miss Chorley's death as the beginning. What if the murderer had done this before and got away with it?'

Reeve scratched his ear reflectively as he turned this over. 'I don't quite get it, sir. What's made you think this?'

Abbs stood, moving the few paces to the unlit grate. Leaning his hand on the mantle-shelf, he absently straightened a spill vase and traced his finger in the dust. 'I don't know, desperation perhaps? We have to find another angle. Why was Miss Chorley in someone's way? That's what it comes down to. Miss Geake's murder was a consequence.'

Returning to the desk, Abbs went on. 'While I'm gone, I want you to find out how many deaths there've been in Seaborough in.. say, this year. It won't hurt to look. When you have a list, we'll go through it together. We'll be able to eliminate most of them at once, so it shouldn't take long. Don't bother with children. D' you know how to go about it?'

'See the Superintendent Registrar for this district,' replied Reeve instantly.

'Good man. I'll see what Captain Selden has to say for himself.' Abbs reached for the *Bradshaw* and a sheet of paper, as he spoke. 'There's something Mr. Emerson said that I want to ask him about. We've no jurisdiction in Hampshire, of course. I shall take up Sergeant Webber's offer of assistance.'

Twenty-five

It had taken much of the day to travel to Hampshire, including three changes of train and a lengthy wait at the busy junction of Salisbury. The county was unknown to him and Abbs was interested to view the changing topography. The latter part of the route traversed the southern portion of the New Forest, with long stretches of wild heath, where ponies grazed and glinting pools lay between woodland.

An elderly gentleman, getting on at a halt, was eager to remind him that *forest,* in its original sense, referred to an ancient hunting ground. In this instance, the desmesne of William the Conqueror, encompassing varied landscape, not only wooded.

Strangers were always surprised, he said, though woods they also passed in plenty, full of venerable oaks and beeches. Autumn seemed further advanced here, with branches almost bare, the ground thick with decaying leaves and beech mast.

The final change was at Southampton. Late in the day for travellers, but he could imagine the porters wheeling trunks and the bustle of passengers. Pushing their way between three platforms, signs directing them to the pier for the Isle of Wight steamer and the Hythe ferry.

The station was busy with respectable men of all description. Browsing at the book-stall, Abbs decided they were clerks and managers, on their way home to the growing suburbs and smaller towns along the line.

When the Netley train pulled out, they passed streets of identical, sooty terraces, their only colour from tin advertisements affixed to end walls. Every now and then, he glimpsed an expanse of water between building-works. This, he knew, from consulting a map on the previous evening, must be the estuary. Southampton sat at its head, lying several miles from the coast.

His destination was situated on the east side of Southampton Water, about half-way down to the sea. As he looked out, the merchant city gradually gave way to wood and pasture, the land for the most part, flat and well kept.

The nights were drawing in, twilight had come on by the time he stepped down at Netley station. Several passengers had alighted. A few went past a ticket-collector at an iron gate, down a rough lane which looked to be the edge of the village.

Someone had made a patch of garden behind railings, where the station name was picked out in white-washed stones. A small waiting-room stood by the gate. Abbs saw that the main station building was on the opposite platform.

Picking up his travelling-case, he followed the greater part of passengers over the brick foot-bridge.

As clouds of steam dispersed and the locomotive slid beneath them, he viewed a trim station, fronted in white stucco, built in the Italian style. The station-master's house was attached. Beyond, stood a signal-box, wherein the signal-man could be seen in the lamplight, a shadowy figure moving to and fro.

The others were streaming through the booking-office, with the plodding familiarity of weary men going home. Most of them would do it, he thought, for fifty years or more.

Waiting by a cheerful poster, advertising *Sunny Southsea,* a uniformed sergeant scanned the faces. He thrust back his shoulders as Abbs walked up to him, saluting smartly. Returning the smile, Abbs was amused at the contrast from his meeting with Sergeant Tancock.

'Would I be right in thinking you're Inspector Abbs, sir?' Receiving confirmation, the sergeant continued. 'Sergeant Thomas Webber, sir, Netley's my patch. My superior, Inspector Ruddock, presents his compliments. He's asked me to welcome you on behalf of Hampshire Constabulary. He's put me at your disposal, to show you round and assist in any way.'

'My thanks, Sergeant. Mine's a flying visit, as you'll have been told, so I shouldn't take you too long from your usual duties. Please thank Inspector Ruddock for his assistance. I'll write a line, myself, on my return.'

'I'll do that, sir. Take your bag? It's only a step. I've taken the liberty of booking you into The Station Hotel here. Not over-large but the best accommodation hereabouts, for all the soot.'

'I'm sure it will do very well, I'm obliged to you, Sergeant.'

'We've two inns in the village that let rooms, sir, but one's on the mean side. Folk visiting the Hospital generally stay here, if they can.'

'Are we far from the Military Hospital?'

'No, sir, down the road there and a short walk along the shore takes you to the main gate. Though it's a fair step, once you're in the grounds.'

'I did wonder if the Hospital would have its own station?'

'Maybe one day, sir, they've everything else. The troops are taken off here but a good many arrive by sea and up Southampton Water.'

'I see. Sounds an interesting place.'

'We're very proud of it, sir, there's none like it. We get a lot of important people come to take a look, Members of Parliament, and the like. You'll see for yourself on the morrow. I understand you need to visit the adjutant's office?'

'That's right. My inquiry is in connection with an officer in the Army Pay Corps.'

Sergeant Webber nodded, his prematurely, bald pate noticeable in the lamplight. He was a vigorous man of about his own age. 'You want the Commissariat then, that's the admin block.'

'I can see your assistance is going to be invaluable, Sergeant.'

'Do my best, sir. Step this way, if you please.'

Having his ticket clipped, Abbs followed Webber through the booking-office, where a fire looked welcoming in the small grate. Outside, he saw a spacious sweep of gravel, The Station Hotel standing on a far corner.

'I'll leave you to settle in then, sir. You've had a long journey, I believe? Might I do anything for you this evening?'

'Thank you, no. I'll be glad to wash the dust off and get something to eat,' said Abbs.

'I think you'll be suited here, Inspector. The landlord's wife does a very tasty steak and oyster pie.'

'I'd be obliged if you'd call for me after breakfast, Sergeant.'

'Will do, sir. Should you need the police-house, it's straight down the road on the left-hand side, just before the shops. You can't miss it.'

'Thank you for meeting me. I'll bid you good-night, Webber.' Abbs watched him set off down the road at a sharp pace. His fellow-passengers had long vanished. From what he could see, Netley looked a large village. The road, lined with fairly recent villas, led slightly downhill in the direction of the water.

He would have liked to go for a walk and get his bearings after supper, but found himself too travel-weary to stir. One fact had been constant at the back of his mind, since he'd learnt it from Mr. Emerson. Captain Selden had paid his visit to his aunt in late September but he'd been expected in the weeks preceding Christmas. His leave had been brought forward.

He'd learnt never to ignore his policeman's instinct, honed by years of careful observation. Something told him, that somehow, this change of plan was significant. It had to be, they'd found nothing unusual in Miss Chorley's life, except her nephew's visit. Selden coming to Seaborough had to be connected with the murders. Everything depended on his asking the right questions.

Twenty-six

A watery sun was breaking through the clouds as they turned into the main street. To the right, Abbs could see a parade of a dozen or so shops, their awnings down and quite a few people about their business. Sergeant Webber directed them left, towards a public-house on the corner, with a row of terraced cottages beyond.

'Netley doesn't appear to be a long-established village,' said Abbs pleasantly, as they walked.

Sergeant Webber beamed beneath his exuberant, waxed moustache. He seemed most enthusiastic about his charge. 'Why, sir, we've abbey ruins at the other end of the village.' He looked back, pointing out the way they'd come. 'What's more, there's a Tudor castle further along, built to guard the Water but that's a private residence.' Setting off again, he touched his hat as an elderly gentleman passed them.

'Mind, you're quite right, sir, there are no more old buildings here. The parish church was built about the same time as the Hospital. Netley's growing, it's considered a desirable place to settle. We've our share of folk living on their own means, who come for the healthy air. There are new houses going up for professional men. They can live in the country and take the railway to town, you see.'

They were now passing the last building on their right and drawing level with a shingle beach, opposite the cottages. Abbs stopped to take in the view. It was a morning of greys and silvers, the wide expanse of water almost merging with the clouds, shimmering intermittently in the weak sunlight. He could smell the salt and hear the haunting cry of a curlew.

'How far across is it?'

'Four mile, sir. There's the steamer off to the Island,' added Webber, pointing.

'The island?'

'Isle of Wight, sir, where Her Majesty's house is. The royal party sail from Pompey, that's Portsmouth.' The sergeant shook his head, as though lamenting the royal household's regrettable lapse. 'We always call it The Island in these parts. Now, here's the main gate up ahead, sir.'

Rather wishing he could be left to himself, Abbs quickened his pace until they reached the imposing double gates, a brick lodge at either side. Large lamps were affixed on top of the gate-posts and a wide drive, edged with young trees, curved beyond.

'We'll need your identification now, sir, if you don't mind waiting. Won't keep you a minute.'

Abbs looked about him with great interest. The Royal Victoria Military Hospital was on a far grander scale than he'd envisaged. The main building was visible away from the shore, set in vast lawns, divided by smaller drives. Red brick, rows of rounded windows, embellished with white stone, the Hospital stood three storeys high. The roof was surmounted by a white dome. A long wing stretched either side of the central block. At the corner, visible from where he stood, another wing stretched behind. He guessed there were further wings around a great quadrangle. The building was very like a barracks.

'All done, sir, you're expected. What do you make of it? Magnificent place, don't you think?' said Webber, without leaving space for an answer.

'It certainly is, Sergeant.'

They set off along the main drive, which took a sinuous path to the entrance. On their right, the lawns ended in a belt of scots pines. Abbs saw a wide, iron pier with its own formal gate, flanked by a pair of open shelters. They were very like the ones on the sea-front at Seaborough.

'That's where they bring the wounded in, sir,' remarked Webber. 'That's why the pier widens at the far end. Course, they can't take a ship in that close. Water's not deep enough near the shore. No, they take them off in tenders.'

'The Hospital is far larger than I expected,' said Abbs. 'I recall reading about it when it opened. When was that, exactly?' Sergeant Webber was sure to know.

'Ten years ago, sir. The Queen was present when they laid the foundation stone, back in '56. There are one hundred and thirty-eight wards, I do believe. Course, they're not full in times of peace.'

'What is that memorial?' said Abbs, turning his back on Southampton Water.

'Ah, now, that's very interesting, sir. It's to the medical officers who fell in the Crimea.'

It would help to be left alone, for a few minutes, to order his thoughts. He was unclear whether Captain Selden was to be found within the building, or at his home. Selden did not live in quarters. He was about to find out, thought Abbs, as they entered the reception-hall, at last.

He was directed to the adjutant's room, where the officer, clad in a scarlet tunic, was brisk and efficient.

'I understand, Inspector, you're inquiring as to the whereabouts of a Captain Edwin Selden.' He handed back Abbs's warrant, which he'd carefully examined. 'And this is in connection with the ah, unfortunate death of his relative?'

'That's correct, sir.'

The officer gave him a keen look, before fitting on his spectacles and untying a manila folder. Removing a sheet of printed headings and columns, filled in with ink, he studied it impassively.

Abbs looked at the painting on the wall behind the desk. Unlike the framed photographs, the subject was not military but depicted a mountainous scene, houses with verandas and lush greenery.

'Darjeeling,' said the adjutant, without raising his eyes. 'To the point.' Replacing the record, he gave Abbs his complete attention. 'Captain Selden has had an unblemished military record throughout long service, principally in India. In the opinion of his commanding officers, he is of good character.'

'That is not in dispute, sir.'

'Good. We don't want any of our number bringing Her Majesty's Army into disrepute. I trust that is understood, Inspector?'

'I'm here to put further questions to Captain Selden, as a witness. There has been a second murder, since his return to Netley.'

'In which case, presumably you wish to ascertain he was at his post here, at the relevant time?' The adjutant removed his spectacles.

'That would be helpful, sir.'

'Understood. Captain Selden comes under the Paymaster's department. He's responsible for an office of pay-clerks. They deal with payments for settling the affairs of soldiers from all over the Empire, sick pay, dependents, allowances accrued, that type of thing, and for the staff, of course. They handle all the bills from the purveyors' department for running this establishment. Although our purpose is medical, we are, in effect, an army base.'

'The scale of the Military Hospital seems remarkable, sir.'

'It is, Inspector. I very much doubt civilians could run an establishment on this scale. We can handle up to one thousand patients here, with the beds at full capacity. Cases may be surgical, medical, convalescent or all three.'

'This is all very interesting, but, forgive me. Is Captain Selden on duty at present, sir?'

The adjutant frowned. 'Captain Selden has not, in fact, returned to his desk since his leave ended. He lives in the village and has sent word he's

196

indisposed. Should this continue, he will be required to attend a medical here to decide if he is fit for duty. I believe that answers your question.' This was said with an air of finality.

'Thank you for your help, sir. I won't take up any more of your time.' Abbs rose to his feet, holding his hat. 'One thing, is it customary for officers to live outside the Hospital?'

'It's not uncommon, Inspector. We provide an accommodation block for all ranks, but once settled, some officers do care to buy a house in the village, particularly if they have private means. One thing we are short of is privacy.'

Abbs was about to leave when the adjutant spoke again. 'Look here, Inspector Abbs, I've no personal knowledge of Selden, only what I've read. But some officers are better suited to admin duties than active service, if you take my meaning. Can you find your way back to the entrance?'

Assuring him he could, Abbs pondered the adjutant's remark as he emerged from the echoing corridor into a lovely autumn day. The sun had come out fully in the short time he'd been inside. Bees were working busily among a bed of fading lavender, where Sergeant Webber was chatting to an orderly.

Breaking off his conversation, the sergeant sprang to attention. 'My word, that didn't take long. Where now, sir?'
Abbs held out a page in his notebook. 'If you might give me directions to this address, I'll need trouble you no further, Sergeant.'

'Can't do that, sir. Inspector Ruddock wouldn't like that at all. My orders are to give you every facility. I'll escort you right to the door and accompany you within, if you wish.'

'Thank you, Webber, that won't be necessary.' He conceded to the inevitable. 'Back the same way, I take it?'

'That's right, sir. Two streets back from the shore road. Did you get all the information you needed, might I inquire?'

'The adjutant was most accommodating. That's a handsome chapel over there.'

'Indeed it is, sir. Now the cemetery...' The sergeant actually lowered his voice, 'that's hidden way over the back of the grounds. Wouldn't do to have it seen from the wards.'

'No, I suppose not. Are the grounds extensive then, behind the main building?'

'Indeed, they are, sir. Would you care to see for yourself? I don't suppose anyone in authority would mind.'

'I cannot spare the time, Sergeant. It's imperative I get on my way back, as soon as my business here is concluded.' Abbs tried to inject a note of regret in his voice. Nevertheless, Webber's face fell.

'That's a real pity, sir. Down that way's the usual offices, you might say, the stables, laundry, stores. I don't suppose you expected them to have their own fire-station and gas-works?'

He hadn't given it any thought. 'I did not, Sergeant.'

'They've a post-office here, a brick-works, it's more like a town than a Hospital. Why the Army even have their own reservoir.' The sergeant broke off to raise a hand to the soldier on the gate.

With some further difficulty, Abbs persuaded Webber to part company near Selden's house. Assuring him he could find his way back to the railway-station, where he'd left his case, and thanking him for his assistance.

The street where Captain Selden lived was quiet and respectable. The semi-detached villas had a few feet of garden, separating them from the pavement, and their front doors in pairs. They were the province of clerks and elderly ladies.

Selden's was distinguishable only by its name, *Muree*, which stood oddly between *Ferndale, Mevagissey* and his next door neighbour, *Lomond*. Abbs rapped the knocker. After a moment, when no one came, he saw the lace twitch in the side of the modest bay window, close by him. The door opened cautiously and his quarry looked out.

'Inspector Abbs.' Captain Selden's voice was flat. 'You've come a long way to find me.'

'You don't sound surprised to see me, Captain.'

'Mr. Jerrold wrote to me. I know about Miss Geake's death.' Sighing, he held the door wider. 'You'd better come in.'

'Thank you.'

'Through here.'

Abbs took in the small hallway at a glance, as Shelden showed him in the nearest door. An etched shell-case was in use as a stand for sticks and umbrella. A console-table held a brass tray and peacock feathers in an ugly vase. Highly-polished boots stood beneath. A looking-glass hung on the dark, patterned paper.

'Do sit down.'

Rejecting the armchairs, Abbs took a seat at the small dining-table by the window. The fire was lit, the room felt unpleasantly warm on such a mild day. A rug was thrown over the arm of the chair with a foot-stool. Possibly, Captain

Selden really was unwell. Hard to say, as he was one of those men who never appeared to look robust.

'Can I offer you tea, Inspector?'

'I won't, thank you, sir.'

'Is that because you've come to arrest me?'

His tone wavered, thought Abbs, between nervy and bitter. 'It's because I've lately had some, Captain. Why should you believe you're about to be arrested?'

'I've no alibi for Miss Geake's death.'

'We require rather more grounds than that, sir. Innocent people very often have no alibi.'

Hope sparked in Selden's eyes and went out again. 'I wish to state, at once, that I did not kill the woman. I'm no murderer, Inspector.'

'Are you telling me that you left Seaborough on the morning we spoke and you've remained here in Netley, ever since?'

'I am, yes. I've been indisposed so haven't yet resumed my duties. In fact, I haven't left the house.'

'How do you manage about food?' said Abbs conversationally. 'You'd been away for some while.'

Captain Selden left off biting the side of his thumb-nail. 'I have a woman who comes in to do the rough work. She shops for me.'

Abbs nodded. 'I've just been to the Hospital and spoken to the adjutant. It was necessary to confirm your whereabouts.' Selden looked down at his hands, placing them beneath the table. 'Fortunately, you do have someone who can vouch for your presence here.' Selden's head jerked up but he made no comment.

Pushing his notebook and pencil across the table, Abbs continued. 'If you'll jot down your daily's address.'

'Look, she only came on my first day back. I'll write it if you wish.' He scribbled a direction and let the pencil fall. 'I know I can't prove my innocence. There would have been time.'

'Well, as I said, sir, not to worry. People don't have proof, more often than not.'

Selden looked properly at him, for the first time. 'How is your investigation faring, Inspector? Are you any nearer finding who poisoned my aunt?'

'Yes, I think so,' said Abbs quietly. 'We've cleared up one or two false leads. It's a terrible fact that a second murder invariably narrows it down and brings the answer closer.'

'I've given it a great deal of thought and still, can find no clue in the events of that last day.'

'Since you left, I've spoken to Mr. Emerson. He told me that your visit was unexpectedly brought forward. You didn't mention this in your original statement.'

'Did I not? I suppose it didn't seem relevant. It's true that my aunt asked me to stay over Christmas-tide and I had accepted.' He hesitated, looking down at his hands. 'After I'd done so, I was offered hospitality, more to my liking. I'm ashamed to say that renewing my acquaintance with my aunt seemed a great chore. One I couldn't avoid for ever, so I thought I'd get over and done with. I told her my leave had been cancelled over Christmas but I could visit her in September.'

'Thank you for clearing that up. What I'd like you to do now, if you please, is to go over everything Miss Chorley planned for your entertainment, during your stay.'

Fingering his half-hearted moustache, Selden considered. 'It's all slipping from my memory. The truth is, I didn't pay sufficient attention when she told me. Life can be one long, dreary round. Endlessly taking your time from the things you actually like doing.'

'You mentioned a dinner party?'

'Oh, yes, she planned that for my final evening. A different set of people from those who came to tea. I don't recall the guests mentioned, except she spoke of the Jerrolds. I hadn't met him at the time. Where else? We were to tour the Hospital. It was built in my grandfather's memory, my aunt's pet charity. I was rather dreading that.'

Abbs looked up from the earlier page in his notebook. Nothing new had emerged so far. 'Why was that, sir?'

Selden sighed. 'Because of my post here, my aunt thought I'd care to go over the Hospital accounts. It seemed terribly high-handed to me. I'm afraid that was her character.' He fiddled with one of the tassels edging the green tablecloth. 'You've probably gathered that my position in the Paymaster's office is somewhat less important than my aunt realised.'

'Can you think of anywhere else Miss Chorley intended you to visit, or people you were to meet?'

'She said something about visiting people near Kempston but I don't recall their name. There was talk of drives to beauty-spots, a concert at the Town-hall. I do care for music, particularly the Italians.' He smiled reminiscently. 'I can recall nothing else.'

'Moving on to Miss Geake,' said Abbs. 'Did you like her, Captain?'

'Liking didn't come into it. She was engaged as my aunt's companion. I scarcely noticed her.'

'Why did you change your mind about keeping Tower House open after your departure?'

'It was a simple act of kindness... for the staff, don't you know? They needed time to arrange their futures. I could hardly put them out on the street.'

'The servants tell me you intended to have the house shut up, directly the funeral was over. After all, why pay their wages to no purpose?'

'Look here, Inspector. You can't call me to account for every little decision. It has no bearing on your investigation. What business is it of yours?'

'My business is murder, Captain Selden. You know, servants see much more than people ever realise. But then, you do know that, don't you?'

To Abbs's horror, Selden's eyes glistened. He studied the curious wall-plaques of Indian faces, as he put his next question. 'What hold did Miss Geake have over you?'

The glass-domed clock on the mantel-shelf sounded the half-hour, as he waited. He could see the resemblance in the two cousins now. It was there in the line of the profile and the same delicacy of manner. Selden hesitated. 'I don't know where to begin.'

'Is your friend here with you now?' said Abbs quietly. Selden's instinctive glance at the ceiling was answer enough.

'How did you know?'

'The boots in the hall. Two pairs, different sizes.'

'You must understand, Inspector, I have a friend staying for a few days, while he finds other accommodation. That's all.'

'Tell me about Miss Geake, Captain. I'm afraid I must know what passed between you.'

Swallowing, his voice low, Selden began to speak. 'She found a travelling-frame, I had. It contained a photograph of a dear friend. By day, I placed it in the drawer nearest my bed. I had nothing to hide but I value my privacy. She searched my things, there's no other possible explanation. Indeed, she did not deny it.' He looked warily at Abbs. 'I don't need to spell out what she said, do I? She was too clever to say very much. I've no idea who killed her, Inspector, but I'd shake them by the hand. She was a vicious female.'

'Did she ask you for money, sir?'

Selden shook his head. 'She only remarked how inconvenient it would be to have to move out, before it suited her. She enjoyed having power over me. I could see it in her eyes. The look a cat has when it's toying with a mouse, but that was all it amounted to.'

'I don't think there's much doubt that she asked your aunt's murderer for money,' murmured Abbs, almost to himself.

'That occurred to me when I received Mr. Jerrold's letter. Do you think she knew who killed my aunt from the beginning?'

'We may never know for certain. I think Miss Geake worked it out over the subsequent days. She may have recalled some small action, which seemed insignificant at the time, and put two and two together.'

'Inspector, I have to ask you, what action are you going to take now?'

'I'm going back to Seaborough, to gather enough evidence to arrest the murderer.'

'I mean about me. I can't bear the uncertainty.'

Abbs studied his notebook. 'I must thank you for your help, Captain. Speaking to you again has clarified my thoughts. Mayhap, being distanced from Seaborough has proved beneficial. There's a lot to be said for standing back.'

Selden looked at him. A tic was fluttering by his left eye. 'My heartiest thanks, Inspector, I don't know what else to say. If there's ever anything I may do for you...'

'Not necessary, sir. I must be on my way but there's something I should like to tell you. It concerns the young photographer you visited with Miss Chorley. I daresay you recall Mr. Philip Winton?'

Twenty-seven

Reeve apparently had the knack of cultivating easy friendships. It was not a talent he had himself, thought Abbs. As a young police constable based in a village, he had known everyone. That was essential in order to do his job, yet he was apart from his neighbours.

His upbringing, the son of a head gardener on a country estate, had set him out of step with his fellows. Not quite one of the village children, sons of agricultural labourers for the most part. Set just a little above the other estate workers' offspring, after being noticed by and put to study with the rector. The unlooked-for distinction had not lasted more than a year. The parents of his fellow pupils objected to his presence among their sons and his extra tuition came to a sudden end.

Reeve was sharing a joke with Dean, as they made tea for the four of them. The sergeant was one of those easy-going men who would make himself at home anywhere, while he would remain an outsider.

Calling in at the police-station, well into the previous evening, he was told the two of them were having a drink in one of the town's taverns. Declining the offer of a mug of cocoa from the constable yawning over the front desk, he'd returned to the Anchor.

When he'd caught up with Reeve, he'd glanced around his room with ill-concealed distaste. Scattered with clothing, periodicals, the contents of pockets and even a paper bag, bearing the evidence of a snack.

On the return journey, he'd had long hours to test his theory. But it was too late at night to give Reeve more than a hint of what he'd worked out in Netley.

He'd suggested the others join them as their local knowledge would be invaluable. Sitting round the desk in Sergeant Tancock's office, where there was more room, Abbs moved some folders as Constable Dean poured out their tea.

'Did you have any difficulty in compiling this list, Reeve?'

'None at all, sir. I had to journey to Kempston, where a lady clerk at the registrar's office was very helpful, once she saw my authority.'

'These are all the deaths in Seaborough this year, not including our murders?'

'There were a few infants as well, sir, as you'd expect, but you said to ignore them.'

'I can't say as I get it, sir. Why d'you want to see them?' Craning his neck, Sergeant Tancock read the list.

Abbs swivelled it a little in his direction. 'A fishing expedition, Sergeant. It struck me that our poisoner might just have had reason to kill previously. I thought it wouldn't hurt to look through deaths in the town. They were driven to kill again, almost certainly because Miss Geake had power of life and death over them. It's possible someone earlier stood in their way and that death passed unquestioned, as Miss Chorley's almost did.'

'If you say so, sir.' Sergeant Tancock looked unconvinced. 'But I don't reckon we've had anyone else poisoned.'

'I'm looking for what appear to be natural deaths, Sergeant,' said Abbs patiently.

'We do things thoroughly in the detective-branch,' said Reeve, a touch of patronage in his manner. Abbs gave him a severe look.

Constable Dean leaned across, addressing him with marked enthusiasm. 'They say murder's easier after the first time. Do you want us to tell you anything we know about these names, sir?'

'If you would, Constable, facts regarding their demise, at any rate. We'll start with the most recent death. A Mrs Mary-Jane Wharton, age at death, sixty-five. Ring any bells, either of you?'

'Wharton,' said Tancock, nodding. 'She lived in one of those houses along Marine View.'

'According to this, she died of heart disease.'

'That's right. Had that watery fat, she did. Her daughter used to push her along the prom in a bath-chair.'

'Do you know if there was any money?'

'She were a widow. Went to her children, a married son and the daughter.'

Abbs considered briefly. 'That seems perfectly straightforward. Elizabeth Marker, aged nineteen? Poor girl.'

Tancock shook his head. 'Don't know of her, sir.'

'Cause of death, phthisis, lung disease in other words. No, there's nothing for us there. The death before that was an Albert Pardoe, aged one-and-forty, cause of death, internal injuries from fall. Dr. Miller again.'

The two Seaborough men exchanged glances. 'No one poisoned him for his money,' said Tancock. 'More likely he died owing.'

'We all knew Bert Pardoe, sir,' said Constable Dean. 'We'd had to take him in a few times. Causing a public nuisance while he was drunk.'

'You mentioned him on the morning the cells were overflowing?' said Abbs, his face clearing.

'That's right, sir. He worked with the same lot, Halesworth's men, the builder's.'

'I recall seeing their cart outside the Hospital.'

'You see them all over the place,' said Dean. 'They're the biggest builders in town. Bert Pardoe fell from the scaffolding on a roof they were tiling.'

'Was he drunk, then?' put in Reeve.

Sergeant Tancock drained his tea. 'Not at work, Caleb Halesworth wouldn't stand for that. No, I talked to them all. Turned out he'd been complaining of feeling bad. His missus were that shook up. I were there when they fetched her, poor body. Just shows, he used to knock her about. Not often, mind, he were a good husband to her.'

'Can a man who takes his fist to a woman be described in those terms?' said Abbs, in the driest of tones.

'He were in his way, sir. You know what they say, *'A dog, a wife an' a walnut tree, the more you beat 'em, the better they be.'* Not that I hold with thrashing dogs or horses,' said Tancock virtuously. 'We've a collecting-box for dumb animals on the counter.'

'Mrs Pardoe's a decent sort,' said Constable Dean. 'She's friendly with my ma. They work together up at the Hospital laundry.'

'How about Joseph Colman, aged thirty-eight? Cause of death, shotgun injuries.'

'We remember that,' said Constable Dean. 'Don't we, Sergeant?'

Tancock grunted. 'B.... fool. Shot himself. Still, that's farmers for you. Always got an easy way out to hand.'

'Why did he do it?' asked Reeve brightly.

He gave no indication of a sore head, thought Abbs, nor did Dean. Whereas, at not yet forty, he was feeling stiff from two days folded in a railway-carriage.

'Woman trouble, what else?' said Tancock. 'He were about to lose his tenancy. He only farmed in a small way, His missus ran off with another man and he let everything go. He took to drink an' all. No one murdered him for his money, that's certain.'

'Before him was Amos Turl?' said Abbs, looking round the table.

'Sorry, sir, never heard of him.'

'No matter. Aged eighty-eight, cause of death, decline. I think we might rule him out. Perhaps I am making bricks without straw.' He saw Sergeant Tancock's face express agreement. 'However, we may as well go through the remainder.'

When they finished, Tancock stretched and got slowly to his feet. 'Anything else you need me for, Inspector?'

'Not for the present, thank you, Sergeant. You'll soon be able to have your room back. We're returning to Exeter on the morrow.'

'Really, sir, does this mean you're giving up? Only what'll I say, should folks ask?'

'You can tell them our inquiries here are concluded for the present. Now, I'd like to borrow Dean, if I may? Sergeant Reeve and I will pay a last call at Tower House and there's one other person we need to see. Dean, can you get me the list of items removed from the house, on the day after Miss Chorley's death?'

'Certainly, sir. All the food was sent for analysis.'

'Thank you, Constable, the list will suffice.'

~

'To think of all the times we've sat at this table and shared a pot of tea,' said Bessie Watkins. 'End of an era, you might say.'

'I don't like change, it's true. I'll miss you m'dear but I wish you well in your new life, knowing you'll be happier.' Patting her old friend's arm, Hannah regarded her affectionately.

'I shall miss you, you've been a good friend, Hannah. You'll write and tell me all the news?'

'Of course and I shall want to hear all about Tunbridge Wells.'

Bessie cut herself a second slice of plum cake. 'I'll be agog to hear who did the murders, that's if they ever find out. I were certain sure Miss Geake poisoned the mistress.'

'I mind it well.'

'Those two detectives didn't stay above a quarter-hour. They went up to the mistress's room but I don't know what for.' She shivered between mouthfuls. 'Tisn't like the same place, you know. Mr. Jerrold's had men in, rolling up the carpets and stacking the pictures against the walls. The library shelves are empty and the furniture's covered in dust-sheets. The rooms are all hollow somehow.'

'What that great place needs is a proper family to take it, with little ones running in and out of the garden. Bring a bit of life up there.'

'Captain Selden didn't want it. I s'pose he has his own life all settled. He'll want the money it'll fetch though.'

'You haven't heard if anyone's buying it?' Busily chewing, the cook shook her head. 'So did the others get suited in the end?'

'After a fashion. Sarah's all right, o'course. That kind always fall on their feet. I daresay her parents wouldn't want her back for good. But they'll take her 'til she's wed, if she earns her keep. She's a good little lace-maker, learned at her mother's knee. William's staying on over the stables for a time, to keep an eye on the property. The gardeners have been paid off. That leaves young Jane. Her mother will take her in on sufferance, but she'll be sharing with her three sisters, and you wouldn't believe how much that girl eats.'

'If you like, I could get Miss Adelaide to ask if any family needs a kitchen-maid? She'd be pleased to get her a good position.'

'I'm sure Jane would take that as a great kindness. Tell her she's an honest girl. She might be slow but she's ever so obliging. Doesn't mind any rough work.'

'I'll ask her directly. She can enquire at the Ladies' meeting.'

'I'm sorry to hear the vicar's no better, and not to hear him preach one last time.'

'It's distressed him terribly to miss a service. And old Reverend Tomlin, who steps in, likes to give a good hour and a quarter's sermon. It was standing outside with Miss Geake's body, God rest her, that made him worse. He talks of saying prayers where she was found, but he can't leave his bed. Who would ever have thought such a thing would come to pass in Seaborough?'

'You didn't sense it, then, Hannah? Before I go, I wonder if you'd just take a look, tell me what you see? Go on, do.'

'Very well, Bessie. I can't promise anything but you know what to do, m'dear.'

Finishing her tea, the cook turned her cup upside down, rotating it thrice on its saucer. Her eyes sparkled with relish as she slid it across the kitchen table.

Twenty-eight

It had been easier than he'd feared, thought Abbs, to get his superior to listen. Superintendent Nicholls's first assumption had been that they'd 'come back with their tails between their legs,' as he put it. Bracing himself for a gruelling encounter, Abbs had put his case for an exhumation order.

The contemptuous outburst had been expected. Nicholls though, was no fool. He'd risen to his high rank by getting results. Known throughout the city as a formidable thief-taker, a murder of quality had rarely come his way. Eventually, Abbs had seen the slow smile spread across his features, the workings of his mind as predictable as a clock.

If Abbs was right, Nicholls could contrive to take the credit. If he was wrong... after causing such trouble and expense on a 'half-baked, crackpot notion,' his time as a detective, at least in Exeter, would be over.

'You realise it'll have to go all the way to the Home Secretary's office?' he'd growled. His cold gone, Nicholls's voice was back to its biting worst. Patiently, he'd said yes and no in the required places, until the Superintendent had agreed to make an appointment for them to see the Chief Constable, at his home outside the city.

There, Abbs had reiterated his inquiry, step by step. Fortunately, the Chief Constable, a former military man, had understood it was the only way to get the evidence that would convict. The telegram of assent had returned from the capital and the necessary arrangements had been made.

Dr. Chisholm, their Exeter police-surgeon, was in their party. Of the Seaborough contingent, only Sergeant Tancock and Constable Dean were to be present. The undertakers were coming from Kempston, it being imperative that Mr. Hicks was unaware of their enterprise.

A dark shadow detached itself from the line of trees along the perimeter and picked its way to Abbs. 'Cold night, sir, still, it's nearly November.' Reeve thrust his hands in his jacket pocket, as he spoke.

'It is but I'm hoping the wind will hold off the rain. I've been watching the clouds blow, they're moving fast. Any sign, yet?'

'Not yet, sir, we should hear them soon. Sergeant Tancock sent me to ask if you'd care for a nip to keep out the chill? He's brought a flask of brandy.'

'Not for me, Reeve. I trust he'll remain alert. We don't want him falling in the open grave.'

Reeve grinned. 'It'll be a nightmare for the men if it does rain.' The church clock began to chime, followed a few seconds later by the one at the town-hall.

As they finished, the faint clop of hooves replaced them in the darkness. 'I'll go and meet them, sir.'

Abbs remained where he was, watching the stars, which were there and not there, as the clouds raced across the sky.

Presently, an irregular line of lights came bobbing towards him like glow-worms, as men, encumbered with equipment and holding up lanterns, drew near. He went to have a word with them, ensuring they had their instructions.

Canvas screens were positioned on two sides of the grave, even though they were a distance from the road. Lamps were hung on poles, sacking laid on the grass and the men began to dig. They worked in silence, save the odd grunt of effort. The man nearest Abbs soon broke off to remove his jacket, the fustian stale with pipe tobacco.

'This is going to take a while, Inspector,' murmured the undertaker. A broad-shouldered man in a heavy cape, he held his lamp aloft. 'I'd recommend a handkerchief when we unscrew the lid.'

After a few words, Abbs wandered aimlessly between the new graves. From a little distance, the glow of lamplight, and the shadows behind the screen, looked like a camp-fire. He waited by a carved angel, its stone cold to the touch. His wife had a similar memorial. Not his choice, it was too elaborate, but her family had wished it.

Back in Exeter, he'd visited Ellen's grave, reading the lines he knew by heart. He'd said a kind of silent good-bye to them both. For he'd finally admitted to himself that he wasn't mourning his dead wife any longer. The dull weight he carried was not grief. Sorry, though he was, that she and the new-born infant were dead. His burden was guilt.

He knew he wasn't the first young man to have mistaken a pretty face and winning manner for something much deeper. Shivering in the chill night, Abbs remembered meeting Ellen, the nursery-maid, travelling with her employers while they visited acquaintance in Norfolk. How quickly he'd wanted to make her his wife.

So much so, he'd transferred to the other side of the country for her. She hadn't been prepared to leave her family and move to Norfolk for him. Within a year, he'd understood his mistake. Everyone had a duty to make the best of their lot in life, and so he had. They'd lived together well enough. He did not believe she had ever known.

A thud of pick on ground recalled him to his surroundings. The bank of earth along the graveside was now considerable. Someone exclaimed as their spade hit an obstruction, followed at once by the chink of metal.

Abbs went to stand with Reeve and Sergeant Tancock. Constable Dean had remained by the gate with the conveyances, lest anyone should wonder what was afoot. They watched the undertaker as he directed his men to scrape the lid clear of earth, holding his lamp lower to read the name-plate.

An unpleasant, sucking sound made one of the work-men shudder, as the coffin, reluctant to tear free from the red Devonshire clay, was lifted sufficiently to get ropes underneath. Finally, after much effort, the box was laid on trestles and the men bent over the screws.

'Wait for the stink,' said Tancock.

Abbs watched the moon above the spire of the chapel, his fists clenched against what they would find. If he was right, they would know at once. Reeve shivered, his eyes intent on the widening gap as the lid was moved.

There was no smell. Dr. Chisholm blocked their view, while the undertaker held a lamp steady for him. Straightening up, he beckoned the two of them to come closer.

'You were right, Abbs. I shall do the tests, of course, but there's no doubt in my mind. Arsenic kills the bacteria in the body that would begin putrefaction. Thus where it is present, the corpse is unnaturally preserved. After several weeks, it should be smelling to high heaven and looking very different from this. Come, don't look so worried, see for yourself.' Abbs and Reeve moved to one side of the open coffin. 'That greenish tinge is a surface mould that's got in from outside.'

The two detectives stared down at the ghastly, waxen features.

Sergeant Tancock joined them. 'Swipe me. I never thought to see Bert Pardoe again.'

Three more days passed, waiting first, for the test results and then for the warrant to be obtained from a city magistrate. Abbs could not rid himself of a bad feeling, a presentiment of gathering trouble. Dr. Chisholm's report had confirmed what they'd seen in the cemetery at Seaborough. Arsenic deposits had been found in the hair and fingernails. The powders, given them by Mrs Pardoe, had been harmless but the box bore a faint trace of arsenic.

In late afternoon on the fourth day, Abbs and Reeve left for Seaborough for the last time, taking with them, burly Constable Franks from the Exeter division. Dusk was falling by the time they descended from the train.

They were met by a sombre Sergeant Tancock and once again, escorted to the small police-station near the sea. Beside him, Constable Dean looked wan and uneasy. Brought face to face with the reality of detective-work, it was not the swaggering adventure Reeve had described.

'I still can't hardly believe it, sir,' said Tancock. 'Begging your pardon, there's no chance you could have it wrong?'

Abbs shook his head, recognising that concern, rather than insolence, prompted the sergeant's remarks 'No chance whatever, Sergeant. I'm certain of the chain of events. The Chief Constable and the magistrate are satisfied.'

'But why finish off Bert Pardoe? How could he gain by that?'

'Pardoe was blackmailing him. He must have seen something while he was working there or possibly, when fetching his wife. We saw Mrs Pardoe on the day we left. Her husband sometimes waited for her on the day she was paid. She found money hidden among her husband's things. She was able to tell us enough to justify the exhumation order.'

'There's plenty in this town will be staggered. He were liked, you know.'

Tancock was talking as though their quarry was already dead. The sergeant's voice faded. There was no more to say. The shadow of the rope lay on the counter between them.

'Where is he to be found, Sergeant?'

'He's not at home, sir, nor at the Marine when we checked.'

There was only one place he was likely to be. Abbs rather thought they were expected. He turned to Reeve, Dean and Constable Franks, waiting stolidly by the entrance. 'It's time to go, gentlemen.'

Rain was coming on, the sea near invisible. He could smell the brine, hear the waves washing the shingle. A lamp-lighter was beginning his work in the square. The trees were bare now, the grass swept clear of leaves, since their previous visit. They'd reached the last weeks of autumn, the year was quietly dying. A sad, reflective time, it always seemed to him, before the gaiety of Christmastide.

When they reached their destination, he left Franks stationed by the main door. The police conveyance remained in a side-street, unseen from the windows. Abbs directed Constable Dean to the rear of the building, with instructions to watch the back exits.

He looked at Reeve, tense by his side, as they stood just inside the entrance. 'Remember, we need a confession. If I read him aright, he's more likely to talk here, than in a cell. I think he'll need to tell someone.'

'They always like to justify themselves,' said Reeve bitterly. 'What if he makes a run for it, sir? This place is a regular warren. He could get away in the dark.'

'He'll come quietly. Where could he go? Ready?'

Reeve squared his shoulders, flexed his fingers, curving them loosely as though ready to spar. 'More than ready, sir.'

The building was very quiet. Lamps were burning dimly on either side of the corridor, a shadow glimpsed through a door. A stifled cough. No one challenged them.

And there, at the far end, was the door on the left. Abbs turned the brass knob, it opened and they were within. The gas-mantle was turned down, an oil-lamp, on the desk, cast a pool of light for writing. A dark frock-coat was hung round the back of the chair.

The room's occupant was standing at the other door with his back to them, gazing out at the rainy night. Slowly, Dr. Gilbert Avery turned towards them.

For a moment, no one spoke. The two detectives remained by the door. Abbs was shocked at the doctor's haggard appearance, his eyes hollowed and red with lack of sleep. He stood in his linen, his cuffs loosened. a wickedly sharp-looking surgical knife dangled from his hand. He let out a hissing breath and Abbs realised that he too, had been holding his.

'Well, gentlemen,' Dr. Avery inclined his head. 'Do I assume you come to consult me and offer you tea?'

'It's too late for that, Doctor,' said Abbs.

Lowering his eyelids for a second, Avery gave a wry half-smile, little more than a twitching of the lips. 'I gathered as much. Really, Abbs, you've learnt nothing about this godforsaken town, if you imagined I wouldn't hear about your late night visit to the cemetery.'

'Why not put down the knife, Doctor?'

'What a soothing voice you have, Inspector. A better bedside manner than I ever did. But I don't believe I will.' Avery held out his forefinger, drawing the point of the knife along its side. A thread of crimson sprang instantly in a line. 'Stay over there, if you please.' He pointed the knife in their direction.

'We're in no hurry,' said Abbs, in a neutral tone.

'You know, I couldn't be sure when you would come,' said Avery conversationally. 'Though I reckoned on your discretion. I waited here for you last evening.'

'We needed the test results on Albert Pardoe's body.'

'Ah, of course. A greedy fool who's no loss to this world.'

'It didn't give you the right to kill him.' Reeve couldn't stop himself bursting out. Glancing apologetically at Abbs, he subsided as quickly.

'Oh, I didn't kill him, Sergeant.' His back to the window-sill, Avery regarded them steadily, his right hand grasping the knife-handle.

'We have enough evidence to see you convicted of Pardoe's murder,' said Abbs. 'His wife still had the box of powders you gave him.'

'You've done well.' Avery shrugged. 'I may have given Pardoe a helping hand but I did him a favour. Put him out of his misery, as I would a dog.' He studied their uncomprehending faces and sighed. 'He was dying, anyway. All right, Abbs, I'll tell you what you want to know. It'll be a relief in some ways.'

Abbs sensed Reeve give a flicker of acknowledgement. He'd planted himself against the door, his arms folded.

'Pardoe was snooping about outside one day. Probably hoping for something left lying around, or trying to spy on one of the nurses. He was a repellent individual who would lie in wait for his wife, on the day she was paid for her work in the laundry here.

Incidentally, Sergeant, if you'd seen the bruises on her arms, you wouldn't be so quick to defend him. He spied in this window and saw me with the safe door open and a cash-box on the desk. He caught me removing bank-notes and putting them in my pocket-book.' Avery's eyes narrowed, as though seeing that day again. 'He let himself in the door here, grinning with pleasure, and set about blackmailing me.

Naturally, I tried my d.......t to convince him I was acting properly. Taking the money to pay in the bank, but he wouldn't have it. We'd had a fête here the previous week, raising money for the new wing. The cash-box contained the proceeds. He was a thief himself, you see, and thought he'd recognised a kindred spirit. It amused him, no end, to see someone of my class behaving like him.

He said it made us equals and we could do one another a good turn.' Avery spat out the words. 'Pardoe was beyond all convincing of my innocence. What made it worse, was he'd seen me at a card-table in Kempston. He knew I was a gambler. I had to give him some money, there and then, to get rid of him. I couldn't allow myself to be blackmailed. You must see that? I felt like a rat cornered in a pit.'

'What do you mean by saying Pardoe was dying, anyway?' said Abbs quietly. He willed Reeve not to say anything that would stop Avery talking.

The doctor made a dismissive gesture with his empty hand. 'While he was taunting me and demanding money, he suddenly doubled up with the gripes. He said he had constant indigestion, blaming it on his wife's cooking. He begged me to give him something to ease the pain.' Avery smiled coldly. 'Pardoe had no fear of me at all. I had a paper containing arsenic compound in my drawer there. It was the work of a second to push it in a box of stomach-powders.'

'His wife could have taken it,' said Reeve, stiff with indignation.

Avery looked indifferent. 'That didn't occur to me, I confess. The compound was sufficient to kill him in one dose. If I wasn't sent for, I knew his death would be taken for gastric trouble. Who would poison a labourer? As it turned out, the symptoms came on when he was up on scaffolding. He lost his balance. I freed myself.

But you wanted an explanation of my remark. I questioned him briefly. From his symptoms, I'm fairly sure he had cancer of the stomach. I'm not as inhumane as you think, Sergeant Reeve.'

'Had you been embezzling the hospital funds for long?' said Abbs.

'Long enough. The subscriptions for the new wing put a lot more money in my way. I thought I'd covered my tracks well.'

'Oh, you did. For a long while, we had no idea.'

'How did you come to suspect me?'

They might have been having a discussion in the bar at the Marine Hotel, thought Abbs. He was aware of Reeve, staring at Avery in disgust.

'When we discovered Captain Selden's arrival had been brought forward. His visit was the only unusual event in Miss Chorley's life. I started wondering if the change in date could have made a difference to someone. We still didn't see who, or in what way, until I went to see Captain Selden at his home. I needed to confirm his whereabouts at the time of Miss Geake's murder, or I might not have done so.' The small amount of colour drained from Avery's features as he listened intently, his eyes fixed on Abbs. 'He told me Miss Chorley wanted him to look over the Hospital accounts.'

'And you pieced it together? Congratulations, Inspector. That arrogant, interfering old woman signed her own death warrant. If she'd been content to leave the Hospital in my hands, I'd have made good the money and she, none the wiser. But she had to show off her charity. I thought I had three months but the nephew, coming early, forced my hand. You might say he killed her.'

Abbs shifted his weight, tension in every muscle. He felt the contempt radiating from Reeve, the greater because he'd liked the police-surgeon.

'Don't come any nearer, either of you. I find myself in no hurry to be condemned. My mind has been a prison these past weeks. I never set out to kill anyone. Events forced this on me.'

The knife wavered, a sudden spat of rain on the glass made Avery flinch. His wrist shook for an instant.

Abbs saw rivulets of water run down the window and half-glazed door. Their reflections seemed to look back at him, the lamplight making it impossible to see outside, where darkness had fallen. He wondered how close Constable Dean was.

Dr Avery spoke again. 'Have you worked out how I did it?'

'Yes,' said Abbs simply. 'We were looking in the wrong direction. Concentrating on the people Miss Chorley saw that day. That was a distraction, like a conjuring trick. You poisoned one of the headache powders you prescribed for her, so you had no idea when she would die. You didn't need to. You would be called in and sign the death certificate. All that mattered was that Miss Chorley died before she could ask her nephew to look over the accounts. But your plan went wrong, when you were called away on the night of her death, and the servant had to fetch Dr. Miller.'

'I knew she'd take the arsenic soon enough. She was always dosing herself for imaginary ailments. Miller had no suspicion. The pompous ass made a fuss out of spite.'

'You claim you never set out to kill anyone,' said Abbs. 'Yet you'd prepared arsenic, had it at hand in your desk. You cold-bloodedly planted poison among medicine for two people. The third, you bludgeoned. That's premeditated murder.'

'I was desperate, I tell you.' Avery's voice rang with anguish. 'Three unpleasant individuals have departed this earth. Weigh that against all the good I've done. I owed money left hand and right. Still do. My house is gone when a promissory note falls due. I've wagered everything I have and lost.'

'You had a pile of sporting papers in here, on the day we met,' said Abbs. 'It didn't seem important at the time, but you swept them away hurriedly, and that made me notice. Then, when I saw you out ratting, you looked like a different man. What happened when your face was bruised?'

'Something you don't know?' Avery breathed shallowly, his chest rising and falling. 'I'd been at a game in Kempston, losing heavily all day. I already owed some people there but my luck had to change. When I left The Golden Lion, I was set upon by ruffians, in the yard behind. It's what happens when you can't pay your debts. I knew then my entire life was collapsing, as surely as a house of cards. To confound my ill luck, Halesworth saw me on the train.'

Reeve had left the door and edged a foot forward, by his side. Abbs wondered if Avery had noticed the bulge of hand-cuffs in the sergeant's pocket. He wanted to stretch out his arm and warn Reeve back. Avery, too, had backed fractionally nearer the outer door. Abbs knew his willingness to talk would not last much longer.

'What about Miss Geake?' said Reeve. 'How did she know what you'd done?'

Avery's face hardened. 'Naturally, she knew about the old woman's powders. She'd given her one that last day, after the guests departed. Eventually, she guessed. There was no proof but the accusation would have been enough. I couldn't let her repeat her suspicions to anyone.'

'Did she threaten to tell us?'

He shook his head. 'Nothing so public-spirited, Sergeant. She wanted money, of course. Doesn't everyone?' He studied their faces, as they remained silent. 'Miss Geake didn't care what I'd done. She hated her employer. She offered her silence, in return for enough money to set herself up. As if I had it...' The doctor began a bitter laugh, that died in disgust.

'What happened to the weapon?' demanded Reeve.

Dashing a hand over his brow, Avery looked exhausted, his knife-hand lowering a little. 'I despatched her with my fishing priest. It's back with my tackle.' His shoulders were slumping. Raising his head, he half-smiled at Abbs. 'I was minded to open the veins in my wrists. They say it's an easy death but I couldn't bring myself to begin. Then I heard your footsteps. No arsenic left, you see.'

'I can't let you...' began Abbs, taking a step forward.

'Stay back, both of you.' Avery jerked the knife at them. 'I warn you, this is scalpel-sharp. I'll use it on one of us, if I have to.'

'Why the gambling, Doctor?' said Abbs. 'You had a respected position in this town.'

'Because I was bored, Abbs.' He flung out his words, his voice rising. 'You couldn't begin to understand how frustrating my life has been. I don't heal people. I've spent years patching the poor, when what they need is money, and lackeying to the fat, idle rich with their imaginary headaches and their gout. Everyone else is on the fiddle in this town. Why shouldn't I have money and live a little? At least, risking everything, on the turn of a card, made me feel alive. At least, I've been no hypocrite. Miss Chorley lived high on rents from hovels in the filthiest rookery in Exeter.'

As his words poured out, Avery reached his free hand for the door-knob. 'I'll not hang, Abbs. For pity's sake, let me die in my...'

Reeve lunged at Avery, intent on disarming him. Knocking Abbs almost off his feet, as he flew past. As he reached the doctor, one hand wrenching his free arm, the other fist raised to punch, Avery twisted sideways, thrusting the thin blade in Reeve's chest.

Afterwards, Abbs felt as though everything had been suspended in time. As he threw himself across the room, in his turn, he caught one glimpse of Avery's white face, as he wrenched open the door and plunged into the night. The door banged and rain swept in.

Crumpled on his side, a dreadful wheezing sound was coming from Reeve's throat. Kneeling, desperately heaving him over, Abbs felt the dark stain spreading across his linen. The knife was not there.

Reeve's eyes were on him. He was trying to speak.

Tearing off his frock-coat, Abbs frantically bunched the material hard against the wound. 'You're going to be all right, Ned. Stay still. Don't try to speak.' Grabbing his whistle, Abbs blew until Dean appeared in the doorway, his face twisted with shock.

Footsteps were running along the corridor towards them.

Thirty

A month later

The impressive edifice of the cathedral loomed ahead of them, its intricately carved west front lit by the afternoon sun. The frost on the surrounding lawns had lingered all day and the sunlight, though cheerful, had no warmth about it.

The man leaving the Royal Clarence Hotel, one of the old buildings edging the Close, was listening intently to the lady at his side. He neglected to offer his arm as they began to stroll to the far end of the walk.

Inspector Josiah Abbs and Miss Adelaide Shaw had drunk tea and crumbled cake, in company with her father, Mr. Shaw having business in Exeter. They had cordially discussed anything, other than the deaths that had taken place in Seaborough that autumn.

'My father will miss his roses.' Adelaide halted by a flower-border, where a few buds hung browned and ruined. 'It's a pity these never had a chance to flower.'

'Will you have no garden in London?'

'Only a very small one, I believe. I have never visited my Aunt Shaw's house. But we shall be happy in Bloomsbury. My father will have his books and he intends to obtain a ticket for the reading-room at the British Museum. He will enjoy seeing the antiquities.' Adelaide smiled resolutely at him.

'I do hope so,' said Abbs. He wanted to ask if he might write to her, but the words remained unspoken.

'With his years, he could not return to his parish duties as before. You saw how easily he tires now. Papa made light of it to you, but we feared he would not come through.'

Abbs nodded gravely, thinking the treasures in the great museums were all very well. But Mr. Shaw would never again explore a hill-fort or find an arrow-head on ploughed earth.

'I'm sorry about your sergeant.' He could see the concern in her eyes as she faced him. 'He was very brave.'

Reeve's foolhardiness d... near got himself killed. As his superior, he felt responsible. Abbs knew Reeve had admired Avery. He'd felt betrayed, determined to arrest the police-surgeon. He blamed himself for not reining Reeve in.

'He received a commendation, last year, for saving a child's life. He snatched a small girl from under the hooves of a coach-and-four. That's why he was promoted to sergeant early.'

'How is he faring?'

'He's on the mend now. They were worried about infection. Fortunately, Reeve's young and strong. He should make a full recovery.'

'He was very kind on the day I found Miss Geake's body. Does he have family to care for him?' Abbs shook his head. To his shame, he did not know.

'Perhaps my father and I might visit him, if he's still in the Infirmary?'

'I'm sure he'd be glad to have visitors.'

'I shall always think Dr. Avery was responsible for ruining my father's health. If Papa hadn't stayed by the body, when he had a chill, it wouldn't have turned to pneumonia.'

Her voice had that hard edge of someone struggling to contain their emotions. She turned away, her face hidden by the edge of her bonnet. Abbs wondered if she would always associate him with that time, with bloodstains and corpses. He feared she probably would.

'I don't believe the doctor intended to wound Sergeant Reeve,' he said gently. 'Everything happened in such confusion. He was trying to get away.'

'I'm sorry, that wasn't very Christian of me. I hope they're all at peace, including him.'

Abbs was silent, remembering that terrible evening when they thought they'd lost Reeve. Sergeant Tancock's men had searched all night. They'd found the knife outside. It was well into the next morning before Dr. Avery's mangled body had been found at low-tide, on the rocks at the foot of the cliffs.

An old lady was scattering seed for the pigeons. A nanny stopped to watch, with her two charges, the children muffled against the cold. Beyond them, a flurry of rooks rose, cawing from the trees in the garden of the Bishop's Palace.

Adelaide lifted her head, watching them soar about the cathedral towers.

'Mr. Hicks has taken Gyp, the doctor's dog. They feared he would pine but he's settled well, Fanny says.'

'That's kind of them.'

'The Halesworths are buying Tower House.' She smiled. 'Mrs Halesworth is very nearly satisfied. Only she would have liked to be head of the Ladies Society and that has gone to Mrs Jerrold.'

And Adelaide had her chance of a new life, though not in a way she would have wanted. She would make the best of it, he knew, and mayhap, she would find someone to marry in London.

'Do you remember Mr. Biggs, Mr. Hicks's clerk? I'm afraid he's suffered a seizure.'

'A lot has changed in Seaborough, then.'

More than she knew. He could not tell her he'd received a letter from a grateful Mr. Winton. His premises were to let again, for he was setting up in Southampton, with an investment from Captain Selden.

And Constable Dean had resigned, finding the nature of policework was not, after all, to his liking.

Reaching the limits of the Close, there was nothing to be done but slowly retrace their footsteps. Reluctantly, Abbs escorted his companion back to the hotel entrance, her gloved fingers briefly in his, as they shook hands and parted.

Touching his hat to an acquaintance, he walked away, skirting the pigeons. He reached the arched gateway, that led to the rumbling carriage-traffic of the county town and the rest of his life.

He would not forget Seaborough and some of the people he had met there. Hesitating, Abbs stood looking back, undecided.

The End

Inspector Abbes' next mystery is *A Christmas Malice.*

December 1873

It took a surprising effort to dress the clothes on the body.

Taking them had been the easy part. No one locked their doors in daylight in the village. Moving like a wraith through the rear yard of the shop premises, turning the handle of the scullery door and inside in an instant.

It was the home of a man who lived alone. A lingering smell of bacon fried in lard, the skillet on the draining-board, a smear of grease along its rim. The rug in front of the range was rucked. The weekly *Lynn Advertiser* on the battered table, folded and propped against the teapot.

Listening at the bottom of the stairs, the door through to the shop was left ajar, the blinds half-down, making the interior shadowed. Shelves of brown, blue and green glass bottles, a wooden mould for pressing pills. The brass scales behind the counter, a large pestle and mortar between two carboys in the window.

Viewing it all from this angle was like being behind a stage, peeping through a gap in the curtains. The quality of silence confirmed no one else was there, though who could be? The more you listened, the more you became aware of tiny sounds, not really silence at all. The tap dripping, then a click as the hand moved on the mantel clock. And once, a faint scuffle behind a skirting-board.

The stairs creaked, so did the wardrobe door, with its escaping odour of mothballs. It was satisfying to thrust his best jacket and new hat into a sack. Then retreat carefully through the cold house, wherein everything was hasty and careless.

Sneak along the path behind the houses, encumbered. But it was too late in the day for women to be beating rugs or shaking dusters from their windows.

Then disappear through the trees to the abandoned shack by the edge of a turnip field. Within living memory it had been the home of an old man. They said he'd been a tinkler who'd settled in the parish. Villagers thereabouts had taken their pans to him, until his fingers had become too misshapen to mend them.

One winter, the wisps of smoke from the pipe that served as chimney, had been seen no more. It was said his corpse had been found frozen on the earthen floor.

The jacket already looked the worse for wear, smudged with flour from inside the sack. It was awkward work pushing and pulling the rigid arms into the sleeves. Fastening the horn buttons with cold, clumsy fingers. The sniff of frost was in the air.

Winter came early to Norfolk and it was imminent. The rich colours of autumn had left the trees, bled into dried husks crumpled underfoot. The birches and ash huddled together, braced for the snow that always came from across the German ocean.

The final touch would be his billycock, tilted at a jaunty angle. A bowler they called it elsewhere. There was no going back now and it served him right. No one about in the last hour of daylight. There was no work needed to bring the farm labourers to this part.

They'd been ditching on the Fen side of the village that morning. Old Bart Swaley and young John Christopher would have downed tools and be making for the Barley Mow by this time. Here, there was no one to see the bitter thing done. Only the black crows picking along the dark furrows.

~

Bishopsgate terminus had been crowded and noisy, with steam belching, whistles blowing and doors slamming on the dark blue coaches of the Great Eastern Railway. This would certainly be the last time he journeyed from there, as the Liverpool Street station was almost finished and due to open early in the new year.

It was a relief to climb into the carriage in readiness to leave the capital. The train, however, was packed with passengers in second and third. He found himself crammed between a window seat and a stout lady, a carpet bag clutched on her lap. A conversation ensuing between the other occupants confirmed, they too, were journeying to stay with relatives for Christmas.

By the time the light dulled across the flat land, on the shortest day of the year, Inspector Josiah Abbs felt an unaccustomed, nervous anticipation as the train approached his destination. It was eighteen months or more since he had seen Hetty. Their first meeting since she had been widowed.

As the locomotive began to slow, he rose to his feet and grasped his travelling case. This was his first visit to the village where his sister and her husband had moved. He looked out with interest, as the swaying motion steadied and finally stilled. Thirty miles or more from their childhood home, Aylmer was situated on the edge of an unknown Norfolk, the county being large and composed of varied topography.

They had been raised in an area parcelled between rich landowners, with prosperous farms, neat estate villages and shooting coverts. Hereabouts, the land skirted the Fens to south and west. Wide, lonely vistas of dark, fertile land, with scarcely a hedgerow or tree. The land was carved by water, dykes, drains and the sullen Great Ouse flowing to the ancient port of King's Lynn.

He was the only passenger alighting on the short platform. The train did not linger. The small country station was scarcely more than a halt. Its modest, single storey building, with Dutch gables, hardly looked large enough to contain living accommodation. Then, all first impressions were pushed aside as his sister appeared in the open doorway.

The diffidence he felt at meeting after a long absence was quickly dispelled by her familiar smile. Abbs felt himself transported back to the school gate. Where his sister would on occasion wait, with an uncanny foreknowledge of the days he intended to slip away to woods and river bank. Rather than coming straight home to attend to his tasks.

He was now taller than her, he reflected as he bent to kiss her cheek. And they were two siblings, instead of five.

'There now, Dora said I'd be late but I made it with five minutes to spare. She's looking forward to meeting you. We'll soon be home, Arthur insisted I take the trap.'

She spoke over her shoulder as she led the way through the booking office, where a bright fire was spitting in a tiny grate.

The stationmaster gave him an appraising look as he inspected his ticket. 'This'll be your brother then, Mrs Byers? Happen we could do with another policeman. We don't get many strangers in Aylmer,' he announced to Abbs, pronouncing it Elmer. 'Good night to you, sir.'

Abbs took his seat in the smartly painted conveyance, with *Chas. Byers, Grocer and Provisions Dealer* in brown lettering along the side.

'What did he mean, Hetty?'

His sister was silent, as she untethered the reins and climbed up beside him to move off. She didn't answer until she'd turned the grey horse and they were out of the station yard, passing a small chapel.

'It's nothing, really. There've been one or two odd happenings lately around the village. Not crimes,' she said, hastily, turning to look at him. 'Only mischief, nothing to concern you at all. I don't know why Thomas said that.'

'You do have a village constable here?'

'Yes, Constable Duffield. He's a good policeman but he's as baffled as the rest of us. You know, you're looking tired and too thin. I don't suppose you feed yourself properly.'

Abbs was amused, reminded of their mother's scolding. 'Well enough, I generally get something on the way home.'

'That's not the same as wholesome cooking. You never did have much appetite as a boy. I dare say you live on bread and cheese indoors. I shall feed you up while you're here and we'll talk properly. I shall want to hear all your news.'

It was easier to speak moving along in the dusk, than it would be seated indoors, especially with someone else in the house.

'Hetty, about Charley's funeral, I'm truly sorry I was unable to visit you in those last months.'

'There's no need, Josiah. A man in your position can't be spared, I knew that and he went downhill quickly. Arthur was here and there was nothing anyone could have done.'

'I'm glad of your letters, even though I don't reply as often as I should.'

'No matter, it's easier for a woman to find time to write. I think you'll like Dora, Miss Stephens. The year's gone swiftly, she's been boarding with me since spring. I do enjoy her companionship and it saves me rattling round an empty house.'

'I'm thankful she came to you. You've plenty of work, then?'

'Yes, indeed, enough and more for the pair of us.'

'You would say if you needed any help?'

'Bless you, Josiah, I do very well and Arthur keeps me supplied from the shop. He's a good man, a mite overwhelming at times,' Hetty smiled mischievously at him, 'but he has a kind heart.'

She held the reins lightly and the horse trotted steadily along the lane, with fields at either hand. The first evening star had appeared, hanging cold and distant above them.

'It'll freeze tonight, it's so clear.'

Looking at the sky, Abbs reminded himself how wide the heavens appeared in Norfolk. Like a dark blanket tucked in over the landscape, making you feel small and insignificant.

'I see the station's apart from the village.'

'We're coming up to it now. By the way, Josiah, best not to mention those odd things to Dora. She had an unpleasant trick played on her. It shook us both up.' Hetty looked ahead again, clearly not intending to say more.

'You can't leave it at that,' said Abbs lightly. 'I'm bound to ask what?'

'She had a parcel.' Hetty continued with some reluctance. 'In a pretty box, the sort that contains an article of female attire. Dora was excited, she naturally thought it was a present. When she opened it, inside swathes of paper, she found a pig's head.' She shook her head at the memory. 'We've all seen them. It was the unexpectedness of it that was so nasty.'

She slowed to turn into a bend and Abbs caught sight of the first lit window. 'I suppose it was children's idea of a joke.'

Frowning, Abbs considered. 'Was it sent through the post?'

'Left in the porch.'

'I won't say anything.'

Privately, he thought it unlikely that village children had dreamt up such a notion or had the means to hand. He wanted to ask if Miss Stephens had done something to make an enemy, but he sensed further questions would be unwelcome. Even so, this had upset his sister and he resolved to learn more if he could.

A *Christmas Malice* by Anne Bainbridge

December 1873. Inspector Abbs is visiting his sister in a lonely village on the edge of the Norfolk Fens. He is hoping for a quiet week while he thinks over a decision about his future. However all is not well in Aylmer. Someone has been playing malicious tricks on the inhabitants. With time on his hands and concerned for his sister, Abbs feels compelled to investigate.

Read more about our books at www.johnbainbridgewriter.wordpress.com

Printed in Great Britain
by Amazon